The Vampires of London

Angelo de Sorr

The Vampires of London

translated, annotated and introduced by
Brian Stableford

A Black Coat Press Book

ISBN 978-1-61227-264-1. First Printing. March 2014. Published by Black Coat Press, an imprint of Hollywood Comics.com, LLC, P.O. Box 17270, Encino, CA 91416. All rights reserved. Except for review purposes, no part of this book may be reproduced or transmitted in any form or by any means, electronic or mechanical, including photocopying, recording, or by any information storage and retrieval system, without permission in writing from the publisher. The stories and characters depicted in this novel are entirely fictional. Printed in the United States of America.

Introduction

Le Vampire by "Angelo de Sorr" (Ludovic Sclafer, 1822-1881), here translated as *The Vampires of London*, was originally published in Paris by Adolphe Delahays in 1852. As its title suggests, and the text briefly acknowledges, the ultimate source of its inspiration was John Polidori's novelette *The Vampyre* (1819)[1], which had been widely misattributed on its initial anonymous publication to Lord Byron, who is scabrously parodied in its leading character. The novel's more immediate inspiration, however, was undoubtedly *Le Vampire*, the second of two plays based on Polidori's novelette to be staged by the Théâtre de la Porte Saint-Martin, presented in 1851.

That second adaptation, by Alexandre Dumas,[2] was a deliberate, and somewhat desperate, attempt to repeat the success of the first adaptation of 1820, written by Achille Jouffroy with additional input by the theater director Jean-Toussaint Merle and Charles Nodier.[3] The ploy was successful; the new adaptation was a big hit, and prompted the production of several new works of fiction playing variations on its theme, of which Angelo de Sorr's was the first, and perhaps the best, although Pierre-Alexis Ponson du Terrail's *La Baronne trépassée* (1853)[4] and Paul Féval's *La Vampire*

---

[1] Included in the Black Coat Press edition of *Lord Ruthven the Vampyre*, ISBN 978-1-932983-10-4.

[2] Translated as *The Return of Lord Ruthven*, Black Coat Press, ISBN 978-1-932983-11-1.

[3] Translated as *The Vampire Lord Ruthwen*, Black Coat Press, ISBN 978-1-61227-004-3

[4] Translated as *The Vampire and the Devil's Son*, Black Coat Press, ISBN 978-1-932983-55-5.

(book 1856, but probably previously published as a serial)[5] were considerably more successful, both of them substituting seductive female vampires for the Byronic male lead.

The reason why the new adaptation of the play was a slightly desperate move is that 1851 was an exceedingly parlous time for the Parisian theater. The revolution of 1848, prompted by food shortages and general economic turmoil, had not cured those ills, and, although it had generated a certain amount of hope that better days might eventually lie ahead, they were conspicuously slow in materializing. The economic chaos continued; many Parisian theaters closed, and those that stayed open had great difficulty filling their halls—a problem compounded when Paris was afflicted, as it had been after its previous Revolution in 1830, with a cholera epidemic. It was not just that the Porte Saint-Martin was in dire need of a crowd-pleasing play in 1851, but in dire need of a crowd.

Playwrights were not the only writers in Paris having a bad time; the publication of books had also diminished drastically, so it is hardly surprising that several prose writers should have been prompted to follow the Porte Saint-Martin's lead, nor that some of them, at least, should have done so in a slightly wry fashion, feeling under pressure to do something that they might otherwise have thought untimely. Dumas had not been at all reluctant to step into the breach; he had very fond memories of the 1820 version of *Le Vampire*, having gone to the first night shortly after his arrival in Paris and found himself sat next to a curmudgeonly gentleman who turned out to be none other than Charles Nodier, loudly dissatisfied with Merle's final version of his dialogue. For Dumas, who subsequently became a pillar of the Romantic Movement—for which Nodier was the chief flag-bearer in the 1820s—and went on to spectacular fame and fortune in that context, the 1851 play was a labor of love as well as a potential money-spinner. Nor were the hardened *feuilletonists*,

---

[5] Translated as *The Vampire Countess*, Black Coat Press, ISBN 978-0-9740711-5-2.

Ponson and Féval, ashamed to take advantage of the vogue, although they did so in a blithely cavalier and somewhat tongue-in-cheek fashion. Angelo de Sorr, on the other hand, seems to have taken the perceived necessity slightly harder, and attacked the task in a more sarcastic fashion.

By 1851, the Romantic Movement, which had taken its first great leap forward in 1830—when its members turned out mob-handed at the première of Victor Hugo's *Hernani*, ready to engage in fisticuffs if need be—had faded into the cultural background. Having once been revolutionary, Romanticism had become ordinary, if not actually old-hat. As the first chapter of Angelo de Sorr's novel sardonically contends, the Romantic had, in effect—by virtue of its success—become prosaic. That created problems for new adopters of its literary ideology, who could no longer pose as dangerous outsiders bidding to overturn an establishment, but were more likely to look like belated jumpers on to a contentedly-rolling bandwagon.

The leading prose writers of the Movement—including Nodier, Hugo, Dumas, Petrus Borel le Lycanthrope, Théophile Gautier, Edgar Quinet and Paul Lacroix (alias P. L. Jacob the Bibliophile)—had explored many of the limits of Romanticism's potential excesses by 1840, and there was little room left thereafter for further melodramatic inflation. Even in the ranks in the ranks of the movement's "foot-soldiers," where such writers as S. Henry Berthoud, Jules Janin, Joseph Méry and Léon Gozlan were to be found, the quest for further originality was still being carried relentlessly forward ten years later, with considerable success, but that only served to emphasize the fact that the scope available to newer recruits like Louis Ulbach and Angelo de Sorr was becoming severely limited.

Angelo de Sorr, having transported his ambitions to Paris from the Midi, like Borel, Méry and Gozlan before him, made his debut as a novelist in 1848 with *Les Filles de Paris*, but inevitably fell victim to bad timing, and found the marketplace infinitely more difficult thereafter. He was eventually to go on to build a substantial career for himself, working as a writer for various periodicals and eventually publishing more than a dozen novels, as well as becoming a successful publisher himself, but it was not until the late 1850s that he contrived to establish a stable presence in the marketplace. He was not alone in his tribulations, of course—the massive disruption caused by the Revolution was further complicated in December 1851 when the president of the nascent but ailing Republic, Louis-Napoléon Bonaparte, staged a *coup-d'état* and proclaimed himself emperor, swiftly sending many of the leading Republicans—including such prominent Romantic rebels as Hugo, Dumas and Quinet—into exile, and clamping down hard on potentially-seditious publication by imposing fierce censorship.

Not all Romantics were Republicans, of course, and some of those who were had never been loud enough in their political affiliation to require censorship, let alone exile, but the political and economic environment created by the coup made any kind of adventurous publication seem hazardous as well as difficult. It is against that background that Angelo de Sorr's *Le Vampire*, given its publication in 1852—although it is clearly set prior to the *coup*—needs to be read, because it would otherwise be difficult to comprehend the remarkable tone of its narrative voice and the deliberate perversity of its action.

Although the title of the novel is singular, Polidori's Byronic vampire is only one of the models employed in *Le Vampire*, and there is a second model adopted therein which has an even more peculiar history. The term "vampire" has nowadays become largely restricted to the practice of blood-drinking, and metaphorical echoes thereof, but it had also been employed, in the context of early 19th century French literature, in a variant fashion—and, just as the Dumas play had given a new boost to the Polidori model, events in Paris in the years immediately following the 1848 Revolution had given a burst of new publicity to that secondary model. It would be inappropriate to go into more detail here, because it would function as a spoiler, so I shall postpone further comment to a footnote at the relevant point in the plot. The important point to be registered in advance is that Angelo de Sorr's novel is not so much about *a* vampire as about *vampires* in a more general sense—in a sense that does not, in fact, include any literal blood-drinking, but which is no less meaningful in consequence.

Like many of the members of the French Romantic Movement, Angelo de Sorr, although fascinated by supernatural materials in legend and literature, was firmly committed—in 1851, at least—to the notion that their time was past, and that they ought not to play a straightforward role in the literature of a positivist era. Several previous adaptations of Polidori's novelette—notably Heinrich Marschner's opera *Der Vampyr* (1828)—largely ignore the neck-biting briefly featured by Polidori in favor of the sexual predation of which he makes much more. Even Marschner's vampire is, however, inspired by a literal pact with the devil, as several of the stage doppelgangers of Polidori's Lord Ruthven had been. The members of the French Romantic Movement were fascinated by the idea of the Devil, but were relentless revisionists, carrying forward an entire tradition of "literary satanism" that included various shades of apologetics. Their interest, however, did not prevent a widespread suspicion that the Devil, even if he were unfortunate enough to exist, had become irrelevant to human affairs. In particular, Jules Janin's "La Soeur rose et la soeur grise" (1937)[6] had argued forcefully that the Devil's temptations could now be seen as a petty and paltry affair, far outshone on the scale of evil by the merely human depredations of the Terror—a sentiment echoed by one of Angelo de Sorr's vampires even while he poses as a maker of a diabolical pact.

---

[6] tr. as "The Good Sister and the Bad Sister" and included in the Black Coat Press collection *The Magnetized Corpse*, ISBN 978-1-61227-248-1.

Although Janin is not one of the several writers directly referenced in Angel de Sorr's novel, *Le Vampire* also echoes Janin's ground-breaking novel *L'Ane mort et la femme guillotinée* (1829; tr. as *The Dead Donkey and the Guillotined Woman*), which reconfigured the *roman frénétique*—a term previously used to refer to imitations of German and English Gothic novels—for Romantic usage, similarly substituting cruel ambition for diabolical inspiration, arguably making it more horrific by making it humanly motivated rather than essentially alien. Janin, along with Berthoud and Borel, was one of the most significant pioneers of the *conte cruel*: fiction sardonically chronicling the horrors emergent from human passions, and the ironies of fate with which such perverted passion often seems to collaborate. Angelo de Sorr's version of *Le Vampire* is, in essence, a nested series of *contes cruels* aggregated into a quintessentially Romantic *roman frénétique*, and its late arrival on the scene ensured that it was compelled to be one of the most excessive and convoluted works of that kind.

The convolution of the novel is manifest in its tortuous plot, but receives its most remarkable extra twist from the manner of its narration; the de Sorr version of *Le Vampire* has one of the most peculiar and perverse narrative voices to be found in 19th century fiction, partly because of its flagrant hypocrisy in continually arguing, on very dodgy grounds, that it cannot possibly be accused of implausibility and flatly denying that the "contumelious epithet" of melodrama might be applied to its relation. As the quoted adjective suggests, the narrative voice is also fond of exotic terminology, sometimes reaching beyond the dictionary for words that no one had previously bothered to coin. Although loquacious when it comes to parenthetical remarks, especially flippantly cynical ones, it is also much given to stubborn understatement in explanation of what is actually happening, with a resultant uncertainty that sometimes leaves a great deal to the reader's imagination, in contexts where the reader can hardly help thinking the worst. Although it protests that it has insufficient imagination to invent anything very extraordinary, some of the scenes it narrates laconically—most notably one in which a young man tries to pimp his sick sister to a resurrectionist while she assists him in haggling over the price—are masterpieces of the grotesque.

The eccentricities of the author were not confined to the pages of his novels; when he was not posing as Angelo de Sorr, Ludovic Sclafer, the son of a family of vine-growers in the Bordeaux region, like to go climbing in the Pyrenees, and he fell into a precipice on one such excursion while *Le Vampire* was in press. His companions reported his probable death, which was swiftly reproduced in local newspapers, and obituaries appeared in Paris; he had, in fact, survived the fall, and eventually got back to civilization, but was either too embarrassed to send a speedy correction or felt that he might get some advantage from his supposed death in terms of sales or critical reception, and did not come clean for some time. In 1857 he disappeared again when undertaking a balloon ascent, again only able to return home after an absence of several days—with the perhaps-inevitable result that no one would believe that he had not got lost deliberately, by way of a publicity stunt. Although he mostly avoided getting into trouble with Louis-Napoléon's censors, "Angelo de Sorr" eventually showed his true political colors during the Commune, when he published the newspaper *Le Trac* [nervousness, especially in the context of performance anxiety] and subsequently wrote a satirical novel, *Ranalalalulu CXXXIV* (1872), about the visit of an African monarch to Paris during the Commune

Although its subject matter is the horror of human malice, and it contains several carefully-elaborated scenes of pure and unadulterated horror, *Le Vampire*, seen as an ensemble, is more a satirical comedy than a horror story and the perverse narrative voice ensures that it eventually reaches extremes of black farce that no previous novel had reached and few have touched on since. It is, as one of the author's footnotes conscientiously observes, a "Procrustean Bed" of a novel, in which respect it was by in means alone—brutal Procrustean carving

11

was a standard feature of the hasty endings of out-of-control feuilleton serials—but in which it set a new standard of deliberate adumbration. Inevitably, that was not to every reader's taste in 1851 and probably will not be today, but it nevertheless makes it safe to suggest that the readers of this introduction will never have read anything quite like it before, and probably never will again, even though I hope to follow up this translation, in due course, with a translation of *Le Fantôme de la rue de Venise* [The Phantom of the Rue de Venise] (1869) by the same author.

This translation was mostly made from the Google Books version of the Delahays edition, with occasional assistance from the Hathi Trust version of the same scan, with unaccountably includes a couple of pages dropped from the Google Books version. Both versions are, however, missing pages 78-81 of the original, although the fact that they start with an even page-number suggests that they cannot simply have been ripped out of the New York Public Library copy which Google scanned. The print-on-demand copies made from the Google scan presently offered for sale by opportunistic "publishers" are also missing those pages. I am extremely grateful to Henri Rossi, who typed out the missing text from the Bibliothèque Nationale copy of the book (which he was not permitted to photocopy) in order that I could complete the translation, and also to Jean-Marc Lofficier, who kindly asked Professor Rossi to attempt to recover the missing text for me.

The translation was made slightly difficult by the density of exotic words, for some of which I have substituted simpler formulations in order to make the intended meaning clearer; in order to be faithful to the style of the original, however, I have been content to reproduce or Anglicize many of them; those which can no more be found in English dictionaries than French ones are mostly easy to construe with the aid of their Classical roots, and I have usually refrained from adding explanatory footnotes.

Other difficulties arose by virtue of the author's evident unfamiliarity with the workings of the British peerage—which causes him, for instance, to overlook the fact that the family names of British aristocrats are not the same as the place names in their titles; the misapprehensions in question were not amenable to correction. I have left most of the supposedly-Scottish surnames unaltered, in spite of their occasional ludicrousness, but I thought it appropriate to change "Kockburns" to the far more likely "Cockburn," although it is conceivable that the eccentricity is not unconnected with the fact the Sclafer later became the lucky publisher of the best-selling Paul de Kock.

Brian Stableford

I. The Corne Verte *Inn*

A large number of small towns exist in France that have not yet been reached by progress. Mores there are simple and primitive, but I cannot affirm that they are any purer in consequence. In these ancient communities, once doubtless bathed by the banks of some stream that has now dried up, or even changed its course, the story of a railway journey is listened to with much greater attention than would be accorded in Paris to an account of an aerostatic ascent.

I rather like those towns, so naïve and ignorant of all the noise that is made in more active circles. Many novelists have said that before me, I know, and many readers, among those who always want something new, will doubtless protest. But, Messieurs—those of my readers who are protesting—I cannot pride myself on writing what has never been said before, and if you desire that, you are certainly not making a small demand. My sole ambition is to interest you. One amuses by means of known facts skillfully organized. The new astonishes.

Oh, you are not ambitious in your demands! A novel is always the same things restated—tell us something new! Messieurs, one does not find that in every century. When Columbus cried "Land ho!"; when Galileo, that Joshua of science, stopped the sun; when Watt tamed the wind on the sea and destroyed distance on land...those men said something new. The novelist tends toward a more modest aim, and does not aspire, so far as I know, to revelation. Psychology is almost his sole study; it is, for him, both distraction and science. As curious as a girl, he ferrets incessantly in the secret alveoli of intimate sentiments, exfoliates lovingly all the layers of unknown sensations, and places a magnifying lens over the tubercles of the heart. Then he reports his observations to those who are interested.

As for me, I consider the novel as a familiar chat with a stranger; except that I chat at my ease and in my own time, without worrying about whether anyone is listening—but I permit those who read me to do the same.

At any rate, I write it frankly, this book is not indispensable to society. One can be a perfectly honest person, exceedingly learned, and never read a novel. These pages are addressed to imaginative young people, leisure-loving people, not to others. And to be sure, I would be enormously sorry if anyone were to waste time because of me. The novel is the fair sex of the world of books; it requires knowledge to frequent it.

But here I am, getting away from my original subject; it is time to close the parentheses. Nevertheless, before continuing, by way of digression, I will confess that, being by nature a trifle butterfly-minded, it is possible that I might, in the course of this narrative, when I bump into some bizarre idea, quit the main line to talk digressively and wander along some side-path.

Perhaps I shall also be reproached for making too much use of the first person. It is not vanity that makes me do it, but it seems unjust and a trifle impolite to me for a writer to attribute to several, by means of a timid "we," the more-or-less-sensate but occasionally grotesque reflections that he might catch on the wing as they cross his mind. Then again, a book with only one signature necessarily has only one author.

The sole merit of secondary writers is to have been personal in their works. I promise, nevertheless, not to fall into any excess of intimacy.

Bazes is a small town that one encounters some ten leagues from Bordeaux as one heads toward the Pyrenees. Its appearance is dirty and bleak. Narrow, pebble-strewn streets, darkened by coverts, lead to a long square in which stands one of the beautiful cathedrals of France.

The inhabitants of the town have some intelligence, which they distribute among themselves by some unknown means.

The rare travelers that stay in the ancient town find a few hostelries there that I introduce to you as inns—for inns still exist, those fine hostelries in which one is poorly served, where there are never enough beds, and where one can tell, in brief, that one is not at home.

Indeed, traveling does not have the same attractions today as it once had. For a start, everyone travels. At Baden one bumps into one's tailor. In the Pyrenees one allows a storm to pass over in a covert that already shelters a creditor or a former mistress—which comes to the same thing. Then again, comfort follows you everywhere; modern hotels cater to all needs. In Liverpool, you are served little Viennese loaves, in Cadiz, oysters from Ostend. It's unbearable!

The proprietor of the *Corne Verte* inn has never been informed of the meaning of the word *comfort*. Nevertheless, travelers stop there, for it is one of the cleaner hostelries in Bazas.

One evening in the month of October in the year 1849, two men, after having dined together, were resting in front of a good enough fire in the common room of the inn.

The room did not offer any visible luxury. The mantelpiece was as bare as a step on a staircase, and at the back, standing out against a tapestry of life-sized characters, was a hexagonal clock whose chime rendered a muffled sound, as if struck in the distance. That bourgeois chronometer gave enormous pleasure to the proprietor's wife. When the hours sounded, it seemed to her that she was hearing the cathedral clock.

The two travelers placed in front of the hearth seemed to belong to the same level of society, but they were not similar in age. One was a young man, the other might have been about forty. They did not say much. From time to time, the younger of the two ran an indifferent eye over the columns of a local newspaper,

Each of the two gentlemen occupied a corner of the hearth, leaving a large space in the middle, which was not vacant. An enormous dog of the mountain breed was lying there. There was nothing remarkable about the animal but his size. Otherwise, his coarse and bushy coat, his long broad paws, his powerful head with small ears, his ill-formed and gummed-up eyes composed a merely rustic form.

Suddenly his sleep was interrupted by an external noise; he raised his head and growled.

"Silence, Mont-Dore!" ordered his master, the older of the two travelers.

After having darted an anxious glance at the door, Mont-Dore replaced his gross muzzle between his paws, and gave the appearance of sleep.

"You have a terrible defender there," the young man observed.

"It's because he can sense someone coming. He's not normally badly-behaved, but I don't know what's got into him today. He nearly bit a couple of people, who hadn't said anything to him. Come on, Mont-Dore, be quiet."

"His bad moods might cause you some trouble, because he's big enough not to let himself be vanquished."

"Ha ha! I think he's found his master recently, though. After a night of vagabondage more than a month ago he came back in the morning with a bite on his leg." Addressing the animal, while patting his head with the flat of his hand, he added: "A wound that doesn't do you honor, Mont-Dore—a wound on the behind!"

The dog only greeted this caress with a dull growl, to which a few reproachful words put an end. Nevertheless he welcomed without too much suspicion a new arrival who came on to the scene through the door of the *Corne Verte*'s common room.

We shall employ the moment when the third traveler was conversing with the hotel proprietor to introduce the first two individuals—who are to play the principal roles in this drama—to the reader.

The one who was sitting to the right, Mont-Dore's master, is named Horatio Mackinguss. The first impression given by the man's face is one of honesty. Those who have the courage to penetrate further into the labyrinth of this book might perhaps criticize that appreciation, but it is just and true—all the more just and all the more true because it unites the generality of examples. Horatio's face bears a frank expression of probity. It is not permissible for me to say otherwise—and that distresses me, not because it might be the case that the real sentiment is hidden beneath a false effigy, which is of little importance to me, but because I find it disappointing that it does not stand out from the commonplace. To write more would be to anticipate the chapters that follow.

Horatio's face was beardless, of an even complexion, pale rather than colored, but of a coarse-grained pallor perhaps caused by the thickness of the dermis. His forehead was broad, slightly bulbous, surmounting bright eyes. A bright eye, with regard to the pupil, is entirely indicative. His mouth was thinly closed, scarcely sketched, beneath a nose irreproachable in form and contour, except that the nostrils offered the distended dimensions that indicate a propensity to exceptional sensuality. The man's hair was thick and soft, and did not curl.

That is the portrait off Mackinguss, the reproduction of the lines and bumps. He was tall of stature, his bearing full of nobility, his manners free and easy, his voice polite. I can also tell you that Horatio Mackinguss, as his name indicates, was Scottish by birth and origin.

Robert de Rolleboise was sitting opposite Horatio and alongside Mont-Dore, whom we have already met. He was a young man of twenty-five, with an intelligent physiognomy and a casual manner. We shall leave it until later to unveil his intimate tendencies.

While the third traveler was busy with the landlord on the threshold of the room, Robert de Rolleboise had put down the newspaper and was looking at him attentively. Then, as the landlord went out, he stood up and walked toward the young man.

"I'm not mistaken? It's really Monsieur le Vicomte de Saint-Loubès that I have the pleasure of…shaking the hand?

"But certainly, my dear Rolleboise! I've just arrived from Cauterets, where I left you exceedingly occupied in rendering yourself incurable of a malady off the heart."

"Oh, Monsieur!"

"That's indiscreet, it's true. How is Madame de Lormont, Monsieur de Rolleboise? Is she still taking the waters?"

"No, Monsieur; she has returned to Paris."

"Oh, I beg your pardon—that's true, you're traveling."

The young man's constrained physiognomy displayed the embarrassment that these words caused him.

Monsieur de Saint-Loubès perceived that. "So, after all," he exclaimed, "people still meet up in inns, as in the days of little duodecimo volumes and coaches that couch!"

"There are still inns, Monsieur le Vicomte, and, as you see, people still have the advantage of meeting therein. As regards me, this is the how and why. This is said simply to offer my excuses for an adventure that might perhaps be taken for a pastiche. Before returning to Paris I had the intention of staying for a few days with my uncle, in Auch. That visit has therefore taken me out of my way. In order to resume it, I have taken a somewhat scenic route. Thus, I came from Gers to Agen, the abode of the poet Jasmin."[7]

"Yes, I know you're ever subject to an attack of poetry. But the waters, although they haven't cured you, must have had the salutary effect of displacing the seat of the malady."

"What do you mean?"

"Before, you were surely a poet in spirit, were you not?"

"Ah! And today, Monsieur de Saint-Loubès?"

"Today you're one…at heart."

Robert made a gesture of impatience, and continued, without any further reflection: "From Jasmin's home I went to the Château de Nérac, where I found a carriage that brought me here. In that carriage I met Monsieur, who is coming from Montpellier, I believe, and is due, along with me, to catch the

---

[7] The Occitan poet Jacques Jasmin (1798-1864), noted for his images of peasant life.

Bayonne diligence, which will take us to Paris. We have had a bad dinner together, and I was just reading a good newspaper—I'm referring to its wit rather than its editing. Now, Monsieur, explain to us in your turn what bizarre event has brought about your entry into the *Corne Verte* inn. If it's to explain the sign to us, you'll be cleverer than our host, and we'll be all ears."[8]

Monsieur de Saint-Loubès brought a chair forward and sat down in front of the fire, to the displeasure of Mont-Dore, who withdrew—not without murmuring—under his master's chair.

The Vicomte was a rich young man. Nowadays, that description is a whole portrait. Furthermore, as he always had been, he combined that advantage with the rare merit of having the sentiment of an innate politeness and opposing in argumentative conversation a ductility of character that cannot be appreciated too highly. I believe that it would be excessive to talk about his moral and political tendencies now, and to sound his convictions and principles—in brief, to carry out a psychological analysis in his regard.

Monsieur de Saint-Loubès dressed well. He wore trousers of a fashionable narrowness, supple and creased varnished boots, and an ample jacket. Let us record thereafter that he had large fluid eyes, good teeth and a Molière moustache.

"Messieurs," said the Vicomte, in a strangely reserved one, "I find myself here in circumstances so unfortunate that I am ashamed to reveal them to you. When I was obliged to make them known to the owner of this grotesque caravanserai, I feared that he would laugh in my face. But first, I must tell you one thing. I am an enemy of the vulgar, and I strive as much as possible to liberate myself from the general laws in which the common herd vegetates. My antipathy is to the prosaic."

---

[8] English readers will probably be less perplexed, knowing that *corne verte* translates as "greenhorn."

"But Monsieur," observed Horatio, "permit me to believe that all three of us profess the same repulsion."

"That's good—but have you noticed that in the last twenty years, things have changed greatly in the realm of the prosaic? Certain men of intelligence have showed it the finger; immediately, the crowd has fled—with the result that the privileged life, independent of heavy ridicule, the artistic circle of old, has become, by invasion, the prosaic world of today! But you'll never understand..."

"Forgive us, Vicomte. Well enough that one could not formulate your idea better than by saying that you are making yourself prosaic in order not to be."

"Bravo. So, when I happen to commit an action that is extraordinary and—oh, my God, let's utter the word, dead as it is: *romantic*..."

"*Romantic* isn't as old as all that."

"So the bourgeois employ it. A consequence of my theory."

"That's very true."

"Well, when I fall into that fault, I'm utterly confused. I therefore beg your pardon for confessing to you that my post-chaise has broken down two leagues from here. Alas, yes—as in a novel by Ducray-Duminil or a drama by Monsieur de Pixéricourt!"[9]

"And to complete the prosaicism, you haven't broken anything!"

---

[9] François Ducray-Duminil (1761-1819) was an author of sentimental and stubbornly moralistic adventure stories, often featuring the tribulations of children, which the disapproving Victor Hugo described in *Les Misérables* as "stupid romances." René Pixéricourt (1773-1844) wrote and directed numerous plays in a similar vein, including some based on Ducray-Duminil's novels, although he also wrote more extravagant melodramas. Charles Nodier thought very highly of him, but the younger Romantics considered him a hackneyed representative of the old guard.

"Not so much as a sprain!"

"Poor Vicomte!"

"What consoles me, however..."

"Ah! Let's have it!"

"Yes, what ameliorates my situation is that the place where my carriage broke down is a frightful spot, devoid of landscape or color. The best part of the ridicule of the bourgeois who are afflicted by such a stupid adventure is that they fall into deep gorges, rebounding from projections in the rock. Fortunately, in my case, it was on a good road."

"Where, if you please?"

"At Beaulac—a frightful name."

"But a very picturesque place."

"No, no—as flat as my hand."

"On the banks of the Ciron. It's very romantic."

"Have pity on me, Monsieur de Rolleboise! And above all...above all, not a word about this in Paris...otherwise, I'll deny everything, and I'll cut you off completely...and Monsieur too."

"But you're truly strange!" exclaimed Horatio, laughing. "What, you don't want to be the hero of a little octavo?"

"Do you know, Monsieur, that my coach-builder abducted his wife in order to marry her, that my tailor was almost poisoned by his son? Today, the bizarre is the ordinary, the exception the generality, the distinctive the colorless..."

"Alas, what the Vicomte says is all too true! Our mores have been so stirred and shifted by the ferments of the century that one dare not advance, that there is not a single drama in life that is as calm as it appears on the surface. Interrogate a stranger traversing the crowd and he will tell you a poignant tale; the woman who is laughing hectically at a feast is feeling her heart ripped by the iron teeth of jealousy, and is bottling up a tortuous episode. Listen to that distant clamor, that vague noise which suddenly troubles your silence; it's a frightful denouement coming to completion, an evil deed surging from the inferno to fall upon some accursed head.

"And if, in fact, we want to descend even lower into the realism of life, pick up a newspaper, that summary of a day's events that a flash of light or hazard has hurled out of the shadows, and every paragraph will be the plot of a drama. Thus, for example, here's a local rag that I was reading just now, the *Glaneur*. Under the rubric of Montpellier there's a five-line article, and in those five lines one could perhaps find five volumes of true history."

"From which one can conclude," added Monsieur de Saint-Loubès, that the most exaggerated novel would be the most tedious novel. If I were a novelist, I'd never write any other."

"Nevertheless," Robert went on, after having searched the newspaper. I don't want to spare you the five lines I just mentioned. Here they are: 'Individuals who are doubtless ill-informed have spread through our town various versions of a very deplorable event. It is our duty to establish the facts in their exact truth. Monsieur le Comte de B   had fought a duel with Monsieur N   , a young man of twenty-one, a student at the École Polytechnique. The outcome was fatal to Monsieur N   . Politics had nothing to do with the cause of the duel.'

"Thus, there is an account of a death, which many people have read indifferently; perhaps a few women have accorded a thought of commiseration for the victim; then, the newspaper having been put down, the matter has been forgotten. And yet, around the cadaver there is a family in mourning, a mother in tears, the ruination of hopes, all faith in the future collapsed!"

"Certainly, Monsieur, in taking that fact as an example, you have been justly inspired. There is indeed a great drama in that event, one of the strangest of dramas, and where you have only perceived the initials, I can fill in the other letters of the names, for I know all the details that led to the duel in question."

"Of course—you've come from Montpellier!"

"And if it doesn't frighten you too much, I could tell you the true story before we retire."

"Oh, this time, I'm doomed!" exclaimed the Vicomte. "On the same evening, to have one's post-chaise break down, to encounter a friend in a dead town, and, to bring the prosaicism to a peak, to hear a story in an inn—truly, that's the height of misfortune! I don't know what I've got into...I'm pinching myself but I'm not waking up! No, I'm not asleep...all in all, Monsieur, I'd like to hear your story...but on condition, Messieurs: that it will be your last joke. Except that I ask you for one mercy: if, by chance, during the unfolding of Monsieur's narration, by virtue of misfortune, my physiognomy and my pose change to the point that my attitude resembles a character of Monsieur le Marquis de Foudras,[10] Rolleboise, my friend, I beg you, shake me very forcefully. Go on—I'm resigned."

"You're decidedly a very amusing individual."

"No, not at all; I'm excessively bourgeois. I know what time the sun sets, and am much preoccupied with the variations of the barometer."

"Ah—what does the barometer say, Vicomte?"

"Variable, my dear friend, variable! We'll have a change of weather, I'm sure of it, for it's high tide this evening at seven minutes past eleven."

"Well, Monsieur, now that the Vicomte's fit has eased, we're all ears. First, can you tell us the names that the newspaper doesn't indicate?"

"Very easily. The Comte de Boistilla fought with Raoul Noirtier. If I did not fear causing Monsieur de Saint-Loubès to suffer convulsions, however, I would begin my story a few years before the event that has provided its denouement."

"I curb my head beneath the law of my destiny," said the bizarre Vicomte, in a piteous humor, while saluting Horatio,

---

[10] Théodore de Foudras (1800-1872) was credited with being the inventor of a new genre of novel, the *roman cynégétique* [hunting novel], pioneered by *Les Gentilshommes chasseurs* [Gentlemen Who Hunt] (1848).

as if to assure him that he did not intend to take his joke beyond the bounds of propriety and politeness.

Everyone lit a cigar. It is said that that is a great help in such circumstances. If the author of these lines were more closely linked with his readers, it would be a pleasure—a duty, even—for him to offer them a Havana.

Before commencing, Horatio Mackinguss, after having looked at one of his two listeners with a certain attention, said: "Forgive the liberty of a reflection, Monsieur de Rolleboise, but if I'm not mistaken, you resemble a person that I've often met in London, Sir Amadeus Harriss. Might you be a relative?"

"Definitely not, Monsieur; I have no family in England,"

"No matter—you're resemblance to the gentleman is striking. But let's get back to our subject.

"Marriage is a lottery that promises a few fortunate results, many unfortunate ones and a large enough quantity of grotesque ones. Thus, on the first of March 1830, Monsieur Noirtier, a young advocate in Montpellier, happened on a fortunate lot, in the reckoning of many people, and even—which is worth just as much—in the opinion of his own heart. He married a young woman he loved, by the name of Valérie.

"Valérie did not even possess the idea of a dowry, but Heaven had imparted to her instead a face that might doom many fortunes. She was one of those imposing, mystic and serious beauties that one dares not love, placid and cold in indifference, splendidly effusive next to an adored head.

"Beside that beautiful woman, the advocate looked out of place. He was a frail young man, not strong by nature, with a physiognomy that was pleasant but weak. Only Valérie had welcomed him. She loved him by virtue of the same bizarre law of the heart that leads handsome young men, vigorous in health and brilliant in fortune, to prefer to the beautiful women who surround them some modest ignored child, insignificant in appearance and mediocre in intelligence. Nevertheless, our two spouses suited on another very well, and as I only have the right of the storyteller, let us congratulate Monsieur and not criticize Madame at all.

"If you will bear in mind that this happened in 1830, and in the provinces, you will permit me to add that there was some dancing at Monsieur Noirtier's wedding. Even today, a considerable number of petty people have not yet abolished the wedding ball, that joyful preface to an exceedingly vulgar novel.

"For fear of running into a bizarrerie of taste—or, rather, an accuracy of judgment—I shall not suggest that Valérie was the prettiest of the woman present at the ball, but she was certainly the most beautiful. Among the men, there was also one who stood out as the most handsome.

"That individual, a friend of the husband, was not French. He was from the United States. His name was Dr. Nohé-Nahm.

"Nohé-Nahm was twenty-five years old, but thanks to his beardless face he seemed younger. Undemonstrative by nature, his movements were accomplished slowly and smoothly, and his passions were not externally manifest. Dissimulation was never readable in his overt physiognomy; perhaps he even possessed the art of veiling insincerity. Nevertheless, the facility of his mores and the ductility of his manners made hum sought-after in society. He had been in love with Valérie but she, by virtue of a feminine caprice, had preferred the young advocate.

"That defeat had not cooled the cordiality between the two young men, and each of them surrounded the other with so much politeness that nothing transpired of it outside the intimacy of the circle. It is true that fatal characters exist on which offended pride has a terrible influence, tenebrous intellects that reflect on a tormenting until the ultimate cry of pain and the extreme stab of anguish, but Nohé-Nahm did not appear to have any resemblance to those sick minds.

"In the course of the evening, he found himself alone with Madame Noirtier. The young man's physiognomy, as always, was calm and unalterable. 'Madame,' he said, with an affectionate and tender smile, 'my wishes are realized: you are happy.'

"'Is it with frankness of heart that you wish me happiness, Monsieur?'

"'Madame, I have only loved once in my life, and I have not been loved. Doubtless, I do not merit it. I am courageous and prompt before firm decisions. My heart has been broken and my love is extinct!'

"'You will be our friend, will you not?'

"'Friendship! Alas, Madame, I am extreme in my sentiments, and I loved you very much!'

"'You're distorting the meaning of my words. I am asking for your friendship; will you refuse it to me?'

"'Friendship is not promised; it is proven.'

"'You are extreme in everything, you say?'

"'That is true, Madame.'

"'I dare not understand you. I dread to question you as to the sentiment that now animates you in my regard,'

"'I will tell you.'

"'When?'

"'When? Oh, a long time from today!' he added, with a smile on his lips, and in a tone of the greatest deference.

"Two years went by. Valérie had a son.

"Among the society that received the young advocate, Nohé-Nahm was regarded as the most familiar and the most intimate. No dissimulation was detectable in his manners, and when alone with Valérie, nothing in his words gave rise to any suspicion that he loved the woman in question. He was a friend of the family.

"1832 was, as everyone remembers, a terrible year for France. The plague that seems to follow in the wake of Revolutions was ravaging Paris and the larger cities of the provinces.[11] The mortality assumed frightful proportions.

---

[11] The great cholera epidemic that reached its peak two years after the July Revolution of 1830 was still remembered fearfully when cholera struck again in the wake of the revolution

"One evening, Monsieur Noirtier felt ill and went to bed before nightfall. As it was more a surfeit of fatigue than a preliminary symptom of disease, Valérie was not worried. Besides which, her salon claimed her. She therefore asked Monsieur Nohé-Nahm to visit her husband.

"When he entered Noirtier's room, the latter—only, as we have said, requiring rest—was dozing lightly. A single night-light offered feeble resistance to the obscurity. The doctor woke the invalid up and took his hands with an amicable smile.

"The wan light illuminated half of the physician's handsome face, and dark shadows struck him. Having been smiling, his expression suddenly became grave and astonished. Without saying a word he lit a lamp and placed it next to the bed.

"'I'm tired, and only need rest,' said Valérie's husband, closing his eyes, afflicted by the light.

"Nohé-Nahm's face darkened; with his two hands leaning on the bed, and his head bending over the husband of the woman he had loved with a vast and contained passion, he said in a slow voice: 'You're ill.'

"'A slight headache, that's all. Sleep will dissipate it.'

"'Listen Noirtier, time is precious. Don't be disturbed, but, I repeat: you're ill.'

"'What is it, then?' asked Valérie's husband, anxiously, sitting up in bed.

"'Are you courageous, my friend?'

"'Speak! How pale you are!'

"'Let's not frighten your wife; don't be alarmed yourself, and I'll save you,'

"'But tell me—what illness do you suppose that I have?'

"'I don't suppose—I'm sure. You have all the symptoms of the epidemic. Within an hour, if we don't make haste, you'll have the cholera.'

---

of 1848, reaching its peak as the present novel was being written.

"Sweat moistened the appalled face of the invalid. His teeth were chattering and his voice as incapable of articulating a word. A malady as destructive as the plague—terror—had gripped him.

"An hour later, Noirtier really did have cholera. During the night, in spite of the doctor's treatment, he died.

"Valérie's despair was immense; people briefly feared for her life, and much longer for her reason. But through the somber mourning that enveloped her, the handsome head of the physician was always visible, who emerged victorious in his double duel with nature. What cares did he not lavish on the woman he had loved! All that a lover might imagine, that a son might suffer, he surpassed. He spent entire nights watching over the stricken head, anxiously following the course of the illness, hopefully observing the progress of the remedy. In a word, he performed a near-miracle; he defied nature and Madame Noirtier entered into convalescence.

"The advocate's death was a double blow to Valérie. Once the paroxysm of the heart's anguish had passed, she saw that the event had left her poor, with an infant son.

"That child offered himself to her eyes as a transformation of the lost individual. Thus, uniting tortured sentiment with maternal love, she created more than love, by adoration, for her son. She bid adieu to the joys of the earth, retired from society with her cradle, and commenced, not without courage a great work.

"In that epoch, the physiognomy of the widow was modified, like the sentiment of her heart. Her beauty became austere. Her languid cheeks paled into a sallow complexion, her mouth lost all sensual expression and her large dark eyes were ringed. She was no longer the beautiful Raphaelesque virgin but the black-clad image, the meager and lifeless head, of the mother of Christ in the old painting by Franck.

"The young woman was poor, as we have said. Her income scarcely sufficed to sustain her modest existence, and that penury frightened her, not for herself but for her son. However, as in any pensive soul, hope radiated in her eyes.

One man had not forgotten her. The friendship of Nohé-Nahm promised protection for her child for the future.

"Raoul's childhood was happy. His mother did not punish him and never scolded him. If he did something wrong, however, she became sad; if it was serious, she wept. Raoul loved his mother as much as she loved him, and as a mother's tears touch a child's young heart, he almost never made her weep.

"Raoul reached his tenth year, the age at which, the cares of a family being most necessary to children, school takes them away. By using his influence, Nohé-Nahm obtained a bursary for his friend's son.

"In order not to be so distantly separated from the person she loved more than anything, the poor mother left her humble country dwelling and came to reside in the town. It was a very sad day for her when it was necessary for her to return home alone, and she wept for a long time.

"His new existence required an excessive expenditure, but the courageous mother, entirely dedicated to her ambitious project, was not frightened by that. She increased her privations; for her son's sake, she became a miser. Her clothes, surrounded by precautions, defied wear and tear; her hats were transformed, but never replaced. It is true, too, that Raoul had white trousers for Sundays, the luxury garment of pupils subject to uniform. For a fortnight, Valérie removed a plate from her table, economized on bread and sugar with a bitter joy, and drank water scarcely tinted with wine, but almost every evening she brought a delicacy to Raoul at supper time, and every holiday, he found an excellent meal at his mother's house. That kind of life—poor but not miserable—lasted for eight years, until the young pupil obtained his baccalaureate.

"We shall not take the trouble to discover or declare whether Raoul did well in class or won a sufficient number of prizes, for a man's serious education only begins when he leaves school. Valérie knew that very well, so that moment brought her a poignant anxiety. A friendly hand, however, anticipated all her steps. Nohé-Nahm, that good familiar spirit, appeared before her one day; he was constantly the same, promising nothing but obtaining, firm in devotion, impassive and mysterious.

"The widow took his hand and kissed it. The man that she had once rejected, she admired that day.

"Without preamble, in a tone that announces a resolution already made, he said: 'Your son, Madame, is about to leave school; what have you destined for him?'

"'Alas, my friend, my plan is to take him to Paris.'

"'You want to make him study law. Well, that's not my opinion. Law is a gulf into which capacities and incapacities are nowadays thrown. Your son is intelligent; we can do better than make him an advocate.'

"Valérie's face was radiant with pride and hope.

"'Place him in a preparatory school for admission to the École Polytechnique.[12] We'll easily pass over the chapter of the expenses those studies will necessitate. I have some funds available; I offer them to you. When he emerges from the École, the government will repay your son, so his future is a certain mortgage for me.'

"The poor mother, moved to tears, could not speak. She seized the doctor's hands and threw herself into his arms. The latter received her without any demonstrative emotion.

"Young Raoul Noirtier emerged as one of the foremost graduates from the École Polytechnique. It would be impossible to describe the joy his mother experienced when he appeared before her. The creation had thus attained the height of the dream. Before her work, Valérie nearly went mad. Nothing could balance that admiration of the mother for her son; it as ecstasy, delirium, childishness, ridiculousness. In addition, Raoul was handsome: a magnificent marble illuminated by a keen intelligence; and, more fortunate than the sculptor Pygmalion, the mother had an animate statue.

---

[12] A college whose primary purpose was to prepare young men for military service, particularly military engineers.

There is, for proud souls, no sweeter sentiment than that of superiority conquered. Valérie had the opportunity to savor it with pride.

"She had, as it happened, a niece as little favored as herself by fortune, but excessive in beauty. Now, it came about that one of those men who, in seeming violation of destiny, combine an indomitable nature with the power of gold, took a fancy to her. His name was the Comte de Boistilla. For a long time he circled the woman, but his lack of success injected a strong dose of vanity into his love; unable to hope of obtaining Valérie's niece for a mistress, he employed a deplorable means, and married her.

"Needless to say, Comtesse Mathilde, in her character and her beauty, contrasted in every way with her husband. The latter loved her brutally, and received in return the fearful submission that certain debauchees prefer to love.

"The Comte never wanted to see her relative, Madame Noirtier—that pauper he called her, who had been stupid enough to prefer an unhealthy cretin to the handsome Nohé-Nahm. Soon, however, there was talk in society of young Raoul's success. Serious men attract the acquaintance of women, those frivolous, and futile beings who find pretty appearances agreeable. So long as obscurity had enveloped the two individuals, no one had bothered to notice the scant liaison that existed between the aristocrat and his relative; that disdain for poor relative even found approval among certain intimates of the Comte. But then, whispers began to circulate. Monsieur de Boistilla was apprised of them; so, advised by his wife, he resolved to invite his young cousin to spend a few days on his estate. That invitation added an intoxication to the self-esteem of Raoul's mother.

"The great day arrived; the happy Valérie prepared her son's almost-military costume, passed her beautiful white hands through the young man's brown hair, and then kissed his forehead, his eyes and his silky moustache. Finally, he departed—but the mother, placed at the window, admired him in the street, utterly joyful when a passer-by turned to look at his costume, or a woman furtively glanced at his proud bearing.

"It was a brilliant autumnal day, the blazing sunlight tempered by an easterly wind that made the leaves tremble, for Raoul had reached the country. He felt happy too. He was twenty years old! For the first time, life seemed independent to him, and the horizon of his thoughts broadened. He was also going to see a beautiful woman, his cousin Mathilde, and like all very young men, he became amorous by anticipation. The amorous are dreamers—and then, what is there to do at twenty unless one dreams? So, Raoul created a portrait of his cousin at his leisure. He saw her tall, slightly corporeal—for young men are rarely smitten with spare girls—her face ornamented with an appetizing mouth, a nose with fleshy lobes and two large eyes scintillating like full wine-glasses

"In his sketch, our genteel cousin was not mistaken; such, indeed, was the Comtesse Mathilde de Boistilla.

"There was to be a big hunt the following day, St. Hubert's Day. That solemnity, unnoticed in towns, had attracted to the Comte's roof a numerous company of noisy hunters. The kennels were resounding with the deep voices of running dogs, and the greyhounds were turning the courtyard into a carousel.

"Raoul was very well-received. His cousin, a cold, hard man, introduced him casually to his young wife, who welcomed him with a smile before which he blushed a deeper red than the flaps of his coat, and to his friends, who passed him curiously in review.

"Monsieur de Boistilla had a violent and brutal character. Everyone in his château took note of his bad moods and dreaded them, his servants and dogs alike. He was one of those men who are said to be good at heart, but whose anger is terrible. In the heat of the moment, they will break one of your limbs, but they will be sorry afterwards—excellent fellows!

"Few women were to be seen in the Comte's drawing room, and none of them could pretend to the title envied by their sex. We are speaking, of course, about the guests. Raoul, crammed full of mathematics, falling into the midst of that unrefined society, did not understand those exclusive minds and conversations in the style of poachers at all. He had a moment of self-doubt—but Nohé-Nahm, who, in his capacity as a doctor, was one of the regular visitors to the house, came to his rescue.

"Dinner time arrived. The Comte was a great eater, perhaps his only quality, so his table was justly reputed throughout the region. Raoul, although he had not reached the age at which an intelligent man becomes a gourmand, was nevertheless sensible of the splendid aspect of the Comte's service. He had been seated between an honest landowner whose fields were undoubtedly much better cultivated than his mind and an old maid of reasonable ugliness, but that grotesque frame did not distress our young friend at all, who was able look across the table at his beautiful cousin. He was at the dangerous age when a man is subject to devastating attacks of love.

"After the meal, digestion, that seductive procuress, murmured mad hopes in a gleeful whisper into the adolescent's heart. Leaning on his elbows, alone at an open window, facing the immense scaffolding of clouds behind which the sun takes so long to set in autumn, he surrendered his imagination to a thousand strange thoughts. All the guests had formed a circle around a center represented by the Comte, engaged in a loud debate about dogs.

"Suddenly, the gracious form of the Comtesse came to stand close to Raoul, but turning her back on the outside for the sake of propriety, her guest and herself. That presence certainly caused the young man a sharp joy, but also, it must be said, a great deal of embarrassment.

"'Well, Cousin, what do you think of our friends?'

"'They're very fortunate, Madame, if you see them often.'

"'Their conversation doesn't interest you, and even the hunt that occupies my husband so much is perhaps not the attraction for you that we would like. Truly, if I did not fear incurring the misesteem of these gentlemen, I would offer to let you remain with us tomorrow, near the carriages.'

"Raoul dared not—or rather dreaded to—express too enthusiastically how happy he would be to sacrifice all possible hunts for the pleasure of remaining close to his cousin. But the latter continued in a more serious tone: 'Listen, Cousin, I'm your elder and your relative, two authorities that permit me to speak to you frankly. I've noticed in you the great fault of many young people in society: timidity, or, if you prefer, self-mistrust. Timidity has the danger that it leads to weakness, and weakness is an incurable illness, as one philosopher says. All these men who are talking so loudly, whose movements are so casual and whose voices are so confident, are twice as old as you. Now, be assured that you possess twice as much knowledge as them, and that at their age, the frequentation of society will have initiated you into more polite mores. In a drawing room, never allow yourself to be influenced by numbers. Intelligence is quite different from figures, grouping does not increase it. Now you're alone in the shadow; enter into the middle of that circle, vigorously give the debate a new direction, and you'd be alone in the light.'

"'Thank you, Madame; I understand the accuracy of your words, and I shall remember them. In any case, I have no illusions. But what you call shadow, when I am close to you, I take for light.'

"The young Comtesse blushed; her beautiful lips were animated by the radiance of a smile, and, abandoning her role as mentor, she resumed playfully: 'Is it at the École, then, that you've learned to address flatteries to women, Cousin?'

"'No, Madame, but it's in your company that I'm learning to be true and to almost to make my sentiments clear.'

"'You're a child, and if you don't speak more wisely I'll withdraw my protection from you. Listen—they're bringing lamps; they're about to open the gaming tables; in order not to find yourself in evident inoccupation, sit down at one of them.'

"The conversation about dogs no longer holding the interest, people were ready to play cards. Mathilde, armed with her richest smile, indicated an armchair to Raoul facing the landowner next to whom he had been seated at dinner.

"It is probable that the cultivation of the fields brings a better return than that of the mind, for Raoul's opponent was getting ready to play for high stakes. There was more gold on the table than silver. The young man's physiognomy was suddenly covered by a blush of embarrassment. His red hears were buzzing. His eyes strayed anxiously to the other tables, where there was not the slightest glitter of any hundred-sou silver coin. And Valérie, the poor mother, had only slipped two five-franc pieces into her son's pocket!

"Women do not think of everything at first, but by way of compensation, when they wish, they divine everything. Mathilde understood the young man's situation, and felt sorry for him. So, while replying to some indifferent remark, she passed close to Raoul and slipped her handkerchief into his hand. The latter unfolded it under the table. It contained a purse. The young man's gaze, although a trifle confused, went to meet his young cousin's gratefully.

"Raoul was a very good card-player. So, after having beaten the first landowner he put a second *hors de combat*, and then a proud squire, and finally a fat notary. Under his hand chattered the silvery voices of gold coins, in such number that he had to arrange them in stacks.

"One man had seen what the Comtesse has done. The cold eyes of that man had paused for some time on Raoul's hands, agitating in the shadow, putting the empty purse in one pocket and the handkerchief in another. That was Dr. Nohé-Nahm. Leaning against the mantelpiece, alone, he watched his young protégé play, but said nothing.

"For twenty years, the woman he had loved had received from him the proof of a true affection, but never the slightest intimate demonstration. He had aided her in the difficult course of her life, without a word of encouragement, without a heartfelt smile. As a child, Raoul had never received a caress or a kiss from him; as a young man, he had never shaken his hand. Raoul received Nohé-Nahm's words as a matter of instruction rather than advice. A romantic intelligence would have suspected a mystery in the heart of that impassive being, but the people who knew him were perfectly sane.

"When Raoul quit the game, he found himself so rich that he did not know where to put his gold. It was, therefore, easy for him furtively to return the purse to his cousin as he had received it, while whispering ardent thanks into her ear. He did not give back the handkerchief, and Mathilde did not ask for it. Perhaps neither of them thought of it, but there are grounds to suspect that the real reason that prevented Raoul from adding it to the purse is that he thought too much of it.

"Retired to his bedroom, our youth did not go to sleep. A fortunate age, when a gifted flower, a squeeze of the hand or the clutch of a handkerchief can enfever the heart and chase away sleep!

"That same evening, Nohé-Nahm wrote a letter, with singular care.

"The following day announced itself with a magnificent sky. Since dawn the preparations for the hunt had been keeping the grooms and the beaters busy. Horses for the hunters and English carriages for a few ladies that were to follow them were waiting in the courtyard. The impatience of the dogs added to the Comte's. They set off. The location of the rendezvous was in the middle of a wooded plain dotted with heaths.

At the most animated moment of the hunt the Comte, gone astray, stopped to orientate himself by means of the voice of the pack, which faded away from time to time. Suddenly, a beater came galloping up and handed him a letter. While letting his horse proceed at its own pace, the Comte read it. His face turned red, his eyes became wild, and with a formidable oath he launched himself into a clearing.

"Raoul was paying little heed to the wolf that was being pursued. Lost in an enclosed fern-brake in the forest, he was savoring at his leisure the joys procured by a nascent sentiment. Sometimes, however, a thought saddened him—for the intoxication was only temporary; the following day, he would return to the austere life that his mother led. Poor human nature: however excellent it may be, a whiff of amour can make it almost ingrate!

"Suddenly, his reverie was disturbed by the arrival of three horsemen who, emerging from a thicket, headed toward him. One of the three hunters—the one in the lead—was the Comte de Boistilla.

"As he approached, Raoul immediately returned a small lace-trimmed handkerchief to the coat of his uniform, unbuttoned at the top.

"'My genteel cousin, is it the government that furnishes you with such cambric?' he said, reaching out to take the piece of fabric marked with the Comtesse's monogram from the young man's bosom. With barbaric composure he added: 'It's doubtless not us for whom you're waiting here—or perhaps we've arrived too late!'

"'Monsieur, that handkerchief was not given to me...

"'You doubtless found it in the forest—isn't that right, my pretty Monsieur—that's how one responds in school. Well, I have a lesson to teach you, my young schoolboy!'

"And so saying, the Comte struck Raoul's face with his horsewhip. The latter bounded backwards and drew his épée.

"'We have no épée, Monsieur, but you have pistols in your saddle-holsters, as I have. Let's get down from our horses and, if these gentlemen would care to summon two more witnesses, we can settle this affair immediately.'

"In spite of the injustice and the brutality of the Comte's accusation, Raoul, who was brave, put off the explanations that he could give until the outcome of the combat.

"One of Monsieur de Boistilla's companions, who had absented himself, soon returned, followed by two hunters. The duel took place.

"The following day, the cadaver of her son was returned to Madame Noirtier. That event was a mortal blow for the poor mother.

"On her deathbed, Dr. Nohé-Nahm leaned over her gasping mouth, and said to her, in his cold and calm voice: 'Twenty years ago, Valérie, on the day of your marriage, you asked me what sentiment I felt for you. I can answer you today. It is hatred. I have killed your husband, I have killed your son, and I am killing you.'

"Two days later, two coffins were lowered into a single grave.

"Messieurs, it is nearly eleven o'clock; the diligence passes here early in the morning; I shall therefore permit myself to take my leave of you for the night. You will not begrudge me that, Monsieur de Saint-Loubès."

"Monsieur, your story has interested me keenly, since I am confident of its veracity. So, if I were to hold a grudge against anyone here, it would only be myself."

"Come on, Mont-Dore, let's go to sleep."

"It's not to address a wry compliment to you in your capacity as narrator, but it seems that your dog was very interested in the incidents of the poor widow's story. He has not slept at all. I even saw his blazing eyes fixed upon us the whole time. Unless I were his master, I would not want to have such an animal in my bedroom."

"Mont-Dore is faithful and devoted to me. With him I can sleep with the door open, my watch and my purse at the disposal of anyone who could take them. Come on, Mont-Dore!"

The dog raised himself up on his four paws and, while following his master, who bowed on the threshold, he uttered a dull growl, at the sound of which the Vicomte moved sideways.

"Well, it only lacks my being bitten by a dog for my evening to be complete!" said Saint-Loubès to Robert when they were alone.

"Would you like to know an idea that occurred to me, Vicomte?"

"I would."

"It's that I strongly suspect that stranger of being one of the characters in the drama he related to us."

"My dear friend, as I've often remarked to you, you make the mistake of seeing the extraordinary in everything. You're more infatuated with the fantastic than…a woman we know; and moreover, your love of it is the more constant. In the conditions in which we find ourselves, that man would have seemed to me excessively eccentric had he not acted as he did."

"He's some storyteller, then, who constructed a moving intrigue on the basis of that newspaper article?"

"Not in the least—he's simply an honest commercial traveler who possesses an old story, already recounted a hundred times over: a melodramatic adventure handed down to him by his father, whose audition he's imposed on us. And now, Monsieur de Rolleboise, let's talk about more intimate things. So you find still yourself under the tutelage of that inconvenient viscera that only serves, in my opinion, to make us commit follies in times of youth and to gratify us with aneurisms in old age!

"Don't let that lightness of expression cause you to suppose an ingrate character. I want to talk to you seriously, as a friend, about that passion. You're blowing tobacco-smoke at me—that's all right; I understand the pantomime, and I don't want to cure you of an affliction of which you don't want to be cured. However, did you know that woman before I met you?"

"I saw Madame de Lormont for the first time last season at Cauterets. I'm in love with her, and I congratulate myself for it. If I did not have that passion in my heart, who would occupy me, I ask you?"

"Yes, I'd also like to find myself in that interesting state of mind—but that would be a frightful imitation."

"After all, that delightful woman has already procured me the dream of delightful hours. Perhaps she will have an influence on my destiny…for good…or ill…it really doesn't matter! When I savor an exquisite wine, I don't worry about whether it will occasion a heart attack, or anything else, in my old age!"

"You reason admirably…as a fantasist. Nevertheless, your fever allows you a few hours of remission, of calm, from time to time?"

"Often, yes."

"Are you in one of those depressions of the heart?"

"Perhaps."

"So much the better."

"Why so much the better?"

"Because we're going to be able to talk."

"Let's talk, then…but over tea."

"Bazas tea! Never. Listen to me. When I met Madame de Lormont in the society of the spa, like many people, I did not neglect to accord her the sort of interest that the sight of a young and beautiful wife in the company of an aged husband always excites in you—for Monsieur de Lormont is old enough to be her father. Nevertheless, not being at all amorous—God preserve me!—I was able to observe at my ease."

"Oh, you're going to torture my heart! But no matter—speak."

"Don't be frightened of jealousy. To plunge that gluttonous sentiment into the soul is to throw a bundle of firewood into the furnace; the flame only becomes more active. Nevertheless, far be it from me to have the intention of offering you the shadow of a suspicion. In a word, what strikes my mind when I recall those guests, otherwise very amiable, is the mysterious penumbra with which they were enveloped."

"That reflection has never occurred to me."

"I can believe it—you have a blindfold over our eyes! Otherwise, if you had cared to observe, you would have been struck by the artistry with which the conversation was kept away from certain subjects. Often, in a seemingly insignificant discussion, a word from the husband threw attention on to another point, or a gesture from the wife distracted the speaker. I have seen Madame pale at a single word, quiver at an exclamation, or the simple sound of a door opening. Never a newspaper on the table, nor ever addressed to someone coming in the commonplace banality: 'What's new?' So, I repeat to you with conviction: between those two persons there exists a great secret, a great mystery!"

"I know people who, in my place, would offer all those remarks as an aliment to their anxious mind—but I have the good fortune not to be made that way. On the contrary, if I were egotistical, I would even congratulate myself on a subject of interior preoccupation that deflects suspicion away from me. So, do you believe that I'm excessively demanding? Not at all. Happy sentiments make me a child again. My reverie is content with the faintest favor. A flower or a smile is a festival in my heart. As you see, being a poet is good for something."

"Your joys are, indeed, weakly ambitious. Like the poor devils who take delight in the vicinity of the Mint in the clink of coins vomited by the machines, or the Savoyards who delight in the fumes from the kitchens of the Palais-Royal, the simple preludes of amour satisfy you."

"You're depressing, Vicomte."

"I'm not amorous, that's all. When I see an intoxicated man, I don't pity him. His joy is false, but it's nonetheless a joy."

"Oh, yes, it's an intoxication that transports me, a splendid intoxication, without lassitude, without brutalization, a reasoned intoxication, felt all the more keenly because I know that it's only an intoxication. Alas, our life is like that! Storm and tempest, then a few lightning flashes, which sometimes open the sky!

"Yes, I love that woman. What does it matter to me who she is? What does her past matter? I love her with all my heart! All my thoughts in the day are of her, all my dreams in the night. The memory of her beauty aliments my passion more than her possession would aliment an ordinary love. One day, Vicomte, one day..."

"Yes, I can guess—you were lucky."

"Oh, you think that I'm going to tell you about one of those favors that count as necessary to happiness! No, Vicomte, no. One day, in a corridor, I dared..."

"To offer her a flower?"

"No, not so much. I dare to take her hand...that hand she did not draw back...and for an instant, we remained there, without a word, without a gesture! Oh, if Heaven had only desired, in that blissful second to stop the course of time and prolong my happiness...but no; she left."

"Admirable, my dear Robert! I'm glad to see you as utterly egotistical as the lovers of the theater. Indeed, would it not have been charming if Heaven had listened to you! But it might not be to very agreeable for many people! So, a dentist is preparing to relieve me of a diseased tooth; at the first creaking of the roots, when my entire jaw is in agony, instead of hastening the extraction, the operator pauses on that pain and makes my torture continue. I blaspheme. 'Oh, Monsieur,' he says to me, complacently, 'have a little patience; it's your friend Monsieur de Rolleboise who has obtained that time should stop on a happy moment that has just fallen to him. It won't be long.' It's very jolly, your idea, Robert, very jolly! Anyway, Madame de Lormont has left the spa, and you're immediately hastening to follow her to Paris. You're very young!"

"You're very old, Vicomte."

"Anyway, we'll talk at greater length about his subject during our journey—for I assume that you'll be amiable enough to accept a place in my carriage."

"No—you'll take me into a realm entirely opposite to the one for which I'm bound!"

"Oh, Robert, my friend, how little you know me to suppose that I would adopt scenic means! Have I not run into enough strangeness this evening? Uncertainty, the unexpected and the extraordinary—but they, for me, are toxic morals that I've never been able to resist."

The two young men stayed up rather late before the last whitening logs, talking from time to time, or meditating, one on intimate memories, the other on puffs of cigar smoke, or nothing, or everything—perhaps the most attractive reverie of all.

Suddenly, the silence was disrupted by two gunshots, doubtless fired in one of the rooms of the inn.

The Vicomte de Saint-Loubès shuddered on his seat. Then starting to stride back and forth in the large room, he cried, furiously: "There! That was all I lacked! After having traversed all the ridiculous phases of the destinies that enfevered imaginations invent, to encounter the heroes of truculent melodramas in an inn! My God, I'm in a fine mess! I'm hip-deep in crime. I can already see myself at the assizes, as a witness! The newspapers will write about my costume, the sound of my voice, whether I've put on weight or am flagging. *L'Illustration* is capable of publishing my portrait! Women will fall in love with me! Oh, my God, my God, what a future!"

At that moment, the landlord came in, half-dressed and very troubled.

"Let me go!" cried the Vicomte. "Has my carriage been repaired?"

"What, Monsieur, go? You fire rifle-shots in my home, perhaps commit murder, and you want to flee! Oh, no, no..."

"What? Are you mad, innkeeper."

"But, I don't know—I hear gunshots and I find a traveler who wants to run away, so I stop him!"

"Wretch! The noise came from the bedrooms."

"Then let's run there, Monsieur, I beg you—follow me!"

"Are you afraid?"

"No, I'm not afraid—but there might be danger and I wouldn't be sorry to avoid it. I'm the father of a family..."

II. Bitten

Horatio Mackinguss had retired to the room that had been prepared for him.

There is no one who, having entered his room at night, when he knows that he is alone, does not return its natural attitude to his body and its true physiognomy to his visage. The man who is serious and self-important in society looks at himself in the mirror and laughs; the cheerful and madcap woman bows her head beneath the weight of a worrying thought...strange to relate, the drawing-room as well as the theater relegates reality to the wings!

Horatio paced back and forth in the room. From time to time, a fragment of a phrase, a word, emerged from his mouth. Then, stopping, as if to fix his ideas, he said to himself:

"Hazard...is it permissible to say that? Hazard, that law of our destiny, that unknown magnet that attracts some toward others, is serving me strangely! That young man has no suspicion that encountering me has thrown him into a new circle, on to a path that would frighten him if he were able to measure the whole perspective with his eyes. So he is linked with me, for I shall see him again. I shall see him again in the home of that woman, Mathilde, Madame de Lormont, with whom he is in love, poor boy!

"Midnight! Come on, Horatio, go to sleep...for you are doubtless asleep, Monsieur de Rolleboise, and you too, Amadeus Harriss, and you, proud and disdainful Olivia, and you, old Duke of Firstland...you're resting easy, without presentiments; and if anyone told you that good Horatio, far away from you, in a little town in France, is awake and thinking of you, that he has invisible threads in his hand that will reunite you—the most improbable means, which will put you at his mercy—you would certainly drive away that insensate thought, that evil nightmare, and you would go back to sleep in a new dream, similarly effaced by the return of daylight. Oh, old Duke, Olivia, Amadeus, sleep, sleep!

"Hazard, I said just now—but, in the same way that certain men encounter fortuitously in life days of unexpected success, there must also be, by virtue of the effects of the same hazard, entire existences that never run into obstacles: I am one of those men. I am the soldier who traverses, safe and sound, the enemy fire in which a hundred of his companions fall.

"Come on, Mont-Dore, don't growl like that; I'm not talking to you.

"Yes, this evening I felt a bitter voluptuousness in returning to that recent work. Twenty years! It took me twenty years, Valérie, but I've satisfied my vengeance! Those honest young men didn't see through me. They didn't even understand Nohé-Nahm. For them, he's a monstrosity, nothing more. Ah…sleep is overtaking me…the worthy Nohé-Nahm is going to sleep."

Horatio lay down. That man, whose face will become clearer later in this book, had, by means of a constant habit of moral agitation, so to speak, satiated his brain. Master of himself, he could stop his thoughts as one snuffs out a flame. Horatio slept like any honest man.

The dog was lying on the carpet. Everything was dark; otherwise, one would have perceived his fur bristling from time to time on his back, and the claws of his large paws tormenting the woolen blanket that served as his bed.

His gasping, anxious breath was produced in muffled snorts. As his master has told us, Mont-Dore had been bitten—but what he did not suspect was that the dog that had attacked him was rabid.

Mont-Dore was feeling the first effects of the disease; a seizure gripped him. And sleep carried Horatio into the fantastic world of dreams.

The dog stood up on his advanced paws, his head extended, his teeth grating. For a moment, he remained motionless thus, his flanks palpitating precipitately. A convulsive frisson ran through his coarse pelt and caused him to bound at the bed, the closed curtains of which stopped him. Nevertheless, he remained standing, his front legs supported on the edge of the bed. His furious and muffled growling woke the sleeper.

Horatio, surprised by that noise and the agitation of the fabric, raised himself up on his elbow and parted the curtains. In the darkness he made out two hot coals fixed upon him.

"Well, what is it, Mont-Dore?"

With one bound, the furious animal launched himself at his master, and then both of them rolled on to the floor. There was a frightful struggle, without cries, without a word: a struggle in which the rage of the one balanced the strength of the other. But the man was to be victorious. Having plunged his left arm into the dog's throat, thus preventing him from biting, he reached out to the mantelpiece with the other for a pistol, and discharged two shots into the animal's breast.

When the two young men, followed by the innkeeper, arrived in the corridor, the door of the room opened. Horatio Mackinguss appeared on the threshold.

"Did those gunshots came from your room?" asked Monsieur de Rolleboise.

"Yes. I fired them at my dog."

"He's bitten you."

"He was rabid. I have three wounds in my arm and shoulder. While I go wash these wounds and apply leeches to them, Monsieur Innkeeper, have a red-hot iron made ready."[13]

---

[13] The novel was written long before Louis Pasteur and Émile Roux developed the first rabies vaccine in 1885. The standard treatment for a bite inflicted by a rabid dog was then cauterization of the wound—hence the demand for a red-hot iron. Not everyone bitten by a rabid dog developed the disease, especially after cauterization, but it was generally believed that the disease could lie dormant for some considerable time after a bite.

III. Two Pistols

There are frightful maladies. When a man is under the threat of those diseases, which science has not yet vanquished, his morale kills him. He dares not advance, for uncertainty lies before him, paralyzing the entire future, extinguishing all his hopes.

Horatio Mackinguss, endowed with a great and active intelligence, had created a laborious existence that incessantly demanded the tension of his mind. To march with firmness and success in that perhaps difficult path, he required a healthy body and a free head. Now, one ever-present thought, impossible to dispel, and wearying, was on his mind. At any minute, a frightful disease might seize him, annihilating the means of a drama whose details perhaps possessed him more than thirst for the result. The bite of his dog threatened to be, for him, Cromwell's grain of sand.[14] So, judging that his morale was the thing most to be dreaded, he resolved to cure his morale.

I shall relate an event here, in a single page. Many, I know, would have extended the scene into a long chapter. As many things remain for me to write, I shall content myself with a more summary reduction.

Horatio was Scottish. The men of that country bear some resemblance to the women of our provinces; they are superstitious. Mackinguss believed in predestination. Doubt was uncomfortable for him; he wanted to gamble his destiny, to interrogate God.

One day, he was alone in his drawing room in Paris. He rang; his domestic appeared.

---

[14] The historian Jacques-Bénigne Bossuet (1627-1704), meditating on the contingencies of history, offered as an example of trivial items on which the fate of nations depend a "grain of sand" (i.e., a kidney stone) that formed in Oliver Cromwell's urethra and caused the infection that killed him.

"Do you know the gunsmith Lepage, William?"

"Yes, Monsieur."

"Go to his shop. There, buy two identical pistols—entirely identical, you hear, indistinguishable from one another. Put them in their box and come back."

Half an hour later, with a pistol-box under his arm, the manservant came back into the room, where he found Horatio.

"Are they identical? Answer me, but don't show them to me."

"Absolutely identical, Monsieur."

"That's good. Take the box into my study; you won't be able to see anything, because the shutters are hermetically closed. When you're in the room, take the pistols out of their box and put them on the table. Go."

The domestic went into the study, convinced that his master was mad. A minute later, he came back into the drawing room.

"You've placed the two pistols?"

"On the table, Monsieur."

"Now come here. Here's a charge of powder, a bullet and a detonator. Go back into the study and load a pistol."

"Only one?"

"You're an imbecile! Hurry; I'll wait for you."

William had soon carried out the order.

"One of the pistols is loaded."

"That's good. Go away."

His face calm, Horatio went into the room, where complete darkness reigned. When he had closed the door he picked up one of the pistols, put the end of the barrel to his forehead, and pulled the trigger.

IV. A Whore?

The clocks, all asleep, seemed to be yawning with lassitude and sounding midnight with a slow and slothful voice. In the middle of the sky the moon, on a cloud—a glaucous pupil in a pale eye—gazed down gloomily over the roofs of the city. It was an autumn night. The temperature was mild, so the streets were only beginning to empty.

A low-slung coupé glided at high speed along the causeway of the boulevards, harnessed to a horse whose shiny coat seemed black beneath the gaslight, like a shadow fortified by steel.

The carriage stopped in the Rue du Helder.

The coachman immediately uttered an imperious guttural cry. Certainly, at that strident voice, al the concierges in the vicinity would have started in their beds. Nevertheless, only the door of a single house opened, and the coupé came to place itself slowly at the foot of a vast staircase.

A young man opened the carriage door and got out. Abandoned to his momentum, he had already climbed several steps when the silky swirls of a woman's dress emerged from the interior of the carriage. Immediately, the gentleman came back, with the rather extraordinary expression of someone caused by distraction to forget certain usual conventions He addressed a word to the coachman, and took the hand of the young woman without further ceremony. Without saying a word, they reached the threshold of an apartment on one of the lowers floors.

Probably by virtue of distraction, again, the young man went in first, without paying any heed to the woman, who followed him. In that fashion, they reached a bedroom. The man let himself fall into an armchair; the woman lay down on a sofa.

A valet presented his master with a card on a silver tray.

"I don't know that name," he said to himself, as he looked at both sides of the cardboard square, traced with imperceptible letters.

"The person is in the drawing room, where he has been waiting for Monsieur since ten o'clock."

The young man got to his feet immediately—but at that moment his gaze fell upon the young woman lying on the sofa. He sat down again.

"Make my apologies to this Monsieur, for not being able to see him for a few minutes. I'm not alone."

The valet went out. Only then did the master come to sit next to the silent woman, whose gaze seemed indifferent to the things surrounding her.

"My God, my dear lady, I have great wrongs to repair in your regard."

"Not at all, Monsieur. You perceived me at your side during supper. You spoke to me at hazard; I replied. You invited me to go with you; I went with you."

"I know. But, forgetful and distracted, I didn't ask you where you lived, and my coachman naturally brought me home. Fortunately, the coupé is still at the foot of the staircase. I'll go inform…"

As he spoke, he extended his arm toward the bell-cord—but before his hand had completed the movement, his gaze fell upon the young woman's face. The face expressed a smile of such strange sentiment that his hand immediately fell back.

"In fact," he went on, "you must have judged my manners quite bizarre. But alas, there is a species of women whose character has become so familiar to me that I have lost all self-respect in their company."

"That's true. Vanity is extinguished before what one disdains. You have loved a great deal, then?"

"A great deal, but only once."

The young man's physiognomy was immediately lost to his companion in a labyrinth of unknown memory.

"You love a great deal today, but you came into the society from which we've just emerged, into the midst of men without morals and doomed women," she articulated, with a gaze full of reproach and astonishment. "So you're not averse to bringing into an impure atmosphere the memory of a person that you perhaps do not dare to name?"

"No; when I emerge from it, my love is increased."

"Yes, when one comes outside into the cold, one appreciates the warmth of shelter more keenly." The young woman stood up—but a hand invited her to sit down again.

"Listen, my dear child; in my life as a young man I've seen many women of your sort, strange and insouciant characters, but I understood them immediately—whereas in you, I encounter a certain distinctive, inexplicable sprit. You're beautiful, but sad. There is in that smile, which can scarcely form, the stain of a tear. During supper, when that handsome white-haired old man intoned an obscene song, all the other women remained serious, while the young men suffered it, but you blushed. When my eyes settle on your face, you lower your eyelids; if my hand approaches, your arm pushes it away—and yet, you're a whore!"

"A whore!" she said, in a repulsive voice. Then, her eyes wandered around the room, and she added, with a nervous laugh that she could not suppress. "Yes, that's true, I'm a whore!"

"Do you live alone?"

"No, I'm with a man."

"Your...father?"

"No."

"Your lover?"

"I've never had a lover, monsieur! Oh, I'm mad to say this, because you can't understand me—and yet, for many days I've been searching for a face like yours, in which there was a sympathetic interest, a voice that did not inject any doubt into my soul. I met you and I chose you. Oh, I had gathered within me all the energy of my will, all the courage of my heart. But now, I'm defeated—it's too late!"

"What are you trying to say to me?"

"No," she continued, as if frightened, and pausing after each word, "No...I shan't speak...because if I spoke, I would die. My sentence would hardly be finished before my left was extinct. No, I don't have the courage to confront that struggle! Adieu, Monsieur—I'm leaving!"

"You're mad, perhaps!" said the man, who was listening to her fearfully.

"Mad!" she said, uncovering her face in that tranquil moment. "Yes, that's true, I ought to be mad, but perhaps I won't be, before dying!"

The young man looked at her for a few moments in silence, but, seeing that there was nothing to reveal the woman's secrets, his gaze became vague, and his thoughts doubtless returned to the places they had quit, for he said to her, after brief reflection: "Forgive me, Madame, if I return to a subject that both of us ought rather to forget. Among all the men at table with us, only one did not speak to any woman. His mouth expressed nothing but disdain."

"That's Horatio."

"Yes, I met him once while traveling, when he experienced an accident—which, it appears, has not had unfortunate consequences. Do you know him well?"

"I don't know him. Many things are said about him, it's true, but..."

"You don't believe them. Are you leaving?"

"Someone is waiting for you."

"Shall I see you again?"

"I'd like to see you again."

"Who can arrange a meeting?"

"Hazard."

"Where do you live?"

"It would be futile to tell you, for tomorrow, I shall be somewhere else. It's known that I'm here... Adieu."

When the strange woman had gone, and the dull sound of the carriage wheels had died away, the young man fell back into his reverie. His keen artistic intelligence delighted in the memory of those incoherent statements, and searched with a bitter ardor through the details of that situation fallen by hazard into the circle of real life. He repeated the woman's conversation mentally, sentence by sentence. Then a skeptical smile brightened his face, and withdrawing incredulously from the initial darkness of the drama, he doubtless concluded that her character was a new variety of the kind of prostitute that only Paris possesses.

The chime of the clock soon replaced him in the course of time. He remembered the person that was waiting for him.

That person was entirely unknown to him, for he paused on the threshold, doubtless occupied in searching the thousand pigeon-holes of the past for the memory of the man in question.

"Monsieur..." His gaze flickered to the card he was holding in his hand. "Monsieur André de Bassens, I need all my apologies, for you are a stranger to me, and, nevertheless, someone who just left me has forced me to make you wait too long."

"Monsieur, the hour at which I have presented myself and the obstinacy with I have insisted on seeing you, are more evident failures of politeness. We have only met once. It was two months ago. I had the advantage of spending the evening with Monsieur de Rolleboise at Cauterets. We found ourselves together at a *bouillotte* table. I'm a very poor card player, so I lost quite a lot of money to you, of which fifty louis was on my word of honor. I had your address, but the next day, when I came to your hotel, I was told that Monsieur de Rolleboise had left during the day."

After saying this, the stranger placed a stack of gold coins on the table. He was a man of about thirty; his uncovered physiognomy offered all the indications of frankness and food humor, but unknown events had modified that propensity with hints of unclarity. The creases hollowed out between his eyebrows spoke of the reflection of a mind often alone, and his large fatigued eyes seemed to have expended all the fire of passion and all the tears of the heart. It was one of those physiognomies that pass unperceived before men, but by which women are always impassioned, because their sex sees through them.

"I remember that evening now, and the departure, entirely independent of my will. I would have written to you to discharge you from the weight of that obligation, but I did not know your name. So, I regret bitterly that the petty debt in question should have troubled you so much—judging by the patience of which you have given proof this evening."

"I will not conceal from you, Monsieur de Rolleboise, that there is another objective that has brought me to your home."

"So much the better, Monsieur, and I beg you to tell me immediately what it is."

"I have arrived in Paris for the first time, and I know no one here but you. I also have on me a letter for an excellent friend of my father, Monsieur de Lormont, but Monsieur de Lormont is not in Paris."

"Indeed; Monsieur le Vicomte has been in Normandy for nearly three weeks."

"You know the family very well, I'm told. So I have come, quite simply, to ask you to be kind enough to accompany me to Normandy."

"Your proposal is all the more opportune and agreeable because I am due to visit your father's friend tomorrow. Thus, it will be with great pleasure that I make the journey. If I can believe society gossip, Monsieur and Madame de Lormont will not be returning to Paris, and will soon be leaving France for England. The difference in climate and change of mores might not suit Madame la Vicomtesse entirely. Young southern heads take fright at London skies."

"But if I can judge by Monsieur le Vicomte's age, Madame la Vicomtesse ought no longer to perceive the caprices of her youth, save in her memories."

"Monsieur le Vicomte got married last spring."

"As a friend of my father, I presumed that he was old."

"I can see that you don't know the family. Permit me then to inform you. Monsieur de Lormont is over sixty."

"And Madame?"

"Madame is not yet twenty."

"Doubtless she loves her husband?" said Monsieur de Bassens, with a smile.

"My God, the nature of a woman is always to love someone, you know. There are more women than men who have not been loved. Having said that, I am not sufficiently intimate in Madame's society to be able to answer your question; only she can do that."

"She's probably a woman of...ordinary beauty."

"She is a beautiful woman."

An observer might have noticed at this point, on the faces of the two interlocutors, an almost imperceptible expression. They each felt it inside themselves, but did not distinguish it in the other. Monsieur de Rolleboise had replied to his visitor's remark in an indecisive, almost embarrassed tone, but an anxious attention was legible in the other's eyes as he listened to the young man's opinion.

"You will admit, however, that to take a wife of an age so disproportionate to one's own, it is necessary either to be very generous or very presumptuous. But, as you almost said just now, a woman is of a nature so malleable, so ready to espouse the opinion of whoever is speaking to her, that it is easy to persuade her that the best husbands are old men. That's a consolation for our latter years."

The conversation continued for a while in digressions entirely irrelevant to our story, and although we could do otherwise, we shall not weary the reader with them.

After Monsieur de Bassens had left the apartment, Monsieur de Rolleboise went back to his bedroom and sat down on the sofa that the whore had occupied, and his mind drifted into a reverie that must have been delightful to his heart, for it led him well into the night.

When his thoughts returned from their vagabond course, his eyes fell upon a little pocket-book placed in the folds of a cushion. It could only belong to the woman who had been sitting there. He looked at it for a moment, unsure as to whether to open it, but, reflecting that he would probably never see the woman again, he permitted himself to seek a few explanations of her odd behavior.

The pocket-book only contained a letter, old, worn and soiled by virtue of having been read many times. It was written in English. Rolleboise, a southerner, did not understand a word of that language. The letter began *My dearest daughter*, and the signature it bore was *Helena, Duchess of Firstland.*

V. An Unpleasant Night

Independently of the portraits that we have yet to paint, a few still remain to be finished off. Let Monsieur de Rolleboise take an armchair, then, and grant us a brief sitting.

Robert was twenty-five years old. Many young men, at that age, still act in a dependent fashion, not yet doing anything by themselves, but Robert had not submitted to that schoolboy existence. His mind had never felt swayed between indecisive eventualities. All the hours of his life had been certain. At twenty he was a man, for a twenty he had found himself alone in life. So, in that epoch, his physiognomy had been suddenly stripped of the irresolute expression of an adolescent insouciant about the morrow. His gait became form and decisive. Practical reasoning, the route of a man of good sense, surged forth in his will.

Physically, Robert not having given in to the bad habits of some young men suddenly released from the shackles of school, who throw themselves into ridiculous eccentricities, had all the manners of comfortable society, heightened by an uncommon dress sense. In brief, he was one of those young heads who, at the entrance to a ball or a fête, causes young women to dream, and whose presence in an intimate circle causes muted irritation to husbands with contorted minds.

These natural qualities notwithstanding, Robert also possessed a certain mental illness that imaginative souls will doubtless appreciate. Rolleboise was one of those young heads imbued with an exaggerated literature in which passions are twisted and tormented to the utmost stab of pain. By virtue of plunging his heart into illusions, he had become one of those imaginary lovers who dream of an excessive sentiment, cataleptic delights and impossible joys: one of those illuminated minds who take seriously the mad ideas of intoxicated poets, absorbing them avidly and trustingly, and then seeking bravely to make them a palpable reality, to make the sunbeam concrete. His mind was saturated to the point of indigestion with all that crazy literature of the nineteenth century. He had sated himself with so many fantasies and novels that he had come, by a thousand hallucinatory gradations, to believe in them.

Real life was capable of shaking his religion, but not of destroying it. When he sensed that his paradoxical and sick ideas were rejected by the simple common sense of the crowd, he accepted that violent blow without a murmur, and as a consequence of his theory. "For human society," he said to himself, "is an orbicular whole composed of different circles. Hazard has determined that I am presently the inactive center of sterile radii. Perhaps, tomorrow, my true sphere will envelop me, and then I shall act."

Thus, in accordance with this principle, the young man's life was a continual displacement. Those women who seek the bizarre and indecisive in all things thought him amiable and witty; those men who only appreciate contained and fixed ideas judged him mad—but Robert de Rolleboise was simply a dreamer, and, in consequence, a fortunate man.

The next day, Rolleboise and Monsieur de Bassens, whose society had immediately become agreeable to him, by virtue of a law consequent upon his inquisitive mind, left Paris together. After a few hours of speed, they reached the sea.

The sea! An immense vastness, at the sight of which one shivers, like an adolescent at the sight of a beautiful naked woman!

Monsieur de Lormont was resident in a property in the region of Caux, a league or two from Le Havre, on the shore of the Atlantic. The individual who had recommended Monsieur de Bassens must have been very dear to the old man, for he received the young man more cordially than a friend, almost as affectionately as a son. Even the young Vicomtesse accorded him a smile of inexpressible benevolence. A woman's mere smile often says more than all the frank protestations of a man.

In the society into which hazard has thrown us, there was no woman other than Madame la Vicomtesse, so she was the focus of all the attention of her commensals.

Mathilde de Lormont was twenty, at the most. She was not a pretty woman. It is even probable that at the age of fifteen she must have been thin and too dark. At twenty, she was a magnificent person. Her dark brown hair, without that frightful gleam which is to hair what make-up is to the face, presented in its suppleness all the soft sinuosities of the comb. A painter would not have been able to find the vaporous shadow that floated around that hair on contact with the dermis, whose pure grain was brightened by the light of an entirely Italian *gustoso*. Her brown eyebrows and long lashes unveiled in her eyes a life rich in splendid passions. A faint blue-tinted shadow surrounded her eyelids and added to the beauty of the face. Fatigued eyes augment a beautiful woman as gaminess augments the taste of venison. Her mouth had conserved all the freshness of youth. The neck of that head offered the fortunate contours of the Milesian Venus and the cerulean tints of Titianesque flesh.

Madame de Lormont was not only a beautiful woman by virtue of the head, that projection of the body. If her face presented lines of dreamy morbidity, one divined more behind the rampart of silk and satin that defended forms and contours to make a lover quiver.

Now, beautiful women, whatever their social situation, require the love of a young man. On the day when Robert had perceived Madame de Lormont for the first time, he had recognized her. She was the conception of his dreams. For a long time he had been in love with her. The presence of the woman, therefore, did not bring any perturbation to his mind.

At his age—twenty-five—any other young man would already have exhausted more than twenty-five amours, but he, predisposed by his foolish and eccentric nourishment, had had but one passion. Mathilde knew that. However, whether out of virtue, or inertia of the heart, she had remained faithful to her husband and her honor. She was not alarmed by the impetuous love, devoid of premonitory symptoms or surging affection, that had gripped him coldly, like a cog-wheel which, having commenced its rotation in a void, continues it crushingly.

Now, it is an irrefutable aphorism that no woman living in a society of men can liberate her heart. If she resists the amour of a young man, the latter must play his part sagely, for he has come too late. We must therefore suppose, honestly, that Madame de Lormont loved her husband.

In the same plane as the young wife, the Vicomte appeared: a handsome head clad in white hair. Hus benevolent physiognomy was often serious when abandoned to the course of his intimate thoughts. Sometimes, far from being alarmed by the assiduous courtesies shown by strangers toward his wife, they seemed, on the contrary, to make him proud, as if they were being addressed to his daughter.

The two spouses had not been in the locality for long. They had come from Paris, although they were only to be resident here for one winter season, and only the sea bathing had attracted them to Normandy.

The other people gathered in the foreground of Madame de Lormont's drawing room are devoid of significance for us, if not for themselves: a few rich merchants from Le Havre, much too exclusive in their habits, and also in their conversation.

In the background, however, in the shadows, appeared a head marked with the seal of high intelligence. It was Horatio Mackinguss. It would be difficult to explain by virtue of what collective secret the sight of that human mask stopped the fleeting thought, deflected the floating thread of reflection, and took possession of the crowd's gaze. That magnetism did not reside in the ample swept-back hair, the grave forehead or the large and staring eyes. However, an imaginative mind would have retained the imprint of that physiognomy; a vulgar intelligence would have considered it stupidly without comprehending the effect that it produced on its primitive nature; and a dream-beset woman would either have rejected the image fearfully or loved it slavishly.

Lord Horatio was one of those men whose fortune one does not dare to calculate and whom poverty would not suit. He never manifested conceit, or confessed his impotence by reason of lack of money.

For the third time, Robert de Rolleboise ran into him—for he recognized him immediately, by reason of having seen him a month before at Bazas, and then again as the silent and grave watcher amid the hectic joy of the late night feast where he had found him by chance. It was whispered in certain circles that the man, having suffered over a woman, had avenged himself at length, mortally; as every person gave a different version of the tale, though, it is as well to suppose that only one man knew the secret.

A sprightly and elegant little old man was dispensing an untiring amiability for the young Vicomtesse, who was secretly laughing at his grotesque contortions and outdated affectations.

"No, Madame, you won't quit the sea before the end of the season, but after your departure, there will be a desert here. You're the most beautiful of the most beautiful women of the coast Are you unaware, then, of a horrible conspiracy? Yes, all the Englishwomen in Ingouville are in league against you, and even threatening to form a redoubtable coalition with the Parisiennes at Frascati."

"But if that's the case, Monsieur Straton, it's truly dangerous for me to live in a place where I have occasioned so much enmity. You'll be for us, I hope, Monsieur Horatio?"

"Madame, I shall be with all the men. In any case, they owe you that assistance; thanks to you, Frascati is less miserable. Yesterday evening, the old Duc de Brissac said that, in order to see you, he scaled the cliffs without a guide or a stick. Finally, there was so much talk about Madame la Vicomtesse that the Baronne de Bléville, on seeing the void left round her, fell into a bad mood, which consecrated your triumph."

"Truly, Lord Horatio, if were to take pride in anything, it would be your speech. Certainly—and I'm convinced of it—

I'm the first woman to whom you've accorded such flattery. Even Monsieur Straton is utterly amazed."

"Madame, that's a mischievous remark that I don't deserve," said the little old man, bowing, entirely satisfied with his reply.

"Seriously, my lord, what else are they saying in Frascati?"

"About you, a great deal; about politics, too much; about trivia, a little."

"And what are the trivia they're talking about?"

"Alas, Madame, they are pyramids of wit that that leave nothing behind, in serious minds but disappointment at having been engaged in such futile matters. Sometimes, however in that rose-tinted picture, a dark and distinct shade appears. Thus..."

"I beg you my lord, don't frighten us.

"What I was about to tell you, Madame, is a scene in an unknown theater, so insignificant that that I would remain silent if I did not consider it a duty to satisfy your desire. Yesterday evening, Monsieur Forlow told us an almost fantastic story—the same Monsieur Forlow who, when he writes to his mistress, signs himself, by force of habit, Forlow and Company."

"And how do you, Monsieur Horatio, know about that particularity?"

"Perhaps it was Monsieur Straton who told me."

"Yes, yes, I heard it from my nephew," added the incriminated merchant. The nephew was not present.

"Oh well! Yesterday evening, Monsieur Forlow told us a strange story. This is it. One of his correspondents in a town in the Midi, whose name escapes me, was murdered a year ago..."

Monsieur de Lormont was then at the table, on the same side as the Vicomtesse. By means of a natural and unperceived movement, he tilted the lampshade toward himself. That sudden inclination enveloped the husband and the young woman in obscurity. Monsieur de Bassens, who was sitting opposite, got up casually and went to place himself in the shadow. Those various movements occurred without anyone noticing, and if we record them here, it is simply an observation of detail that might be reckoned overly conscientious.

Lord Horatio went on, staring into the penumbra: "The murderer was condemned to death. But the bizarre thing is..."

"Ah! Let's have it..."

"Yes, the bizarre thing is that on the day fixed for the sentence to be carried out, the jailer found nothing in the cell but a cadaver."

"But my lord, that happens every day. There are facts so commonplace that I skip over them every time I encounter them in a newspaper, such as fires and shipwrecks. Truly, you're terrible in your choice of stories. Tell us instead about the amusing incident that revealed that Madame de Graville wears a wing."

"Ah! Madame, Monsieur Straton will tell you that, with all his mordant and satirical wit. For myself, I'll stick to concluding the adventure of Monsieur Forlow's correspondent." The lord went on, obstinately: "So, nothing was found but a cadaver, but, strangely enough, that cadaver, whose head was almost consumed by the gunshot that had delivered death, was recognized to be that of an old man."

"Aha! The murderer was a woman, no doubt?"

"No, Monsieur Straton, but the murderer was a young man."

"That's extraordinary," said the Vicomtesse, getting up, "but it's a shame that you don't have a denouement to tell us."

"Justice is searching for one, Madame."

The conversation begun by that subject then extended into a labyrinth so sinuous, its thread so twisted in a knot so tangled and inextricable, that it would have been impossible to return to the starting point phrase by phrase, circuit by circuit sand link by link.

The path taken by a casual conversation is a bizarre thing; the extravagances of an invalid in delirium are no more chaotic. Everything proceeds in zigzags. A chance word throws you in a new direction. Thus, after having emerged from the cell, the chatter paused for a moment on the luxury of a dancer, and that new subject led to a discussion of California, from which it took flight for an entirely antipodean location...

Robert de Rolleboise had drawn apart from that circle, whose comments were indifferent to him, and he leaned on the still of an open window, dreaming. To dream, for a man in love, is almost to possess. The curtains, detached from their loops, hid him completely from the sight of the people gathered in the drawing room. Solitude is the first lover of those in love; she initiates them and prepares them for the great joy that is promised to them.

The landscape that extended before the young man's eyes was beautiful. Facing him, from the height of the cliffs of the Cap de la Hève, was the ocean, illuminated by a white lunar light. All along the shore, where the waves were breaking noisily, semaphores and lighthouses shone like stars. And in the background, far away, on a narrow spur of land, a few dull lights appeared, and a few black houses—and that tiny space contained Le Havre, one of the richest cities in France, the port of Paris.

Robert absorbed the vast effect of that scene, but did not admire it. Entirely given over to his amour, he did not have the leisure to squander his time in sterile reveries. Besides which, he knew that although he often felt the effects of poetry, he was not a poet for that. Then again, his crudescent passion had attained a paroxysm so material, its physical joy was becoming so tangible, that the dream and the illusion were left far behind.

The two windows of the drawing room were both open. On chancing to glance at the other one, Robert made out a woman's head at the contiguous window. Immediately, one of the windows was abandoned. As soon as the Vicomtesse perceived the young man's presence, she made as if to withdraw. The latter retained her.

"Oh no, don't go! Don't cast despair into my intoxicated heart like that! Stay here, alone with that landscape that extends before us, that I might be happy."

"Poor Robert, still the same folly!"

"Still the same love, still the same joy when I'm near you. Oh, believe me, this great passion, this fervent faith that my heart has invested in you, is not a vain caprice, a simple young man's fantasy. It's my entire life that your face has taken on. Oh, that makes you smile...and yet, Madame, through you I might live or die. Above all, don't believe that I am telling you all that my heart feels, that I'm depicting for you all the vertigos wit which my head is seething—oh no, I couldn't! For I can't express the love, I can only feel it...I'm a lover, not a poet. Oh, for pity's sake, don't go, don't withdraw your hand from mine; stay in this fortunate breeze, which brings me all the intoxications of your face!"

"Shut up, Monsieur."

"Yes, that's true, I'm a madman, an idiot. I'm talking like an adolescent escaped from his mother's arms...let's lower our voices."

"What, let's lower our voices!" the young woman exclaimed, at that imprudent phrase. "Monsieur de Lormont is two paces away from us, and you dare to express yourself in that fashion!"

"Oh, I beg you, never, oh never, pronounce that name! It's a word that obsesses me, which my fearful hand repels in my blackest dreams. No, that man could not bear a grudge against me, for that man cannot love you."

"Durable and devoted affection is not a fever, Monsieur."

"A fever! Listen Madame, I saw you for the first time in the Pyrenees, at Cauterets, and that sight was an entire revelation for me. I followed you to Paris. Faithfully, I placed myself in your path, my thought attached to yours by an intimate affinity as strong as that attaching lightning to a magnet. You were living in retreat, in religion; I waited for you in church.

You left Paris; here I am beside you. Tell me, do you believe that I love you or not?"

"Robert, I beg you..."

"It's me who is imploring you, and you ask me for pity! No, the new life that is transporting me is so vehement, that passion that exalts me so impetuous, that your loving nature cannot resist its magnetism. In this silvery light your head is very beautiful, Madame! Oh, you, too, have pity on me!"

And the young man, drunk with joy, leaned further toward the visage of the young woman, whose halting respiration caused her pale lips to part.

Robert did not savor the ecstasy into which his senses were plunged for long. Pythagoras informs us that the dogs of the Nile drink on the run, for fear of crocodiles, and advises us to do the same with the cup of pleasures; a foreign hand, doubtless by virtue of that precept, suddenly came to shake him in his intoxication. A vigorous arm drew him back, and, before he could think of offering any resistance, he found himself back in the drawing-room outside the curtain.

A man was still holding him; it was Lord Horatio.

Robert, his expression furious, was about to demand an explanation for that strange abruptness when the lord, without saying a word, indicated the old man's hand, which was lifting the curtain.

"Mathilde, I've been looking for you for ten minutes. These gentlemen are asking for a little music."

"Sing! Alas, I can't!" said the young woman, in a low voice, quitting the embrasure.

"Madame, we implore you," said Horatio, advancing toward her. "If it can possibly serve to activate your determination, I will even offer to accompany you."

The Vicomtesse replied with a smile of worldly graciousness, and, supported by her husband's hand, went to the piano.

In that brief interval, the Scotsman turned round and said, in a low voice, to the mute young man: "Child—would you rather it had been Monsieur de Lormont who pulled you out of your distraction?"

"Monsieur, I don't know for what reason or with what objective you acted in that fashion, but I thank you for it."

Monsieur de Bassens, who had spent the entire evening mingling with the company of merchants and shipwrights of compassed intellect, talking business and politics as best he could, came over to Robert. "Do you know, Monsieur de Rolleboise, that I have a good mind to surrender you to Madame la Vicomtesse's vindictive resentment. You told me yesterday evening, without conviction, even in a banal fashion, that Madame de Lormont is beautiful—but you must have meant magnificent, I assume!"

"Isn't she?" the young man agreed, dazedly.

"Do you know that individual sitting next to her?"

"I'm seeing him for the third time. He's a Scotsman."

"One of those gentlemen told me that he's mad, another that he's in love—which is almost the same thing."

"In love! That man is in love, you say!" Robert said, unguardedly, while looking at Lord Horatio with blazing eyes. "Did they tell you with whom?"

"I'm assured that he's infatuated with the ten or twenty millions attached to the hand of a young Englishwoman."

"But is that certain?"

"Not only do I know the sum of the fortune, but also the name of the young woman, thanks to Monsieur Straton's kindness. It's Olivia, the daughter of the Duke of Firstland."

"Firstland!" said the young man, putting his hand to his forehead. "I've seen that name somewhere, but I can't remember where."

The various conversations having ceased, the circle had gathered around the piano, at which Madame de Lormont was seated.

"What will you sing for us, Madame?" asked Lord Mackinguss, scanning a few scores that were scattered on top of the instrument.

"I don't know, my lord—whatever you please."

"Oh, don't demand so much of us, for then it we should all need to vote," observed the owner of a whaling ship with an epigrammatic wit.

"Do you like Meyerbeer? Here's cavatina on which my hand has fallen." And the Scotsman hummed the admirable cantilena of the fourth act of *Robert le Diable*:

> *Robert, you whom I love*
> *And who received my faith,*
> *You can see my fear...*

Recognizing the notes that the musician was causing to vibrate with an authority and a sardonic languor, the young woman went pale. She picked up a score at random, as a last resort.

"I love Donizetti," she articulated, faintly.

"You know that the collection is at the binder's," her husband said to her. "But no matter, you render the piece that Monsieur has chosen admirably."

Robert leaned on the back of an armchair facing her, his eyes motionless and fixed, waiting for the woman he was devouring with his eyes to begin. Entirely intent on his idol, he had not paid any attention to the preludes, and did not know, in consequence, what the Vicomtesse was going to sing.

Mathilde began.

At the first word, on hearing his name, the young man shuddered under the influence of the illusion. The voice was imploring, sympathetic, intoxicating. When she came to sing the word "mercy" her eyes met Robert's, as if by chance.

The latter could not bear the apparent lamentation of the song, stood up, and marched back and forth in the drawing room like a madman, or a wild beast in a cage.

The song continued. The voice rose to dazzling and vertiginous heights. One sensed that the singer was trembling, exhausted by her ardent pleas, putting her last effort into that final cry of mercy. It was the complete image of passion, and there, where the artistry alone ought to have been admired, the young man, transported by his fiery imagination, saw reality.

The instrument also cried in anguish. The keys quivered beneath steely fingers. And the poor amorous young man, lost in the wave of vertigo, received those sounds like a poignant jeer that the musician was causing to snigger in his ear. He was insane. Unable to stand any more, he let himself slump on to the windowsill, which was marked for him with an ineradicable memory. With his head in his hands, forcibly isolating himself from the sound, he tried to conquer the energetic calm that often arrives after turbulent sensations.

When he uncovered his face, his eyes were pensive but tranquil, his cheeks pale but untrembling.

Let's look at things coolly, he said to himself. *What has happened this evening has hurled me on to the threshold, preventing any retreat; it's necessary to go in. Love is a war. There's a Latin proverb which says that fortune favors the bold. Now, in the life of a young man, timidity is more than a fault, it's a moral defect. I've been running after that woman for a year now; that's enough. I can only see the future as far as tomorrow, not beyond.*

The Scotsman captivated the general attention. In the theme, which he ornamented with brilliant variations, and for the commercial ears lent to him, he showed talent—but something that no one noticed, including Rolleboise, was the expression of mockery legible on his serious face, accompanying the melody of the master who, tormented and maddened by a bizarre fantasy, was twisting the fantastic notes into mocking plaints and peals of thunder.

It was during these ironic crepitations, which everyone was seeking to understand, with the same false obstinacy as a stranger attempting to find in an unknown language some relationship with his own, that Robert left the room. Having already been to the house several times, the turnings of the staircase and the direction of the corridors were familiar to him. Having arrived at the upper floor, he placed his ear near the keyhole of a door and his eye met obscurity.

He entered rapidly, without making a noise.

The curtains drawn back from the windows permitted the moon to pour all its rays into the room. The young man, thus illuminated, saw his image reflected in a mirror, and was afraid.

His face was as livid as a head by Zurbaran, his hair moist and untidy. There are moments in life that sometimes decide an entire existence. Robert understood then that what he was doing would lead to unknown but tremendous consequences.

Indecisive, he vacillated momentarily, wondering if he had not been imprudent to force his destiny thus, to hurl a kind of blazing torch into the unknown. But his eyes, becoming accustomed to the half-light of the apartment, showed him the Vicomtesse's bed raised up on a platform. He breathed in the intoxicating atmosphere that floats in a woman's boudoir and destroys any hint of wisdom in a young man's heart.

The scene in the drawing-room came back to his mind, already decorated with the embellishments of memory. He was in the theater; he resolved to finish his role.

First, by virtue of a certain self-mistrust, he sought, not to retreat but, on the contrary, to be unable to turn back. He remained motionless for a moment; then, hearing voices outside and footsteps on the staircase, he said to himself, satisfied and seeking to deceive himself: *Now it's impossible!*

Then, rejecting the past as concluded, behind that barrier, he accepted the future at the point at which he found it.

There is in all human actions, especially in love, a material fact that cannot be avoided. Thus wanting first of all not to be seen, he needed a safe retreat. The choice of that retreat was the grotesque aspect of the drama.

In fact, in the circumstances, it was not an easy thing to find. The curtains at the windows had not been let down. And besides, on a beautiful moonlit evening, does not the imaginative mind of a woman like, before going to sleep, to reflect in silence on the emotions of the day? Then again, above all, he wanted to remain upright, for if he were to be discovered, he wanted at least to be found in a dignified stance. It is scarcely probable, in fact, that a woman might surrender to a lover who appears to her under a bed, from which he emerges awkwardly, covered in dust, not having the leisure and opportunity to explain. It is impossible, too, that she might retain her laughter before someone she finds crouching, huddled or flattened out like an anatomist's skeleton, in a cupboard. Now, in love, laughter is not a good augury.

Robert understood all that. Thus, after having ferreted in all the corners several times and moved around all the items of furniture, he stopped in front of the curtain of a door that seemed to have been locked for a long time.

Thus hidden, the young man waited for more than an hour. During that time, he understood, tremulously, all the inconveniences of his scabrous position, and seriously reflected on how precarious his situation was. The most trivial cause might inspire suspicion: a creak of his shoe, a sneeze, a rumble of his stomach, or a temptation to cough.

But midnight chimed, and while he was still occupied in anticipating all those dreads and avoiding all those accidents, the door opened and the apartment was illuminated. A chambermaid came in.

At that moment, a reproach stung his heart. He was about to dishonor a man and perhaps ruin a woman. Hidden, he had waited in a covert for a suitable opportunity to steal an old man's love. But alas, all thought of wisdom murmured very quietly in the face of the boiling of his fever.

Mathilde came in.

"Open the windows, Lucrèce; the night is magnificent."

In the greatest silence, and to his intimate satisfaction, Robert applauded himself for having refused to take refuge in the curtains at the window.

"I haven't seen Monsieur de Rolleboise."

"Madame I believe I saw him going up an hour ago, I can't see any light in his room; he's undoubtedly gone to bed."

"Who is getting into a carriage in the courtyard?"

"That's Monsieur Mackinguss."

"I'll go to bed later; you can leave, Lucrèce."

"Madame won't need anything else tonight?"

"No, I'll get undressed myself. And then, you wake me up every morning during the best of my sleep."

"I'll await Madame's orders."

"Don't come until I ring."

The Vicomtesse remained alone, leaning on the window-sill. Robert, breathless and thanking Hell for all its favorable dispositions, was about to show himself, but the young woman was speaking; it is always useful to listen to a young woman's monologue.

"It's past midnight. All the windows have fallen into darkness; the domestics are asleep; I'll wait for him."

The young man had every right to be bewildered. Those words, which he did not comprehend at first, caused him to shiver.

The Vicomtesse opened her door cautiously and looked out into the corridor; then the partly-opened door opened more widely. A man came in.

It was Monsieur de Bassens.

The young woman threw herself into his arms.

Robert shuddered with a moral horripilation; his teeth grated and his hair was moistened by a cold sweat.

VI. Until Tomorrow

The next day, at breakfast time, Rolleboise was the last person to appear in the dining room, tranquil and cold. His face was livid. One night appeared to have aged him ten years.

After great mental shocks, repose, even inertia, is necessary. By virtue of a slowly-matured reflection, Robert found himself calm. He said little, and his voice had no emphatic expression. He gaze was free and easy, devoid of stiffness or sarcasm.

Monsieur de Bassens was chatting with the old Vicomte, rarely addressing a remark to the young woman. In fact, that man, whose character always placed him in the shadows, did not appear to be very talkative with respect to women.

As he left the dining-room, Robert offered his arm to the Vicomtesse. He was silent, impassive.

The latter said to him in a bantering tome, even affecting to speak loudly: "I really think, Monsieur de Rolleboise, that you have adopted the task of initiating us in advance in the compassed stiffness of a gentleman. Monsieur de Bassens, whom one would certainly not reproach for an overly expansive character, is less dismal than you."

"It's necessary not to judge a man by first appearances. I have reflected much on that last night, Madame."

Rolleboise went out.

Without saying a word, without turning his fixed gaze aside, he marched straight ahead. His thoughts were active and seething, for his pace quickened.

After having traversed the plateau of the Hève, he found himself on the edge of the cliff, facing the flat green sea. His arms folded, his haggard eyes wandering over the clefts in the dunes, he spoke to himself slowly.

"For twelve months I have loved that woman, distracted myself from any other thought for her; for her I have plunged my life into an ideal and chimerical dream—and yesterday

75

evening she treated that love as madness, that passion as fever! Oh yes, it is quite mad, quite insane, indeed, to attach ourselves thus by the heart to a woman, that mockery of God. I say it now, coldly, without anger: I do not love her, I do not hate her, I do not scorn her, but, no matter, I would pay dearly for the joy of having her one day at my feet, submissive and supplicant, and having no pity! I was frightened by my temerity and my joy, and I believed in that scene in the song, whereas all of that was nothing but a comedy. of which I was the fool, the buffoon at whom people laugh..."

His course, like his mind, was in disorder and had no goal. To counterbalance the disturbance of his head however, it was necessary to keep his body moving and give himself a fever.

He descended the cliff, without precautions but without danger, traversed the valley of Sainte-Adresse and then climbed up the coast of Ingouville.

It was early; the coast was deserted.

The young man having walked a long way on difficult terrain, physical fatigue got the better of him. He sat down on a wooden bench under large beech-trees. In front of him, the landscape offered all its riches to distract his thoughts.

The mouth of the Seine extended all the way to the blue coast of Basse-Normandie. It was high tide. Le Havre, the size of a handkerchief, emitted sailing ships and steamers through the gullet of its harbor-mouth, which covered the sea all the way to the horizon, to the sky. But Robert did not even deign to glance at the tableau extended at his feet. It is necessary to be virtuous to be disturbed by a landscape, even when one can watch the sun rise.

A carriage passed in front of him. He did not look up.

At the edge of the coast the horses stopped and a man got out. He gazed at the sea momentarily, over which large shadows of clouds were running, and then came back to where the young man was sitting. He sat down on the same bench.

That presence doubtless irritated Rolleboise, for he paraded his eyes over the haven ill-humoredly, but did not glance at the other.

That man, however, was not unknown to him. It was Horatio Mackinguss.

"Sad young man, unfortunate amour."

Robert turned, recognized the Scotsman, and did not greet him.

"If I'm not mistaken," Horatio continued, "you're twenty-five. It's therefore been ten years that you've been moved by or for women, and yet you're still at the stage of adolescent naivety!"

"What does it matter to you, Monsieur?"

"Perhaps more than you think. So, young man, you love Madame de Lormont?"

"No, Monsieur."

"You hate her, then; it's the same thing."

"I don't love her, nor hate her, Monsieur."

"That's good; I prefer that. So, you wouldn't want to have that woman your power?"

"To possess her, no,"

"To avenge yourself."

"Yes."

"Well, Robert, I can give her to you."

"You! In fact, it's not impossible that you've been her lover."

"Oh, my God, I've hardly addressed a gallant word to her."

"You're motivated by the Devil, then, my lord?"

"Child, let's leave the Devil where he is, if he's anywhere. The Devil is an idiot who can do nothing, a fool who immodestly takes responsibility for a few trivial human peccadilloes, but who isn't a match for the most mediocre of mortals."

"It's futile, then, Monsieur to take pleasure thus in the spectacle of an offended heart; I want to be alone."

The Scotsman stood up and, favoring at the young man with a profound and pitying gaze, he smiled. Then, placing his hand on Robert's shoulder, he said to him, in a grave and slow voice, becoming more animated as he spoke:

"Rolleboise, what I'm saying to you are not vain words. You loved the Vicomtesse; doubtless she has wounded your vanity, and you have stood up angrily. That's good. Is it not the case, young man, that a woman is a terrible incarnation when one cannot tame her? Is she not all that is most cowardly and most cruel in the human species: the woman who shamelessly, incessantly, insults, and from whose insult one can never recover? Does your mind never revolt, therefore, in considering this society in which woman is the mistress and man always the slave? In which, before a frail child that could be crushed in one hand, it is strong and powerful men who bow down? Have you not often quivered at the thought of those hatreds, those quarrels that sometimes lead to death? Tell me, have you reflected on that once during long nights of despair and jealousy."

"The ultimate spirals of the Inferno are no worse than the tortures I have endured in silence, without making a sound, in the darkness."

"Oh, you're not listening to me! Well, young man, know that there is a circle in which things do not happen like that. There, woman is not a distraction but a goal. Rich, you will make her a means of vengeance; poor, she will edify your fortune. Instead of lying down feebly at the feet of a mistress, you will see her imploring beneath you, and you will not love her!"

"But, to speak thus...you have never loved, then?"

"Loved? Yes, once."

"And the woman by virtue of whom I'm suffering today, I would have at my mercy?"

"Not only that, but you could give me to her afterwards."

"For that, what would I have to do?"

"Come among men who will serve you, and obey only one."

"Who?"

"Me. Above all, don't think that I've come here to satisfy in you a hatred that is indifferent to me, to avenge an offended vanity. No, I need you, that's all. Moreover, I won't haggle over your resolution. In accepting, you would lose all will."

"But I'd be dependent on you!"

"In this world, one always depends on someone more or less worthy than oneself. At present, a woman holds you under her sway. I'm not accusing you of a fault, merely stating a fact. Besides which, remember that in acting solely for me, many others would be acting for you. To punish the mockery of a man, you'd put your life, our family and your honor at risk; will you therefore do nothing to avenge yourself on that of a woman?"

"Mockery? Yes, it's easy to call it that. Who are you?"

"Who am I? I'm Lord Horatio Mackinguss, nothing else—your traveling companion, that's all."

"And by accepting your conditions, I'm not undertaking to commit murder, theft or besmirch my honor?"

"Do you take me for a brigand chief?"

"Perhaps."

"But my friend, they no longer exist except in women's novels. Don't worry, nothing that you rightly fear will be imposed upon you."

"And that woman will be delivered to me?"

"Oh, truly, you're making me weary! I'll repeat it one last time. Not only that poor woman, but any other, if you wish: the young woman who scorned your first love, and many others besides."

"I accept."

"When are you returning to Paris?"

"This evening."

"Be at the English Tavern tomorrow. We'll dine together."

"And there I shall know everything?"

"Everything."

"And if your conditions aren't agreeable, and I no longer want to?"

"Then," Horatio continued, in the same calm and cold tone, "within an hour, you'd no longer know anything. Until tomorrow."

Five minutes later, the carriage had gone along the coast, and Robert found himself alone.

That scene, which might have thrown a more candid mind into turmoil, had given the young man a salutary strength that provided a diversion from the past.

"So I'm not mistaken, then!" he exclaimed. "Fictions are indeed becoming reality!"

VII. Stout and Porter

The next day, at seven o'clock, Robert went into the rooms of the English Tavern in Paris. The person he was to meet here was endowed with one of those physiognomies that rarely pass unperceived in the crowd. His gaze therefore fell upon that of Horatio, who was sitting at a table in a rather crowded part of the room.

Facing him, an individual with a face unknown to our young man was drinking. He was an Englishman, or a Scotsman. His face expressed bonhomie and insouciance. His cheeks were as pulp and rosy as the sugared fruits that confectioners display in the first days of the year. The hair growing on his head and the two bushy lateral side-whiskers climbing into the tortuously convoluted shells of his ears were a reddish blonde, like beer. His cravat, of an entirely British whimsy, was knotted like the horns of a snail, supporting like tusks two collars of a more lanceolate form. His frizzy eyebrows, and his nose like a turbaned Moor, made his features a droll assembly.

"Monsieur de Rolleboise," said Horatio, "May I introduce my friend Sir James Cawdor, Baronet. Sir James, Monsieur Robert de Rolleboise."

The two men bowed, and Robert sat down facing Lord Mackinguss.

"What do you drink, Monsieur de Rolleboise?" asked Cawdor, abruptly.

"I don't know—something strong. What's that?" he pointed at several bottles, s empty as soap-bubbles.

"Oh, that's the eternal drink of the eternal drinker. Sir James comes to France for Bordeaux wine and goes back to England for Jamaica rum and Madeira."

The man about whom this was said could not have paid less attention o his friend's definitive words had he been deaf. The waiter had just deposited a large bottle in front of the young Frenchman—one of those bottles that one can drop without breaking it, with a vast label, like those one sees on tins of English boot-polish.

"What's this frightful black beverage you've ordered for me?"

"You need a tonic, so you've been served stout. It's a corrective useful in important circumstances."

Robert filled his glass with the thick dark liquid, on the surface of which a jaundiced foam formed, and emptied it rapidly. In the meantime, Horatio riffled through an English newspaper. Then, having folded it to display an article, he presented it to Robert.

"Read these few lines; you might find them interesting."

The young man took the newspaper, cast his eyes over it, and immediately returned it to the lord.

"Excuse me, but I don't understand English very well."

"Oh—you'll have to learn. Did you hear, Sir James—Monsieur de Rolleboise doesn't understand English."

"We'll teach him," the Baronet replied, simply, who appeared to employ his mouth for other things than talking.

"If Monsieur de Rolleboise cares to listen, I'll translate the *entrefilet* for him. That's what you call it, isn't it?"

"Perhaps. I'm not a journalist."

Robert put his elbows on the table casually, and waited for the Scotsman to begin.

"It's written from Carluke in Scotland. 'A few leagues from Stonebyres, an old castle stands on the Clyde. The ruin is known as the Castle of the Falls, and belongs to Sir James Cawdor, Baronet, but that gentleman never sets foot there. The manor thus uninhabited is, the local people assert, haunted on certain night by evil spirits, with the result that the country folk have debaptized it of its original name and commonly designate it as the Castle of Vampires. Indeed, they claim that at certain times, on dark nights, the windows are illuminated redly, the chimneys smoke, horses whinny and men sing. Nevertheless, what is certain is that, on the day after the supposed nocturnal assembly, or the day after that, on several occasions, the cadaver of a young woman unknown in the neighborhood has been found near Stonebyres Falls—and several nights after that, the grave accorded to her in the village cemetery has been violated. At any rate, the traveler who visits the ruins does not see or hear anything; it remains to be determined whether these murders...' I shall refrain from translating the writer's reflections. Well, Monsieur de Rolleboise, what do you think of that? Do you believe in vampires?"

"But I presume that Sir James could clear up the matter better than anyone else, since he's the owner of the Castle of the Falls."

Sir James, retrenched in his imperturbable phlegm, took no more notice of the young man's words than if his name had not been mentioned.

Robert had almost emptied his bottle of stout, and a faint intoxication, serious and grave, was acting upon him. At first he was frightened: dread had seized him on feeling that he was penetrating into the mysterious and perhaps criminal life to which he had pledged himself. At that moment, however, things and objects took on a new form. He felt his brain enlarged and his mind clarified by a strange lucidity. The round face of Sir James appeared to him as a farcical fantasy, a caricature by Hogarth.

"Robert," said Horatio, "superstitious beliefs are often merely an exaggeration of the truth."

"Which is to say?"

"Which is to say that the inhabitants of Lanarkshire are perhaps not mistaken, Monsieur de Rolleboise."

The Scotsman's eyes had settled upon those of the young man like a red hot iron on a wound. Under the influence of that powerful magnetism, Robert could not turn away.

Horatio continued: "Let's see, Robert—would you like to be a vampire?"

By means of a violent effort, Rolleboise detached himself from the action of that man, like a drunken sleeper fighting the nightmare that holds him by the throat, and cried out, in a muted and contained voice: "No, never."

"So you don't want to see the magnificent Mathilde again?" said the lord, with mocking ease and carelessness. "You want to quit life at twenty, without having expressed all the bile in your heart, before having rendered scorn for scorn? Oh, young man!—she's a very beautiful woman, though, a brunette of splendid passions, of frantic embraces. Will you renounce reality before having the echo in your ear of that amorously-inflected voice, after having received in your ardent imagination her words of love; will you hurl into the abyss of oblivion her intoxicating caresses, her ecstasies?"

"Silence!" cried Robert, covered in cold sweat by a terrible memory and standing bolt upright, as if galvanized.

But the terrible empire that Horatio exercised upon him caused him to sit down again, slowly, falling heavily into his seat as if pole-axed. By virtue of his intoxication, he saw Mackinguss's face in magnified proportions. The latter's physiognomy cast a violent fascination over him.

The Scotsman continued, with an expression that Robert distinguished as an infernal mockery: "Undoubtedly, you've known those joys! She has accorded you everything that her love could lavish, and you no longer want it!"

"Milord," said the young man, in a slow and somber voice, squeezing the arm of his interlocutor, "give me to her for one day—one hour...no matter...not to love her, but to avenge myself upon her, and I'm yours. But for mercy's sake, deliver me from this fatal fluid that is circulating in my veins. Don't look at me like that, for I shall go mad, and I want to have my reason."

Defeated, he let his head fall on to his arms, on the table.

"Sir James," Horatio said then, in a low voice, to his neighbor, "did you hear the reading of that article?"

"I heard it."

"They might, in fact, have found a cadaver or two: that of the proud Duchess of Grasslow, who preferred to throw herself into the Clyde, and that of Countess McGrahor, choked by a fit of anger, but I've never been able to understand what they mean by these violated tombs. It's a palpable fact, though; it must be true. It's necessary to seek and find the explanation for that mystery, do you hear me, Sir James?"

"I hear, Milord."

"Tomorrow morning, you'll depart for London with Lord Lodore and him"—he pointed at the young man who was still collapsed on the table. "You'll receive your instructions tonight."

When Robert got up again, his physiognomy was calm.

During that entire scene, the Baronet had not had any expression on his face connected with what was happening before his eyes. He was still drinking imperturbably. The bottles he had emptied were on the next table, arranged as for a game of skittles.

Horatio and Rolleboise stood up. Their companion, seriously occupied in watching a plum pudding sizzle in the blue-tinted flames of rum, paid no attention to their departure. When they arrived in the street, Robert was preparing to leave on his own when Horatio stopped him.

"Get into my carriage."

Robert did not raise any objection, and sat down beside Lord Mackinguss.

Horatio was the younger son of Earl Mackinguss. On the death of his father, his brother profiting from the privilege accorded to the eldest sons of the family, had taken possession of his ancestral fortune. It was not one of the meager patrimonies that still exist in France and which only serve vanity. The old Earl's fortune might have been twenty or thirty million; that was what he had received from his own father and he transmitted it to his son intact. In fashioning the character of the two brothers, nature had certainly taken no account of the different positions that awaited them in society, but nature does not have the leisure to reflect on such matters.

Edgard was miserly and avaricious; Horatio showed himself to be a true aristocrat in all respects. He had not wanted to follow any of the careers that serve as a refuge for the younger sons of families. So, at twenty, with one of the finest names in Scotland, he had found himself devoid of a fortune and any legitimate expectations. But Horatio was, by nature, one of those men who, braving their destiny, excel in everything. He traveled for a long time, even staying for a while, it was said, in the south of France.

On his return to London he had attracted some attention. He possessed superb horses, fine, admirably-bred greyhounds which, mantled in blazoned velvet, ran before his charger in winter around Hyde Park, but he was not known to have any association with women.

In fact, Horatio had never been in love. He scorned that sentiment as enslaving, and could not reconcile it with that which predominated in him and brought out all his strength: pride. Unlike many others, whom pride has doomed, pride was Mackinguss's salvation. It was an impetuous passion that he needed to satisfy, and, the thing most necessary to that objective being a fortune, he had to become rich. For him, honor was simply a reputation that it was necessary to conserve.

In the course of this drama, we shall dig deeper into the hidden fibers and the intimate life of that man.

VIII. While Passing Close to a Cemetery

A Londoner—an inhabitant of London, an entirely tangible and positive intelligence—finds nothing in the night but a period of interrupted activity that nature imposes and consecrates to repose. He is, therefore, quite amazed to see Parisians living more in the four or five hours that precede midnight than in the whole of the day. He does not understand that artificial existence lit by gas, for an Englishman is more prosaic than a number; he grants nothing to fantasy. He wants proof of everything. The slightest innovation in his mores caused him to faint. By virtue of that uniformity of mind and invariability of action, he becomes in France an infallible thermometer. By virtue of the effect that contact with an Englishman produces on a man, you immediately know that latter's character. However, when Londoners are in Paris, they throw themselves head first into that feverish life, simply to satisfy the bizarre law that drives every foreigner to exaggerate the spirit of his nation.

In London, therefore, ten o'clock is much more advanced hour of the night than one o'clock in the morning. in Paris. The shops, closed for a long time, no longer provide a glimmer of light, and the theaters will soon render to sleep a population quite bewildered by having been gripped for four hours by the eccentric seductions of art.

Ten o'clock had just chimed on all the clocks in the district when a young man, seemingly coming from the direction of the Queen's Theater, went through the passage, dangerous for pedestrians, that leads from Pall Mall to the Strand via Charing Cross. In London, carriages travel very rapidly and are never illuminated. It therefore requires courage to venture into the darkness and the mud of the Charing Cross intersection.

When the individual that we have already seen indecisive on the pavement of Whitehall had reached the Strand, he signaled to a coachman who was sleeping nearby and climbed into his cab.

"Corbett's Lane," he shouted, in a singularly high-pitched voice.

"Yes sir," replied the coachman, confidently, gathering up the long reins that passed over the hood of the cabriolet and arranging himself at his ease on his high-set seat.

The horse departed at a rapid trot. Having arrived at the entrance to Fleet Street, the coachman let his courser settle into its own rhythm, and, opening the upper panel of the carriage, he tapped respectfully on the young man's hat.

"What do you want?"

"Beg pardon—your honor wants to go to Corbett's Lane?"

"Didn't I say so?"

"I heard—but where does your honor place that street?"

In London, a coachman does not know the city; it is always the traveler that informs him. When the latter is a stranger and it is dark, one goes at the whim of the horse. Carriages are hired according to the distance traveled, so it is probably that coachmen lose nothing by pleading ignorance. The case that concerns us, however, was not typical. In a curt and clear voice, the young man gave him directions. After leaving all the little streets around Saint Paul's, they crossed the Thames at London Bridge and went into the poorer districts of the city.

In complete contrast to Paris, when one advances into the poorer districts of the English capital the houses become smaller, and often present nothing but a ground floor to the street. On the other hand, the subterranean parts become more profound. There are immense substructures divided into floors, where day only ever ventures wearing a cloak of darkness. In Paris, the class of poor and needy working women lives in mansards and attics; in London, it goes to earth in cellars.

Having reached Rotherhithe, the coachman had further recourse to directions. They were then in the vicinity of Blue

Anchor Lane, a street cut across by the Greenwich railway line. There was little to be seen but uninhabited tracts, some of which are not yet built up. At that unsocial hour, everything was silent and somber, except that, at intervals, a few locomotive whistles announced the city limits. Nevertheless, it was excusable that the coachman did not know Corbett's Lane; being scarcely built, its corners did not yet bear indicative plaques, for lack of houses to which they might be attached.

The cabriolet stopped, and the young man got out. After having spoken briefly to the coachman, he strode briskly into a narrow and puddle-strewn side street. Beyond that alleyway was a square, or rather an empty space, unpaved and entrenched, such as one finds on the edges of all great cities. Nearby, there was a circular wall, inside which grew tall trees mingled with pale gray columns like stripped trunks. That was New Cross Cemetery.

The young man went along the wall and then, turning left, approached a small isolated house, squat, old and black. He doubtless had a key to the door, for he went in without knocking. He probably knew the people in the dwelling, because, with no light and without even groping with his hands, he stopped at a staircase to which we would gladly have devoted a few lines had it not been lost in a darkness that would have made the shadows of an interior by Ribera seems bright by comparison. The individual went up a few steps and then, having reached the first floor, turned the key in a reluctant lock and opened a second door. He went in.

The room was poorly lit by a lamp. At the back, behind the furniture, silent battles were in progress between the irritated shadows and a few feeble glimmers painfully obeying their orders. The furniture of the room seemed more bizarre than poor.

The chilly walls were covered with a tapestry, holed in many places, whose weave only conserved races of color. The cold air that the door disturbed as it closed again agitated the whole of the tapestry and caused two ragged portraits to oscillate momentarily, which had been continually surveyed in their giltless frames by the geometric threads of several generations of spiders. The mouths of the individuals thus represented had been smiling for a century—a strange kind of smile for a painter to leave to a family, which seemed to be incessantly mocking the dolors of existence!

The only substantial item of furniture apparent to the eye was a dresser with drawers, bulging like the flanks of a Dutch galleon, ornamented with carvings reminiscent of an old man's wrinkles, and bronze plaques designing winged dragons, which writhed around locks in burlesque and menacing contours. The chairs, outdated in their form, bore no more resemblance to one another than those in a second-hand dealer's shop. A bookcase in black wood paled by time and dust was directly adjacent to the tapestry, its shelves crammed with ancient volumes and wads of crumpled yellowing paper.

Near a massive table, covered with a cloth with effaced designs, sitting in an armchair with a low seat and a high back, was an individual who appeared to be alive. He was an old man of a stiffness and decrepitude that would have delighted Hoffmann. He was enveloped in a tight-fitting sulfur-colored dressing gown, which, while hiding his arms, gave him the appearance of a mummy from Memphis. His coiffure consisted of an ample black wool bonnet, to which a vast green cloth visor was fitted, like an awning over a door, projecting its shadow over the entire face. The man's face was not wrinkled, but his desiccated and taut skin was yellowing over his jutting bones like Cordovan leather nailed to a drying frame.

When the door opened, the old man's head rose slowly above a book, and two small gleaming eyes peered into the darkness.

"You see, Antares, I haven't made you wait," the young man said, sitting down on a chair from Shakespeare's century. He put his hat on the table. His abundant hair was parted on top of his head like a woman's.

"I'm always at your orders, Olivia," the man replied, without shifting, as motionless as a sphinx. Then he added, in a tone of dry mockery: "Is the Duke in god health. These old men of war always live to be a hundred."

"Listen, Jew, I forbid you to talk about my father. If I've come here, it's for me to talk and for you to listen. It might be necessary one day for me to unearth a more miscreant Jew from the sewers of Saint-Giles, in order to rid myself of Antares."

"Don't joke like that, Olivia. You've come; I'm listening."

"Antares, I've come to talk to you about affairs of the heart."

"Aha! The heart, Olivia! Talk to me about the Talmud, present me with a Hebraic difficulty...but the heart is a language I don't speak."

"I want to talk to you about two men."

"Olivia is in love! Poor human nature—how delirious it is!"

"I didn't mention love, Antares."

"You mentioned two men. You love them?"

"I don't know."

"They love you, then?"

"Yes."

"That's a very bold response, Miss," the old man said, sniggering. "Anyway, I know these two men. He first is Amadeus Harriss..."

"You know Amadeus. His fortune is large. And I owe him my life."

"Oho!" said the old man, with scant consideration.

"But for him, I'd have perished in the waters of the Clyde. Nevertheless, it's not that reason which will make up my mind."

"In your opinion, what is his character?"

"His character irritates me. He's certainly a weak man, but he's unsuitable."

"The second, Olivia, Lord Horatio Mackinguss, is the man you need. Horatio is weak, submissive and good. Furthermore, his will is negligible; he'll be your slave."

"Antares, I'm not taking a husband to renew with him the existence of the French fabulist's Philemon and Baucis."[15]

"Don't worry about that, Miss; you mention a fabulist; we'll find without any effort, in some French romancer, the means of cutting through that difficulty."

"Let's talk about France, Antares."

"What has Olivia decided?"

"Will you answer to me for that absence?"

"Madame, I've done as you asked; I've even offered my advice."

"Answer my question: Ophelia will never reappear?"

"Only the dead never reappear, Miss."

"Oh, Antares!" said Olivia, getting up impatiently. "I'm wicked, it's true, but I don't want to feel on my conscience, do you understand, the weight of my sister's tomb!"

"There are, however," the old Jew continued, unmoved, "deaths that closely resemble the effects of maladies..."

"Antares, don't torment my already excessively barbaric mind like that!"

"One might die of hunger in two years, Olivia."

"That's horrible!"

"Ophelia is your elder, Miss," he continued, in a sly and ferocious voice.

Olivia, her eyes somber and her brow furrowed, strode back and forth in the Jew's room. The latter, utterly indifferent to that agitation, contrasted with his own quietude, returned with real or feigned attention to his reading.

The "young man" picked up his hat. The old man raised his hooded head then, and said reflexively: "Miss Olivia, I might, for ten thousand pounds sterling, consent to..."

"Wretch! After all I've done for you, that's how you ruminate a treason!"

---

[15] The Classical version of the fable of Philemon and Baucis is found in Ovid's *Metamorphoses*, but Jean de La Fontaine produced a version in verse that became much better known in France

"I'm a Jew, Olivia; I do business with everyone."

"Antares, wait for me here in two days, at the same time. You'll receive my decision."

"Entirely at your orders. Good night, Miss Olivia."

Left alone, Antares closed his book and uttered a little dry laugh, which must have singularly bewildered the silence extended through that monkish chamber. He took off his garment, his bonnet and his eyeshade, and carefully removed his white hair—and in the old man's place appeared a man of about forty, of the meager but strong constitution. He stuffed papers into the pockets of his black coat, and shut others away in a drawer, blew out the lamp and went out.

When Olivia left the little house, midnight was chiming on the clock of the railway station on the Dover line.[16] The night was dark, as all nights are in London, when the moon only appears for a few months in summer. That evening, however, it was perceptible through a gap in the heavens near the horizon, brand new, like a fingernail-clipping of the sun.

Olivia soon reached the wall of the cemetery. Suddenly, she thought she distinguished a dark object on the crest of the wall. The young woman was too strong by nature to be susceptible to fear, so she kept going forward.

A shadow was distinctly perceptible gliding along the stones. It was a man who had just climbed the wall. He was dressed in black. His face stood out, pale and wan, and in that spectral face two fires sparkled.

Olivia gazed at the motionless man crouching on the wall for moment, and then, without a shudder, continued walking. The hired carriage was waiting at the end of the narrow street.

"Where to now, sir?"

---

[16] There was no railway connection between London and Dover in 1850, but a proposal had been put forward to extend the line from London Bridge to Greenwich all the way to Dover; it never happened. It is unclear which station is being cited here; Corbett's Lane Junction was the most important intersection on the line but did not have a station to board passengers.

"My hotel," replied the strange individual, whose sex only we know.

"Which is, if you please, your honor?"

"I'll get down in Waterloo Place."

IX. Hamlet

The Duke of Firstland was the last descendant of an ancient Scottish family. He owned a chain of mountains and lakes in the region of Inverness, and a few islands in the Hebrides. His fortune did not surpass twenty million francs, but because the old man had simple tastes, content with his life in retreat, like an austere and grave mountain man, the income from that sum was sufficient for him to maintain with honor the rank of his name and his clan. However, the old Duke was not happy. His frank and benevolent face had lost all radiance of joy; his mouth had forgotten how to smile. Always alone in his apartments, and dejected, his mind seemed to be dwelling in a hidden dolor, and enveloping its sad thoughts with resignation.

The Duke had married twice, but not with impunity. His first wife had died two years after the birth of a daughter. The husband mourned his Duchess, for he had loved her tenderly, and then forgot her somewhat, for he was young. Youth cannot anticipate. In brief, the Duke, after forgetting the dead, forgot himself.

To marry once is audacious; to entangle oneself in a second marriage is folly.

Two years after the death of the Duchess the Duke married Ophelia Cockburn, who soon rendered him he father of a second child. His first child, Ophelia—who, by a strange coincidence, bore the same name as her stepmother—was three years old at the time of that birth. The new daughter received the name of Olivia.

The Duke was not happy with that second Duchess; her character clashed with his. In thought, he returned to his first attachment, and as his daughter Ophelia was the earthly personification of that stolen soul, he poured the sum of his affections over her innocent head.

Fifteen years went by.

Ophelia, grew up in her father's company, and, like him, was deceived in her amour. Her soul impoverished of joys, the young woman seemed bathed in an atmosphere of sorrow, and melancholy weighed constantly upon her head. The Duchess did not like her, and her younger sister had the same sentiments toward her as her mother.

Ophelia was eighteen when the somber Firstland Castle was the theater of an event unusual in a region of primitive and rude mores. One evening, the Duchess did not appear. They waited for her all night. The mountain was lit up with torches, but the following day was spent in fruitless searches. Finally, at dusk the day after that, the Duke, on going to a remote room in the castle, perceived a stiff body suspended in mid-air. He drew closer, alarmed. It was the Duchess, hanging lifelessly from one of the ceiling beams.

At the news of that death, Olivia became somber, but did not weep.

No one could suspect a crime; a suicide was inexplicable.

After the day of that event, Ophelia, more melancholy and pale than ever, wandered in solitude and avoided all society, even that of her father. In the soul of the latter, a terrible conflict was raging—one of those disturbances in which reason trembles. Olivia approached him, whispered in his ear, and he shivered. His haggard eyes arrested, staring at Ophelia's white immobile face, with widened eyes and the mysterious expression of a sad and lamentable reverie. She, mute, seemed to be allowing her gaze to return to the past.

The Duchess had left no indication to explain a fit of madness of despair, but a piece of paper was found close to her on which these lines were written:

Reverie is a shade of sleep; sleep is a shadow of death; to dream forever, it is necessary to quite the earth. Ophelia.

The nebulous form of those lines did not fit the character of the person who appeared to have written them. Then, one evening, Olivia, sitting at the feet of the old Duke, who was weeping, observed that the handwriting on the piece of paper was not her mother's. The old man became as frightened as a child at the sound of that acidic and suspicious voice. The gesture of his hand asked for mercy, tearfully pushing away the monstrous phantom of truth that rose up before him. But there was no pity. Olivia set beside the note a letter written by the young Ophelia, and the Duke shivered at the identity of the handwriting.

At that moment, a living statue passed through the hall. She stopped in front of those two individuals and, extending her slender arm and her pale hand, said: "On the memory of my mother, one the honor of my father, I swear that my hand never traced those lines."

On retiring for the night, the poor father perceived in a deserted gallery a shadow praying before a portrait of a woman, that of the first Duchess—and the old man, his face somber, passed by without looking at his daughter.

That night, at two bed-heads, there were bitter tears and no sleep.

Every day, Olivia penetrated further into her father's confidence; every day, Ophelia seemed to draw further and further away from the center of that loving sphere.

Olivia did not weep, as we said, at the time when her mother's corpse was discovered. Those few words almost dispense us from making a portrait of the young woman in question. However, it is probable that the Duchess, deceased so mysteriously, would not have wept either, at the death of her child.

Olivia resembled her mother. She was envious, jealous and malevolent. One simple circumstance caused her to hate her older sister. One was addressed as Miss Firstland, the other merely as Miss Olivia.

The Duke loved Ophelia, for it is difficult to remove from one's heart a rooted and embodied affection, but her presence troubled him. He avoided her. In hours of doubt, he stood up against the frightful infiltration that Olivia's suspicions injected into him—but the fatal fluid soon returned to plunge him into poignant anguish.

One day, the old man was passing slowly through a room when he saw his daughter motionless in front of him, her arms open and her physiognomy imploring. Their eyes misted over, the poor father fell into that beloved embrace, and mingled his tears with those of his child. A minute went by, an indescribable interval of happy remission, and there was no sound save those of halting sobs and tears.

Suddenly, through his tears, the Duke perceived the somber and fatal physiognomy of Olivia.

Then, detaching himself from that embrace, he fell to his knees and cried, in an imploring and desperate voice: "Ophelia, my child, tell us the truth!"

"Oh, my poor father," replied the young woman, "I'm very unhappy."

The next day, at meal time, Ophelia did not come to sit down beside her father. They searched for her for a long time; they did not find her.

Without saying a word, the old man, as white as his hair, went up to the high room where death had already revealed itself. There was no one there.

A few mountain folk said that during the night, they had perceive a white shadow on the rocks of the mountain, leaning over the torrents of the Findhorn, and that that pale shadow had suddenly disappeared from sight.

The old Duke shed tears for a long time, and dressed in black. His daughter threw herself into his arms; her eyes were dry, but, covered by his own tears, the old man did not perceive that.

Four years later, the Duke quit his mountains, his forests and his pale days, witnesses to his dolors, and came to London. His daughter was approaching twenty, and she too was soon to leave him.

At the moment when we pose our pen on the threshold of Firstland's town house, Miss Olivia had not yet finished dressing. The Duke's daughter, let us say without being subject to any unfortunate prejudice, was a beautiful individual. The coloring of her face had all the delicacy of the tint that one can only compare to the color of milky tea. Her prominent forehead overhung her eyes, beautiful in form but brightened by a harsh expression. The apparent lobes of the nose and the slightly curt corners of the mouth testified to the woman's pride, and repelled weak and timid characters at the first glance.

Her shoulders and arms were bare and her beautiful honey-blonde hair hung in ringlets almost down to her elbows, lost in the treasures of feminine frivolities whose technical names only interest dressmakers—and our literature is not so exclusive.

On a sofa, an old woman as sitting—Olivia's customary companion, to whom she referred as her aunt. The woman was tall and spare—so spare that by placing a light behind her body, previously stripped of its inflated fabrics, one would surely have been able to read the small print in the columns of the *Morning Chronicle* through her.

The furniture of Miss Firstland's bedroom was in good taste, for it came from France. The young woman had a dressing table in front of her, lined with yellow satin in the form of a baldaquin. At the back was a mirror, also framed, by lace set in the satin. The double-leafed table-top was covered all the way to the edge of the hem, and concluded in a cloud of powdery lace.

To one side, on a table admirably decked with Italian mosaics, stood a water-jug and its bowl. The jug was the work of one of our principal Parisian artists. Its urceolate flanks were decorated with the veins of leaves and buds of flowers, which swelled the walls of porous earthenware. The handle was formed as a leafy branch of an exquisite pourer, on which a child was chasing a lizard. The hand already held the animal captive, for it would otherwise have dived into the water, which almost undulated on contact with its frightened head. On the front, beneath the overlapping canthus, two cherubs were painted, each holding in one hand the Firstland coat of arms, surmounted by a ducal crown. The bowl that received the water was posed on the branches of an oak whose trunk supported the base. Under the branches of the tree an obese ox was ruminating, on the neck of which a young bare-legged cowherd as leaning. The bowl was gold, the rest solid silver.

A young chambermaid with skin as white as candle-wax and turquoise eyes was giving the young woman the final attentions that her toilette required.

"So, you understand, Suky, that my aunt's people saw you talking to a horseguard in St. James's Park."

"He's my cousin, Miss. His father's house is next door to my mother's, in Ipswich. We were engaged when the government took him away from his family."

"Know, Suky, that I don't want my women to be seen talking to men who are strangers to my father's house. When you want to see your cousin, go to Ipswich. What do you think, Aunt, of this pale flighty person who frequents horseguards, men six feet tall, under the pretext of going to chapel to hear the Reverend Simpson? Miss, if you take it into your head to watch the parade in St. James's again, don't come back."

"But..."

"I'm talking to you, not asking you questions."

The young woman shut up, and could not hold back a large tear that swelled up in her long lashes, vacillated fearfully, and fell on to her mistress's shoulder. Olivia saw that in the mirror, and before poor Suky had time to wipe it away, she stood up, pale with anger and disgust. There was a golden pin shining in her fingers. Without saying a word, she plunged it into the maid's arm. The latter uttered a faint cry, but her tears dried up.

"Slut, you deserve being thrown out on the street with no bread! Go on, quickly, clean my shoulder."

The desolate maid, the skin of her round arm red with blood, had recourse to all the perfumes that the bottles and flasks on the dressing-table contained.

"Wipe your arm—you'll soil me."

The aunt, distracted from her reading by the incident, put down her book. "Perhaps my niece has forgotten that Sir Amadeus is in the drawing room."

"I think, my dear Aunt, that Sir Amadeus will be kind enough to wait until I finish dressing."

"Can't you receive him here, now?"

"Amadeus less than any other, Aunt. And you can be sure that my husband will never enter my apartment without my permission."

"Not all men, my niece, are so supple in their character. A husband's manners are sometimes coarse."

"I shall render him supple. Oh, don't think that I want to be like a zero next to a one beside the man I marry, and that I'll consent only have the value by virtue of a number."

"As a woman, I can only approve. In any case, you'll find in Amadeus the man of your desires, and that's fortunate, for there's nothing so terrible as two imperious characters that collide with one another."

"Collide! I don't collide, I knock down. That's how I'll act with any man. Oh, I don't have an intelligence as facile as that poor Countess of Landsdale, who wears the cashmeres and jewels that her husband's mistress disdains. It's scandalous! Ring, Suky."

"It's necessary, however, Olivia, not to abuse the empire that you can exercise over Amadeus' heart. Thus, it wouldn't be appropriate to act in that way with another man—Horatio, for example."

At that moment the door opened and a young woman appeared.

"Hannah, go inquire of Andrew as to the health of my father, the Duke of Firstland. You mentioned Horatio, Aunt? Oh, he's different; I would simply tell him to come back at a more convenient time, or better still, admit him in here, ask him to pass me a white pearl to refresh my face, and to perfume my handkerchief." So saying, the young woman allowed a disdainful and scornful smile to wander over her lips.

"He's a handsome man," observed the aunt, shamelessly.

"And above all, a good man," said Olivia, with the habitual haste of any young woman who does not want to appear to stop at certain physical considerations. "Truly, it would be cruel of me to take such an individual for my husband!"

"Milord the Duke thanks Miss Firstland," said Hannah, who had just come back in. "He is in perfect health."

"Very good. Now go tell Sir Amadeus that I shall have the honor of seeing him."

The young woman went out backwards.

"I haven't told you about the dream I had last night, Aunt—or, rather, the nightmare. In my sleep, I remembered all that we were saying yesterday evening on the subject of those supposed vampires of the north mentioned in the *Times*. I was at the Castle of the Falls, and someone threw me as I slept into the torrents of the Clyde. A strange people, ours! The Scots always need to aliment their imaginative spirit with fantastic and supernatural stories!"

"Doubtless there are a few brigands who benefit from the quality of the extraordinary with which their misdeeds are clothed. The other day, at the French ambassador's, I met the worthy Sir James Cawdor, the owner of the Castle of the Falls. He was quite alarmed to discover that his rock is afflicted with vampires."

"It's certain that Sir James doesn't resemble a vampire like the one depicted for us by Byron—or rather Polidori. After all, everyone judges individuals in his own fashion. Thus, the other evening, the Countess of Landsdale spoke to me about Horatio in an utterly false fashion, introducing to me in colors that certainly aren't his. In fact, she said something that made me laugh uproariously. 'That man,' she confessed, 'represents for me the fatal physiognomy of Lara!'[17] Poor Horatio! I must tell him about that calumny. Aunt, I await your pleasure to go to the drawing-room."

---

[17] *Lara, A Tale* (1814) is a long poem by Byron, sometimes alleged to be quasi-autobiographical; the persecuted hero eventually dies in tragic fashion.

Sir Amadeus Harriss was a young Englishman dressed entirely in black, with the exception of his cravat, which was a blue-tinted white in the most aristocratic manner. All in all, there was nothing that distinguished him from any other man.

When the ladies came into the drawing-room, the conversation was devoted to banalities to which Miss Cockburn, the old aunt, put an end by settling into the utmost depths of an armchair to envelop herself in the immense pages of the *Times*.

"You seem anxious, Sir Amadeus. There's a pained expression on your face that is not habitual to you."

"Alas, Mademoiselle, you know that a constant melancholy always reigns within me: shadows of the heart, less somber when I'm in your company. But I don't want to talk to you about it, for your mockery is not a remedy."

"Always your imaginary dreads! You'll soon be sadder than a second-rate poet who sighs a sonnet to the moon every evening. Don't worry, Amadeus, these fictitious apprehensions will fade away with the years."

"I don't believe in the years," the young man added, supporting his head in his hands.

"Affected presentiments!" the young woman mocked. "My Aunt Cockburn didn't believe in the years either, when her soul found itself in bondage to an elegant private secretary of George Canning, whom she perceived for the first time in the halls of Westminster at the last session of the trial of Warren Hastings.[18] Now she believes in the centuries. Always the same folly!"

"My malady is here," the young man continued, tapping his forehead. "The events with which human existence bristles frighten me. I know them too well not to fear, not for my life, but for my reason."

---

[18] In April 1795—implying that the Aunt must be in her seventies.

"To cure you of that sentiment of moral weakness, you need to abandon yourself entirely to a determined and vigilant friend."

"That's a very painful renunciation, Miss. However, I wouldn't refuse the hand of a woman who invited me to lean on her."

"Yes, Amadeus, on the path in which vertigo afflicts you, trust in the footsteps of a faithful guide."

"Faithful!" murmured the young man, darting a bitter glance at the young woman. "That's a very presumptuous word in a human mouth! For you see, Miss Olivia, I'm a creature that love frightens. Suspicious of myself by nature, I'm jealous for that reason alone."

"I don't understand you, Sir Amadeus," said the young woman, visibly furrowing her imperious brow.

"You're darkening your expression, illuminating your gaze, whose glare wounds me—but no matter, I want to tell you everything."

"Oh, Sir Amadeus, don't tell me a dream; I'm fearful of that kind of story."

"A dream! You're right—there are frightful dreams! But in fact, and it frightens me, what I have to tell you is a reality. On waking up this morning, Miss Olivia, I found this letter, addressed to me, on my table. I broke the seal and this is what I read..."

"I'm listening, sir," said the young woman, straightening her disdainful expression.

"*Sir, if you would like to know where Miss Olivia Firstland goes at midnight, dressed as a man, you can be informed. Come this evening at a similar hour to the vicinity of Westminster Abbey. A man will introduce himself to you. Follow him.*"

"And the signature?" asked the young woman, calmly.

"Oh, a strange signature."

"What is it?"

"*A vampire!*"

"And the reading of this anonymous letter is presented to me as a form of interrogation, sir?"

"Perhaps."

"Well, know, sir, that I never lower myself to giving explanations to someone who does not have the right to demand them, especially when the cause of it is ridiculous. After all, it wasn't clever of you to show me the thread of this melodramatic plot in such a manner. You've been invited to discover the truth. Go."

"I shall," the young man replied, rather dryly.

"Only, before you confer in this way with nocturnal spirits, reflect on the consequences that might follow. You have a weak head, sir."

Miss Olivia got up and went over to her aunt, still wrapped up like a monster bouquet in the pages of her newspaper. The young woman's head was inclined, her forehead pensive, and her lips could be seen trembling in an expression of muted nervous irritation.

"But that's frightful!" murmured the old woman, burying herself frantically in the noisy pages of the *Times*.

"What's happened then, Aunt?"

"My dear child, it's inexplicable! Since French mores came to corrupt our decent and religious habits, anything can be expected!"

"A Chartist conspiracy?"

"No, an immortal and sacrilegious occurrence. Words cannot decently explain such a monstrosity! In sum, three nights ago, in Kensal Green Cemetery...or, rather, Highgate...no, no, it really was Kensal Green...I have it here. Oh dear...I can't find it now. This paper is so big!"

The young woman, abandoning her aunt to her uncertainty, redirected her attention to the door-curtain, which a domestic had just lifted in order to let someone through. The old Duke came in, leaning on Lord Horatio's arm. The old man, slightly stooped, was grave beneath his sparse white hair.

Horatio Mackinguss had an entirely new appearance; if it had not been for his name, we would not have recognized him.

His extinct gaze was directed at the ground; his stupidly creased face was covered with a mask of astonishment, and his mouth seemed momentarily to contract into a pout of disappointment. A hint of native bonhomie extended over his face. Horatio rarely visited London, and the people he saw there had no connection with the Duke's family, which was rather distant from the social whirl.

"But my dear Horatio," Olivia's father continued, after the usual polite greeting, "if you had only consulted me in his matter, I would immediately have dissuaded you. Sir James Cawdor has just made the best deal of his life. Would you believe, ladies, that Mackinguss has just bought the Castle of the Falls and its dependent rocks, at a high price? My poor friend, it's a property that will bring you nothing but old wives' tales!"

"But remember one thing, Duke—the castle is famous today throughout the three kingdoms. People visit it, like Holyrood, Stirling and other royal residences. And what the Duke of Hamilton did in Edinburgh, why should I not do, with more justification, in Lanarkshire?"

"But instead of visiting your castle, my lord, people will avoid it! Fortunately, if you take a wife one day..."

Horatio shot Miss Olivia a vigilance expressing the most honest love that was ever in a virtuous heart.

"Yes, we can certainly hope that, in the event, Milady will alienate that haunted rock from you, if only because of the nocturnal spirits."

"Miss, if ever I have the good fortune to marry a wife, I shall be at her orders."

"You profess excellent sentiments, my lord. So, you admit that you would be an obliging husband—in the best sense of the word."

"My God, Mademoiselle, I treat myself thus; how could I be any different with others, especially those I love?" And the honest gaze continued to wander with a tinge of bliss over Miss Olivia's cruelly mocking person.

The Duke and Amadeus, who was sitting in the light of a window, were chatting together.

"Have you any news to tell us, my lord?"

"Alas, Miss, I don't know of any," Horatio immediately replied, modestly, as if embarrassed in close proximity to a woman.

"You'd be very kind, then, to read me the *Times*."

"Gladly, if that would interest you."

The old woman emerged from beneath the vast tent that covered her like one of those vast village pastries that are shielded from the sun.

Horatio took possession of the paper and turned the pages over and over with his unintelligent hands, with an awkwardness that would have made a clown at the Adelphi Theater jealous.

Finally, the poor suitor began—but the young woman soon stopped him.

"My God, my lord, what an odd way you have of reading! You're quite inexorable. The cheerful news you read as if at a funeral, and delight in the narration of the most horrifying crimes. What are you thinking about as you're reading?"

Horatio set the paper down with a grimace that was charming in its stupidity, and his honest and timid eye returned to his question. After breathing in deeply, he sighed.

"Lord Mackinguss, I suspect you of being in love with me."

Horatio lowered his head and blushed clandestinely.

"Well then, do something for me."

"Everything I have I lay at your feet, Miss."

"Sir James Cawdor, the gentleman with which you've just concluded your last artistic affair, has assured us that you've never learned a word of French. Is that true?"

"Quite true, alas, Miss."

"He also told us that there is one particular word that you pronounce in an amusing manner."

"I believe, Miss, without boasting, that I pronounce them all like that."

"Come on, don't be so modest, and say to us, quite seriously, *turlututu*."

"That's true—I recognize the word. My friends, after drinking claret, have often made me pronounce that bizarre locution, but they've never been able to give me its meaning in English."

"Well, I shall be more generous than your friends; it means *I love you*."[19]

"It's a very pretty word," he remarked, with a benign and trustful smile.

"Learn it well—look, here it is written down."

Olivia place a piece of paper before his eyes on which the word *turtlututu* was written in pencil. Horatio looked at it momentarily with profound seriousness—that English seriousness which tickles the French sense of humor so much—and then, twisting his lips into an elongated spiral, the uttered the loveliest *toulioutoutou* that had ever been pronounced.

Olivia, without pity for her poor admirer, burst out laughing. Even the Duke and Amadeus could not resist, on hearing Mackinguss—who, ardently desirous of pronouncing the word in the French fashion, rendered the side-splitting *toulioutoutou* every time. Horatio maintained a painful gravity.

All that laughter was, however, drowned out by the jaw-cracking racket of the old aunt, who, tormenting her zygomatic muscles frantically, was choking with joy, and making whistling noises with her old cheeks, as dry and withered as an English roast.

It was Sir Amadeus who stopped laughing first, took pity on his rival and changed a subject that was scarcely worthy of causing the ladies' hilarity. "I was just explaining to the Duke, Miss, my disappointment at not seeing you at Covent Garden this evening."

---

[19] It is actually an onomatopoeia supposedly echoing the sound of a flute.

"Yes," the Duke added, "Sir Amadeus is leaving for Brighton after dinner. But we'll see him again tomorrow, in the evening, at least." And the old man shook the hand of his presumptive son-in-law affectionately

"Oh well," said Olivia, lightly, "we'll ask Lord Mackinguss to replace you in our company."

Horatio bowed profoundly as a sign of joyful assent. And, shaking the young man's hand in the English fashion, he said to him: "Believe sir, that it is with happiness that I accept Miss Firstland's invitation."

The young woman stood up, and, passing close to Amadeus, whispered to him: "Be careful, Sir Amadeus. Vampires are abroad in London, and you have a weak head."

"If it were not others, Miss, it would be you who would render me mad...for that is my destiny; I sense it!"

X. Covent Garden

It was a nice enough day in London. A fine, imperceptible drizzle, a damp and smoky mist, spread a pale and troubled light over the great city. The sky, a leaden gray, weighed heavily upon the dome of St. Paul's, a construction that appeared all the more colossal because the summit of its cupola was bathed in a cloud that the eye could not pierce. English monuments have a strange aspect. Beneath the low, pale sky, the stones do not take on the burnished color that the sun gives them in Spain, nor the earthy layer with which the rain envelops the old cathedrals of France. In London, tall edifices always seem to be struck by a nocturnal light; the columns are black on one side and a chalky tint on the other. Those somber layers are produced by the black smoke of coal, and the pale parts by the washing of wind-driven rain. On seeing St. Paul's thus by night, one would think it an effect of the moon, and by day, in the thick cloud, one might think that it were clad in snow.

Leaning out of a house in Grosvenor Square, Robert was directing his inert gaze at Westminster Abbey when he heard someone calling behind him.

"You can't stand at the window like that, Sir Robert," said a voice from inside.

"What! I'm not even allowed to get a little air!"

"But sir, in London, one never takes the air at the window; that's a bizarre habit of southerners, utterly unknown here. You never see a head at a window in any circumstances, not even on the day of a Chartist demonstration."

"Do you know, Sir James, that the life you're imposing on me is tiresome?"

"I know," the other replied.

"I've been in England for nearly a month now, and it's only permitted to me to go out in the evenings, always enclosed in a carriage. In truth, I couldn't make a tour of this square without going astray!"

"Take it from me, Sir Robert, that one never goes out by day in London. This evening, we're going to Covent Garden."

"Yes, I know, to a deep and dark box. We'll arrive when the actors are already on stage, and we'll leave when there's no longer anyone about but the horseguards. Can you explain to me, finally, why I mustn't be seen?"

"No, Sir Robert," Cawdor replied, with his habitual phlegm, "it's not necessary. Only, reflect on one thing: if Lord Horatio acts thus, it's in order to keep his promise to you."

"Or, rather, say that I'm the instrument of some treacherous scheme. But I also recall that Milord gave me his word not to soil me with any crime, nor even an evil action—for if it were otherwise, Sir James, believe me, I'd be able to recover my will and stand up against that man, all-powerful as he may be."

"That's a deadly thought you have there, Monsieur Robert; the moment when you contemplate it seriously won't last long for you. A cadaver for which no one will search will never return to the surface of the Thames, Monsieur de Rolleboise."

"That's the stuff of melodrama, Sir James, and nothing more."

"No, Monsieur Robert, it's merely drama, pure and simple. By the way, I'm going to give you some news that concerns you, and which all London already knows."

"All of London is occupied with me, then?"

"I mean by that the whole of the aristocracy."

"Well, what is this news?"

"It's that you're on the point of getting married, Sir Robert."

"Me, getting married!" exclaimed the young man, utterly bewildered.

"Yes, you, Monsieur Robert de Rolleboise."

"From what novel, Sir James are you taking the sentences that you're throwing in my face?"

"I never read novels."

"Well, I beg you, speak to me seriously."

"I always speak seriously."

"But you're saying crazy things!"

"Not in the least."

"Insane things."

"Listen young man," Cawdor went on, with perfect amiability, "please don't attach a futile astonishment to every word I address to you. I say: you're about to be married. That's sufficient, it seems to me, and you have no objection to raise."

"Oh! Well, if that's the way it is, that's different!"

His hands behind his back, Robert marched back and forth in the room at a precipitate pace. Internally, he was revolting against the complete renunciation that had been imposed on him. Finally, appearing to accept his role, he said to his interlocutor who was still sitting quietly: "So, I'm to be married."

"You're to be married.

"That's good..."

"Oh, indeed!

"That's very good...but to whom, pray?"

"I don't understand, Monsieur Robert."

"You don't understand! But it seems to me that I'm talking French."

"That's precisely why, Monsieur Robert; you keep on forgetting that you ought no longer to know the French language."

"But I warn you your idiom fatigues the throat so much, your words give me such cramps in the gullet, that I'll have laryngitis in a week."

"Your gullet will become more pliable. You were asking me, then, Monsieur Robert?"

"The name of the person to whom you're marrying me."

"Pardon me—first of all, it's not me that's marrying you."

"Oh! Who is it, then?"

"You, of course, my dear sir."

"Really?"

"And furthermore, I can tell you that you're very much in love."

"In love, me?"

"Hyperbolically."

"Well, so be it: I'm madly in love. But again, with whom?"

"You're marrying the daughter of the Duke of Firstland."

At that name, Robert seemed to remember something. "Firstland! Yes, I remember encountering that word somewhere. That's it—a letter written in English that that woman left in my home. In fact, I can read it now."

Immediately, he rummaged in a drawer and took out a small pocket-book. It contained a letter. He scanned it rapidly.

"*My dearest daughter*...signed: *Duchess of Firstland.*" His physiognomy became somber and his forehead creased.

"Mr. Cawdor..."

"Sir James, I beg you."

"Sir James, my honor must emerge intact from these strange circumstances in which I find myself..."

"My dear friend, you talk to me constantly about your honor like a tiresome adolescent with heartache!"

"So," the young man continued, "I shall not marry the person you've named to me."

"Very good, Sir Robert."

"Because she's a kept woman!"

"Very good, Sir Robert; we have no objection at all; in fact, it's in order to break off the marriage that we're going to Covent Garden this evening. Furthermore, I promise you that we'll leave the hall before the public in the stalls and the upper boxes—and above all, before the horseguards."

The door of the room opened. A person that is unknown to us came in. "I have the honor of greeting Monsieur de Rolleboise," he said, coldly.

"Your servant, Lord Lodore."

Lord Lodore performed the same functions in regard to the young Frenchman as Sir James Cawdor, but he was a person of a completely different character. He had a strange appearance: he was tall and thin. He was entirely dressed in black, and his coat, always buttoned, did not allow any trace of linen to show through. His pale blond delicate hair, sparse, delicate and receding, left the whole of his wan, bony and naked face uncovered. His hollow sea-green eyes remained immobile in a heavy stare. His short snub nose, pale lips and mouth announced a man of mysterious, even barbaric mores. In brief, he had one of those physiognomies that are transformed in fits of passion, becoming terrifying when flagellated by the whip of a brutal sentiment.

Horatio counted on that man as on himself, but he had never understood him. There was a constrained reserve between them when they were together, especially on the part of the master. Often, the latter's magnetic gaze tormented the surface of that mysterious soul, searched the profound shadows of that sinuous mind, racked the angles of that unknown character, but in vain. Of all that he had tried to vanquish, only the interior of that man was still obscure. Nevertheless that which he had attempted on his subaltern, the latter had never attempted upon his superior, and he was to Lodore that he was to everyone: an enigma. Lodore was the inert body that stopped the ray but without reflecting it back.

"Monsieur Robert, your barber is here."

On the threshold stood a black shadow, wearing a face of automatic immobility. His legs were so thin and his feet so long that one might have thought him a bust of a mannequin in a black coat supported by two scythes.

In the deepest silence, the barber began his work. Sir James, phlegmatically extended on a sofa with his hands joined on his belly and his two thumbs rotating, watched him gravely. Lodore, standing with his arms folded, had leaned against a sideboard. Only the razor was active.

But the barber, almost without movement and entirely without a sound, disappeared. He was immediately replaced by a manservant equally diaphanous and silent. The latter took possession of Rolleboise and began dressing him.

"But these aren't boots that you're putting me into! I'll never have the leisure to explore the extremities. They're two ridiculous promontories!"

"You're mistaken, Monsieur Robert—those boots fit you admirably."

"Indeed! But you're now submitting me an impossible problem. Your English boots will never reach the extremity of the tunnel of this garment. It's a simple rifle-sheath that you're giving me for trousers!"

"First of all, Monsieur Robert, you must perceive, from the blush rising to your manservant's cheeks, that the last word of your sentence is out of place."

"As you wish, Sir James, but your *inexpressible* is utterly grotesque. I can't get it on without powder. I really don't know why you're dressing me in this fashion today."

"My dear Monsieur Robert, this is, however, a garment that has emerged from the hands of Stultz.[20] After all, it's necessary to dress you like everyone else. If you go out in London with a well-made inexpressible, you'll attract the gaze of passers-by, and it's not polite to stand out."

Nevertheless, by means of hard work and many precautions, the prudish valet had succeeded in covering his master with that shocking element of masculine attire. Then they went on to the jacket.

"But I'll have something other than that thin black jacket?"

"Not at all. The black jacket is sufficient for everything here. It is, in any case, the most graceful and most comfortable of garments."

"But you'll freeze in winter with your graceful jacket."

"In winter, we button it up. The English never take more trouble than that."

---

[20] Johann Stultz was Beau Brummell's tailor of choice. He died in 1832, so Cawdor is speaking metaphorically.

"Well, so be it, we're in autumn. My gloves?"

"If you go to a ball, they'll perhaps be given to you. Otherwise, never."

"I'll have red hands, Sir James!"

"That's true; but also, this winter, you'll have blue ones."

"Gentlemen, I perceive that there's a role underneath all this that I don't know, but which has fallen to me. I'd like to know, however, whether it will ever again be permissible for me to dress appropriately, as in my homeland."

"Tomorrow, Monsieur Robert. Will you please get used to tilting your head slightly to the left, and losing all petulance from your stride. Are you satisfied, Lord Lodore?"

"He's the very image," the Englishman replied, making a tour of Robert and examining from every angle. "If possible, however, give your voice a more guttural accent."

"Yes," said Sir James, "and if anyone greets you outside, reply with the head and the hand, but don't take your hat off; it's not customary here."

"Again, if, in a corridor—at the theater, for example—you nudge a lady with your elbow while walking, you continue on your way as if nothing has happened. In London, one doesn't waste time with all those ridiculous banalities customary in France."

"Messieurs," said the young man, in French, his brow furrowed, "I suspect that you're going to make me commit some kind of infamy."

The two Englishmen looked at one another as if they did not understand. Robert repeated the same remark in their language.

The only response he received was from Sir James, who said, emotionlessly: "Yesterday evening, Monsieur Robert, in Lady Landsdale's drawing-room, I saw a person of your acquaintance—or rather, two persons, for Madame de Lormont was accompanied by a handsome young man."

Pale with anger, and his eyes fiery, Robert tapped his foot and said to his companion-guides: "Now, gentleman, what must I do?"

"More guttural, please, more guttural," replied Lord Lodore coolly.

"If Monsieur Robert will come to the dining room, we'll dine."

The three men left the room, and the clock struck six.

That evening, Covent Garden Theater was putting on a performance of a German opera, perhaps *Fidelio*. The crowd was quite numerous. The Duke of Firstland's box was facing the stage. Miss Olivia was in the front with her Aunt Cockburn, who was clad in a dress inflated like an aerostat—for Englishwomen, who are generally a trifle plump, are obstinate in the belief the hooped skirts are still being worn in Paris, as of old.

Horatio Mackinguss was sitting in the second row, beside the old man.

Olivia looked round anxiously. "Oh my God! That superb bouquet you gave me, Milord—I've left it in the carriage."

"Andrew will go to fetch it for you."

"Oh! A bouquet that a valet has handled, perhaps sniffed! How can you be so naïve, milord?"

"I'll go myself, Miss."

The proud young woman granted him a smile in payment for his kindness. Horatio gazed at her in a fashion that was as eloquent as it was honest, and departed submissively in search of the bouquet, without paying any heed to the slightly mocking laugher that the aged Miss Cockburn addressed to him.

The young woman's attention was momentarily captured by the stage, but he eminent of her great fortune and beauty soon brought her back to more vain ideas. Her arrogant gaze looked disdainfully downwards.

Near the forestage, a low and profound box appeared to be occupied. Nevertheless a man came to stand against a column and paraded his gaze around the room. On perceiving that pale face illuminated by two eyes whitening in the shadow, the young woman shuddered. She recalled the nocturnal encounter near the cemetery. Those phosphorescent pupils stimulated her

117

memory. Immediately, stood against that column, she recovered a fatal resemblance to the head of the man supported by the wall of the necropolis—but she turned away, because the two fixed rays departing from that petrifying gorgon face settled on her.

At that moment, Horatio came back into the box and humbly handed the flowers to Olivia.

"Thank you, Milord! Would you be kind enough to add to the trouble that I've caused you that of telling me the name of that sinister spectator standing on his own in front of that dark box?"

In his awkward haste, Olivia's suitor drew his opera-glasses from his pocket so rapidly that they escaped from his clumsy hands, fell on to his knees and were about to roll between the legs of the old aunt, who immediately set out to protect her modesty. These incompetences, committed in public, irritated the proud young woman. Finally, the poor lord, red with intimidation, aimed his binoculars at the individual who was as motionless as a statue.

"Certainly, I know the gentleman. That's Lord Lodore, Miss."

"Do you know him well?"

"No, ladies, but if it would please you, I will impose myself upon him so much that I'll be able to tell you about him knowledgeably."

"Oh! You misunderstand, Milord. I have no need of police!"

Fatigued by Lodore's stare, the young woman looked down at the flowers that her hand, irritated by the Comte's incompetence, had already maltreated. As she considered them attentively she discovered a note rolled up in the corolla of a white camellia. Poor Horatio came under suspicion. In fact, without any emotion, the young woman turned round and said, in the most natural voice, but a trifle coldly: "It's legitimate for you to talk to me, Milord, but I haven't authorized you to write to me. Take this note out of my bouquet and do so dexterously, if possible."

"In truth, Miss," said Horatio, blushing, "there might be a piece of paper in your flowers, but I give you my word that I am not the guilty party."

Without saying word, the old Duke unrolled it, unsealed it and passed it to his daughter. "Since it's addressed to you, Olivia, read it."

Without taking the note from her father's hand, the young woman ran her eyes over the lines.

Beautiful as one is, one always has a rival. Sir Amadeus Harriss will give proof of that tonight. A Vampire.

The young woman frowned and resumed her position, leaning on the rim of the box. "Tear up that paper, Father," she said, simply. "My Lord, do you perceive anyone at the back of the box where Lord Lodore is standing?"

"I believe I recognize Sir Amadeus therein, Miss."

"Alone?"

"I don't know, but I can only see him. In fact, if I'm not mistaken, he's just gone out."

This was during an *entr'acte*. The door of the Duke's box was ajar.

"In fact, I can hear his voice."

"He's in the gallery," Horatio observed, looking into the corridor, where several people were passing by. "Sir James Cawdor is with him."

James Cawdor was indeed walking along the exterior passage, with Robert de Rolleboise on his arm. The young Frenchman seemed to be impatient, and was speaking rather loudly in a high-pitched voice.

"I repeat to you that it shall not be, Sir James."

"Sir, permit me to tell you that that determination is not based on any plausible reason. It is also folly."

"No, I tell you; come what may, I shall never marry the daughter of the Duke of Firstland!"

"But why, Sir?"

"Why?" said the young man, indignantly. "Because Miss Firstland is what we call in Paris a *lorette*: a whore. That's why, Sir James!"

XI. Your Reason

Midnight was chiming in all the belfries when Amadeus, emerging from Whitehall, reached the statue of George Canning. His black jacket was buttoned up all the way to his white cravat, and his face appeared leadenly pale, with a bluish tint.

Night has a real influence on certain imaginative minds. Their anxious gaze suspects the shadows, their brain becomes overactive and an insurmountable nervous fear takes hold of them. Intelligent and indolent brutes, however, have no apprehension of darkness; in fact, never going beyond reality, their conception cannot surpass the circle that surrounds them, no matter how tight it might be.

Amadeus had courage and determination. He had, therefore, vanquished a forceful native timidity. He would have confronted death coolly in a duel, or a battle, but it was necessary for him to prepare that artificial strength. Taken by surprise, he weakened. By night, a simple story rendered him as pusillanimous as a child—and yet, he experienced a bitter enjoyment in procuring such fictitious apprehension. Like the German poet, who placed a woman beside him to reassure him during the hallucinatory fears that his fantastic conceptions communicated to him, Amadeus created at night, by the confusion of all the sounds of the day, phantoms and chimerical apparitions that frightened him. In brief, while traveling, he never feared attacks by armed hands in the streets of cities; he walked without any concern for thieves and bandits—by day he would traverse a deserted forest unarmed—but in the evening, in his bedroom, he feared the presence of a man under his bed.

He had often tried to cure himself of that eccentricity of temperament, but his nature had always weakened against his strong resolution. Nevertheless, this evening, under the gaslight, he did not fear any apparition. However, the stylistic strangeness of the letter so extraordinarily found beside him when he awoke, the signature that concluded it, the choice of rendezvous in the tumulary stones of Westminster, and the very hour of midnight, once so influential, all accumulated in his febrile brain, which was racing.

Like all unhealthy minds, however, Amadeus was in love, and like all those in love, he was jealous. The poor young man had no presumption, no high opinion of his personal worth. Ingenuously, he attributed his fortunate position in the world to chance. Chance is a very peculiar guide. Amadeus knew that, so he professed great self-mistrust. In spite of all the passion he felt for Olivia, but dared not express, he was still more astonished to be loved than not to be. So, jealousy combating dread, Amadeus appeared at the rendezvous at the appointed time.

Scarcely had he taken a few steps in the vicinity of the ancient basilica than a hand was placed on his shoulder without him having perceived anyone. Was it some statue descended from its niche that had come to advise him to flee, or some gargoyle with a batrachian head crawling around him to mock his fear?

Having turned round, however, he saw a human form facing him.

"Sir Amadeus Harriss?"

"That's me," he replied, confidently.

"Will you kindly come with me?"

"I will—but who are you?"

The man took off his hat and indicated the black braid that surrounded it.

"You're a manservant? Whose manservant."

"Mr. Harriss', sir."

He's an idiot, he thought. "I'll come with you—go on ahead."

After a quarter of an hour of walking through streets and squares that Sir Amadeus had never noticed, having only rarely had occasion to traverse the district in his carriage, his guide arrived at a seemingly rich house. They went in. The young man was introduced into a drawing room.

"Whose house is this?" he asked, again.

"It belongs to Mr. Harriss, sir."

The questioner gestured impatiently. The valet, however, was dressed very respectably, and nothing in his placid physiognomy was suggestive of madness. Amadeus, almost deluded by the natural appearance of things, wondered whether he really might be under the influence of a strange aberration.

The servant continued: "If Milord would care to wait for a moment. Here are the evening papers. Having spent the evening at Covent Garden with the Duke of Firstland, His Honor has doubtless been delayed longer than he anticipated.

"Indeed! Let us avoid equivocation, if possible. Do you know who I am?"

"Sir Amadeus is His Honor's—my master's—brother."

"What! Your master's brother! My brother is dead!"

"Sir Lewis will be here soon. Your Honor will recognize him."

"That's all right—I'll wait," the young man said, not understanding the enigma at all.

The valet bowed and disappeared, backwards. His footsteps were inaudible. One might have thought that a panel in the corridor had absorbed him into the wall. A bright lamp, the light of which was softened by a frosted glass, was burning on the table. Amadeus sat down next to it, and, more to put on a brave face than to seek a distraction, he picked up a newspaper and started scanning it with his eyes.

Robert de Rolleboise had, however, returned from the theater. In a room adjacent to the one in which Olivia's fiancé was sitting, he was listening to the instructions of his two companions, Lord Lodore and Sir James Cawdor.

Rolleboise was striding back and forth, with the gait that is like the pendulum of active thought. Lord Lodore got up, when slowly toward him, posed his long bony hand on his shoulder, and looking at him with his staring eyes.

At the sight of that wan face, and the contact of that hard gnarled hand, Robert stopped, as if at the behest of a switch.

"So you're still forgetting the renunciation you swore, Robert? We don't like to find our will indecisive, and tonight, you are our will. You've heard us, Robert: if you hesitate for a second, if a single inflexion betrays your voice, you must assume your ignominy and your death. Think about Mathilde. Think about yourself. Are you ready?"

"I am."

"Good—you're awaited."

Robert left the two men and found himself on the threshold of the room where Amadeus was waiting. The batten of the door was open; only the curtain separated him from Harriss. He lifted up a flap of the curtain silently, and his gaze fell upon the man sitting next to the lamp. Silence itself would have considered that scene attentively.

At that sight, Rolleboise was gripped by an involuntary seizure; he stepped back, and the heavy pleats of the curtain fell back. But a hand gripped his arm. In the shadows, in the background, behind him, he perceived the imperious and impassive face of Lodore. He went forward, and this time the drape fell back behind him.

Amadeus, alerted by the rustle of the fabric, saw Robert standing in front of him. Frightened, he pushed his chair back and retreated.

Calmly, Robert walked toward him without saying a word.

Amadeus put his hand over his eyes, as if to dispel a hallucination, but in vain. His image continued to advance. He was breathless. His livid cheeks moistened with sweat; the blue veins in his forehead swelled, his vision blurred.

A door opened behind him; he went through it, calling for help in a halting and choked voice, and, losing his head, ran through corridors and staircases, and finally arrived in the street.

Robert was still following him.

Outside, the locale was deserted, silent and dark. Terror had such a firm grip on Harriss that he continued running, at random, in unknown directions. But when Robert, or rather his shadow, gained on him, he almost ran backwards. His head was bare. Whenever he passed some faint light, he appeared as pale and distressed as Hamlet before the phantom.

In the darkness, a few paces behind Rolleboise, following the shadows of the walls, came a third person, who, at times, uttered a word or phrase of stimulation.

In that fantastic course, the two men were so close to one another that Amadeus, with his hands extended, repelled his phantom

"Who are you?" the poor panic-stricken man articulated, with feverish emphasis.

"A vampire."

"A vampire!"

"Yes, who wants to live as you do, love as you do. I'm Lewis, your dead brother. I emerge from my tomb every night."

"You want my life!"

"What would I do with it? No, it's not to draw life from the living that I emerge...the dead don't want to live."

"Lewis, if it's your shade that is pursuing me, mercy! Have pity on your brother!"

"A vampire never has pity. Fear not, Amadeus—I don't want your blood!"

That voice reached Amadeus' troubled ears monotonously and without living inflection. While speaking, the two men were still moving.

"You don't want my blood! What do you want, then?"

Robert leaned further toward the young man; his magnetic gaze seemed to penetrate his troubled brain, and he said, in a slow voice, as if carrying out a real operation: "I want your reason!"

"My reason!" cried the unhappy victim of pursuit, covering his face with his hands, as if to defend himself against any attainment.

"Yes, your reason, your reason! I can feel it entering into me...animating me...enlightening me! Yes, yes, I'm taking it from you, I'm taking it from you. Can't you feel it leaving you?"

Alas, in fact, poor Amadeus' brain was very ill. His reason, already deeply troubled, weakened under that moral torture. For the unfortunate man, thus pursued, it was not a frightful dream but a supernatural, infernal reality that was acting upon him.

Before that tortuous anguish, confronted by that visage decomposed by agony and intelligence, Robert too suffered a flash of vertigo. It was his image, it was him, who was struggling thus in the midst of a delirium plunging him into the abyss of madness. He was frightened, and paled in his turn— but his arm was seized by a hand of steel; a word fell into his ear like a drop of liquid lead into cold water, and he shivered at that violent pressure, and straightened up, galvanized by that mysterious word.

Amadeus was still fleeing, but his pace was staccato and irregular; he was vacillating, like a drunken man, and could do no more. Sometimes, he paused, perhaps to seize a glimmer in the obscurity of his intelligence, but then the dead, sepulchral voice of the vampire buzzed in his ear, with no variation of tone.

"Your reason, your reason! It's abandoning you…it wants to come to me…your reason, your reason!"

The man's tone penetrated to the depths of the poor insensate's brain, and echoed their sonorously, as if in emptiness. He shut his hallucinated eyes, stopped his buzzing ears, but he still saw his image and till heard those avid words: "Your reason, your reason!"

Exhausted, almost dying of fright, he fell inert into a profound doorway. His eyes opened atonally; he looked at Robert for a moment and said to him, with a burst of laughter that was prolonged like a note that takes a long time to fade away: "You'll give it back to me, Lewis, won't you?"

The unfortunate man was mad.

The individual who had remained constantly in the shadows throughout that scene came to stand before Robert then. It was Lodore.

"It's frightful, Milord, what you've made me do here!"

"No one requires your opinion, Robert. For the moment, I request the assistance of your arm."

The two men picked up Amadeus' body and carried it away. The poor insensate was still laughing stupidly. Rolleboise was holding him by the arms; in consequence, he could only see Lodore.

"Where's Lewis?" the madman asked.

"Lewis has gone to the woman he loves, Olivia."

The unfortunate fiancé did not understand.

"Now," Lodore continued, "We're carrying you to be buried in Lewis's tomb."

"That's true," he replied, in a melancholy fashion, letting his head slump on to his breast. "Since I've lost my reason, I'm dead. But he'll give it back to me...yes, he'll give it back."

They stopped at the door of a large house and deposited their burden there.

"This is where he lives," said Lodore. "Set him down on the doorstep and knock loudly."

When that was done, the two men disappeared around the corner of the square. They could hear the poor madman's insane laughter for some time.

XII. The Old Duke

The words pronounced in the corridor of Covent Garden Theater by Robert de Rolleboise had been heard in Miss Firstland's box. Soon afterwards, the carriage that was carrying the young Frenchman was overtaken by the Duke's. As they came downstairs, Olivia, overcoming her anger, had said to Horatio: "My Lord, if you were a man of courage, I'd do you the honor of asking you to avenge that insult, but..."

Horatio did not flinch before this proposition, of a rather depreciative nature. He simply replied, in a tone as indifferent as it was naïve: "I should think so, Miss."

The young woman looked at him with disdain and pity, and then returned to her irritation. The man's phlegm revolted her; she would have liked to be able to whip that composure and inertia with her seething wrath. Like one of those weak minds ever nonplussed in the face of the violent agitations that shake others, Horatio bowed, embarrassed, at the carriage door that closed in front of him.

The old Duke did not say a word, but the pallor of his visage revealed a poignant internal suffering. His forthright character, forged in the proud and arrogant mores of Caledonia, remained somber in the presence of his offended honor. He, who possessed in the gallery of his ancestors a portrait of Bruce, and through the distaff line, a Balliol, had been insulted in a crowded theater by some malevolent petty lowland laird, who had become a merchant, a lawyer, or whatever, and grown rich in consequence!

His silent thoughts, however, contrasted with Olivia's spasmodic irritation; she did not say anything, but her bitten lips emitted an occasional impatient and angry articulation. The lines of her superb forehead were twisted into profound and taut furrows. Her respiration whistled in her flared nostrils, and her teeth were audibly grinding. Her hands were crumpling her gloves and the remnants of the poor bouquet

were scattered all over the oilcloth-covered floor of the carriage.

Only the old aunt spoke, racking her brain stuffed full of
Bible verses with eccentric hypotheses and impossible suppo-
sitions, always falling back on her favorite theme, the rascality
of men.

The Duke embraced his daughter and retired to his
apartment. He expressed the desire to be alone. His manservant left.

The old man loved Olivia, but the affection that united
them had never led with her to the anxious intimacy that gives
the heart a particular delicacy of sensitivity. In the young
woman's daily life there were many respectful formalities that
she never neglected, any more than she neglected to say a
prayer in the evening as she was about to go to bed. Most of
the time, the aged father received these attentions through the
intermediary of a servant, and replied to them in the same
way.

Pursued by the insomnia of senility, however, huddled in
his bedclothes, the Duke sometimes shed slow tears. It is a sad
and lamentable thing to see tears in an old man's eyes! Were
his dark nights illuminated by the glimmer of an extinct affection? Did he feel a faint expansion of the soul at the memory
of a lost perfume? Was his ear still ringing with a familiar
sound, as he distinguished a sigh in the plaint of the wind? Did
his deluded eyes construct a formless phantom in the darkness?

Often, his dreams transported him into wild locations,
atop sheer crags, and he saw torrents, heard the rumbling of
the cataracts of the Findhorn, and then the fall of a pale apparition that was lost in the white foam of the pouring waves.
Then he woke up with a start, breathless, and the tears continued his dream.

But that night, he was no longer a man defeated by age
and dolor, an old man indifferent to the events of life and living in the past, like the polar peoples illuminated by the aurora
borealis. He seemed to have cast off the burden of age and to

have grown in stature. His eyes, almost always extinct, settled in a grim fixity, and his precipitate tread was firm on the deadening carpet of the room.

"An insult to my face, in a crowd, where everyone could hear! That old man, they must be thinking, is a crumbing ruin whose initial debris is already in the tomb, so one can insult him with impunity! Ah, young men, do you think that, as a joke, perhaps for an infantile snigger, you have the right to insult a father like that, to tarnish his name? Not so!

"Honor, in my country, is a rock that supports a fortress. The fort might crumble, but the rock remains unshaken; perhaps you will kill the old man, but that is all! The sword that made our name illustrious, the formidable claymore that one of my forefathers chipped on the battlefield of Sheriffmuir and another reddened at Culloden is still in my hand. I am still capable of handling it, and of covering the yellow rust that is corroding it with blood!

"Truly, I despise those frail pygmies who, with their shrill voices, emit words that wreck a family! I feel humiliated by not having knocked down one of those weak, degenerate men that throw mud at you disrespectfully. The abasement of great human things! How many monuments have been diminished by the slow corrosion of time? Everything noble decreases.

"Thus, the first of the Firstlands, at the head of his clan, fought beside William the Lion. When all his men were lying with their faces to the heavens, he shared the fate of his king. Later, before Norham Castle, when Balliol was crowned, a single chieftain retired to his mountains, refusing to recognize himself a vassal of England, and that warrior's name was Hodge of Firstland! One of my ancestors left his blood on the field of Falkirk, followed Wallace in the forests, over the seas, in battles, in tempests, and died with him on the English scaffold. Another forefather fell at Sheriffmuir, leaving his son nothing but his honor and his claymore. I have the portrait of a Malcolm!

"And—shame and derision!—before those tombs, after those generations of giants, when the last of the Firstlands is reaching the end of his days, he has to combat an insulter of women! A child whom the weight of a highlander's sword would crush!"

He fell silent. That lightning-flash of memory, coming thus to strike his ulcerated heart, galvanized him with a few violent shocks, but he soon collapsed, inert. The stiff hand of old age gripped him again. He fell to his knees, his white head in his long thin hands.

"And I am not loved!" he exclaimed, still tearful. "I find myself abandoned here, as if in a tomb! I wander, like a tumulary statue detached from its pedestal. Olivia! Alas, I'm her father, that's all. And, tormenting thought in which my soul weeps, never in her company have I experienced the intumescence of the heart, the confident and intimate joy that I once experienced! Meanwhile, it would have been ineffable to feel my solitary soul penetrated by an affection as resplendent as an incense rising up in the cold atmosphere of a temple! But, alone on this earth, a man of effaced mores, I no longer have any refuge but the tomb. Alas, one is also alone in the tomb!"

His damp face was raised, and his gaze settled on an ivory Christ facing him, on a black background. The Duke professed the Catholic religion of his ancestors, before the advent of the grim John Knox, who preached the gospel by having priests and cardinals murdered, and plunging statues of the Virgin into rivers, with the pleasantries of an exceedingly reformed wit: an apostate who had a Bible in place of a heart, a man with arid eyes who lived without emotion in the palace of Holyrood, with a queen at his feet, who felt a woman's tears on his cold hand and had no pity!

The old man's physiognomy suddenly calmed, and prayer, the imploration never rejected, brought him the relief that is so powerful in misfortune. After having prayed he calmly stood up, He headed for the back of the apartment and drew back a silk curtain descending over the tapestry, uncovering a portrait. That canvas depicted a pale young woman with a sad and loving expression. Before that painting, art that makes itself felt by means of sight as literature makes one see by means of sentiment, the old man wept again, but his mouth designed a smile.

"Ophelia, my poor child, why did you leave me? Me, your old father, who would have forgiven you if you were guilty... Guilty! Oh, forgive me for speaking thus before a tomb! You are in Heaven now, in the real abode of our dreams! Your Heaven is so resplendent that your eyes stray toward the infimal shadow in which your poor father is suffering! I've asked God to send me the assurance of your happy existence, and I feel it taking hold of me. No, I won't listen to certain frightful dreams, which depict your shade floating, with lamentations that the echoes repeat, in the growling waters of the Findhorn. Oh, if the thought were not an evil, and its execution a crime, I would go to die myself where you extinguished yourself! Our two shades would be together...!

"Listen, poor Ophelia, I often have ideas of happiness that frighten me—they're doubtless sallies of the intoxication of my sick brain—that you might still be alive! If one day, your unfortunate father could weep in your arms, his white head on your blonde hair, full of those perfumes of the spring of life, oh, my Lord, for that moment of intoxication I would give many centuries of my sojourn beside you! Those words are a sacrilege, but you'll forgive them, my Lord, for if I love her so much, it's because she's my daughter...

"Dear child, I recognize you—there are your dreaming eyes, always searching the lowering sky for a trace of blue, your mouth smiling sadly as it speaks, softly, words that I can still hear! And your beautiful blonde hair, which spreads on golden curls over your pale shoulders. It's said that the hair is conserved as well as the bones!

"But no, you're still in this world; I'll see you again one day; I want to believe it. I'll fix my attention on a not-too-distant epoch, and I'll await your return. Oh, if madness could deceive me to the point at which I could believe that I would see you again, I would want to be mad! Alas, before this image, which I love, I forget everything: the present, the past, the stains that my honor has received!"

His visage became somber again, and after his moth had deposited a kiss on the portrait, his hand allowed the veil to fall again. His head was weary, and a poignant pain was encircling his brain. He opened his window and leaned on the sill, bleak and pensive.

The deserted street was illuminated by gaslight. The old man's mind went back to his daughter. With a bizarre stir of profound affection, he reproached himself for having abandoned the portrait so promptly for a somber distraction. Like a mother who fears that she has not put enough love into the caress given to her child, he returned to the beloved image and kissed it for a long time, addressing puerile remarks and heartbroken comments to it. Then, filled with his thoughts, he returned to dreaming of that affection, which, like all such, cost him so many tears.

At the very end of the street, in the distance, two lights appeared. Soon, the rumble of an approaching carriage became audible. It was going to pass in front of the house. Indifferent to external things, the old man watched it coming, content to feel his gaze reclaimed by the approach of the horses. They were traveling rapidly. Suddenly the Duke went pale, uttered an exclamation, and leaned out of the window, his gaze avid. But the carriage had disappeared and the sound of its wheels faded away at a corner of the street.

At the window of the post-chaise, the poor Duke had distinguished a woman's head—and that woman, yes, was his daughter, his Ophelia!

For an hour he remained motionless, thunderstruck and inert. When he raised his head, a sad and discouraged smile was wandering over his lips.

"It was an illusion! I possessed you too mindfully, my poor child! It was a flash of lightning for which I thank God, for I believed in it, for an instant!"

He fell back on to the low seat of his oratory, and prayed long into the night.

The next day, after tormented sleep and a painful awakening, the Duke headed for his daughter's apartment.

"Olivia," he said to her, "yesterday evening, your honor was attacked in my name, and my name in our honor. There is in our blazon an open hand, which signifies frankness. We are going to knock on the door of the man who committed the insult. According to what he does and says, I will offer him that hand, open, or closed on the hilt of my sword. I'll wait for you."

"I'll accompany you, Father," Olivia replied, simply, her pallor testifying to the passage of a violent anger.

A short time afterwards, the old man, leaning on his daughter's shoulder, gravely came down the stairs of his house.

It is very rare in London, especially in the older districts, to see houses preceded by courtyard or event overt coaching entrances. The sidewalks are generally very broad, and it follows that on days of rain and mud, which are not rare in the locale, crossing the sidewalk to reach one's carriage is, for ladies, much more terrible than in Dover or Brighton. It is an inconvenience difficult to obviate. One's shoes can perhaps be protected by having a carpet extended on the exterior flagstones, but in misty and foggy weather it is necessary to have recourse to a manservant skilled in maneuvering an umbrella. On the evenings of balls, one erects a temporary tent. Comfort among our neighbors is entirely internal and stops at the door. The outsides of their houses, like their clothes, have a modest and simple appearance, but inside, they are richly furnished and solidly nourished.

That day, the atmosphere was a cloud, which, having descended unceremoniously from the gray sky, was wandering at its ease through the streets of London. Although it was the middle of the day, ruddy lights were perceptible in the depths of the shops through the fog.

A carpet was extended over the sidewalk, leading to the footstep of the Duke's carriage, and, by virtue of the respect that the aristocracy of birth or money still obtains in England, the passers-by were pausing or making detours in the roadway.

The old man and his daughter appeared on the threshold of the house.

At the same moment, a young man with a strikingly beautiful woman on his arm, who was talking and laughing loudly, cleaved through the crowd of idlers and casually came across the carpet extended over the public pavement.

That young man was Robert de Rolleboise, as we saw him the previous evening in the foyer of Covent Garden.

On perceiving him, the Duke went pale and his cheeks quivered; he leaned more heavily on his daughter, as if to intercept her gaze. When Robert and his merry companion were on the carpet, the former casually took off his hat and saluted the old man and the daughter in a mocking fashion. The crowd opened up on the opposite side, and the two individuals vanished into the fog.

"Let's go back in, Olivia," said the Duke, in a cold tone, leaning on his valet, Andrew.

The proud young woman had clearly perceived the salute of the young man, of whose fatal resemblance the reader is aware. Without disturbing her father, she went back to her apartment alone, in which outbursts of an ill-contained rage could be heard from afar, gradually fading away.

Back in her bedroom, the Duke sent his servants away, sat down at his writing-desk, and traced the following lines with a firm hand:

Sir,

I shall not soil my pen by describing your conduct. All is finished between us. I regarded you as my son; as a father, I curse you. If you have lost your reason, I feel sorry for you; if not, I offer you my breast and hand you my épée.

Duke of Firstland

When he had folded and sealed the piece of paper, he put his white-haired head in his hands and wept.

"Sad days, fatal hours that light and sound my old age, I receive you without blasphemy. My Gehenna is on this earth, and the tomb will deliver me from it. Alas, all that I loved has quit me. The heads that should have seen my fall have inclined before me, and I always find myself alone with my memories, with a tomb, with God! My first affections, where are you? Crushed by time, alas, and flown away in dust.

"I still believed in that man. I said to myself confidently: *He will be my son; Alone and orphaned, he will love an aged father*—and now I am betrayed, abandoned, felled by the sickle of an insult. Alone, alone, I am alone in weeping. Like old Ossian, our Homer, I see them all fall around me! Oh, my God, this is my prayer: take terrestrial affections away from me, purge my heart of all perishable attachments; they give me nothing but tears.

"I sometimes squeezed his hand; that recalled me to earth; and now, my hand will fall back empty, and no one will raise it again. Alone! Alone! They have all abandoned me, those that I loved..."

The curtain of a door was lifted up at those last words, and a man came slowly toward the old man inclined over the Christ, and took his hand.

The Duke raised his head, inundated by tears, and looked at the man momentarily. His tears redoubled, and he fell into the other's arms, crying: "Mercy, mercy, you who have had pity on a poor father! Oh, my last hope, let me call you my son! I shall love you dearly!"

Alas, we have to write an exceedingly barbaric sentence now. That man was Lord Horatio Mackinguss.

135

XIII. Poor Madman

The apartment into which the reader is invited to enter now was as gloomy as dusk on a rainy day. The shadows slept at their ease in the profound folds of the curtains, and the precipitate tick-tock of the clock trotted lightly over the broad zone that leads to eternity. The atmosphere arrived in the lungs warm and heavy.

On the tables, the sideboards and the chimney stood an entire congress of pharmaceutical vessels, pale and lukewarm. Spoons, standing in half-full cups, took their footbath standing to attention leaning on the walls. Teapots, spouts forward, were conversing in low voices with the resonant rim of some glass alarmed by an exterior noise or attentively reading the labels on bottles and vials.

The previous night, Sir Amadeus Harriss' valet had found his master lying on the threshold of the front door. In England, however regular the mores of an individual might be, if one sees an extraordinary disturbance in him, one immediately say to oneself, quite naturally: *He's drunk.* The gentleman was, therefore, carried to his bed, tea was prepared for him, and that was that, until morning.

The next day, the doctor who saw him immediately declared that he was suffering from a complete ablepsy. Then, convinced that the deterioration of the intellectual faculties was not derived from any physical cause, he treated him in accordance with his theory.

At the moment when we enter the sick man's room, a man was seated at his bedside. His cold gaze rested on the young man extended on the bed. A few slight spasms notwithstanding, Sir Amadeus seemed calm, except that a continual muscular stir wandered over his lips. One might have thought that he was conversing with an invisible being, the phantom of his enfevered dreams. He was not asleep. His atonal eyes were open, his eyelids immobile. However, his hand shifted and slipped over the edge of the bed.

Another hand seized it.

"Well, Amadeus, how goes it?" asked the man maintaining the vigil, in the indifferent tone in which one addresses a man in ordinary health.

"I heard a voice...can one talk in the tomb, then? Who's there?"

"One of your friends."

"Yes, on earth one has friends, Ha ha!" And a slow, faint and insensate laugher flowed from the pale lips.

"I'm Lord Mackinguss."

"I don't know you."

"Horatio."

"Horatio—no, I don't know that name."

"I had breakfast this morning with someone you know."

"Not a friend; I have none."

"With your brother."

"Yes, yes, my brother Lewis. Ha ha!"

"He tells me that he has your reason."

"But he's going to give it back!" Amadeus exclaimed, suddenly. "He'll give it back to me, and then...I'll come back...where? Oh, I don't remember!" He fell back on to the pillow.

"He's marrying Olivia; it was your reason hat advised him to do it."

"Olivia..."

"Your fiancée."

"Olivia. I've heard that name, yes? Back there, in a dream...but I don't have my reason..."

Suddenly, the unfortunate sat up; a flash of lightning, a coherent idea, seemed to traverse the void of his mind, and he said, in a low voice, placing his warm hand on Horatio's arm: "What time is it?"

"Eternity."

"Ha ha! Yes, eternity, here. It's the eternal hour around which I must rotate now. But on earth?"

"Noon."

"Well, remind me in twelve hours...we'll go out...we'll go to Westminster Abbey. There, perhaps Lewis will give me my reason back."

"Perhaps," said Lord Horatio, in a dubious tone.

"What do you know about it?"

"Perhaps Lewis can't return your reason."

"Why not?"

"Because he's lost it."

"Lost it! In one night!"

"Certainly. He's getting married!" Lord Mackinguss followed that remark with a mocking laugh, which the invalid did not perceive.

"Well, we'll take someone else's."

"That's not easy."

"Do you have your reason?"

"Since I'm with you, I can't have."

"That's true, we're no longer on earth. Oh, I had a very bizarre dream, very bizarre. I'll tell you about it. Listen...let me remember..."

Supporting his poor head on his hand, he tried for some time to find the thread of his dream. Still impassive, Horatio waited for him to begin.

"Well? This dream?"

"Yes, here it is: My name was Amadeus Harriss; I was on earth, rich, happy, for I was in love with a woman...down there, the love of a woman makes one happy. Her name was...Olivia...yes, I was to be her husband. Then, a suspicion fell upon my heart like a black stain; I doubted the young woman...when...I woke up."

"Well, Lewis has taken possession of your dream; he's marrying Olivia."

"Wait," the insensate continued, who was not listening, but pursuing the memory of his dream. "She went out at night, dressed as a man. A vampire knew it..."

"She went to see him."

"Do you think so?"

"It's certain. Then, this vampire stole your reason, and now he'll marry your mistress."

"Yes, that's true, Lewis told me that he was a vampire. Oh, my poor dream...my poor dream...!"

And the unfortunate fell back on the pillow, which he stained with a tear. "Friend?" he said, suddenly.

"What do you want?" asked Horatio.

"My head's on fire...ice."

Horatio maintained a barbaric immobility. The sick man was delirious. Before that poignant spectacle of a man fighting against madness, however, he yielded to the powerful sentiment of humanity that pushes us to help someone who is suffering at our mercy. He picked up a cloth impregnated with cold water and placed it on the invalid's forehead. The sedative action took effect immediately.

Gradually, the bed-ridden young man's gaze lost its fixity and wandered around him, as if to get its bearings. The poor insensate sat up effortlessly, and held his head suspended over his bosom momentarily, like a sleeper emerging from a torpor.

"Yes, I remember: yesterday evening, I was pursued...frightened by my image...by a man bearing a strange resemblance...I still love Olivia...but no one's mentioned her to me. Where does she go, then, at night, dressed as a man?"

"Amadeus, is it your dream that you're still telling me?"

The invalid paid no attention to those words. He spoke slowly, gathering his scattered and confused ides with great difficulty. "No, I didn't know whether Olivia was deceiving me. But why would she, so beautiful and so imposing, love me, so feeble and so fearful in the world? There's also a man who prowls around her, a handsome man at whom one sometimes laughs...but about whom one also dreams, perhaps, thereafter."

"Well, that man is me," said Lord Mackinguss, presenting himself in front of the other, apprehensive that the symptoms might signify a return of reason.

"You!" said Amadeus, staring at him.

"Well, all that is a dream."

"A dream...no, for I understand now. You're Horatio. Yes, I recognize you...you're handsome! Also, I made a reflection, after..."

"A reflection? On whom, sir?"

"On you."

"Ah! And what did you think?"

"Yes, yes, I told myself that in order to be what you appear to be, you were simply too naïve yesterday...oh, I'm recovering my reason...but my head's on fire. A little ice, my lord."

"There is no more."

Lord Mackinguss had stood up and was marching back and forth, his brow furrowed, his expression dark. Suddenly, he stopped and his hand fell on a phial containing a thick yellow liquid; he reflected. That man, implacable for a woman, especially after an offense, was reluctant to kill someone. The end did not frighten him, but the means appeared to him to be atrocious and vulgar. To rid oneself thus of an individual who is a hindrance, when one has a little intelligence, is an imprudence worthy of a man of the people submissive to coarse mores. The law strikes poisoners, but pays no attention to those who drive you mad.

Alas, in the course of this fatal life into which we descend, there are always helpful events that cure moral perplexities fully. A valet came in carrying a silver tray.

"There is a letter for Sir Amadeus, my lord."

"That's all right. Leave it there."

The valet went out. Then Horatio put the phial down and went to the bed.

"Amadeus."

"Ice!"

"You'll be given some."

"My head's splitting."

"Here's a letter. Will you be able to read it?"

"A letter from whom."

"I don't know."

"Look at the signature, I beg you. Who brought it?"

"I've just perceived it on a table."

"Like the first, then! The signature?"

"The Duke of Firstland."

"Ah! I'll read it. Give it to me."

The young man seized the letter avidly. He read it, and his face changed.

"*Lost your reason...all is finished between us...*oh! My God! I'm falling back into the night of my ideas, memory is fading away, everything's effacing...it's not a dream...my reason is lost, then! Everyone is abandoning me! Oh, yes, I was Amadeus...Olivia was beautiful...the old man loved me...ha ha! Dream! Illusion! I'm in the tomb, forgotten! We're going to Westminster, my lord!"

"We'll go this evening."

"And in my dream, a sensation came to me that I named...the name's gone..."

"Love?"

"Yes, love. *All is finished between us!* What does that mean? That's true, I'm dead...well, I want to rest in peace. Listen, friend, don't wake me up, let midnight chime...for now that my dream is lost, I don't want it anymore! No, I no longer want my reason!"

And the poor madman fell back on his pillow, murmuring a few works of an old Scottish ballad, which he mingled with bizarre words and burst of insensate laughter. A man clad in black came in, came to the bed, and considered the invalid briefly."

"Doctor, do you think he'll recover his reason?"

"Never."

XIV. The Gold Coin

Amadeus Harriss did not recover his reason. His heart lost sentiment, oblivion enveloped his brain. In the sad night that fell upon him, his extinct eye might have distinguished two shadows leaning over his bed—the Duke and his daughter—but he took them for two phantoms and did not recognize them.

Nevertheless, in the course of his moral paralysis, a few glimmers of reminiscence, a few slightly less heavy clouds appeared from time to time. Then too, when the clock struck twelve, whether it was day or night, he sat up in his bed, asked for his clothes, his carriage, and gave the order to be taken to Westminster Abbey.

Alas, they were his best moments, intervals of madness that were merely more distinct, less confused.

He went into a sanitarium situated in the cheerful abode of Richmond.

Physically, however, Amadeus flourished. His limbs became robust, his cheeks swelled; he was a colossus. Everywhere, one finds that proof of disjunction between matter and mind, the lees and the pure fluid. Nature always commits illassorted marriages between the stomach and the brain. Thus, if reason succumbs, the survivor flourishes and fattens, like an heir refloated by an opportune succession. Benevolent human nature, what beautiful mastodon products it will offer if intelligence is lacking!

Miss Firstland had little room in her heart for tender sentiments. Did she mourn poor Amadeus? I cannot answer that question. At any rate, the good Horatio became the faithful companion of the old Duke, and remained submissive to Miss Olivia's feet.

Now, it would be unjust to infer from any scene that I have produced before your eyes, reader, that his manners were ridiculous, and that he passed in the Duke's society for a simpleton—far from it. To begin with, he avoided society, for he said that he was very timid, and now his mind was blissful, because he said he was very much in love. All in all, his exterior was more suitable than that of feeble Amadeus. His character might be brittle, but he was a handsome man.

Now, Miss Olivia, proud and vain by nature, could not be attaching herself by the bonds of matrimony to a husband of ludicrous and common manners. Horatio, in spite of his simplicity and malleability, was presentable and wore a handsome mask. He might be less rich than Harriss, but he had an old name. No matter how inert a heart might be, how hard as a character and how ferocious a soul, there is still, in female nature, a moment when a woman allows herself to be overtaken by a victorious sentiment.

That is why, one day, the news spread through the drawing rooms of London that Miss Olivia Firstland was marrying Lord Horatio Mackinguss.

For herself, for her heart, the Duke's daughter had only ever seen that man at her feet, for the heiress had a kind of beauty too severe too severe to insinuate reverie into a young head in quest of love. She possessed purity of line, the fortunate elegance of contours, but her eye was not loving, her mouth never designed any smile originating from the heart. Her beauty intimidated amour.

Nevertheless, that did not prevent her, and with good reason, for having a high opinion of her marble visage; for, in the final analysis—and I am speaking here in general and digressively—there is no woman who, no matter how horrible she is, frankly admits her ugliness. There are a great number who nobly recognize a modest beauty in themselves, but there are even more who are privately convinced that they possess the ideal type of beauty, the model of statuary. And, indeed, those poor women, living on the sentiment of charm, would be too desperate if it were otherwise. Let one laugh in accordance with the illusions of the poet!

All the ceremonies of that high society wedding had taken place in London. I shall not tell you the abrupt names of the notabilities of the court and the aristocracy that were scrawled on the contract. We shall also pass over in silence the details of the dress, the expression of joyful sentiment etched in the physiognomy of the bride, and the hint of constraint and sadness that ought to have been painted on the face of the husband—strokes of the carmine-dipped brush that it is time to proscribe and necessary to abandon to the placid brewers who ride benignly through the grassy pathways of a lactescent literature: insupportable barbets who yap in the distance on the threshold of their impotence in the setting of the modern novel, building, with the patience of mosaicists, lukewarm and abbreviated works whose only décor is a cottage and an arbor, and whose only characters are a pale young woman and a naïve and fatalistic young man.

But let us return to our canvas, that word being taken in the humble sense of the weaver.

That evening, a numerous and resplendent company was assembled in the Duke's drawing rooms. The presence was noticed of Edgard Mackinguss, Horatio's older brother, descended from his mountains to attend the wedding. The more we look at that man, the more we think that we have seen him somewhere before. A vague memory tells us that he has already appeared among our characters in some background. But it is a resemblance so confused that we abandon it. The continuation of the story might perhaps enlighten the night of our memory.

Edgard had one of those faces whose ever-wandering eyes never look you in the face. Although he was only forty, the skin of his face looked old. His thin and rigid nose, pierced by two narrow slits, and his eyes, lost in loophole cavities, inspired mistrust. The man said little and did not engage in chitchat, for his sober conversation remained aridly in the reality of figures. He avoided the glare of candles, and when his face was shadowed, his taut mouth stretched into an indefinable smile. The man's mockery communicated a singular apprehension.

There was no dancing, but there was gambling.

Sir James Cawdor, more vermilion than ever, blossoming in his bicuspid collar, leaned contentedly on a flexible item of furniture. He was chatting quietly with a beautiful woman sitting beside him.

"Well, Sir James, I believe that it will be easy for you to return to your property at Stonebyres."

"Be assured, however, Milady Landsdale, that Lord Horatio is quite satisfied with that acquisition. Workmen are toiling there already. At any rate, he's something of an artist; he loves the supernatural. The Castle of the Falls will suit him admirably."

"I believe, Sir James, that Milady is less inclined to poetic ideas than her husband; perhaps you are aware of Miss Firstland's character."

"I have heard talk about it, Milady, but young women have their caprices."

"When one inherits them from one's mother, it's a true nature. Poor Amadeus has gone mad."

"I don't believe in stories, Countess. Sir Amadeus is mad, it's true, but it's a matter of his organization, that's all."

"You don't believe in stories! That's what everyone says here. Oh, what a contrast with Paris. There, all men are poets."

They say so, at least Milady—but, fortunately for them, they're mistaken. An entire artistic people is as impossible as a monument that is all sculpture and ornamentation."

"Baronet, who is that tall individual talking to Milord the Duke?"

"That tall individual, Milady, is Horatio's brother: a highlander who lives in the midst of his clan, as in the olden days, in a fortified castle."

The young bride, leaning on her aunt's arm and giving her hand to her brother-in-law, Edgard, was coming from a room adjacent to the drawing room. She came to stand near the Countess of Landsdale. In an interval of attention, Olivia leaned toward her neighbor in a familiar fashion and said to her, with a slightly mocking smile: "Well, Countess, as you can see, I'm marrying Lara."

145

Among all the men in the assembly, Horatio stood out. He was no longer the timid and supplicant man in love of the preceding scenes. His head was erect; his physiognomy revealed a character of firm determination. In the midst of all gazes, his eyes were distinct, dark and fiery. At that moment he appeared in the background, talking to an individual who was listening with his head tilted. Dark shadows deepened the accentuations and protrusions of his face. His mouth had an imperious expression and his speech was incisive.

The Countess put her hand on Olivia's and leaned toward her, gazing in the direction of her husband. "Have you ever perceived that expression on Milord's face, Olivia? Well, study that expression, which is not false."

The young woman reflected, her eyes resting on the man, and made no reply. She stood up. Sir James, having perceived those few spoken words with his indifferent bonhomie, adroitly brought the Countess of Landsale back to a distracting conversation.

Suddenly, Olivia was accosted by a person whose expression was one of fearful astonishment. It was a young woman. Lady Mackinguss immediately extended her hand, with a welcoming smile. "I'm truly delighted to find you in good health, my lovely stranger. How is Monsieur de Lormont?"

"Miss Olivia—oh, I would like to be able to give you that title—let's talk about you."

"My beautiful Mathilde, you seem upset."

"Is that the man you have married?" Her hand indicated Horatio.

"Yes, my beautiful friend, that's the man I have married," the young woman replied, dryly.

"Olivia, you don't know, then, what that man is?" Madame de Lormont said, in a low and precipitate voice, taking the Duke's daughter to one side.

"He's simply Lord Horatio Mackinguss, my husband. A poor fellow in love, whom I might perhaps have married out of pity. I can confess that to you, as a woman and a friend."

"That man has never loved you, Madam!"

"And what gives you that certainty, my beauty?" replied the young woman, her mouth imprinted with a bitter smile and her voice slightly tremulous.

"No, that man has never loved you, for he has never loved anyone; his heart is dead."

"My beautiful friend, I fear that poor Sir Amadeus' malady might be spreading."

"Amadeus! Oh, yes, I know, he has removed him from his way. Oh, it's a terrible role that that man is playing, Madam! Do you not know, then, with what he is threatened? Do you not know about the adventure that befell him one night in an inn?"

As Sir James Cawdor was nearby, Madame de Lormont continued speaking in a low voice, which only Olivia could hear. Before the words of the young woman, who was in full possession of her reason, the young bride paid serious attention to her for a while. Her anxious eyes seemed to be scrutinizing the probability of a mystery in Horatio. She redirected her thoughts back into memory.

Lord Mackinguss had perceived the conversation of the two young women.

"Do you want to know what that man is?" the Vicomtesse went on. "Well..."

But Madame de Lormont's eyes had met Horatio's gaze, and she fell silent, as if petrified. With his eyes still immobile and robustly directed forwards, Horatio marched unhurriedly toward Mathilde and Olivia. He drove back their vanquished and inert gazes, and as he came forward, the rays of his fiery eyes seemed to penetrate like two blades into those astonished heads. The two women, maintained in silence, recoiled instinctively as he approached.

When he was no more than two paces from Mathilde, he showed her his right hand.

There was a gold coin shining between his fingers.

Madame de Lormont, going pale, collapsed into a chair, and her visage sank into her hands.

XV. The Branches of Macduff

The Duke's drawing rooms emptied before midnight. Edgard had an apartment in the house, but he nevertheless went out with the other guests.

Olivia's father, leaning on his son-in-law's arm, retired to his bedroom. On the threshold, Horatio shook the old man's hand; the latter embraced him.

In the bridal chamber, Olivia, lying motionless on a sofa, her pensive head supported in the palm of her hand, was waiting. The old aunt, walking around, occasionally uttered an exclamation, or a hypothetical phrase. Her niece could hear her, but made no reply. A blonde chambermaid with an exuberance of flesh that would have made a seminarist quiver came in laden with candles to announce Lord Mackinguss.

The young bride made no movement, and the aged Miss Cockburn let the guillotine of silence fall upon the neck of a sentence she had hardly begun.

Horatio, appearing beneath the folds of the parted curtain, took possession of the scene displayed before him with a single glance. Everything was still. Only his foot, tormenting his supple and shiny boot, produced the noise that is the male equivalent of a woman's rustle of silk.

The old aunt resumed walking, her skirts inflated and as noisy as an aerostat being filled, and frightened the white flames of the candles with the displacement of the air.

Without saying a word, Horatio advanced toward an enormous bell-rope and pulled it. Immediately, with the promptitude of valets in the theater, Suky and Hannah were framed in the gilded woodwork of a doorway.

"Light the way for our good Aunt Cockburn," said the husband, simply, kissing the old maid's hand, as dry as a papyrus.

The latter, having kissed her niece, went out, clucking a few inaudible words that were probably borrowed from Biblical verses. Tea and the Bible provide the dualism of old Englishwomen, the two spirits that fight over them. The Bible promises them Heaven beyond the tomb; tea offers it to them on earth. A life without tea is Hell beforehand; without the Bible it is Hell afterwards.

When the two spouses were alone, Olivia straightened up on her seat, turned haughtily toward her husband and said, in a slow, barely-contained voice: "I don't like actions that are decked out in mystery. Will you, therefore, Milord, please explain the burlesque scene that you played a little while ago with Madame de Lormont."

Without paying any more heed to those words than if they had not been spoken, Horatio took a few sealed letters from his portfolio and set about perusing them. The young woman was irritated by that disdainful indifference. She got up, with a nervous abruptness. Her gaze animated, her lips pale and parted over her clenched teeth, she came to stand arrogantly and imperiously before the seated man. The latter did not seem at all anxious.

The Duke's daughter said: "Milord, there are young women whom one surrounds before marriage with urgent concerns, frail children to whom one attributes a false importance, and who, when they acquire the title of Milady, permit themselves to be treated with protection but without respect. Don't count me among those facile minds. I have not married in order to abdicate my will.

"A character that thought of colliding with mine would be ridiculous if it were inferior; if equal, I would overturn it. I am not, believe me, a woman sighing with love, who lies down at a man's feet asks nothing of him but a smile in order to be happy. Know that between you and me there is a distance that is difficult for one of us to cross. I will bear your name and live in your house, but it will please you to submit to my will and subordinate your orders to mine.

"Reply, then, to my question, Milord: what do those stupid affectations that Madame de Lormont adopted before you signify? Have I unwittingly taken a magnetizer for my husband?"

Olivia, leaning on the back of Mackinguss' chair, had spoken slowly, as if to favor the infiltration of every sentence into her husband's obtuse intelligence. The latter, however, while listening, had not ceased to scan his correspondence. When the young woman stopped, Horatio continued reading. Before that obstinate indifference, the beautiful lady knew what to think, but not what to say.

In the end, the lord gathered up his letters and replaced them in his portfolio. That done, he stood up and finally condescended to look down at the young bride—but with a gaze so ardent and forceful that she lowered her eyelids.

"Ah!" he exclaimed, suddenly, raising his head. "It's good to stand up straight, to brace one's spirit, so long curbed, to render the voice its strength, the gaze its energy. You asked, I believe, whether your husband is a magnetizer; be assured, anyway, that he is not a simpleton. Between us, you say, there is a great distance; that is true. To look at me, raise your head.

"Madame de Lormont is too communicative; I maintained her discretion, that's all. Now, don't ask me what there is between that woman and me, because it does not please me to tell you. It's a quarter to midnight; be ready in a quarter of an hour."

"What do you mean, sir?"

"I'm telling you to be ready in ten minutes; we're going out at midnight."

"Going out? Now? And where do you intend to go, if you please, at such an hour on such a day?"

"Firstly, Madam, remember that I am the one who has the prerogative of asking questions here. You will do as I wish. When I go out, if I desire it, you will go with me. Furthermore, you say 'such a day.' Do you think, then, that it pleases me to dress gaudily, with my spouse, as my tailor might do, and invite friends and neighbors for that great work. Not so, Madam, those are not my mores.

"Oh, perhaps you have thought that poor Horatio was etiolated by love, that he dreamed of Olivia every night: the worthy Mackinguss, the faker of sighs, who amused you, at whom that frightful she-ape, that night-owl Cockburn, laughed! Oh, that laughter, that mockery, is still ringing in my ears! My wrathful blood is pulsing in my veins; it is a vengeful host spurred by fire, an all-consuming tidal wave advancing. Oh, you have not recognized the man approaching you!

"Well, I am casting away the branches of Macduff and marching against Macbeth! Love! You thought that I was in love! Ha ha! Love is a word that I have erased from my heart, Madam. Love is a weakness, an abasement, which does not suit me. A suspicion of love brings a blush to me face! A lover who sighs is, in my eyes, like a starving man who has no bread. Now, I never implore, I never extend a hand.

"I know your character; you are one of those women who, conceited by their face and their fortune, take pride in making men spin like weathervanes, of extinguishing their will, of dispersing their energy. Then, when they become supple, and you see them at your feet, the gaze dead, the forehead vanquished, the mouth imploring, you lash their hearts with stinging words, bilious and scornful gazes, and barbaric laughter. And you are right, for those men are cowards.

"I too have simulated idiocy; I have played stupidity; I have sensed, with a bitter and violent sensuality, my pride ripped until it bled, racked and twisted until the last jet of anger. I have coiled myself up in rings, like an irritated serpent—and now, I am standing up again! Oh, you do not know what Horatio Mackinguss is: that simpleton, that fool, who will repay you a hundredfold, dolor for mockery, torture for dolor. You too are proud—so much the better! I want to knead your pride, trample it underfoot, stifle it beneath the mud."

Horatio Mackinguss, great and terrible, marched as he spoke thus toward the young woman, who recoiled at his approach for the first time, pale and frightened. Having bumped into a chair, she collapsed into it, conserving a captive fixity of gaze upon that man. The latter held her thus mute under the irresistible action of his fiery eyes and his suddenly transfigured physiognomy.

Eventually, she tore herself away from that invisible grip, her bosom heaving, and the chair that was supporting her was shoved backwards. Then, raising herself up to her full height, she looked him in the face. "You do not know what I am; you do not know what I can do."

"I know what you are, and I can do more than you will ever be able to do. That is an advantage over you, because you do not know what I am."

"Milord, I do not put on theatrical airs and strike dramatic poses; I do not require for my aid all the furrowed brows of melodrama; I do not fling overinflated and sonorous speeches in the face, but ordinarily, I attain my ends. Be careful, Milord..."

Horatio did not even accord those words an indifferent smile. He rang.

"You're going with me, Madam."

"Going with you! Where, if you please?"

"You'll find out."

"I want to know now."

"Madam, you use there a term that it is necessary to erase: the first person."

Two male domestics of the most gleaming blackness were standing on the threshold. Horatio offered his arm to his young spouse; she leaned on it without proffering a word, without offering any gesture of resistance. Olivia, above all ridiculous opposition, acted appropriately before her servants.

Without any deference, Milord sat down beside Milady.

The carriage rumbled for nearly three quarters of an hour through the streets of London. The night was misty. The moon appeared palely through the nebulosity of the air, as if it were englobed in the frosted glass of a carcel lamp. They passed over Waterloo Bridge. The gaslight, stifled by the fog, was clad in ruddy and apoplectic tints.

The carriage went on for a long time, and finally reached Bermondsey. A few streets later, it stopped. During the journey, the two spouses had not addressed a word to one another, or glanced at one another.

"We've arrived, Milady," said Horatio, offering his hand to Olivia from outside.

"Where are we?" she asked.

"In a place that you might recognize: Corbett's Lane."

"Corbett's Lane! And where are you taking me, in such a district, almost outside the city, entirely uninhabited."

"Pay attention to two things, Madam: we're in the presence of a valet, and you're interrogating me."

"Yes, Milord, I'm interrogating you, because I'm not your slave."

"But Madam, you must be under an illusion at this point, if you suppose me to be as naïve as a student in Gower Street."

At the same time, having taken Olivia by the hand, he helped her down. It was one of those hidden struggles that sometimes occur in high society, which take on courteous forms and smiles grimaced by wrath. Thus, the young woman appeared to get down supporting herself lightly on her husband's fist, but in fact, Horatio's hand was gripping her wrist like a steel ring, and, without apparent effort, pulled the recalcitrant beauty out of the carriage; then, seizing her by the arms, he dragged her by the same method into a side-street through which my reader might already have passed, and said to her in a voice to strike a chill into the heart:

"Does it not seem to you, Madam, that I bear more resemblance to an amorous abductor carrying his beloved away, than a husband who is doubtless assumed to be lying in the conjugal bed?"

"You bear more resemblance to Satan accomplishing a cowardly work."

"Very good, my beautiful wife—you're beginning to know me. Indeed, be sure that if Satan has any influence over human actions, Hell is conspiring in my favor.

They soon reached the wall of the cemetery, of which they only followed the tangential line that brought them to face the small, solitary and rickety house. On recognizing the place to which she had come in disguise, Olivia had a troubling presentiment.

She had entered without knocking; Horatio entered the same way. When the door was closed, she followed him without hesitation up the somber staircase, and he walked with a confident stride. On the first floor, the man opened a second door and let the young woman pass before him.

We have already given a brief description of the redoubt. Nothing had changed. The lamp was lit, the old man was reading. On hearing the door open he raised his head but did not budge from his seat.

"Antares, Lady Mackinguss."

"Yes, yes—Olivia has followed my advice. Tee hee!"

The young woman leaned against the bare stone of the fireplace, resting a glare of malediction upon the Jew. Her face was pale and her cheeks quivering. That irritated physiognomy, that hatefully blanched mouth and the fire of her eyes made a strange contrast with her splendid diamante head-dress and rich wedding-gown.

"You're a dastard, then, Antares!"

"Tee hee! My dear Olivia, I work for everyone."

"Madam," said Horatio, extending arm, "To cut this dialogue short, you will chat to my Jew at a more opportune time. I haven't come here for the two of you to get your hackles up. Time is pressing, so take a seat and keep quiet. Antares, here I am, married to Miss Firstland; I congratulate myself that Milord the Duke is satisfied with the alliance. Where is Ophelia?"

"Your marriage having taken place in accordance with your desire, and that comminatory presence appearing to me to be more imprudent than useful, I had the young woman taken back to Paris."

"What have you done, Antares?"

"Nothing, but I've given my opinion: it's more imprudent than useful."

"It's a tried and true means, it's true. It's necessary to act now."

"Which is to say?"

"Which is to say that when something is no longer useful and its existence might prove harmful, one destroys it."

"Milord, you're an atrocious man," Olivia articulated, in a vibratile voice, her white-gloved hand directed menacingly at Horatio, "but since you have drowned my heart in hatred, I reject all thought of luxury and fortune, all consideration of pride; I shall save my sister and doom you!"

"Antares, we're talking to one another. Later, I'll make Milady understand that it's stupid to turn against oneself weapons sharpened for others. How long can that life last? For I want an end without consequence, without precipitation, continuous and sure."

"Milord, we'll guide that existence for twelve months; no one will have any suspicions, not even the victim. Tee hee! My dear Olivia, you ought not to hold anything against me, for, after all, you also desired that denouement, but dared not perpetrate it. Well, a friendly hand—Milord's—is executing your desire before you have even expressed it. It's simply a gallantry on your husband's part. You therefore owe one another gratitude, not threats launched flamboyantly in irritated words."

Horatio strode back and forth over the dull carpet. By virtue of that movement, the agitated air brought disturbance to the papers set on the table.

Olivia stood up. "Milord, when will it please you accord me a little repose?"

"Yes, Antares," Horatio immediately went on, without otherwise paying any attention to his wife, "we still have work to do, a dark and dense future that it is necessary to cut through without dread. To arrive at these results, we shall call upon all the assistance of my imagination and your atrocious soul. I'll forget the past; that's our concern; I'll no longer pay any heed to Ophelia."

"I'll leave for Paris as soon as I'm free."

"Yes, but before then, we need to plot a new drama."

"I know," said the Jew, looking at Olivia, who was almost terrified by all these machinations.

"Or rather," the aristocrat continued, "it's necessary to take up threads from afar and attach them to present situations. You'll occupy yourself with that. It's Mathilde that I'm talking about."

"I've thought about that, Milord, but for all these things, I'll need money. With the money, I've sworn to you to accomplish everything. Thus far, everything has succeeded; the future will be the same, but I need the gold."

"You shall have it."

"A great deal of gold," said the Jew, his eyes lit up.

"Be careful, Antares—I'm not a woman, and one only plays with me once in life."

"I'm your servant," the Jew replied, humbly.

"That's good—don't forget it," Horatio replied, haughtily, taking Olivia's hand. "Now, Madam, we're leaving, if you please."

Without paying any further heed to the Jew, who had plunged back into his papers, they abandoned the hovel. The carriage was waiting in Corbett's Lane. As they approached, the coachman woke up, and the horses, anticipating the whip, twitched their ears. They departed at a rapid trot.

A quarter of an hour later, the newlyweds returned to Firstland House.

On the threshold of her apartment, the aristocrat took Olivia's hand and said to her, in a low and penetrating voice: "Now, Madam, you know who I am and who you are. Amadeus is mad; Ophelia is going to die. If you pronounce a single, word, if you express a shadow of suspicion, the daylight will be extinguished for you. I desire a peaceful night."

XVI. Suky in Profile

The day after the preceding scenes, after a sleepless night, Olivia got up with the apparent calm of victorious reflection. Her mind had settled upon a line from the cripple of Newstead: "Deep vengeance is the daughter of deep silence."[21]

A few days later, Lady Mackinguss left the house of her father, the Duke, and came with Lord Horatio to a fine house in Grosvenor Square. In the brilliant society that visited the young bride, no one had any suspicion of the intimate drama of the two spouses. They often went to see the old man, who scarcely noticed the changes that had take place in his son-in-law's behavior.

One cold damp morning, Lord Horatio, in his bedroom, was chatting in front of a blazing fire with an individual methodical in body and placid in mind. That individual, seated solidly in an armchair like a Japanese divinity, his knees forming a right angle, and the palm of his hand on a perpendicularly-held cane, was articulating his sentences slowly. A light-colored wig covered his prudish baldness, and the shells of his ears seemed to be stopped up with wads of cotton wool.

"Certainly, Milord, in that case, I believe in the congenial fact. Besides which, your health and your age immediately reject the idea of an adynamia. Now, Staab, in his *Treatise on Edeology*,[22] speaks of a woman almost octogenarian who, after

---

[21] Lord Byron, who had a slight club-foot, was resident for some time at Newstead Abbey; the quote is from the verse play *Marino Faliero* (1821)

[22] The doctor, in the satirical tradition of Moliére, is deliberately employing jargon that is partly improvised; there is no such treatise, and some of the subsequent terms employed are nonsensical. Edeology is, however, the scientific study of the genitalia, and it is possible to infer from the doctor's jargon

an illness, or, rather, a bizarre salacism and a furious hysteria, experienced all the symptoms of pregnancy. Now, the subject with whom we are concerned is one of the less well-known obscurities of nosography. We can, however, with the authority of the Swedish edeologist, attempt a means."

"Certain?"

"Perhaps."

"That's a dubious adverb that I hate."

"But the doctor continued in the same tone and the same idiom: "Certainly, you are not an assodic man. The astynia that we fear is not a consequence of acrasia. Your senses have not attained that asthenic limit which engenders frigidity. Thus, I believe that by essaying an iatric prophylactic, and abstaining from demulcent nourishment and improlific labor, we might perhaps obtain an acataleptic solution. As I am no polypharmacist, I shall concretify all these considerations in a single magisterial formula. You are doubtless following a sage hypnology?"

"I confess to you, Doctor, that I don't entirely understand what you're saying."

"No matter; I was asking whether you had established within yourself a slumber in rapport with your wakefulness."

"I sleep very little."

"That's good," said the doctor, getting to his feet. "So, I shall search profoundly for the pathognomonic signs of this latent asthenia, and once the principle is attained, you'll be submitted to an abundantly phosphoric medication and an ichthyological nourishment, and we shall vanquish the result, conquering a real impregnation. I have the honor of saluting Milord."

---

what kind of a problem it is that has led Horatio to consult him. Asthenia means weakness—in this instance, presumably, sexual impotence...although Horatio's subsequent monologue and a subsequent revelation in the concluding explanations suggest, behind their careful cloak of euphemism, that he has not always suffered from that problem.

When the physician had gone, Horatio, his forehead anxious, marched slowly back and forth in the room. In his velvet gown, his head and neck bare, the man was perfectly handsome. His small, pale and stiff hands tormented the enameled golden beads of his heavy girdle, and he whipped the backs of the chairs that were within his reach.

"Truly, I don't know what prompted me to adopt such slow and roundabout means. That man, at any rate, with all his fancy words, cannot reassure me in the least. All his science is based on hypotheses, all his endeavors run into doubt. Strange mysteries of nature! I'm healthy in mind, robust in body, lively in health, and yet, I can only destroy. Thus, I will be victorious in everything. Amadeus will have fallen before me; I will have softened like wax my rebellious and malevolent wife; and now, alone, with her, I'm no longer anything. Ha ha! Derision! Yes, I see, everything in me, in the physical as well as the mental, in conspiring against that woman. Heaven has stamped me with a seal of malediction! It has thrown me upon the earth, fatal, incomplete, that I might do evil. I shall accomplish my destiny!"

Horatio fell silent momentarily. The lines of his face almost softened, a negligent smile brushed his lips, and he said, slowly, with a bitter melancholy: "And yet, when I was young, I dreamed of things unknown, of a woman's smile, of a lecture of love! I was handsome...as handsome as an Albani adolescent, and I believed!

"Then, one day, I loved; but I was not loved. That moment was, for me, an entire revelation. What a capricious and eccentric thing the heart of a woman is! Unknown desire, an ever-uncertain, sometimes monstrous dream! Yes, I understood human life then. To false hearts and ridiculous bodies, young women confide themselves! There are, no doubt, for them, in those indecent contrasts, those disparate forms, the burning joys of unrelieved sensualities!

"Then again, I often ask myself whether, on the threshold of life, the evil angel, to provide himself with bizarre spectacles, does not deposit in the ears of those failed men a magic word, a perfidious charm, to attract and conquer women. Those clownish couplings must delight him! Well, I too want to give myself those hideous spectacles, those infernal joys! Ha ha! Yes, I was unloved, and, enraged, I became evil. I wrung my heart and castrated it. Oh, what splendid intoxications I feel within me before the bloody torment and the poignant anguish of a woman! But alas, I have perhaps used up all those enjoyments!

"Thus, I have taken pleasure in injecting passion into the bosom of a virgin; for, more powerful than Mephistopheles, it is still permissible for me to feign love. I have observed the incoherent gradations of love, my heart has raked all the fibers of that young heart, I was envious and irritated by her ecstasies; but also, the tears, the perplexities, the despairs, oh, how that palpitating anguish intoxicated me! Yes, I have ripped many of them thus, those young women's hearts; the outburst of my laughter have dissipated many dreamy illusions, and those memories enchant me!

"However, less fortunate than the vampires who pump life from the living, I have not felt the reawakening of my soul! In the ecstatic intoxications, I have remained somber. I have, however, employed violent revulsives, robust stimulants, I have submitted myself to dilaniatory galvanisms! Often, before elevating myself in the ethereal nimbus of these chaste childish passions, I plunged into the miry gutters of physical decrepitude and moral corruption. I bathed in the Phlegeton of vice, tore my flesh in infamous enjoyments and excessive sensations. Then, emerging therefrom, I placed myself suddenly beneath the pure breath, before the celestial gaze, of an angel of youth, love and faith, and felt nothing!

"Oh, when once the heart is dead, it is forever! And yet it is my credence that to love, if only for an hour, would save me! But no, I'm accursed, evil. Alas, if I had been able to love, I would have been better. Better! Which is to say, obscure, unhappy, poor, the humble younger brother of Edgard Mackinguss!

"It requires great virtue to be good, today. Amadeus was good! What a sickening spectacle humanity is! To those who want to succeed, an evil genius presents itself, which never deceives them: a fatal voice that breathe false blandishments; a hand that, harpooning them in the abysm of false destinies, raises them up above the inclined crowd. Oh, when a man appears on the surface, do not ask him whence he comes, nor seek the traces of his passage!

"To be complete, to gather in oneself all means, all strengths, all powers, only two things are necessary: beauty and malevolence. I am handsome; I am malevolent. I have a face; I have no heart. I overturn men and their works; I march bravely, in a magnificent and deadly voice, trampling an affection or destroying a hope at every step, leaving behind dolor and wailing, and now, nature presents herself against me in hr turn. Well, I shall violate nature; I shall throw down a challenge to her impotence!

"Oh, I take no pleasure in these conflicts; they are artificial intoxications that will wake me up one day, will perhaps make me more malevolent—and the more malevolent I am, the stronger I shall be!"

Like all men of powerful will, Horatio stopped talking abruptly, and his face immediately became calm.

He leaned pensively on the window-sill, his gaze wandering outside at random.

In front of him, the garden of his house extended; and a ray of sunlight, having succeeded, no one knows how, in filtering through a cloud, lit up a district of London. It cheered up the flowers, rummaged around in the trees, and spread brilliantine over the glabreity of the foliage.

It is a sad sight, that of a damp, somber place suddenly struck by a sunbeam! The dark and verdant earth; the trees shedding their foliage and corroded by spongy mosses; the dirty stones, glistening with the slime the slugs and snails leave behind them; the yellow and sticky salamanders retreating, dazzled, to their viscous lairs; all of that hurls cold and unhealthy nudities at the eyes; it is reminiscent of an old man,

161

lost in his decrepitude, sickly, and grim to all joy, who suddenly produces, lovingly, the grimacing shadow of a smile.

However, in the midst of that withered and sickly landscape, solidly framed by four high walls, someone was walking, with a pensive tread, whose youth and suavity of form contrasted pleasantly with the backcloth and its details. It was one of Lady Mackinguss' maids. Her head, supported by her hand, was doubtless laboring over some serious thought, for she paid no attention to the ray of sunlight that was playing treacherously over her blank face. A dreaming woman, a loving heart!

Horatio stared at her. His expert eye immediately discovered a suspicion in her appearance. A suspicion, in that man, was the certain prelude to a verity. He followed the young woman momentarily with his gaze, and a slight serious smile strayed over his lips.

But the surly cloud, coarse and unpolished, closed its skylight, and the sun went back into the heavens. Immediately, the young woman, frightened to find herself in such a sad tableau, fled in her turn.

Horatio rang.

An admirably-cravated valet presented himself at the door, immobile and silent.

"William. I'm going out in a quarter of an hour. Tell Bertram to hitch up the carriage.

The valet disappeared, backwards. A minute later, Horatio rang again. The same mute apparition was framed in the doorway.

"Ask Suky for news of Milady, and let her bring it to me herself."

During the brief interval that William employed in carrying out that order, Horatio became impatient. A man of restless activity, he could not bear gaps between his actions. But the valet introduced into his master's apartment the young woman we saw just now in the garden. One of the two automata left. Horatio darted at the timid child one of those gazes that plunge into the heart, setting aside all deception. The young woman shivered under the inquisitive gaze.

"Milady thanks Milord."

After a moment's reflection, Horatio said abruptly, as if on a whim: "How old are you, Suky?"

"Twenty," the soubrette articulated, faintly.

"Are you not related to one of my servants?"

"Yes, Milord," she replied, blushing.

"My huntsman, I believe."

"No, Milord, it's Bertram, the coachman—my cousin."

"Oh yes, very good! A former horseguard."

"Yes, Milord," agreed the poor child, as red as a slice of roast beef.

"Turn sideways, Suky, so that I can see you in profile."

Utterly confused, the soubrette turned slightly. Horatio considered her with an observant seriousness that did not, however, express any suspicion.

"That's all, Suky; tell my valet to come and dress me."

Left alone, Mackinguss resumed his thoughtful pacing.

"I wasn't mistaken," he murmured. "Another blunder that nature hastens to impose on those who are frightened by her gifts. Certainly, when I took that life, that Olivia, whom I hate, I knew the moment when the obstacle loomed up; but obstacles have never stopped me. Perhaps this one is stronger than me, and I would be mad to break it down. Oh, no matter—I'll take a lateral path and get out of it. The old Duke's descending into his tomb, the death of his last daughter will precipitate him into it. Thus, I'll have a child; I need one; I want one. Because a child is twenty millions. Twenty millions! Alas, the twentieth part of that sum is the summit of the hopes of many families, and for me, the entire sum is merely a first step! But the means? Oh, the means are frightful! Bah, it's the idiotic and intoxicated man of the people who, unwittingly, sets fire to the barrel of gunpowder that is to blast a king! The means disappears with the iron and the shrapnel."

Half an hour later, Lord Mackinguss, superb and proud, unhurriedly went down the front steps of his house. An open carriage was waiting at the bottom. With his foot on the foot-plate, buttoning his glove, he glanced at the coachman, Bertram.

Suky's cousin is a handsome man, he said to himself, as he sat down on the flexible cushions.

XVII. To be a Father

Social life consists of a facile mask, which everyone employs and about which no one worries. To wear the mask well is to be in good company. For that, it necessary to possess a little aptitude—which is to say, to have the intelligence to avoid the angles of others and blunt one's own asperities; in a word to make one's character supple. For certain already-feeble minds, it is a school of depravity; others, more robustly tempered, acquire malleability and strength therein.

Before strangers, Horatio and Olivia were polite. Their voices sounded affectionate; they spoke with a smile. People congratulated the old Duke on his son-in-law, and old prudes grimaced ludicrous compliments at Olivia on her happiness.

To every marriage there is a backcloth of active old women, urgent and extensive, which is sickening to behold. Perhaps that superannuated medley renders the thing more comical, which is an advantage; but that shameless cackling, that vilely malign gaze, that smile, contorted like a broken-down machine—the entire refrigerant assembly—gives rise to profound thought.

Alas, all those decrepit harpies have also had their wedding days. One day, joy came to smile upon their smile, putting on a semblance of removing a veil, of showing them a magnificent perspective, resplendent with light, and whispering to them, to the accompaniment of a heartbeat, that that was the future. Thus, of all those joys, of all that future of felicities, all those hours of intoxication, nothing remains but wrinkles, a withered form, and a repulsive appearance. By way of a souvenir, those women no longer have anything but a smile in which disillusionment and apathetic, morose doubt are visible.

Yes, that old tableau tells the truth! That is life stripped of dreams, the heart impoverished of love, the flesh inert, devoid of desire. Oh, take that glacial appearance away from young heads; take down those antique hangings; do not display it thus, to mirror that extinct past, that sniggering lie, to those who still believe!

By dint of feigning understanding in society, the two spouses came, by means of a secret armistice, almost to conserve their role in privacy. That was all the less difficult for them because they encountered one another so rarely. Then, like two actors going into the wings together while finishing the refrain of a song, they continued to smile and speak as falsely as possible. All in all, they both had too much intelligence to affect a futile physiognomy of hostility, an aversion that was continuous without being noisy. Their characters were not surly, and by custom, they liked life to be comfortable and dignified.

Since the commencement of this story, the season, as well as the events, has moved forward. We are now in the middle of winter, becalmed in fog. The Thames is as yellow as ocher, as choppy as a troubled sea.

I like that cold atmosphere, that sad aspect of the city of London. Life there is contained, material and pensive. The air that strikes the forehead renders the brain vigorous. Everything is dismal; no one laughs; the crowd is not cheerful; outside, there is nothing, everything happening indoors. For, I confess, in matters of pleasure, I am an egotist. Public festivals irritate me, joy on all faces annoys me; I am silent before that movement. For certain sentiments, I am not in harmony with the majority, but only with a few individuals. I like contrasts. A random effect of the moon, an ugly husband with a beautiful wife, a first-year student striking the poses of a politician, a financier making a witty quip, a vaudevillian weeping amorously—all those things fill me with delight.

In London, intoxication is reflective, folly is reasoned, passions are solved like an equation. One is debauched coolly, one frequents vice routinely, as devotees go to church. Thus in the morning, by virtue of a hidden cause dependent on the atmosphere, one says to oneself: *This evening I shall get drunk; tonight, I shall procure a brunette with big feet; I shall dine in the French style and I shall horsewhip the waiter.*

Now, in my opinion, that is the true way to sense life. In acting thus, programmatically, you enjoy all those things in the imagination, and the hope renders you joyful. Men who are virtuous in fits and starts, and excessive by caprice, have atrocious intelligences, hearts on which one cannot count either for generosity or for vice.

In Paris, love is distracted; in London, of its own accord, it expands to vertiginous proportions, magnifies itself and plunges you into a hallucinatory limbo.

In Paris one first takes care of the details, and afterwards, the capricious imagination lacks the force of transform realities; thus, eccentric minds cannot fashion the finished creations to their whim, always searching for an unknown form. In London, passion is a fluid that changes everything at the whim of caprice, which shows human nature through a prism.

It was, then, one of those winter evenings during which it is good to have wealth, health and amour. If I were not too humble to permit myself to address a wish to someone who is as dear to me as rare, that would be the triad that I would wish for my reader. But let us not touch on those abrupt subjects, those ill-sounding expressions. Talking politics is perhaps one of the surest symptoms of rickets.

Horatio and Lady Mackinguss, each seated at one end of a sofa of such flexibility as to make a Drury Lane cockney leap with fright at the thought of pitfall traps, were chatting about futilities and trivialities. In front of them was a thickset porcelain table with gilded flaps, furnished in a similar fashion to the one Queen Victoria sent to Saint-Cloud and on which Louis-Philippe played cards on summer afternoons.

The two spouses were laughing as they talked, which has the right to surprise us, and taking tea together, which should not astonish anyone.

"Well, Milord, the poor Countess had to ask after her husband this morning in all the police stations in London. You know Lord Landsdale's character—a trifle mad."

"Yes—what we call an eccentric and the French an original. What new folly has got into his head, then?"

"Yesterday, on coming out of the Queen's Theater, he had his coach draw up on the sidewalk at the bottom of the steps, and once having climbed aboard, ordered his coachman to continue along the sidewalk."

"A charming idea."

"It was late, and the street seemed dirty, so the unified flagstones seemed very suitable. A mob of policemen chased him. They caught up with him under the galleries of the Quadrant. He had traveled along the sidewalks of Pall Mall and Piccadilly, going through two bazaars and three passages. It's said that he tussled with a horseguard."

"A carriage traveling through a passage at high speed must have a delightful effect. After all, that joyful idea could only germinate in his brain, for it's not the first. Can you imagine, Milady, that Lord Landsdale was seized one day, while out walking, with an attack of amorous passion for a young woman wandering alone in the Avenue de Champs-Élysées in Paris. He pursued her all the way to the Arc de Triomphe. There, the young woman, in order to escape his hybrid speeches, plunged into an empty omnibus. The Count immediately got on after her, and paid for all the places, saying that his family, composed of fourteen persons, was waiting in the Avenue. The conductor lifted up the placard saying FULL and set off. It was a Sunday; it as starting to rain. The Bourgeoisie of Paris, in their best clothes, pursued the empty omnibus, advertised as FULL, with their cries and gesticulations. The imperturbable conductor repelled them from his foot-plate, and with the greatest self-composure, indifferent to all the noise, the Earl slowly pronounced, in French, protestations and offers of an entirely British kind. The adventure of that omnibus has always seemed quite delightful to me. A cup of tea, Milady?"

"By the way, what has become of Sir James Cawdor? We don't see him anymore."

"Sir James is in Scotland, Milady; perhaps we'll see him there. Do you know, Milady, that you are, in everyone's opinion, one of the most beautiful women in London, and it would be crazy for us to employ our time quarreling. I love you ardently this evening, Olivia."

The young woman looked at her husband with a dubious smile, which was soon lost in a microscopic cup of China tea.

"Ah! What, then, do your previous words signify, those assurances of inertia of the heart?"

"It was a joke, Milady, and eccentricity of an English husband."

"And all those machinations unveiled in Antares' house—also jokes?"

"Yes, they were the proofs of the freemasonry of married women; I repeat, I want to love you. Your hand, my beautiful lady."

"Here it is, Milord."

"You have the hand of a queen, Olivia, and certainly, if nature did not mock human beings, we would have beautiful children. Have you not always desired a child, Milady?" Horatio spoke daintily, as he nonchalantly turned over on a cushion, his gaze tender and slightly false.

"Oh yes; a child was the dream of my life, but..."

"Well, Olivia?"

"But you don't love me; it's another hope disappointed," she said, with an almost dubious pout of the same nature as the marital smile.

"And what assures you that your dream has not been mine? If I said to you...but would you believe me...? If I said to you that everything I have done to have you, I have accomplished in order to realize two dreams: to love you, and one day to be called *Father* by a voice that would call you *Mother*..."

And those two individuals delighted themselves with that thought, with accents of verity to make them both burst out laughing before that comedy, so simply played.

"And then," Horatio continued, proudly, "he would be rich, richer than the younger son of a family could ever be! We would give him honors and buy him titles! For, since our brother is obstinate in living like an osprey in his manor in

Argyle, I would take his place in society. Do you understand, Milady? I want you to be the foremost beauty of English society, and to be noticed at court this Christmas. I shall appear in Scottish costume, with the tartan of my clan and an eagle-feather in my cap; I have the right."

"And of all the lords from beyond the Tweed, you would be the most magnificent, Milord."

"A cup of tea, Milady?"

English prudery offers an exhaustible fount of gaiety. The eye valiantly lends its participation to anything, but the ear jibs at the slightest amphibology. Thus, on the great days of court reception, the Scottish lords come in their national costume, which, as everyone knows, leaves the lower legs, the knees and a part of the thighs bare. Now, young misses know no greater shame than pronouncing the word "trousers" but do not blush at the nudity of those who have none.

"What time is it, Milord?"

"It will soon be midnight, Olivia; you're tired; place this cushion under your head."

"Yes, I can feel sleep overtaking me. That's strange!"

"Our walk in Hyde Park has evidently wearied you."

"That's true, we came back late. Lady Melrose was very pale..."

"I knew her when she was very beautiful, in Lisbon—but that was ten years ago."

"Yes, Autumn will not come again for her. What has become of Lord Melrose?"

"Oh, I don't know. It's said that he's pursing a French dancer."

"They both lead a quite extraordinary existence here."

"Quite ordinary, you mean. Thus, in Lisbon their conduct was exemplary."

"But they never loved one another."

"That's exactly why. They were seen regularly, every evening, in their box at the theater, like two fortunate lovers. I knew the whole secret."

"Ah! From whom?"

"In truth, from one of those monks who sing masses in the morning in their convent, and choruses of *Robert-le-Diable* in the evening—for it was, in that era, the opera in vogue in Lisbon. Lord Melrose entertained the leading dancer and Milady...guess."

"You're going to tell me a wicked calumny."

"No, but a very amusing item of gossip. The pale and nebulous lady entertained the bass tenor."

"That's scandalous. Oh, I'm very drowsy!"

"Olivia you're adorable laid back like that, on that cushion; your physiognomy becomes dreamy, and my dreams become reality in our company! I love you thus, my beautiful angel; lie back!"

Horatio prepared another cup of tea with particular care. Olivia drank it mechanically. Her head fell back on the cushion; her eyelids drooped; her breathing became regular; she fell asleep. Her husband watched her sleeping, and his mouth expressed a victorious smile.

He rang. Suky and Hannah appeared.

"Put Milady to bed, and, if possible, don't wake her."

The two chambermaids, assisted by Lord Horatio himself, carried the young woman to her bed, undressed her and put on her night attire. She was still sleep. Her beautiful head was lost inertly in the waves and alveoli of the pillow's lace. The mute maidservants did not permit themselves to be astonished by that strange sleep.

"Let Milady sleep tomorrow morning, until she summons you. She won't need anything tonight. I'll be here. Go to your rooms and go to bed."

The two soubrettes bowed respectfully and went out. The calm and regular breathing of the sleeper was still audible.

After considering his beautiful wife momentarily, Horatio said to himself, with a cold smile: "When one makes war, it's necessary to bite one's bullets."

XVIII. Here one can get dead drunk for eight half-pence

If London does not have boulevards and quais like Paris, by way of compensation, in numerous sink-holes, it offers all the ignobilities of the Place Maubert.

To start with, one encounters loud and shrill debauchery in the neighborhood of the docks, in Wapping and Rother-hithe: the semi-honest vice of a population of sailors, material philosophers indulging, in a libertinage of brief joys, the realization of ardently elaborated dreams—men vicious in fits. For a month they are drunkards, occasional thieves, grotesque gallants, passionate boxers, delighting in thrusts of the dagger; then the sea reclaims them. Retempered by toil, they become sober and strong again; sourly, they impose exciting privations upon themselves, overburden themselves with fatigue, and dream during tempests of tranquil beds and joyous insomnias; and then, one day, they come ashore, as avid as wolves. They become utterly disreputable, but they lack leisure; the sea, their grim mistress, always recalls them.

Now, we have too low and too poor an opinion of the Place Maubert to compare it to such paltry districts, where vice is only a fantasy, a caprice, a mild purgative. The veritable cloaca of the hideousness of London, the tableau in which the putrefying colors and green tints of filthy passions are displayed naked and flamboyant, is the district of St. Giles.

By day, the population of those streets, the faces blanched by the chilly fog, appear at the ventilation-shafts of cellars. By night, everything outside is silent, but underground, frightful beings, afflicted by all deformities, the residues of human beings, swarm in suffocating lairs in we do not dare to raise the curtain on fetid conceptions and filthy scenes that we cannot present to the reader before having softened them.

The square of Seven Dials is an intersection into which seven black, muddy, sooty and smoky streets vomit forth. It is a neighborhood of Jews, second-hand clothes merchants and organ-grinders, the Montfaucon of prostitutes and the plebicule of thieves.[23] There, the cellars are more densely inhabited than the houses. One climbs outside. The stairway is a ladder, the door the opening of a ventilation shaft. These openings, drainpipes of all fetidities, serve as conduits, chimneys, windows and gutters.

Now, in these dens, smoke is not an inconvenience; on the contrary, it is a luxury; it keeps one warm. One seeks out a cellar where cooking is done, from which the smoke has difficulty getting out. Only the regulars can survive there. It is known as a "divan."

No matter what the season, in streets full of nauseating odors, everyone is barefoot. One sees human forms there that pretend to be women, with broken pipes in their mouths and wearing men's hats. The men are all in black jackets but have no shirts.

One of the most ignoble streets in the vicinity of Seven Dials is Monmouth Street. Part of it, almost all of one side, is inhabited by second-hand clothes-dealers. Their merchandise hangs outside along the shop-fronts, the entrances of which they block like hides drying on the hooks of a tannery.

On the side opposite these suspended rags, among the numerous subterranean taverns that can be distinguished, there is one less visible and more crowded than the rest. After having lifted the trap-door entrance, one descends a wooden stairway. When the trap-door opens, it gives a feeble light to the interior, which is always illuminated by a dull lantern and the ruddy light of a few coal braziers—but atrocious voices immediately protest against the daylight that hurts their eyes, like ospreys exposed to the sun. The trap-door is dropped, and the murmurs cease.

---

[23] The Gibbet of Montfaucon, in Paris, was famous for centuries as a place of execution; "plebicule" is an improvisation from a Latin term referring to an orator who appeals to the common herd.

Slightly above that bizarre entrance, on the wall, a sign is written in faded gray letters: *The Foxes' Den.*

Scarcely has one descended a few steps into that hole, which bears some resemblance to the orifices through which certain men disappear into the sewers of Paris, than one can read a significant advertisement traced in red letters: *Here one can get dead drunk for eight halfpence.*

Drunkenness—that's what these men demand! A few drops of a fiery liquid will transfigure an individual. Real things fade away, the veil of forgetfulness unfurls like a cloud, and on that canvas the gaudy hues of the mirage are vigorously daubed. It is a new life. Sensations are multiplied a hundredfold. The inert and stupid man of a moment ago utters witticisms effortlessly; his heart wakes up; unknown sentiments animate him; his body experiences wellbeing; his delirium has the appearance of an intoxication. Poor human nature—how it lets itself go!

It is a truly sad spectacle, that lumpen body violated thus, that intelligence stirred by galvanism. The observation of those men has always attracted me. What expansion! What joy! Follow one. Just now, he was a null being, a dead mind, lying down, incapable, sad and grim; now he is singing, speaking, pursuing an imaginary conversation; he loves, he hates; he is good, wicked; all his strength is in his head; his legs buckle; the body, unable to do any more, begs for mercy, and drags itself through the mud, but the head caries it away pitilessly, relentlessly. His brain, at odds with his hopes, squeezes them, crushes them and tramples them.

Alas, of all those who use up their health to realize a dream, to satisfy a passion, the drunkard is perhaps the wisest. Unable to attain the prey, he amuses himself with its shadow. Poor incapable and feeble minds, let us leave them to their illusion! But that lucid intelligences, broad minds, might go to seek in drunkenness the exaggeration of their faculties, that their imagination might strike the regions of madness, that is a blasphemy, that is to tempt God!

At the moment when we courageously descend the ladder of the tavern, it is night outside, but that circumstance of timing is, for those who are dreaming in the Foxes' Den, as indifferent as it is unknown. The majority spend months drinking, sleeping, laughing blissfully, quarreling with the courage of the drunkard who has left all vaunted valor behind. For them, it is neither day nor night, it is always dull. They snigger when they look at the hands rotating on a clock whose numbers have been erased, whose chime, annoyed not being heard, has committed suicide. In fact, for the habitués of this place, there are only two opposed hours that affect them. Their pockets indicate them. When shillings clink therein, it is time to come in; when they are empty, it is time to leave.

In the dives of Paris, one does not speak, one howls. In English taverns, people look at one another, and make ignominious signs at the gnome who is serving, but no one says a word. One dreams, one talks to oneself. The scene that we are about to describe is merely an ordinary one that we are catching on the wing, a continuous physiognomy dependent by chance on the action of our drama.

The first room is square, low-ceilinged, and damp-floored. Tables and benches are scattered all around. Men are smoking and drinking; their eyes are staring sightlessly, their mouths blossoming in implied laughter.

At the back of that cellar, through which we are going to pass, is a second trap-door almost constantly raised by day in order to receive light from the first room, and by night to give alms to the latter of a few ruddy gleams. The stairway is made of stone, the steps are viscous, worn and rounded, but a rope sustains you. That modest railing has never been seen, but one divines it.

The lamp stuck to the wall facing the second stairway illuminates that second floor of the cellar greasily. Anyway, the second room has the same dimensions as the first. When the eye has adapted to that penury of light, it distinguishes, placed all around, those prudish partition walls commonplace in English restaurants. Thus, each drinker is quite alone in his cell, entirely devoted to his beverage and his drunkenness.

We shall not go as far as the divan. Not that the colors that strike the atmosphere that one breathes there would be terrifying to my reader, but, unfortunately, literature is not a questionnaire. We know that the reader is more avid than the writer, but whatever one says, there is no need, like the torturer with regard to the victim, to spare the palette, to interrogate the pulsations of his arteries.

Anyway, we are not directing our characters; we are following them, that is all.

Now, I say this loudly: these pages sadden me; these depictions bring doubt and discouragement to my soul. Whatever one might believe, it is with irritation that the novelist, in a corner of his vermilion canvas, gives birth thus to a somber scene in the comedy of life, in which scorn sniggers victoriously, and in which insult is addressed to the Creator.

Yes, it happens that the man of dreams and fictive life has occasion to plunge his bare arms into the mire of vice, momentarily to disturb fetid gases and impure reptiles; he sometimes descends with courage into the gutter of low scenes, and vertigo does not grip him. It is the man in question that you see, sad in the midst of drunkenness, calm and cold in the orgy, as pale and Dante in the circles of Hell. He, alone perhaps, is strong in his reason, for, of all the souls acting in this fantastic drama, he is the unique spectator—he, alone, must return therefrom!

In the depths, through the orifice of an ascendant sliding door, one can confusedly distinguish moving shadows. The noise of vessels is audible, but no voice rises up. In the cellar in which we find ourselves, almost all the partitioned compartments are occupied by men and women, and one even sees a few young women. Everyone has a pewter mug in front of them, and drinks from it from time to time. In London taverns, there are neither plates not glasses.

Nevertheless, the Foxes' Den is a tranquil place, an honest establishment, as indicated by the sign written on the wall near the lamp: *No Fighting.*

In the midst of all these motionless drinkers, the gazes that pierce or fall, a lanky shadow is stirring: an individual whose long arms swing like flails, whose head has all the ugliness of a mascaron or the outlet of a gargoyle. He is the Ganymede of these men.

The memory of that gnome carrying a tankard in each of his large and greasy hands—those hands that one does not shake, but squeezes—the thought of that vampiric face, excites the hearts of the drinkers more than the laughter of a mistress. That being is known as Pander. Whether it is his name or a contumelious epithet, I do not know. At any rate, he answers to it.

Suddenly, down the stairway from the first room, a man fell rather than entered the one in which we have paused. He was a mariner—so said his tarry garments and his hat, with a rim broader at the back than the front. He was singing a song in bad English. A joyous laugh burst forth from the ochreous bars of his teeth.

"Ah! Here's the palace of joy! Hello, friends."

No one replied.

"Oh, the English—always dismal, as sad as the face of broken wind."

"Ah! Where has that dog of an Irishman fallen from? Throw him a potato and shut him up!"

"A potato, you old Leicestershire badger! That's not on my menu today. Hey, Pander the Fox, come and greet the friends!"

"Shut up! What do you want?"

"What I need, you old Dead Pudding-Face, is to rid you of one of your tankards and squeeze it in my hand."

"Oh, it's you, Mr. Droll, delighted to see you. What can I get you?"

"What, you species of mizzen mast, do you think I'm dying of starvation? Know, then my dear screeching chicken, that I have in my right pocket a smoked herring at your disposal."

A third loud voice resonated under the vault. "Now then, Pander, you dog, not content with cheating the customers, you're annoying us further by talking nonsense with that villainous Irishman."

The drinker who expressed himself thus was as tall as a ladder and his eyes were ablaze.

"Villainous!" said Droll. "I demand that the honorable personage retract that false expression. I'm a good fellow, the proof of which is that I'm squeezing the hand of that wheezy badger Pander."

"What do you mean, Mr. Rabble, cheat the customers?" said Pander, after liberating himself from Droll's amicable grip.

"I mean, ignoble Jew, that I came in here on the assurance of your sign. I've handed over my last four pence and I'm not drunk. To abuse the confidence of a master of tongues like that is a crime."

"Is it my fault if you eat? The house engages to get you dead drunk, but on condition that you don't eat."

"I haven't eaten anything, Pander, you thief!"

"I saw you, for I have my reason, me. You took a potato out of your pocket and a big plug of tobacco, and then you ate them both. Ha ha!"

"You're a thief, I tell you; you put water in your bitter instead of vitriol."

"Come on, Mr. Rabble, calm down—you're disturbing the repose of these gentlemen, and the honest conscience of that dried cod, my friend Pander. You called me villainous, well I'll return that insult to you in the form of a second pint of four penny bitter."

The master of tongues stood up, astounded by that prodigal generosity, and threw himself into Droll's arms.

"Come on, Mr. Rabble—you're weighing upon me too much."

"Yes, young man, like a balcony on a caryatid. Be my caryatid! Be my son!"

"Oh, as to that, no, Mr. Rabble, I'll never be your cantharid, it's too tiring. Sit down, and let me make this honest Pander party to my plans. Tell me, Pander, what do you say to yourself when you go to bed?"

"I don't go to bed."

"What would you say to yourself if you did go to bed one night?"

"You're annoying me, Mr. Droll; I'm wasting my time with you. Tell me what you want, and I'll serve you."

"Oh well! Handsome and estimable Pander, if, one day, beaten by contrary winds, you go to bed after having battened down the hatches, say to yourself, with conviction, this consoling sentence: *All that a man can desire on earth—which is to say, kegs of bitter—I possess! I'm a happy man, and I thank you, Lord!*"

"Are all the men of your country as loquacious, Mr. Droll?" demanded the dispenser of bitter.

"Pardon, Mr. Droll, but I believe I recognized in one of your periphrases the offer of a pint of bitter, and yet this dear thief Pander is as unmoving as a granite sphinx."

"Calm down, my friends. Honest Pander, here in this purse...ha ha! You recognize it! You grimace at the sight of it...!"

Pander sat down on a three-legged stool. In that new position, his arms hung down, allowing the two empty tankards he was holding to touch the floor. The Irishman smiled momentarily at his leather purse.

"Here, there's ten shillings inside. Take five, plus four pence, and listen to what I want. I'll be staying here for a week. Every morning, you'll place before me a four penny pint, and the same every evening."

"Mr. Droll, you're forgetting me!"

"Mr. Rabble, you, who are a master of tongues, for the moment, master yours, or I'll forget you inevitably."

Mr. Rabble shut up in the face of that threat, but his eyes were hypnotized by the Irishman's leather purse.

"You won't eat," said Pander, not in an interrogative tone but as a simple observation.

"I have a herring, a herring that comes from Jack Foxon's tavern in Newcastle. When the week has gone by, I'll see what I have to do. Oh! Also take the price of a pint of bitter for this thirsty individual. Now go away."

Droll sat down beside Rabble. Rabble had a repulsive and grotesque appearance. His head was bare, and his thick russet bard grew as it pleased over his cheeks, left fallow. A hideous physiognomy: one of those heads that frighten you, because they speak of the filth of the gulf into which a man might fall. The seal of vice and all its ignoble and purulent leprosies sniggered with an atrocious seriousness on that visage, lit up by an inert intoxication. His overly tight black jacket, with holes at the elbows and shreds at the wrists, left bare a bony breast covered with abundant villosities, like the hide of a goat. His trousers, as shiny as if they were varnished, could not reach the coat and scarcely descended below the knees of his thin extremities. His calves and feet were naked.

Pander had carried out Droll's orders. Two pewter tankards were already receiving the caresses of the Irish mariner and Mr. Rabble, the professor of languages.

"Ah, I recognize this liquid! Long live the Foxes' Den and its bitter! Do you know, Schoolmaster...?"

"Professor, sir!"

"As you please. For a professor, you seem to me to have a poorly armored stomach. It ought to be lined, nailed and copper-bottomed, like the *Coquette*, my last three-master."

"I drink this like milk, like a *bavaroise*."

"A what? You're speaking Chinese now."

"I'm speaking French. A *bavaroise* is a mixture of milk and syrup, of which Parisians are very fond. But that damned Pander's bitter seems to me to be velvet in the stomach."

"Pander, you wretch!" cried the loquacious Droll. "Send us a little smoke this way; it's as icy here as the coast of Northumberland."

"I tell you, Mr. Droll, that Pander deserves to be sent to Australia with the deportees. Would you believe that just now, he laughed in my face when I asked for a foot-warmer! You've come from Newcastle, Mr. Droll?"

"Arrived yesterday evening, respectable Mr. Rabble, on the *Coquette*, laden with coal for a company in which I have no interest. I was in Newcastle for a month."

"Is the bitter good there?"

"Unknown. Gin, whisky and potatoes, that's all. I was at John Foxon's tavern—a very intelligent fellow. He's invented an apparatus, a device for giving one an appetite."

"Ah!"

"Yes, Mr. Rabble, it can hollow out your stomach in a minute. How many potatoes could you eat, Professor, if you forced yourself?"

"Hum...perhaps four pounds."

"Well, John Foxon could immediately put you in a state to eat another four pounds."

"The wretch would make me return them, perhaps?"

"Not at all. On the contrary. This is it, in brief. Do you smoke, Mr. Rabble? Tobacco?"

"Tobacco!" said the later, fetching a short blackened pipe out of his inside pocket. "I have smoked it, but now I'm as fond of dried leaves or grass. Pander, you frightful dictionary, bring me what I need to refill my pipe."

"Ah! Pander furnishes you with tobacco?"

"Just me, yes."

The ignoble Pander brought the professor a piece of coal. The latter crushed it with his tankard. He collected the powder thus ground in his hand and filled his pipe with it. Pander spread a layer of embers over the matter, and Mr. Rabble stated smoked tranquilly.

"Ah! You smoke coal?"

"Always."

"And it doesn't trouble your digestion?"

"Never...not that I do any. Well, John Foxon's device—when are you going to explain it to me? Not that I want to use it, but it might be curious."

"He attaches a piece of string to the ceiling of his tavern. At the end of the string is a lump of lead twice as big as a bullet. Underneath it is a chair nailed to the ground. The placement is calculated. The sated individual sits in the chair, puts his head back and opens his mouth as if he had a tooth to offer to a dentist. By means of a spring, the ingot falls from a height straight into the throat and descends all the way to the required depth."

"That's very ingenious."

"It's called the stowing-lump. Bitter's nothing compared with that for hollowing out your stomach."

Droll had emptied his tankard. His tongue became confused and his eyes wandered; he leaned heavily on the table.

"And you disembarked with a pocketful of crowns?"

"Yes, crowns. Four shillings and four pence, there's my crowns. What ruins me is love. I'd be capable of giving my herring for a woman. Listen Rabble, are you my friend?"

"Your brother—call me your brother!" exclaimed the expansive linguist.

"You're my friend! Well, then, let's make confidences. Rabble, are you in love?"

"In love...no—but someone once was with me."

"When you had a shirt. Listen, my friend, I'm going to tell you some things...horrible...frightful...about...about..."

"The Comte de Neuilly?"[24]

"Neuilly...don't know him...about...Pander."

---

[24] Ange-Achille de Brunet, Comte de Neuilly is nowadays best known for the oft-reprinted memoirs of his years as an émigré in England, which were published in 1863, but he was notorious in that capacity long before then. His father had been master of the royal stables before the Revolution of 1789.

Suddenly collapsing on the table, the Irishman remained motionless, dead drunk—intoxicated, or poisoned, as the English expression justly has it.

The professor paraded a profound reflective gaze over him, speculatively.

But, through the coal smoke that is blinding us, suffocating us, and which all those torpid, brutalized, drunk individuals are breathing contentedly—not forgetting Mr. Rabble, who could smoke an entire mine of it without being nauseated—we can distinguish, confusedly, three individuals who are coming in: two men and a woman. The latter is clenching a black and oozing pipe between her broken teeth and leaving a column of smoke behind her, like a pyroscaph. The odor of tobacco, among these individuals, is like perfume in society: it announces the presence of women.

There was only one empty booth—the largest of all; they sat down in it.

Let us begin with the woman, not out of courtesy, but simply because one has to begin somewhere.

She coughed frequently, perhaps deliberately. Her respiration seemed noisy and abrupt. Sin and gin had stunted, withered and atrophied her like the dried cadavers of a family killed by poison that are exhibited in the ossuary of the Saint-Michel crypt in Bordeaux. She might have been seventy, but might only have been twenty-five. She was wearing a battered hat.

Oh, the sight of those English hats has always been a great joy for me. I often ask myself, where do they come from? When was the day when someone looked for it, impatiently, during a brilliant walk in Hyde Park or a fête at Windsor? The odyssey of an English hat is strange.

Perhaps it saw the light of day in Belgrave Square and crowned the beautiful blonde head of a peeress. Then, one Christmas Eve, was it not called to embellish the laughing face of a chambermaid celebrating in City Road? One morning, I think I remember, did it not appear to me, after many vicissitudes and transformations, on the alert head of some soubrette at the Adelphi Theater? Yes, that night, as cheerful as its mistress, it fancied a cup of tea, and received it. Alas, since that midnight feast, its star has faded! It swept away its flowers and ribbons; the dull and crimpled appearance of its bonnet saddened it so! However, one still perceived it, dealing squarely—not so say cubically—at Greenwich. Rumor has it, that it coiffed one day a turned-up nose, shiny hair on the head, and ineptly annealed ringlets, dry and slack, which might have cost six shillings. On coming back, it was crumpled against the funnel of a steamboat on which two Englishmen were boxing. It lay down in a tavern, a spirit-shop in which, after libations of porter and stout, it took part in a dishonest tourney that threw it down into the lowest class of hats. For a few winters it served on the Dover-Calais ferry; then, one day, it saw itself in the role of shopping-basket. Some time afterwards, an infatuated waterman picked it up in a market for some river-portress. Finally, I find it again in a tavern in Monmouth Street, in its primitive form...

In England, hats offer far more cases of longevity than in France. I have never had the privilege of witnessing the end of a hat or a black jacket; that is a very rare event in London.

The dress worn by that interesting person had forgotten its original form and color. The entire lower part was yellow with mud and the upper part black with dirt. That rag formed the woman's entire costume; her body had acquired an utterly diaphanous degree of thinness. Needless to say, she was barefoot. In St. Giles, and most particularly in Monmouth Street, footwear is unknown. Even the second-hand clothes-merchants have none on display.

That sickly individual, clad at such little expense, called herself Miss Mob. It is a name fairly widespread in the taverns of London. Its significance, moreover, never contrasts with those who bear it.[25]

---

[25] The novel's original readers would probably have known what "mob" signifies in English, and were at least as likely to have been aware that Mob is the name attributed to the person-

Miss Mob's neighbor was her brother. His thinness was suggestive of an escapee from and anatomical museum. The third person had a face as pale as the reflection of an alcohol flame, and his eyes were so red that it made one feel ill to look at them.

Scarcely had they sat down than the great Pander loomed up before them, giving his mute physiognomy, as far as possible, the form of a question mark.

"You need three bitters?"

"Three bitters!" said Mr. Mob, in a scornful tone. "What do you take us for? We consume *à la carte*."

"Me, I want a bitter," Miss Mob articulated, dully.

"You hear—a bitter for my little sister, and a pot of gin for us."

With two strides, Pander plunged back into his lair.

"Well, Mr. Digger, what do you say to my proposition? Does it suit you?"

"No, not at all," the pale man replied. "Your sister might drag it out for another month."

"But Mr. Digger, you don't know her! A month! What do you say, little sister?"

"I say that Digger is a crow who wants to cheat us."

"Listen, sir," Mr. Mob went on, raising the pot of Holland's gin to his companion's lips. "Let's make a deal for twenty shillings."

Mr. Digger started, and his teeth clocked on the pewter pot.

"Don't be afraid; if I speak thus, it's to your advantage. Count me twenty shillings. The lord mayor's election is next week. Well, if it isn't finished by then, I promise to give you a shilling every morning until the liberation. Is that reasonable?"

---

ification of Death (as an old crone) in Edgar Quinet's Romantic classic *Ahasvérus* (1834) (available from Black Coat Press as *Ahasuerus*, ISBN 978-1-61227-214-6.

"To begin with, Mr. Mob, I only need a demi-cadaver, and if I take your sister it's simply for her torso; the rest I'll leave. My colleague Raven might take it."

Mr. Mob and his interesting sister were nonplussed. The latter had drunk her pint of bitter; the apples of her hollow cheeks lit up like pomegranates in autumn. Her respiration wheezed noisily.

"What do you say, little sister?"

"A person with self-respect, Mr. Digger, doesn't let herself be sold piecemeal. All or nothing. I've always said that it was a bad idea, Mob. Treating with these vagabonds is an impoverishment. To conclude a deal for a crown, it's necessary to ply them with two shillings' worth of drink."

"Come on, Digger, be reasonable: it's a good opportunity you've happened upon; don't be too voracious."

"Voracious!" cried the resurrectionist. "That's easy for you to say. In any event, nothing bad will happen to you, while I dream every night—or, rather, every day—about ropes around my neck!"

"But Mr. Digger," Mob protested, "you're forgetting our arrangement. I'm undertaking to bring the cadaver of my little sister to you personally, on the evening of her inhumation. Oh, I suspect that you don't get an offer like that every day."

"And once you have my money, who will force you, I beg you, to scale the cemetery wall to go and finish a job paid for in advance?"

"Digger, we're both honest men, whatever might be said in certain places. Give me ten shillings now, and ten more when I hand over the body."

"But I never—no, never—pay a pound for a demi-cadaver!" exclaimed the resurrectionist, despairing of the bad business that was being set before him.

"I want to sell you all of my sister, sir! All of my sister, do you hear? Oh, but I know what they give to someone who denounces a resurrectionist!"

Mr. Digger, raising himself up to his full height, seized his neighbor's neck. Mr. Mob went blue in the face. His little sister seized the beer-tankard. The pale man withdrew his hand, letting the brother go, and said down again calmly.

Miss Mob, softening, took the resurrectionist's hand and said, persuasively: "Come on, Mr. Digger, take my head too. I've been mad for two years, I must have a deposit."

"A deposit, a deposit...that doesn't reassure me at all. So much the better for whoever ends up with your head, but me, I can't make it pay. In any case, if I consent to deal with your brother, who isn't reasonable, it's simply because of your chest. Come on, let's finish now and shake hands afterwards. See, Mr. Mob, here's a crown...plus half a crown...which is to say, three half-crowns, more than seven shillings. Well, bring me your sister in a week's time, and you'll receive as much again."

"Fifteen shillings! My poor sister, don't you feel humiliated?"

"Mr. Mob, I wouldn't make that deal with just anyone, believe me. Oh, ours is a hard profession!"

So saying, Mr. Digger counted out on to the table, making each coin resonate, seven shillings and sixpence.

At that metallic sound, the professor raised his head and pricked up his ears like a horse at his master's voice.

Mr. Mob's eyes were sparkling like two fireworks. The bargaining power of that silver, under the influence of the alcohol, which was making him spasmodically drowsy, tormented him.

"Very well, Mr. Digger; in a week you'll give me the same."

"Make sure it doesn't drag on any longer; otherwise, my colleague Raven might get in ahead of me with the man of science concerned."

"Have no fear."

"What if you buy her another bitter?"

"Another bitter...hmm. That's four pence!"

"Listen, Mr. Mob, if I say this, it's simply in your own interest: above all, don't get caught. Besides which, I could give information against you. Oh, yes, our profession is bristling with difficulties."

"And lots of fragments of bottles on the crests of walls eh?"

"Don't joke like that, Mob, my dear friend. Without the help of the vampire, I'd probably have been hanged a long time ago."

"What vampire are you talking about?" asked Mob's brother curiously.

"Ours. We don't know him otherwise."

And Digger, his mind excited by intoxication, adopted a mysterious expression, as one does on approaching a fantastic tale.

"Yes, Mr. Mob, when we want a cadaver, this is what we do. At nightfall, we get into a cemetery—Kensal Green, Highgate, Nunhead or New Cross, it doesn't matter which—and we wait."

"For the cadaver?" asked Mr. Mob, in a pleasantly inebriated tone.

"For the vampire."

"What form does it take?"

"We call him that to designate him, that's all, He's a man."

"Like me?"

"Yes, but better. All black, except for his eyes, which shine whitely like those of a frightened cat. We never see him arrive."

"I understand; he lives there."

"No; one might think he emerges from the ground. Suddenly, he looms up in front of us. He walks; we follow him. At the slightest sound, he disappears. Where? No one knows. He vanishes. A tree hides him; he fades into the wall of a tomb."

"Oh, Mr. Digger, you're frightening me."

"Furthermore, in his presence, the guard dogs shut up. He knows the places better than us, and he always stops in front of fresh graves."

"Truly, Mr. Digger!" said the listener, looking around anxiously.

"It's in your interest that I'm telling you this. In which cemetery is Miss Mob being buried?"

"New Cross, since she's from Lower Deptford Road."

"Well, climb over the wall on the side opposite the main gate. Close by is a white marble tomb on which an open Bible is sculpted. Stand behind it, and wait."

"What will I see?"

"At about midnight he'll pass slowly by, arms folded, pensive. Anyway, you'll see his pale face."

The two men, prey to an infectious fear, drew closer to one another, focused on their subject, avid for details. The woman, collapsed on the table, could not hear them.

"You follow him. He knows the new graves. You'll see him crouch down in the place where Miss Mob has been buried; you won't hear any sound. Only, gradually, the body of the vampire will sink into the earth, descend beneath the surface, then disappear into the hole."

"What does he dig with?"

"I don't know. Perhaps with his hands. Then, shortly afterwards, he'll come out of the ditch and look for another. You go after him. Your sister will be out of her coffin; you carry her away."

"And the man has never spoken?"

"Man! He's not a man, Mr. Mob, he's a mysterious being, something terrible, the sight of which chills my blood with fear. Ah!"

Suddenly, the resurrectionist stood up, fearfully, his back to the wall. His face was distressed, his eyes, horribly open, seemed to be confronting a sudden apparition. Without saying a word, he climbed up on the table, leapt over Mr. Mob and his sister and disappeared from the tavern, uttering a scream of fear that caused all the numbed heads to rise up.

Mr. Mob could not comprehend that panic. So, to reassure himself and chase away the memory of the picture drawn by Digger, he poured over his lips the last drops of gin left at the bottom of the tankard.

In complete contrast to many, Mr. Digger did not find boldness and courage in gin, for what had troubled him to violently was not, in appearance, very frightening. An individual had just appeared on the threshold of the room, followed by two other men.

The first individual was tall, thin and endowed with a strange face. We recognize Lord Lodore. After him came Sir James Cawdor, whom we identify quite readily, although some whim had given him the idea of sticking a moustache over his lips. The third man, tall and handsome, is unknown to us; he wore livery.

All the booths were occupied, as we mentioned previously. The gentlemen therefore had the privilege of sitting down at the table that the resurrectionist had just fled, and where the worthy Mr. Mob was still drinking.

The gait of the men, especially the one who was wearing a long gray frock coat with blazoned buttons, seemed slightly attained by inebriation. Sir James was agitated by a mad gaiety. When he spoke, he affected a strong French accent. Lodore was tottering slightly, but, as always, maintained a great sobriety of speech.

In two bounds, Pander was beside them, his neck extended and his arms oscillating.

"Three bitters?"

"Bitters!" cried Sir James. "What do you take us for, islander?"

"For customers, perhaps?"

"We drink wine! Do you hear, taverner? That is, at least, the desire of my two friends, James and Bob here. And real wine, because I know it; I'm a veteran of the horseguards, and I despise beer as much as I despise the infantry."

Ordering wine in Monmouth Street is like asking for a glass of nectar in one of the cafés on the boulevards. So Pander, a man who never allowed himself to be taken by surprise, immediately replied: "You want wine. I can get it for you, but it will take quite a long time. We have first-rate stout, and gin that would make a Quaker laugh."

"Well then, bring us plenty of gin—too much gin," cried James, with the expansive tone and enthusiasm that one only finds in the estaminets of Paris between eleven o'clock and midnight. "My dear Bertram, I regret, in truth, only being able to offer you Hollands, but we have a proverb that says that the most beautiful girl in the world can only offer what she has."

"Sir is French?" asked Mob, lured by the quantity of gin that Pander was about to bring.

"Yes, Monsieur, French by birth, joyous companion by taste, and coachman by profession, as is my friend Bob, whom you perceive silent by my side."

"I like the French a lot."

Sir James shook his hand, and passed it to Bob, who also shook it.

"Gentlemen, I present to you, lying here, Miss Mob, my sister, a person who will be charmed to drink to your health when she wakes up. Isn't that right, Miss Mob?"

"Very good, sir, but don't wake her; your sister is wearing a very pretty hat and has a charming name."

"Oh, my God! That name doesn't really belong to us."

"Ah, it's a pseudonym. It's very wittily chosen."

"Since you're French, Mr. James, tell me how it's said in your language?"

"Oh, My God, as in English, except that it isn't pronounced in exactly the same way."

"Oh! They say *Moub*, perhaps?"

"No, they say *canaille*."[26]

"Canaille… yes, that's true, the pronunciation isn't exactly the same."

---

[26] *Canaille* does, indeed, mean "mob" in the sense of a riotous crowd or "the masses," but its range of meaning is wider than that of the English word, and its subsidiary uses are blatantly insulting, implying criminal rascality and base vulgarity.

Pander deposited a vast tankard of gin on the table. James paid a fabulous sum, in Mr. Mob's eyes. The immense pitcher passed from mouth to mouth, but the liquid appeared to diminish considerable more after the swigs taken by Bertram and Mob than those taken by Bob and James.

Mr. Rabble, however, had not been drinking for some time. Gazing at the Irishman Droll, lying dead drunk beside him, he was reflecting. His reflection must have been sinister.

Gradually, one of his hands disappeared under the table. But the mariner sat up suddenly, darted a suspicious glance at him, articulated a few incoherent words, took his purse, placed it in another pocket, and lay on top of it.

Mr. Rabble had a bizarre smile, if one could call that labial contraction a smile.

Scarcely had he fallen back on the bench than Droll plunged back into the torpor of inertia and intoxication. Then, effortlessly and without making a sound, the professor of languages seized both the sailor's wrists with one hand, and with the other, encircled his neck with an iron grip. The unfortunate man's body twitched several times, his limps quivered, and then it was all over. His face turned blue.

Surreptitiously—simply to avoid attracting the attention of the drinkers in the opposite both—Mr. Rabble plunged his hand into the pocket of the strangled man and took out the leather purse.

He summoned Pander in a thunderous voice, demanded a bitter, and shelled out the price. The latter was not in the least concerned as to where the professor had got the money. He served him, and retreated into his frightful lair.

Mr. Rabble had a happy thought, which made him smile. After having searched two pockets, he brought out the smoked herring. Five minutes later, the bitter was drunk, the herring was eaten, and the master of tongues left the Foxes' Den utterly joyful.

Perhaps it might give rise to criticism to recount that monstrous incident thus, as a simple observation, in parentheses. Now, it is not whimsy that suggested that form to us. By means of that simple sketch, we believe that we are depicting the true physiognomy of crime as it is perpetrated in great cities. No crowd, no cries, no torches. Every morning, the Paris Morgue and the London "bonehouses" open their doors to men murdered the previous night. Why? For something trivial: a word, an insult, a sou. And all that is done without noise, coldly, as a perfectly simple thing.

The dead do not talk. That is the reason.

For individuals descended so low, the life of a man is nothing. Thus, Rabble left enchanted with the deed he had just done, and went to drink all night in another tavern. Amid the clouds of his intoxication, a slight hope floated gaily: perhaps he would find another man with a few shillings in his pocket—but such encounters are rare, and Mr. Rabble would be saddened by that if he were not a little drunk.

As for Droll, who would worry about him? He would stay there for a few days; people would assume that he was drunk. Then, one evening, Pander might perhaps notice that his tankards remained full, would shake him and laugh uproariously one seeing that he was dead. The bitter had killed him, people would say. He was a child.

And Mr. Pander would take back his intact tankards, delighted at having been paid in advance for a consumption that reverted to him. In the evening, the stiff cadaver would be taken away, and it would all be over. Mr. Rabble would go back to the Foxes' Den, the event would be recounted to him, and he would listen as if it were news, for he would certainly have forgotten the neat trick of which he was the author.

In those filthy gulfs, crime is no longer crime; it is a familiar thing that does not interest or astonish anyone.

"So, your revolution overturned more than one coachman in Paris?" said Bertram, whose moist eyes were glittering more than carbuncles.

"There's no longer anything but omnibuses and allegorical chariots!"

"You were right to come to London, but it was a mistake for all of you to come. The English are no longer grateful. Have you driven much, Mr. James?"

"Ten years in the stables of a banker. After February,[27] I went into service with a bookseller who'd become some kind of minister. He dressed me ridiculously, and my service was very tiring. He drove himself; in the meantime, I was obliged to lie on my back, arms folded. That position gave me headaches and hurt my back. All the rich are in London, people were saying everywhere; so I came to London."

"And do you think, my dear James, and you, my dear Bob, that I fell right away into the seat of Milord Mackinguss' carriage? Oh, make no mistake, my friends—to arrive there required a lot of politics. It was love, my friends, yes, love that led me there. Have you ever been in love, Mr. James?"

"Ho ho! Have you ever been in love, Bob?"

"Ho ho! Have you ever been in love, Mr. Mob?"

"Ho ho!" repeated the latter. "Have you ever been in love, little sister?"

Miss Mob, still lying down, did not reply.

Bertram was still drinking. Sir James studied him with shining eyes and a jovial smile spread over his illuminated face.

"One day," the genuine coachman continued, "I was on sentry duty in Whitehall, motionless on my motionless horse. I'm talking about the time I was in the horseguards. Now, no woman passes along Whitehall without darting a glance at the two horseguards on duty. It was forbidden for us to smile at them, but one day I disobeyed the order for my cousin, Miss Suky. The next day, on parade, I saw Miss Suky again. A third day, I saw her hat in a path in St James's Park. That day, I was alone—which is to say that I didn't have my horse. You wouldn't believe, my friends, how inconvenient the society of a horse can be, sometimes.

---

[27] The month of the 1848 Revolution.

"You've never been in love, so I won't talk about my happiness. Miss Suky is very pretty, but then she was better. It's always the consequence of a fortunate love. In brief, her mistress, Miss Olivia Firstland, having also experienced the need to come to a conclusion, by means of intelligent maneuvers, I found myself at the mead of milord her husband's stables. Use the same means, my friends, and you'll be in no danger of not succeeding. After all, since you're so amiable to me. I'll be very obliged to you and your friend for life."

"You still love Miss Suky?"

"Tee hee! After the spirit-merchant, she does well! But my dear friends, you know that I have to be back by midnight. We've already had quite a party together—well, let's go back together."

The handsome Bertram and his two companions left Mr. Mob and his sister and started up the difficult stairway of the tavern. When they emerged from the ignoble place, the air in the street surprised them. The coachman staggered slightly, sometimes suddenly straightening up with braggadocio. His speech was halting and his sentences rarely reached their terminus—an undeniable warning for alcoholized tongues. Sir James, with a very amicable generosity, and although he was only a little drunk, still approved of him, pushed himself upon him, laughed with him, and even more stupidly than him. Lord Lodore followed silently.

Before reaching Grosvenor Square, they made several halts in the spirit-shops of Regent Street. Bertram was still talking to everybody, about everything.

"Listen, James, you're my friend, so I want to share everything with you. Tomorrow, you'll climb up on to my seat with you...you can take the reins of one horse, I'll take those of the other. Yes, that's it—Milord will never be better guided, will he?"

"And Bob, my dear Bertram. You're forgetting Bob."

"Bob too...all three on the seat...we'll gather the reins and the whip in our six hands...it will be a touching sight...Milord will weep...the passers-by will weep. Yes, that's it, it's settled...Miss Suky's waiting for me...she's very beautiful, Miss Suky! Ha ha! How Milord will be driven tomorrow with his three inseparable coachmen! His friends! For, after all, he's our friend too, isn't he, James. Yes, Suky loves her cousin Bertram...and the ex-horseguard loves his cousin Suky. Where are we, my good friends?"

"Grosvenor Street."

"Grosvenor Street...yes...we're nearly at the square. You're coming in, my friends, because we're never, never going to be parted..."

To all these statements James replied with approvals and hyperbolic protestations. They went into the house. Bertram had one of his friends on each arm. He allowed himself to be led. They did not encounter anyone on the way.

Lord Lodore opened a door and pushed Bertram into a room.

"But this isn't Suky's room!" he exclaimed, turning round.

"You've lost your memory."

"Oh, my dear friends, don't make any mistake! Don't you know that there's a room under this roof in which Lady Cockburn sleeps? Oh, damn! An ex-horseguard in such sheets!"

"Is your heart not speaking to you, Bertram?"

"Well, my dear friends," said the former horseguard, very serious, leaning on his companions, with his finger on his forehead, "one thing worthy of note is that intoxication embellishes everything. Thus, except for Bob, who is still ugly, everything seems beautiful to me. This room, which I find very ordinary every evening, presently appears magnificent! I'm breathing unknown perfumes!"

"But it's always thus, my dear Bertram. And Suky— you'll find her more beautiful still."

XIX. A Night with Cleopatra

The clock chimed ten. Olivia had not yet woken up. None of her maids had come into her room. The curtains of the bed were parted, and Horatio, sitting in an armchair placed beside the bed was watching her sleep.

Lady Mackinguss' bedroom, its walls hung with good taste, also presented four modern paintings: four fantasies framed in costly wood, as remarkable for the bizarre excavations of the chisel as the canvases. Gilding had been pitilessly proscribed, for nothing is so unworthy to surround a work of art, of no matter what character, as a gold-clad frame, like a priest in his stole, spreading yellow shadows like the outside of a diligence.

The young woman remained enveloped in the penumbra of slumber. Her lips contracted silently, as if replying to àn interior sensation, and her eyes shifted beneath her closed eyelids. Horatio did not hasten to wake her. He got up discreetly, went to sit down at an open writing-desk, and wrote the following letter:

Robert,

Lord Lodore has always been, so far as I am concerned, a tenebrous man. To see into the depths of his soul it is necessary to illuminate them. Every night he goes out. Where does he go? I don't know. I want to know. Tomorrow, from eleven o'clock until he goes out, you will hide some distance from his house. Follow him, no matter what time it is, no matter where he goes. Above all, remain invisible. After completing that task, it will be permissible for you to go back to France for a time.

When Horatio had sealed the letter, Milady woke up. An observant eye easily recognizes, from the physiognomy of a person emerging from sleep, the character of the dreams that have occupied them during the night. The lineaments of Olivia's visage seemed softened, her cheeks were warm, her eyes moist and her lips slightly swollen. She immediately extended her hand to her husband, who came back to take his place beside her bed.

"Have you been there for a long time, Horatio?"

"I never left you, my beautiful angel."

"Oh, what a strange sleep!" she said, slightly confused, and glad to find things in order. "I don't remember anything. I went to sleep yesterday evening, I believe, on the sofa."

"Yes, your chambermaids put you to bed, almost unconscious. Was your sleep tranquil?"

The light in the apartment was faint. The curtains cast their shadow over the young woman's face.

"Oh no—quite the contrary! Tormented!"

"Happily?" said the husband, leaning toward her with a smile on his lips.

"Happily! Oh, Horatio, I have had such dreams…!"

"Olivia, if, instead of a dream, a seductive reality had come to watch over you, to lull your sleep, would you love me a little?"

"Yes, I remember—you passed through my dreams like a shadow…you spoke to me. I tried to reply, but the leaden hand of sleep closed my mouth."

"No, Olivia, it wasn't sleep that closed your mouth!"

So saying, Horatio planted a kiss on his wife's beautiful hand.

"And then," she continued, caressing her husband with a tender gaze, "I sensed with regret the awakening awaiting me. I would have like to sleep forever. But also, your voice was so strange!"

"A loving voice, Milady, is not an ordinary voice."

Olivia was silent, doubtless savoring internally the memory of that night, mysterious for her, frightful in reality.

Feeble human nature! A little wine, a little love, and it is transfigured. This woman, who feigned harmonious accord with her husband yesterday, has been taken over by her role.

Pride has been forgotten, hatred blunted. Instead of being alarmed by the artificial sleep that has been procured for her, she misses it. Horatio does not flinch. He rejoices in his work. Before the atrocity of his action, at the sight of that amorous languor, he does not feel jealous!

"Have none of my maids come?"

"They'll come when you ring."

"Is it very late?"

"No—only eleven o'clock."

"What were you thinking, sitting next to me, when I awoke?"

"You wouldn't believe it."

"Perhaps."

"Guess, my beautiful lady."

"You weren't thinking about me."

"No, about more than you."

"Oh! And why is that?"

"I was searching for a name."

Olivia smiled, but the smile was cold—or, rather, mechanical. Gradually, she was recovering her inherent nature, and emerging proudly from the happy limbo into which a seductive incubus had perhaps plunged her.

"It's a serious matter, the choice of a name, Olivia."

"That's true, the name influences the destiny."

"An unsuitable name is like a ridiculous garment that one is obliged to wear for a lifetime."

"Well, I haven't been searching, but I've found one."

"Ah! And what is it?"

"We'll name him after his father."

"After his father?"

"Yes—don't you want that?"

The husband laughed secretly, but he immediately suppressed that treasonous snigger.

"Does that name not sound badly in his mother's ear?"

"You're wicked, Horatio, and you don't love me!"

"Beautiful Olivia, we love one another equally, you may be sure."

"I've always doubted it."

"For you to believe it, is it necessary for me to say it?"

"Yes."

"Well then, *turlututu*. Haven't you told me that that is its French significance? It's very fashionable today to throw a few foreign words into our speech."

That word broke the charm. Olivia frowned, darted a glance at her husband in which the bile was evident, and fell silent again. Lord Mackinguss stood up with an entirely British air of insouciance.

A tumultuous noise erupted outside. Precipitate footsteps were heard, and female screams.

"What does that signify, Milord?"

"I don't know, Milady, but someone will tell us."

Horatio shook the bell-cord, and—which almost never happened—rang twice. Hannah appeared, her face distraught, panting.

"What's happening, to make all that racket before Milady has rung?"

"It's Bertram the coachman, Milord, who's been found dead in his bed."

Horatio was not in the least astonished. The more precipitate events around him became, the more he affected calm. He left Olivia's room, whispering to himself: "Dead! It's quite simple. Has he not had his night with Cleopatra?"[28]

---

[28] The reference is to Théophile Gautier's classic story "Une Nuit de Cléôpatre" (1838), translated into English by Lafcadio Hearn as "One of Cleopatra's Nights," with whose ending the great majority of the novel's original readers would have been familiar, and hence able to appreciate the malevolent sarcasm of the remark. I have, necessarily, used a more brutal translation in the chapter title (which has "Le" rather than Gautier's "Une") and in this final line (which substitutes "sa").

XX. The Vampire

Lodore lived in Snow Street, an ugly, curving little street near the crossroads of Holborn Hill. His house had a troubling physiognomy.

Like its owner, Lord Lodore's apartment was mysterious. It consisted mainly of a room so profound and unequally lit that the distant items of furniture could only be made out confusedly. Beneath black curtains so heavy that they oscillated for a long time after the draught from the door had struck them, hid a squat, flat bed. Hard and hypocritical couches had never accommodated any woman.

The apartment was devoid of luxury. No frame or canvas ornamented its wood paneling. Only, we know that there existed in the depths of an alcove a painting in a strange style and colors as wan as the resentful penumbra that bathed it. That engraving doubtless rendered some funereal episode in some novel with a dour and sepulchral setting.

There are characters that never open up, men always mysterious even to themselves, as suspicious of silence as they are of sound; such was Lodore.

Nevertheless, on the evening when we enter the house in Snow Street, inexplicable ideas were flowing through the brain of that man. His bony face was contracted and agitated; his eyes were fiery, like phosphorus. He was marching back and forth in his room, unhurriedly and silently. The curtains of the alcove did not stop him; he was engulfed in the darkness, and for a moment the room seemed abandoned, but gradually, the curtains stirred and he moving shadow suddenly reappeared.

Now we are facing a head that we scarcely dare to sketch: an individual for which it is necessary to skip the details and dash off incomplete strokes. We have shoved him back into the distant shadows, into the dark background of our tale, but still we dread that he might be too prominent.

Now, that monstrosity, which frightens us, that moral infirmity that we fear to display, has not emerged from our imagination, as you know.[29] The novelist, in all the debauches of his imagination, is his dreams of strangeness, would never have been able to attain a similar conception—but he has plunged his hand courageously into realism, and hazard has led him to an atrocity, a barbaric buffoonery of nature.

There is a word that causes tremefaction, even terror, for some, but is still quite inoffensive for us, which the victorious reader, the reader more positive than a number, who reads novels with a grim eye, throws in the face of the writer: implausibility! That substantive will not torment us today, because it will not be us to whom it will be addressed.

Lord Lodore was still marching—or, rather, gliding. A lamp as calm as an academician's brain was spreading its motionless light.

---

[29] The author inserts a footnote here: "Our readers have doubtless not forgotten the strange affair of Sergeant B***, which aroused so much excitement in the medical world at the end of 1849. A book can only pencil in the margin of one of its pages what the newspapers have set forth before the whole world." The novel's original readers would immediately have recognized this as a reference to the still-notorious case of the grave-violator Sergeant François Bertrand, dubbed "the vampire of Montparnasse" by the newspapers reporting his erotic fascination with the dead bodies of young women; he was caught in June 1849, court-martialed and executed. The term "vampire" had previously been used with reference to a grave-violator in the French translation of a story by E. T. A. Hoffmann, who was a great favorite of the Romantic Movement's writers (1813). Modern readers might be familiar with Guy Endore's classic novel based on the Bertrand case, *The Werewolf of Paris* (1933), although that transplants the events of the story twenty years forward in time.

Lodore did not speak much, so his voice did not have a determined, sure timbre. His speech commenced softly but, in becoming more animated, grew louder.

Gradually, a murmur troubled the silence; the marcher's gait became jerky and halting. He spoke.

"Yes, when I examine myself coldly, I frighten myself. The more I advance into the night, the more my resolution fades, the more my will weakens. I'm devoid of strength, devoid of energy, before that deadly power; it's an accursed hand that shoves me forward, and I can't avoid it. However, I want to stop, to throw myself out of this frightful path, to regenerate myself! I've made an oath to do it. Out of respect for myself, I'll keep it. Yes.

"Yes, I'll suppress that monstrous passion, the thought of which, in moments of calm, makes my hair stand on end. I won't go! Oh, I'm unfortunate! Perhaps there's a remedy, but I dare not ask for it. Perhaps there exists a man who can cure me, but I don't know him. Oh, if they all knew, they would be appalled by me, and wouldn't feel sorry for me. And yet, it's not a madness; I'm calm; I have all my reason. Oh! Oh, despair! The calmer I am, the more that abyss attracts me, the more my horrible dreams excite me!

"Certainly, there are two natures within me. By night, I'm no longer the same; I'm transformed; I forget, and a frightful scene looms up before me. Obstacles open up before my footsteps, dolors fall silent, my eyes are magnetized...

"Then, afterwards, I wake from a tormented nightmare, from a wearying night, and I'm afraid of my dream. Dream? No, reality! And for ten years, I've been like this.

"Oh, I remember it, the day of that frightful revelation. I was twenty years old; my senses were still dormant. Why? Oh, because I was ugly, the smiles of women were not addressed to me; I felt the mockery falling, burning, on to my heart. Yes, you laughed at me, at my ill-made face, at my somber and malevolent mind. But on nights of anger and fury, who then is avenged, my beautiful dreamers?

"But how did that thought surge from my brain? Mystery. It was a somber day, I was passing a church; the knell was tolling, funereal hymns could be heard, and I felt a shock. From that moment, I was lost! Oh, I'm very unhappy...!

"It's midnight, the weather is black, the streets are deserted; yes, yes, that's how I need the nights to be! Oh, a fatal intoxication is taking hold of me, that darkness attracts me, my brain is emitting waves of hallucinating illusions.

"I'll go.

"Yes, I'll go again tonight, my last; after this, it will be finished—yes, finished forever. Human weakness! How I deceive myself...

"No, if I go there this evening, I'll go tomorrow, and then the following night, until the end. I'll have the courage, the strength. I'll stay. Yes, the struggle will be terrible. My fatal nature will crush me in a robust grip, but I'll vanquish it...!"

The unfortunate man, his head in his clenched hands, appeared to be fighting with an impetuous obsession, a vehement attraction. He mistrusted himself. As his resolution weakened, he called upon the aid of a material barrier; he closed and locked his door, removed the key precipitately from the lock and threw it into the street. Then, having violently closed his windows, he said to himself, in a low and hesitant tone: "Now I'm locked in, I won't be going out!"

He went into his alcove, threw himself on his bed, and everything became silent.

Passion is coercible, but like vapor; compression multiplies its force a hundredfold.

Half an hour went by. The curtains stirred; a shadow emerged from the obscurity. It really was Lodore, but his physiognomy was no longer the same. Calm was extended over his face, animated by a slight expression of strange sensuality. His eyes were piercing; the struggle was over.

He advanced tranquilly toward the door, and, unable to open it, braced himself against it. The hinges grated, the lock and bolt screeched, but, in spite of an extraordinary strength, the door remained unbreakable. Twice the man circled his room, his cage. He hoisted up the window and plunged his gaze into the street. Houses in London are not high.

Coldly, without fever or precipitation, he went back to his bed, brought out the sheets, rolled them into a rope, and, attaching one extremity to the window-sill, threw the rest outside. As calm as if he had been stepping over the back of a bench, he stepped over the dormant balustrade and, holding on to the unfurled sheets, slid down almost to the ground. Entirely in his right mind, he searched for the key that he had thrown out, put it in his pocket, and headed, without haste, along Farringdon Street toward Blackfriars Bridge.

Lord Lodore advanced at an ordinary pace, his head inclined before him like someone reflecting, or rather, taking pleasure in the futurition of an event. He went down Great Surrey Street, turned left on to London Road and engaged thereafter in the long perspective of Kent Road. The clock on the platform of the Dover Railway Station chimed one o'clock.

Lodore walked for a long time, but without haste. Finally, he stopped, almost outside the city, in front of a wall: the wall of New Cross Cemetery.

The atmosphere was still; the murmur of the great city had died down. Had it not been for the fog of ruddy clouds over London, one might have believed oneself in the heart of the country, far from human beings.

It is not so many years since cemeteries were established in London as in Paris. Before then, people were buried in churchyards—the grounds of churches. That custom is still observed in English towns, but, judging with reason that those nuclei of pestilence placed in the heart of a great city might have a harmful effect on public health, four necropolises were opened outside the city limits. New Cross Cemetery is the most modest; it is London's Montparnasse.

The Anglicans devote no great pomp to their dead. A simple stone on which a Bible verse is engraved, or, more rarely a truncated column; that is all. The touching cares that is observed religiously in France, especially in Paris—tombs covered in flowers, the continuity of life that seems to pursue the dead to the depths of the tomb; all that relates he memory to strangers—is unknown in England. The pathways are lined with black cypresses and green fir-trees.

In the obscurity, Lodore's shadow was confused with the dark wall. His silhouette appeared momentarily on the crest. He reached a cypress and slid silently to the ground.

Since his departure from Snow Street, from time to time, a discreet shadow had appeared in the distance behind him, following him through the night, vanishing when he stopped. That shadow climbed the wall in the same place as the lord, and like him, melted into the branches of the cypress.

Now, Mr. Mob having had the misfortune to lose his little sister two days before, in spite of his apprehensions regarding a more distant end, was waiting that same night in a corner of New Cross Cemetery for the vampire to come and exhume the cadaver, as the resurrectionist Digger had told him to do. He had been there for more than three hours, and his impatience increased every time the clock chimed—but he deceived himself as to the slowness of the time by letting his imagination caress in advance the hours of happiness that awaited him subsequently.

In fact, was not Mr. Mob to receive, on delivery of the cadaver, seven shillings and sixpence, and did not such a sum promise indescribable joys in the cheery abode of the Foxes' Den? He calculated with leisure and joy the number of bitters that the sum in question promised. Thirty bitters!

But the time flew, and the vampire did not appear. The eye, adapted to the dense obscurity, distinguished in the distance the black boles of trees, the flat branches of firs, the gray columns of tombs. By virtue of an excessively taut fixity, inert objects sometimes seemed to take on living forms. The shells of Mob's large ears, always at war with his hat, resonated with unfamiliar rustles. Gradually, his creative imagination stimulated his thoughts; the only living being in the midst of a population of the dead, he was afraid. A frisson passed over his head; his gaze became troubled; his own movements frightened him.

In the background of that black canvas, a shadow stood out, and advanced; Mob recognized it as a man. One might have thought him a poet dreaming in the evening amid the pathways of a park He was walking slowly, looking ahead. Above his black costume, his face stood out like the marble of a tomb in the night of cypresses.

Fear took possession of Mob. For fear of attracting the vampire's attention, he did not want to breathe, but that appeared to him to be difficult.

The place indicated by Digger was good. From the height of a swelling in the terrain, it overlooked the entire slope of the cemetery devoted to humble burials. The freshly-filled-in grave of the little sister stood out for an expert eye, blacker than the others.

When the vampire passed close to Mob, the latter thought that he recognized him, but in the disorder of his mind, he could not bring back to memory the circumstances that had already placed him in front of that face. The strange man suddenly lost his height, and advanced into the field of graves crawling. Mob's troubled eyes could scarcely follow him. He stopped in a place not far distant from his sister, clung to the ground like a leech, and sank into it.[30]

The dead woman's brother did not budge from his observatory. Suddenly, however, his attention was attracted in another direction. Along the same pathway that the vampire had followed, another man came. He went by quickly and was soon lost in the cypresses.

That human presence disturbed Mob. Perhaps it was a resurrectionist, with whom he would have to dispute his little sister. At any rate, as his imagination always traveled at a very

---

[30] Graves were shallower in 1851 than they are nowadays, but even so, there seems to be something suspiciously supernatural about Lodore's ability to exhume bodies without the aid of a spade.

placid pace, the dead did not frighten him. He did not even accord a thought to all the tenebrous things that might be passing in the silence of the cemetery. The good brother only aspired to two things: to be out of New Cross Cemetery with his little sister on his back, and to go into the Foxes' Den with seven and sixpence in his pocket.

Lodore suddenly emerged from the ground and finally crawled toward the place where Miss Mob was resting.

The man who was following him drew nearer, and, in order to hide from Lodore's view, descended into the ditch that he had just abandoned.

At the bottom of that ditch lay an open coffin, and in the coffin was a cadaver.

Robert—for it was him—lit a muted lantern that only projected its light downwards, leaving the orifice of the hole dark. The body lying there was that of a man.

The man's eyes opened.

Rolleboise froze,

With a convulsive movement, the dead man stood up in front of the living one, his gaze haggard, touched the walls of the ditch by way of reconnaissance, and, without saying a word, suddenly launched himself out of the hole.

The buried man was nude, and his shroud scarcely covered him.

During that strange mute scene, Mob had courageously slid closer to his sister's grave, abandoned by the vampire. He had only to pick up the cadaver. On emerging from the grave, he ran toward the wall, and ran into the first exhumed individual, who was running on his own.

Mob recognized that phantom as Bertram, the coachman from the Foxes' Den.

The apparition stimulated his fear, and his pace. He bounded like an antelope. Arriving at the foot of the wall, he threw the cadaver over to the other side, where it as heard to fall on to the road. Then, clinging to asperities in the stones, he hoisted himself up on to the crest.

Behind him, Bertram climbed up, enveloped in his white sheet.

Mob, seized by the leg, uttered a cry and fell back, stunned, into the cemetery.

Bertram passed over the body and leapt down outside, on to the flaccid body of Miss Mob.

XXXI. A Case of Love at First Sight

Let us return to Paris. We shall encounter one of our characters there, Robert de Rolleboise.

It was not without a secret anxiety that the young man returned to the society that had suddenly lost sight of him. He was frightened of the expansive existence that suddenly succeeded the contained life in London. The gaze of the crowd weighed upon him.

They days had flown by. The wound inflicted on his pride no longer offered more than a scar that had almost faded away. His heart only gave the occasional thought to Mathilde. His passion was extinct; but the events into which a fatal hand had drawn him frightened him. Hanging on to the jagged edge of the gulf, he shivered under the influence if vertigo. Like many men, he had been able to dream about a strange and romantic existence, but the reality of the dream overwhelmed him like a nightmare. What would he not have sacrificed to destroy that past, to extract himself from the circle that retained him? But he had only traversed the laborious part of the drama; the supreme moment was still in store for him, and in advance, he took pleasure in that vengeful contrivance.

Paris, dream; London, reality. Here, one desires; there, one loves.

There is on the banks of the Seine a class of idle young men who employ their youth exclusively with amour. That, at least, is what they name the brutal and cavalier sentiment that runs its course in certain boudoirs. Then, one day, weary of women of pleasure and the divinities of the theater, inert in the company of plaster faces and chloroformed hearts, they marry. And, utterly bewildered, they consider their young wife as a phenomenon. They believe themselves to be disillusioned by the spectacle of love, but have only seen its décor. Their mores are ignorant of preludes, mysteries, the great silent joys that the heart procures as it blossoms.

But what is sad is that, after having lost faith in the realities of youth, those poor individuals return to their province, pose as miniature Richelieus or Brummells, and calumniate the women of Paris. For them, Paris is the Breda quarter; their fêtes are limited to orgies in the establishment of a restaurateur renowned among grooms and whores—which is to say, respectable chambermaids and kitchen-maids abducted from their antechambers and kitchens.

The behavior of those young bourgeois comprises a buffoonery that has always amused me, broadly combing the two elements of burlesque: the stupid and the ridiculous. While handsome "sportsmen" court hetaerae and actresses uglier than themselves, cretins and simpletons attack real women and succeed. And the spectacle of those things constitutes one of the great entertainments of the century!

Watch one of them pass by, those beautiful girls as pale as hothouse flowers. Her mouth is disdainful, her gaze limpid and mendacious. She laughs falsely at the young man who is talking to her. The whole crowd admires her. The adolescent darts a fearful glance at her; the man sends her a piratical wink, which she grasps; the old man stops and turns round shamelessly. Oh, she is very beautiful, very splendid, that pale young girl thus displayed by her mother.

Now, adjourn to the moment of the great action of a woman's life, marriage. She will appear palely that day, because the poor virgin will still be pure—she will only have loved her confessor; a stupid and dirty language-teacher; an old "lion" wearing a wing-collar; a valet in her father's house!—and the beautiful girl marries a churl, a Thersites whom she will love and pamper, and who will render her jealous.[31]

In hours of reflection, Robert was frightened on the past. His pride was no longer bleeding. It was necessary for him to gather up all his courage.

---

[31] Thersites is a Greek soldier featured in the *Iliad*, represented by Homer as vulgar, lewd, dim-witted and ugly.

Nevertheless, there remained a love that he had not experienced. A woman had driven him mad, but his heart whispered to him that a virgin heart might make him happy. Happy! Alas, had he not descended into a circle where hatred alone could preside over his dreams? Could his heart be reignited? He marched despairingly in his fatal path, cursing the evil hour during which that pitiless genius had seized him.

Certainly, there are beings—I do not say human beings—who live without love, who laugh at those who love; individuals occupied in raising and lowering, looking at a woman as one does a landscape, or uttering at the sight of her a stupid exclamation, like those people who wax coldly ecstatic before a painting or a melody they do not understand. Such men are either superior minds or imbeciles; superior minds are rare.

Robert did not understand the life beyond love, but he neither was he so poor in dreams as to accept the limit. Besides which, in the intelligent milieu in which he lived, and in which one extracts from existence all the sensations it contains, it was impossible for him to remain inert.

In Paris it is necessary to be a tradesman, to understand double-entry book-keeping, and to read about the day's parliamentary session in the *Moniteur* every evening, in order not to be carried away by the torrent of the passions. Robert's life, fortunately, was sheltered from commerce; his high intelligence distanced him from politics; he had nothing left but society.

Now, society frightened him, but the quest for isolation only augmented attention. Like the man who faints in the street, who needs air, and whom the crowd stifles by surrounding him, so he too feared the gaze of the curious crowd. In fact, he had been noticed. The grim and mysterious young man, always face-to-face with an obsessive thought, occupied some and intrigued others. Some thought he was in love, others that he was mad; he alone knew his misfortune.

Incapable of overcoming his destiny and adapting himself to the necessities of a new life, he fell into a moral depression. The social world lost sight of him. Solitude took possession of him: the brutal Parisian solitude that labors so violently those who plunge into it and renders them idiots or makes them strong.

One day, Robert was coming out of the galleries of the Palais-Royal; he was pensive and morose: it was one of those sad hours in which thought weighs upon the brain with all the density of reason, moments when noise is uncomfortable, crowds inconvenient.

Carriages were going past in both directions, rapid and ardent. Robert threw himself into the Rue de Valois. That somber quarter, a block of houses ripped by three or four tortuous dead-end streets into which one dare not venture, distracted him. His inquisitive and curious gaze sought to penetrate the obscure alleys, to divine the interiors of the smoky dwellings. He was pleased by that sudden tranquility. He was waking slowly, his head nodding thoughtfully.

A face appeared at a window. Robert's gaze fell upon that face. It was a woman.

Indubitably, there is a real affinity, a tendency to rapprochement, between certain individuals. There is a fateful law that regulates us, which we call chance, a mysterious and occult attraction that guides us. Robert was subject to that influence when, the following day, at the same time, he traversed the same street, the Rue des Quinze-Vingt. He had not thought about that fact, had not waited for that moment to go out, but nevertheless, while he was thinking about other things, his steps led him to the same place. Why was the woman also leaning on her window-sill at the moment when he passed by?

Perhaps by chance.

Robert noticed that it was a young face. Before turning the street corner, he looked back. The following day, a second observation was planted in his brain. The face combined two advantages: youth and beauty. This time, when he turned round, the young woman withdrew slowly.

In his existence, as he had arranged it, that apparition was an event. He reflected upon it. Love is an endemic disease that most commonly strikes young people between eight and twenty-eight years of age. It is not a dangerous infection. Nosology can oppose several efficacious remedies to it, but not one preventative. It is the complete opposite of cholera.

Was Rolleboise in love? No. But perhaps he felt a faint premonitory symptom of the disease. A slight vapor floated over his errant thought. He went back to the Rue des Quinze-Vingt.

Once, the window was closed. For the rest of the day, Robert was sad; in the evening, he recognized, fearfully, that he was in love.

Generally, an illness that does not threaten to lead to the tomb does not attract anyone's commiseration. All that people say is that you won't die of it. The misery doesn't count for anything. People are frightened more by a sudden death than a trespass laboriously conquered with the aid of an entire pharmacopeia. That is, surely, a poor employment of pity. Thus, I feel as sorry for those who suffer from love as I do for those who suffer from toothache—which is saying a lot. And it is doubtless because it is terrible that the former are commonly referred to as lovesick.

So, Robert was in love, dazedly in love, solely on the strength of a face. There are people who consider love from a very restricted viewpoint. A head seen face-on is sufficient for them; they would never think of falling in love with a woman of whom they have only seen the back of the head. The genetic instinct is a buffoon. Given that, I am not far off believing in second sight in amorous matters. A lover, of course, on the simple perception of a gaze, a smile, builds in his mind without errors, by means of perception, the hidden things: the body, the mind, the character. He continues the lines, and if a defective reality looms up before him, it is only after the vanishment of the phantom created by love and the fall out of love.

Rolleboise had forgotten everything. The form of his character, alone, took pleasure in the strangeness of that love. So he marched prudently in that emergent passion.

The young woman thus perceived at a dull window of a large poor house had a sickly beauty. Her pale face was crowned with abundant and delicate blonde hair. Her pure forehead thought without dreaming, her eyes opened softly and sadly, and her mouth, slightly bitter, like a despairing smile spoke of a loving heart slowly dying. When the young man passed by she gave him the gaze that a prisoner accords to a ray of sunlight that falls into his darkness, and perhaps her physiognomy took on the defeated expression of a soul incapable of belief in happiness.

Oh, of all doubts, that is surely the most heart-rending, the only one that poisons all hope!

The young man loved her in an austere manner—because there are women for whom one desires celebrations, laughter and noisy joys, and others to whom one devotes solitude, a heart that is the echo of her heart, a silent ecstasy, a sad smile, a tear. Such was the form of his affection. He had divined the heart of that woman, and without worrying about the mystery that might surround it, his soul had submitted effortlessly to that serious contemplation, that mystical ravishment. In any case, the surrounding objects always influence the nature of a nascent sensation.

So, in those days, his heart lived in containment, delivered to a corrosive torment; furthermore, the sky was gray and heavy, the street was deserted, the house black, the window poorly garnished, and all of that built a somber frame for a thoroughly melancholy physiognomy.

Alas, the amour illuminated thus by the reflection of a tear is perhaps the truest of all, the one most intimate to the soul.

A powerful magnetism, that of the radiant eye! A strange fluid that penetrates the body, calming or galvanizing! How many times has a young woman dreamed all night about the gaze of a young man who has passed her by, a stranger she knows that she will never see again?

Thus, Robert and his melancholy unknown woman gazed at one another; two invisible rays had met, and, from that moment—or, rather, that commotion—on, a revolution had taken place within them.

Antipathetic rays repel. No matter how beautiful a woman might be, it happens that one remains insensitive to her gaze. Then the two characters are in conflict. We shall not hesitate to formulate an incontestable axiom here. Never retreat out of weakness from a woman whose gaze has acted upon you, because, if you persist, that woman will love you.

Without saying a word, at all hours of the day, those two young people united their thoughts. Every evening, they both entered into a happy dream, and in the morning, in the penumbra of sleep, savored their dream drowned in a demi-reality.

The sensations of the dawn of love are the sweetest. The perfume intoxicates more than the taste. That is very sad, especially for gourmands. And who is not a gourmand in everything, except for idiots and aged Protestants?

However, although he was in love, Robert did not behave stupidly in his happiness. Taking pleasure in the flowers and scents of the road, he walked slowly. One never sees an intelligent man hasten the denouement of amour, precipitating its phases. Some of them even slow down the preludes, idling in a situation that pleases them, enjoying a sojourn in an unforeseen incidence. But few women understand that strategy. Less sage than us, they disrupt all our plans. Women do not know how to love.

After all, love is not a cheerful thing, and I prefer caprice, for the same reason that vaudeville sometimes pleases me more than poetry. For every love one has many caprices! Love is sentiment in the form of an ingot; caprice is the same sentiment in coin.

Thus, when Robert had experienced all the first sensations, and minutely triturated the last essential grains, he thought about taking a forward step. One day, having penetrated into the Rue des Quinze-Vingt, he darted a glance at the houses facing the one inhabited by the unknown woman.

A painted board set over the lintel of a small narrow door, indicated a furnished hotel: one of those mysterious, obscure hotels in which disquieting things must necessarily be happening. A modest name, a crude sign washed by the rain, a dark alley closed by a grating that clicks as it closes. The windows are always veiled by red or yellow curtains; no hand ever moves them aside; no face ever shows itself there. I have always thought that strangers never go into those hotels, that they are exclusively haunted by beings apart, who scent the place and are known there. It is always in those establishments that strange suicides are accomplished, and arrests of shady politics are made. This one was entitled Hôtel de l'Aunis.

Robert went into the black alley uncertain as to whether he would go any further, but as the latch of the gate closed, the familiar sound was heard by a species of old woman, who immediately stuck her head out of the panel in the door of the lodge. One might have thought it the head of a condemned woman emerging from the guillotine beneath the blade descending in its groove.

Robert had a respectable appearance, so the concierge looked at him suspiciously. He asked for a room on the third floor at the front. The old head was retracted at two voices whispered. Eventually, after a brief interval, a woman less aged than the first, slightly better dressed, with one of those faces that look as if they have been dragged through nettles, grimaced an all-purpose smile and syrupy gaze at him. That oozing individual came out, not just to bring a light, which was certainly necessary, but to guide the important individual—who represented six or eight five-franc pieces a month—to the spiral staircase.

As they went up, the young man heard doors opening discreetly behind him and curious shadows venturing on to the landings. Undoubtedly, they were astonished to see a stranger seriously requesting accommodation. Only Paris has places of that sort: hotels where no one stays, cafés where no one eats, shops in which no one ever buys anything. Where is the new lame spirit who will tell us what goes on there?[32]

Finally, the young man was introduced into a room exactly similar to all furnished rooms. The piece was not discussed. Left alone, Robert advanced discreetly to the window protected by duty curtains and sprinkled with fly-specks. Across the street, the young woman was leaning on the window-sill.

The heart of our amorous young man was beating as if to burst. The human heart is like the pendulum of a clock, but less well-regulated.

It was the same beautiful faced glimpsed from afar, even more beautiful, but also, perhaps, sadder. Nothing was happening in the street, so it was occupied by a dream alone.

Now, what do young women dream about?

Then her indifferent gaze stopped on the window in the Hôtel de l'Aunis, still closed. She perceived a face and went pale. Alas, poor Robert immediately saw the beautiful apparition disappear.

He waited for an hour, but the window did not open again, and no shadow glided over the curtain. It did not matter; he considered himself fortunate. She had gone pale and withdrawn at the sight of him. The latter circumstance announced that he was recognized, but the former whispered suggestively to him that he was loved.

Robert strode back and forth in the room, joyfully. His radiant heart transformed the miserable luxury shivering around him. The furniture seemed less dull, the lithographs less grotesque. He graciously welcomed the landlady who brought him candles, illuminating her rubefactions with an unctuous smile.

---

[32] The reference is to Alain René Le Sage's *Le Diable boîteux* (1707; tr. as *The Devil on Two Sticks*), in which the amiable limping demon shows the young protagonist what is going on beneath the roofs of a great city.

She presented him with a large open book, the pages of which were lined in both directions and bore printed instructions. Unused to these sorts of lodgings, the young man did not understand the hotelier's gesture. The latter demanded his name, his age, his profession and birthplace. Robert counted out the price of the rent, and asked the proprietress of the Hôtel de l'Aunis, as the orthography of his name was rather arduous, to inscribe her own in its stead. No protest was raised at that strange arrangement, and the young man, left alone, blew out his candles. It was night, but the window opposite did not light up with any glimmer.

The evening went by; eleven o'clock chimed; the noises of the Rue Saint-Honoré and the vicinity of the Palais-Royal began to die down.

Rolleboise opened his window quietly, but remained in the darkness of the room. Seated in an armchair, his gaze fixed on the windows of the house opposite, he meditated. In fact, it was the first time that he had deigned to raise his head to look at a woman in a window, and what he had never felt in the society where reserved young women position themselves on days of repose, an unknown caused him to experience. After all, that intrigue presented itself as the first chapter of a novel; he had accepted it for that sole reason. But his heart was also in commotion, and Robert was one of those rare men who are slaves to that viscera.

He savored his love. Left to itself, his imagination gave birth to pyramids of hypotheses and built splendid castles in Spain untiringly.

Keen intelligences enjoy absence more than presence; their dreams surpass reality. Only geometric heads can delight in possession and utter hurrahs of joy. For the latter the honeymoon rises honestly on the horizon, but for the former it makes its first appearance at the zenith and, in consequence, is always bound to descend. Women are disheartening; they always love in accordance with the same system and pass immutably through the same phases. I have always suspected them of never venturing into a passion without a thermometer.

Finally, a light appeared in the mysterious room. A shadow was outlined on the curtain. Robert, endowed with the second sight that nature accords to the amorous, recognized the person who possessed his thoughts. Then a larger silhouette came to place itself beside her. The movements were prompt, the lines clearer; it was a man.

Young Rolleboise was ranked among those who are not jealous. He felt his love so strongly, had such belief in the power of sentiment, and had such scant doubt in his heart, that the presence of a third person did not disturb him. He could have looked savagely at a beautiful woman already possessed that his senses desired, but for a child that his soul adored, nothing could shake his adoration.

The large silhouette disappeared, and the light with it. The clocks chimed midnight. The sky overhead was one of those fine nights at the end of autumn, and the moon was spreading its pale radiance over all the houses on one side of the street; the shadow protected Robert's window.

The window opened silently, the young woman leaned on the sill and looked up at the heavens. The white light struck her pale face. She seemed to Rolleboise as beautiful as a Madonna, and he applauded that, for, in spite of love, the vanity of a lover is always flattered by real beauty. The young man devoured her with his gaze, and fascinated her with all his soul, so the young woman, yielding to the attraction of that vehement magnetism, allowed her gaze to descend into the obscurity.

She could see. Love multiples all the sensory faculties a hundredfold.

She tried to withdraw, but in vain; her gaze was riveted, held by an invisible bond.

Without the aid of a light, Robert traced a few words in pencil on a card. In the darkness, his hand fell on a few flowers, perhaps forgotten the day before by happy lovers, and which were wilting sadly in a blue vase. The life of a flower is sometimes a novel. That poor bouquet was attached to the card, and its helpful weight carried the piece of paper to its destination. Immediately, though, the woman disappeared and the window closed.

Robert left the Hôtel de l'Aunis excessively happy.

Then, stopping as if seized by a sudden reflection, he said to himself: *I've met that woman before!*

XII. A Morsel of Bread!

That unknown woman fallen thus into the life of Robert de Rolleboise resided, as we have said, in a third-floor apartment in a house of mediocre appearance. Her room was neat, cold and poor. The walls and floor offered their gray nudity disagreeably to the eye. The furniture, shameful in its insufficiency, was shabby and ugly. The bed, as sad and narrow as a coffin, did not invite repose.

The morning was coming to an end. The young woman was sitting at a table, pensively. One could remark in her clothing the dilapidated luxury that announces a decline in fortune, a memory at which present poverty sniggers. Her black satin dress had pale patches and was frayed in the arms. A simple headscarf covered her shoulders. Her face, admirable in the purity of its lines, displayed pallor and distress. Of everything surrounding her, only her hair had conserved its beauty, ornamenting her head like a sultana's turban.

It was ten o'clock. At times, the young woman repressed involuntary yawns. She was not yawning out of boredom.

In front of her, on the table, there was a card, on which a few lines written in pencil appeared. Her large blue eyes could not tear themselves away from that name. Her mouth, which had perhaps forgotten how to smile, nevertheless designed a softened line, and her bosom sometimes rose with secret aspirations. Gradually, her head leaned forward, and her mouth placed itself on those penciled lines. She remained bent over thus momentarily; then, when she straightened up, her physiognomy was covered with a blushing expression of confusion.

"It's really him!" she murmured. "Alas! As long as he doesn't recognize me!"

But a noise that was doubtless familiar became audible outside. The card disappeared. The door opened. A man came in.

The second individual, tall, with a thin but strong constitution, might have been forty or fifty years of age. His dry face bore an expression that was more austere than sad, and his gaze was illuminated by an indefinable gleam.

"You went out early this morning, Antares," said the young woman, in an affectionate tone.

The latter approached her, and kissed her forehead before replying.

"Vainly, alas, my poor Ophelia," he said, in English. "I've knocked on many doors, addressed myself to many hearts, but without success. No matter—I shall save you; I want to; I've sworn to do so!"

"Today, when so many miseries weigh upon the city, for what can you, a foreigner, hope?"

"Oh, don't try to shake the moral strength that sustains me! Dear Ophelia, you cannot know how much affection I bear for you! Thus, there are terrible hours when, alone, I would kill myself, but for you, I resist. Yes, it's when the memory of the past comes to harass my brain!"

"Let's not talk any more, good Antares, about extinct times."

"Beautiful child," he went on, leaning the blonde head against himself, "you'll forgive me, I know, but my memory cannot efface them thus! Also, I didn't know you; I was unaware of the sweetness of your heart, the purity of your soul, on the day when I listened to the deadly proposition that threw you into my life. But soon I had a revelation. When I was told to extinguish your existence, I shivered at the thought of that crime, and I came to love the victim that I had wanted to doom. You'll forgive me one day, won't you, Ophelia, for the violence committed when I pushed you into a world of vice and infamy. I only considered you then as an ordinary young woman, whom pleasure would immediately conquer...you had been calumniated...and then...I was paid! Oh, no matter; I was infamous, Ophelia, and you will only forgive me when I have saved you...for I shall save you! Oh, to give you bread, I will resort to crime again, if necessary..."

"Oh! Don't say that, Antares!"

"Have you eaten this morning?" he asked, sadly.

"I was waiting for you. Have you?"

"Can you think, child, that I would eat out there, when I know that you're suffering here? Is there any of yesterday's bread left?"

"A little, I think," said the young woman, in a heart-rending tone. And, having risen to her feet, she took a small piece of dry bead out of a cupboard—a quantity scarcely sufficient for a little child.

"That's very little," said Antares, with a painful smile.

"Eat it all—I'm not hungry."

"Oh, don't have recourse to a lie to hide your need from me! You scarcely ate anything yesterday evening. Poor child! At your age, it's deplorable not to be able to nourish oneself."

"I don't go out—how to you expect me to have an appetite?"

"Appetite! Yes, when one has enough to eat one calls hunger appetite. One dares not make use of the veritable word!"

Antares divided the piece of bread, but unequally. He placed the larger part in front of the young woman. That portion weighed less than an ounce. The morsel he reserved for himself was equivalent to two mouthfuls. But the generous child immediately rejected the larger piece and took possession of the smaller one.

"Oh, please—you've been walking all morning, you're tired and you're giving me almost all of the bread!"

"Don't refuse, Ophelia, I beg you...you're weaker than I am."

But the poor child fell at his feet and looked at him with an imploring expression. Her large blue eyes, full of tears, spoke of so much generosity, that Antares did not insist. He ate the larger part. The young woman swallowed her bread in two mouthfuls and drank a mouthful of water as well.

That insufficient nourishment only served to reawaken torpid hunger.

Hunger! A frightful monster that devastates cities, a shameful need, which often takes hold of infants in the cradle, tortures them throughout their lives and only releases them to the grave. There are people who make a profession of being hungry, who hurl that word at your pity, pursue you with that banal lamentation, to whom one gives without commiseration. Those, one only pities partially. The man in a blouse, the woman in rags, hold out their hands by virtue of habit; one gives to them; and the following day, they start again. But those wearing suits, those with hats, from whom can they ask bread? Shame retains them in the shadows, in the unknown obscurity in which frightful dramas swarm. Hunger has horrible accoutrements when it knocks on certain doors.

"Have you any news from London?" asked the young woman.

"From whom? From your sister? From your brother-in-law, Horatio Mackinguss? He's more false and barbaric than Olivia. They're powerful. At the slightest word, the merest gesture of a threat, we'd both fall, my dear Ophelia! To ask for alms is to reveal that one is alive, and death alone protects us from them. Oh, if your father were still alive we could go to him, but..."

"He's dead. The only one who loved me!"

"Yes—he thought he would find you again on high."

"Alas, my only refuge is with him!"

"Don't add that sad thought to the sum of your anguish, my daughter. Come on, be brave! I'm going out again."

"Where are you going?"

"I don't know, but we need bread. If necessary, I'll employ the ultimate means, but I'll get some."

"What will you do, then?" asked the young woman, anxiously.

"I'll put out my hand—I'll beg! I'll search the crowd for an honest face, a man who might be a father; I'll tell him that I have a hungry child; I'll beg him; I'll weep—and if ever he too has experienced misfortune, he'll listen to me. This evening, Ophelia, you'll have bread."

After having pronounced those words in a tone of desperate affection, the man who called himself Antares took her in his arms, kissed her forehead, and left.

When she was alone, the young woman picked up the carafe of water and took a long draught. She was in that frightful period of hunger when thirst is predominant.

Noon sounded at the Palais-Royal and the Tuileries; the sun warmed up the atmosphere outside. The sky was blue, but the Rue des Quinze-Vingts remained somber at all times, and the interior of the room cold.

Many hours had gone by like that in the life of that woman. She had been hungry for several months, and her nourishment became more insufficient every day. She saw the companion of her life regularly, twice a day. Every morning and evening he came to extinguish, with an interior tear, the glimmer of hope that was reborn the following day. The day went by silently, like the night. She would have seemed less neglected in a prison; in a prison, she would have eaten. Here, no one spoke to her; she had nothing to distract her: no noise; no book. She was scarcely twenty. At that age, one delights in following a dream through chimerical sinuosities, but a dream, a sterile desire, cannot satisfy and leaves nothing after it but lassitude and disenchantment.

She went to her couch, and from beneath the cushion on which her head had rested her pale hand withdrew a few flattened flowers. Where had those flowers come from? She would not have admitted it to anyone, even herself. Those dead flowers were laid on her table, where they rejoined the mysterious card. Leaning on her elbow, with her head in her hand, Ophelia looked at them for a long time. She forgot her hunger.

"Alas, is it not a helpful force, a benevolent consolation that Heaven is sending me? Always, in my somber night of misery and suffering, close beside the memory of my poor father, who doubted his child, I perceived a smiling image in my heart, a phantom that I loved. And a secret voice told me that it wasn't entirely a dream, but the reflection of a reality! Yes, I took him for my good angel, and I believed in him...

"Then, once, one evening, among men and women that I didn't understand, when I wanted to run away, frightened, I recognized my beloved phantom. I stayed...he was near me...serious, like me; his smile was sad and pensive. Then, I don't remember any more. I had a fever. I was carried away...he was still close to me, calm and tranquil...we were alone...then, everything vanished! But I still dreamed about him.

"The voice of the dream told me that he would come back...and he has...these are his flowers, this is his card...every evening, I see him again, but I'm afraid! He seems more beautiful to me what when he appeared to me in the guise of a phantom. Antares doesn't believe in phantoms. When I talk to him about one of our Scottish beliefs, he laughs in a way that makes me feel ill.

"Yes, it's really him, he tells me that here in these two lines. He dreamed about an angel! Me too...oh, thank you, Lord, thank you, for the help and happiness you've sent me!"

Ophelia stood up and took a step toward the window. Discreetly, her finger lifted a corner of the curtain, demanding just enough room to place her eyes—but she withdrew immediately, very pale.

The poor child, paling at emotions that make one blush!

What had she seen? Did she even know? At the same moment that her gaze had risked itself, an eye had also ventured forth in a corner of the curtain at the window opposite. The two gazes had met. But all of a sudden, a vertigo had passed over her eyes, objects appeared to move, and she fell into a chair. She drank.

Those symptoms of weakness were attributed to an emotion of the heart. The unfortunate child had forgotten her hunger, but the hunger had not forgotten her!

She fell back into tangible life. Nervous oscitations gripped her, atrocious cramps tortured her breast, where a continual fire maintained an artificial thirst. The pains frightened her. She shivered under the influence of the vertigo. It seemed to her that she was about to faint on to the bare floor, and the thought that she would lie there, without help, gasping with hunger, gave her a desperate resolution.

"He'll come back this evening, as he did yesterday," she said to herself, "without money and without bread. And if I don't eat, will I die tonight? Oh, I don't want to die now! It's impossible for me to die of hunger; I haven't done anyone any harm, and I've had nothing but tears in my life! It would be unjust for me to expiate some great sin, of which my conscience is innocent and which someone else committed! Yes, I'm going to go out; the warmth of the sun, the noise, will give me courage. Then, how shall I not find something to eat in this great city, where everyone eats? Oh, I hate this bare, cold room, where nothing smiles at you! Warm air, life, sunlight!"

She went out with the urgency that a person gripped by suffering and wanting to numb it puts into everything. Scarcely had she crossed the threshold than she felt stronger. The change of location distracted her mind. Having reached the middle of the alleyway, near the door, she stopped; then she advanced slowly, looking up. The window at which the young man had appeared was closed; the curtains fell over all the corners. The young woman launched herself out into the street.

In the distance, tall trees appeared crowned with sunlight. It might have been four o'clock.

The Rue de Rivoli was quivering with the noise of carriages, horses, and the crowd. All of it was rolling, galloping, talking, laughing. In the midst of that movement, that luxury, those cheerful and serious faces, indifferent to the poor girl going by, Ophelia was stunned. Confused to find herself unknown and alone in that society, she traversed the isolated parts of the wood in the Tuileries, went past the Place de la Concorde and found herself facing the great avenue of the Champs-Élysées. Leaning on the parapet of the sunken gardens, she waited for the carriages to leave her a passage in order to cross over.

The sun was setting behind the trees, which were ablaze. A dry and bitter wind had covered the earth with a litter of yellow leaves which crackled underfoot. The baldness of the high branches was reaching the last boughs.

The poor famished child, darting needy glances from side to side at the merchants' shop-fronts, where gnarled loaves of spiced bread and planispheres of mediocre maca-roons were on display—but she would have preferred bread. When she reached the Carré Marigny, she no longer felt strong enough to go on. Where was she going? Would not hunger, her constant companion, pursue her everywhere?

A dazzle troubled her sight. Pale and exhausted, she leaned against a tree. Her eyes closed. A solitary and idle stroller mistook her for one of those mute mendicants who do not ask, but whose supplicant expression implores alms. By way of caprice, or rather, commiseration, he placed a ten cen-time piece in the child's hand and continued his stroll without suspecting that he might just have saved the life of a dying woman.

On contact with that gloved hand, Ophelia reopened her eyes. Her cheeks colored with shame, and overcome by emo-tion, she plunged into the dark part of the wood. The place was solitary; no strollers appeared. The poor, grateful girl knelt down next to a bench and thanked God.

Having finished her prayer, she returned to the streets with a firm tread via the Madeleine. She stopped in front of a baker's shop. Several people were making purchases. Her ti-midity forced her to wait until they had gone. She went in. A certain sentiment of delicacy forbade her to have the two sous' worth of bead cut into two, so she took it in one piece. It was well-gilded, very appetizing, but also very small! Neverthe-less, she did not want to touch it. Her heart had not forgotten that her protector was also suffering, and was perhaps humili-ating himself for her sake. She permitted herself to smell it, though. The little piece of bread was embalmed!

Alas, that was all she had of it!

Her precipitate pace soon brought her to the vicinity of the Palais-Royal. A certain energy sustained her. He would not be long in coming.

A man was following her. He was immediately recognizable as an Englishman; his costume and gait announced that. On looking more attentively, however, we recognize Sir James Cawdor, Baronet.

Although she was wearing garments of excessive simplicity, one divined on sight that Ophelia was a beautiful woman. Her figure, above all, stood out, remarkable in its delicacy and noble distinction.

Sir James looked at her with satisfaction. An entirely British indulgence wandered over his face and shone in his eyes. The Baronet, as we have said, had a rather significant temperament with regard to women. Sir James is one of our great resources.

Paris was lighting up; the shops illuminating. The Englishman drew alongside the young woman, looking down at her with a searching gaze. He began to speak, slowly and phlegmatically.[33]

"Oh yes, I was most delighted, very glad, to meet you. You are, indeed, magnificent"

Ophelia crossed the street and continued on her way on the opposite sidewalk.

"Oh, you can't run away! Your hair gives me pleasure, a great deal."

"Monsieur, I beg you!"

"Great pleasure! I'm in love with your hair! Don't be frightened by my language...I'm English, and, moreover, an eccentric man. I have the habit, when I encounter a woman who pleases me, of taking a souvenir from her. Oh, don't be afraid, I'll pay for the little souvenir—I always pay."

"Monsieur, I truly don't know..."

---

[33] The original text renders Sir James' subsequent speech in bad French, with occasional English intrusions, so the effect is somewhat lost in translation.

"Ah yes! You don't know what an eccentric man is! Listen, don't walk so quickly; the pavements are very narrow in Paris. Yes, yes, I'm in love with your hair. The other day, I met a shopgirl. Her nose reminded me of another...another that I loved too much! She had one of those big boxes in her arms, for storing hats and dresses. I bought it from her for a souvenir of her nose. Yes, I went back to my hotel, London Hotel, well content, with my box under my arm. I shall keep it always!"

Ophelia returned to the sidewalk she had quit, but the Baronet was too smitten with "his" hair to abandon her thus. The young woman looked at him with a gaze so supplicant that he should have perceived that it was inappropriate to speak to her in flirtatious Britishisms, but how could an Englishman understand what a Frenchman never divines?

"Oh yes, your hair, it was, upon my word, very pretty! I want a souvenir, a little souvenir, and I'll leave you tranquil.

The poor child went into one of the dark passages in the vicinity of the Palais-Royal. The intrepid Baronet followed her into it.

"Oh, you're very amiable, Miss, Mademoiselle, to come here, where no one can see us. But I still wanted it, the souvenir of your hair and you. Look, give me your little piece of bread."

At that word, Ophelia wrapped both hands around her little treasure.

"Oh, have no fear, Miss, I wanted your little bread, it's true, but when I take a souvenir, I pay for it right away. I paid very well for the hat box. Here's a brand new Republican coin. I've paid five francs fifty centimes for it. They're very rare, these coins...I've bought many of them for my country. Go on, give me your little bread, I promise you to carry it for a long time over my heart, upon my word!"

Before the young woman could prevent it, the eccentric man had taken possession of her bread, leaving in its place a five franc piece. Then he disappeared.

After arriving in the street, Sir James threw the piece of bread into the gutter.

Ophelia did not know what to think of that originality, which was worth so much money to her—enough to live for at least four days. She gathered up her remaining strength and started walking in search of a bakery. She was so weak that at every moment it was necessary for her to lean against a wall. The slightest impact would have knocked her down. Her ears were ringing, her breast was burning, and stabbing pains were laboring her head.

Finally, she reached the door of a shop.

The merchant, possessed of one of those fat round faces announcing the absence of imagination, was lounging on a bench covered with red velvet and constellated with nails that had lost their gilt.

"What do you need, my lovely child?"

"I'd like a loaf of bread," the unfortunate starveling articulated, faintly.

"Ah! Mademoiselle is English; I know that accent. And here's one, as fresh as your face and perhaps as warm as your heart, eh? Should I weigh it?"

"No need." So saying, Ophelia deposited her coin on the counter.

The baker looked at the coin attentively and dropped it on the counter two or three times, where it rendered a dull, flat sound. In spite of his gallantry, the shopkeeper did not joke about hundred-sou pieces.

"What's this you're giving me, Mademoiselle?"

"Five francs."

"Five francs! Damn, it's not worth the heat that it would require to melt it down, this money." And with four of his fat fingers he folded the piece in two. "It's lead, my lovely child; I don't know whether or not you've been deceived, and you ought to thank me for not verifying the fact with the Commissaire of Police—but there are affairs one doesn't want to get mixed up in. Here, my young Englishwoman, here's your five francs."

The poor woman, struck with confusion and despair, stood there inert. She was still holding the four-livre loaf in her hands. The baker took it off her and guided her by the shoulder back to the sidewalk with a mocking honesty.

The feeble child, overwhelmed by shame and desperate, was at the end of her tether. She felt numb. Her legs were buckling. It was dark. It was the hour when the streets begin to fill with that idle, curious, intentional population of men who look around and women who take up positions in front of window-displays—the moment when Paris digests.

So, Ophelia, perceiving that people were looking at her, abandoned the noisy places. She was then at the intersection of the Rue de Richelieu and the Rue de Neuve-des-Petits-Champs. A damp and somber passage opened nearby. She went into it, went down a few steps and set forth into dirty and solitary streets by which the Palais-Royal is encircled.

She walked, or rather dragged herself, slowly. From time to time she sat down on steps. She wept,

Oh, there are complications of misfortune that would make the hearts of angels blaspheme! If the first alms had come from God, what evil will had caused that false coin to fall into her hand? How could her good angel, in whom she believed, about whom she had so often talked to her father, have witnessed such miseries? His influence must be very feeble not to be able to lighten the soul confided to his guard from the weight of her anguish!

But the poor wretch only shed tears. She dared not doubt.

A violent vertigo suddenly rose to her head, almost causing her to fall down. Her hand clung to one of the iron bars of a wine-merchant's shop. Behind those bars as a window that supplied daylight to a room where people were eating. A red curtain fell over the panes, but imperfectly.

By chance, Ophelia directed her troubled gaze into the interior of that room. A single man was sitting in front of a table on which several dishes were fuming. He was eating and drinking tranquilly.

It was Antares.

The young woman thought at first that she had been deceived by a resemblance, but a more attentive examination allowed her to recognize her companion in misfortune perfectly. Her first impulse was to fly toward him, but after reflection, the poor fearful creature did not dare. Her pure soul was incapable of suspicion, but, struck already by so much suffering, a victim of so many infamies and crimes, she had come to repress, timidly, the impulses of her heart.

However, a sudden thought, which she immediately forgot, came to her mind. Would she, in Antares' place, have paused tranquilly like that, to eat alone?

No matter—her lips did not form any reproach. Nevertheless, without daring to confess the reason to herself, she dared not go in.

The idea that her protector was not suffering like her, and hope, that deceitful mistress of which one cannot get rid, which awoke smiling, gave her courage, Courage treacherously imparts strength as intoxication creates wit.

Ophelia reached the galleries of the Comédie-Française, and a few minutes later, she went into her sad, cold room.

The sight of those four walls, where she always suffered, in body and in soul, was heart-rending. Her breast was burning. The cold water made her feel better.

Seven o'clock chimed. Her languid gaze went to the window, her pale hand raised the curtain. The window opposite was open, but no one was there. She went to her couch and let herself fall upon it.

An hour went by—an hour in which each second was a dolor.

Finally, there was a noise at the door. Antares came in. As we have seen him on the morning of the same day, his face wore a despairing, discouraged, fatigued expression.

Ophelia sat up on the couch and, without saying a word, extended her arms. The imploring pose of the young woman, whom hunger was killing, would have moved the most gangrenously egotistical heart.

Without responding to that touching invitation, Antares collapsed on a chair.

"My poor daughter," he murmured, in a slow and heart-broken voice, "I'm desperate! I've asked, I've begged, I've extended my hand, my eyes have wept. All in vain—no one turned round! They pass quickly, in order to forget quickly, before the man who implores!"

"And since this morning…?"

"I've been walking."

"Since his morning, you haven't eaten?"

"No. Now, it's finished; I have no more hope. As I crossed the Seine, I thought about hurling myself into it, but a memory revived my courage."

The young woman, her head slumped over her breast, made no reply. Before the desolate expression of that man, she doubted. But her eyes could not have deceived her. A horrible mystery was lurking behind that traitor's mask. So, she asked, in a fearful voice: "You must have suffered frightfully?"

"I've been suffering for a long time." Antares' voice emerged somber, almost grim. It was the tone of an unfortunate man rebelling against the perseverance of a fatal destiny.

"Of hunger?" she asked, more directly.

"Hunger! Yes, it's a long time since we had breakfast! That's true, I forget, in the tortures of my soul, all personal pain. I'm weary. Perhaps sleep will silence the hunger!"

"Are you not thirsty?"

"Thirsty? No, I'm hungry."

That response was a revelation for Ophelia. Antares was deceiving her.

Before the monstrosity of that drama, she shivered. It was a flash of lightning illuminating her entire past. That man, so unshakable in his atrocity, capable of such frightful hypocrisy, frightened her.

She forced any inquisitive word back into silence, for fear of illuminating suspicion in her torturer—for the man who was making her die of starvation might kill her for a word.

Her body collapsed on the bed and her eyes closed, as if yielding to sleep or a faint.

Antares believing it to be a commencement of death-throes, got up silently and headed for his room, like an actor returning to the wings.

When the door had closed, Ophelia sat up in the darkness, as white as a corpse. Kneeling on her couch, she prayed; but her prayer was short, because vertigo took possession of her.

As silent as a shadow, the young woman walked to the window, struck by the rays of the moon. Her eyes, adapted to the darkness, immediately distinguished the face of the young man facing her. She opened the window silently.

At the same moment, a note attached to a bouquet fell at her feet. Ophelia did not unseal the letter, but with a pencil she wrote on the envelope: *I have dreamed of my good angel. May I hope for protection, respect and help from him?*

The bouquet went back to fall at Robert's feet.

"Yes!" exclaimed the young man, in a low voice, across the narrow space of the street.

"Who will answer to me for you?"

"I swear to you!"

"On what?"

Robert went back into the room, and two seconds later, threw into Ophelia's room a little locket containing a minia-ture. The paper in which it was wrapped contained these lines:

This is the portrait of my mother. If I deceive you, spit on it, break it and throw it in a gutter!

The young woman ran to the door. With all possible pre-caution, she opened the latch, stopping at the slightest grating sound, trembling that she might see the door of Antares' room opening.

How frightened she was on hearing the same sound in the other's door!

A hand was slowly turning the handle.

Antares was not asleep and was introducing himself into the presence of his victim, perhaps in order to witness the final act of his work.

In the face of that danger, Ophelia maintained her composure. Covered by the rumble of a carriage, she opened the door and launched herself on to the wooden staircase.

Robert was waiting for her in the street. She flew toward him, took his hand and drew him away, crying: "Run!"

They marched at a rapid pace, without speaking, for a quarter of an hour.

The exhausted Scotswoman stopped.

"You're weakening!" said the young man, putting his arm around her.

"Oh, save me!"

"Yes, but what do you need? Speak!" Robert cried, bewildered by the mysterious proportions that his adventure was taking on.

"Accord me what I asked of you…give it to me…and then, leave me alone…stay away…without seeing me!"

"But tell me what you want!"

Ophelia straightened up, by a last effort, extended her arm toward a shop, and in a croaking, avid voice, she cried: "A morsel of bread!"

XXIII. Antares Divided

The person whose hand was turning the handle of the door did not hear Ophelia go out, because, after her departure, the metallic noise continued with the same discretion.

Scarcely five minutes had gone by since the young woman had disappeared when someone came up the stairs, and stopped on the threshold of the door, which had been left ajar.

It was Sir James Cawdor.

The Baronet had almost taken the narrow corridor preceding the apartment when, on perceiving that someone had opened the door of the room in which Antares slept, he stopped.

A few seconds later, the door began slowly to rotate on its hinges. Undoubtedly, Ophelia's companion was not expecting such an encounter, to judge by the pallor that suddenly overtook his face.

Sir James' amazement, although it was of an entirely different nature, was no less, and was inevitably translated by a very British guttural exclamation. "Oh! That's strange!"

"Shh!" said Antares, dragging the gentleman into his lodgings and immediately closing the door that he had opened with so much precaution.

"But there's no mistake!" the Baronet exclaimed, again, looking him up and down repeatedly as if he were stitching him with his visual ray. "It really is in the presence of the Earl that I have the advantage of finding myself?"

"Himself. Well, what do you want?" said the pretended Jew, ill-humoredly.

"I was expecting to meet someone named Antares here."

"So was I. I didn't find him. He's probably gone out."

"This really is his apartment?"

"I suppose so."

"That's strange!" observed Sir James.

"Not at all, sir. We've both come looking for someone who's absent, that's all."

"That's true. I'll wait, then. Nevertheless, forgive me, Count, for the perhaps inconvenient singularity of my observation, but your costume is quite bizarre. It's doubtless by virtue of eccentricity that you're wearing a blouse in Paris?"

"No, sir."

"Ah!"

"I have reasons for that, unknown to you."

"Ah!"

"Sir down sir."

"Ha ha! I've already thought of that, Milord, but it seems to me that our friend Antares' room is as insufficiently furnished as a theater waiting room. And it's cold in here."

So saying, the Baronet sat down phlegmatically in front of a fireplace in which two microscopic brands covered with ash were reminiscent of two glow-worms having an intimate conversation.

"Something that I've noticed before, Milord..."

"Ah! What?"

"Yes...is he striking resemblance that exists between you and Antares."

The Earl did not reply. His arms folded, his face contracted with impatience, he was walking back and forth.

"It is, in fact, the same face. On placing a wig on your head, and spectacles on our eyes, a dressing-gown on your body, I'm convinced that we have no need to wait for our friend."

After these words, Sir James emitted a little snigger, which left no doubt in his interlocutor's mind.

"Well, what do you want with me?"

"Listen, my dear Antares, or Earl, if that second appellation rings better in your ears, believe that I only owe to hazard the discovery of this little mystery."

"I know that, sir. Hazard is our deadliest enemy."

"So, to put us at ease with one another. I propose that we put an immediate end to the subject. I have many creditors, Milord."

"That's an error, Sir James."

"Ha ha! It's perhaps better to be on my side than theirs. Gambling and amour have ruined me, Milord!"

"But two members like you could ruin us."

"After all, a secret that I sell is a letter in the fire, a word that falls into an abyss."

"However profoundly one buries a secret, Sir James, as you know, reeds always grow that the wind interrogates."

"Reeds don't grow in abysses, Earl Antares," said the Baronet, smiling. "And hen, I'm not as stupid as the kind of Lydia's Figaro![34] At the great Festival of Fraternity, I perceived, around the chariot of industry, a young allegorical virgin who claims that I need two thousand pounds sterling."[35]

"And you don't know that the Earl and Antares are one?"

"I'll never have known it."

"That's good, Sir James."

"Do you know, Milord, that we're playing a terrible trick on Lord Mackinguss?"

"Ha ha! How do you come to be here, Sir James?"

"Don't you have any wood?"

"No."

---

[34] The reference is to one of the myths concerning King Midas, whose ears were transformed into those of a donkey by Apollo; the king's barber, the only man who knew the secret, sought to free himself from the pressure of keeping it by digging a hole and confining it there—but reeds grew on the spot and whispered the secret to the wind.

[35] The 1848 Revolution was followed, on the 24th April, by a great Festival of Fraternity, the procession of which concluded at the Arc de Triomphe; there is a famous painting of the event by Jean-Jacques Champin. The event was repeated three times on the anniversary of that first occasion, but did not survive the coup of 1851.

"Too bad—I'm shivering. I've been in Paris for two days. This afternoon, out walking, I saw Miss Ophelia in the Champs-Élysées."

"You're mistaken, Sir James."

"I'm never mistaken. I'm too clever for that. Have you been with her all day?"

"No."

"Well, I'll go on. A man gave her alms. Five minutes later, your companion in misery was coming home tranquilly, with bread in her hand, like an honest housekeeper. I took the bread off her."

"All this astonishes me."

"Astonishment is a fault. I'm never astonished."

"It's true that I didn't question her this evening."

"I was at The Théâtre-Français a little while ago. The thought that the young woman might be able to eat made me feel uneasy—but I was sleeping peacefully when I was woken up by the noise of the curtain."

"Going up?"

"No, coming down. Then I remembered that Antares lived in this street, as you had written to London, and I resolved to come and warn him myself about the straying of his young protégée."

"That was an excellent idea, Sir James."

"Yes, a fifty-thousand-franc idea! It's cold in here, Milord."

"I already told you that I don't have any wood."

"Sit down then. You're performing the function of a fan, quite unnecessarily, walking back and forth like that. Remember that you've taken the name of a fixed star. Well, where's the young heiress?"

"There—in the next room."

"What is she doing?"

"She's dying. When you came in I was going to see whether it's over."

"Ah! Very good. I'll expect you in the morning, then."

"That's too soon. To my distress, I'll be very busy."

"You will, at least be free in the afternoon. I'm staying in the Rue de Rivoli, at the usual hotel. I'm intending to leave for London the day after tomorrow, for a baptism."

"Lady Mackinguss has already given birth?"

"I don't think so, but the event will probably take place this week—it's been more than eight months."

"That's true—it's eight months since their wedding visit. I asked for a year. Horatio will be satisfied. Would you like to go and see?"

"No, no—these spectacles trouble my digestion. I'll return to my stall. Until tomorrow, Lord Cashier."

"Good night, Sir James."

Antares took the candle that was burning smokily, and lit the way for his unwelcome visitor as far as the staircase.

As he came back he went into Ophelia's room. Standing in the middle of the apartment, he listened. Not a breath could be heard. He approached the couch.

No one was lying there. He ran to the window and looked in the gap behind the bed: nothing.

His face became pale, his hand tremulous. "Ah!" he said, in despair. "This is a fatal hour in my life—an hour in which I've made two mistakes."

He disappeared down the stairs.

XXIV. The Hanged Woman

Our characters are not easy to follow. In spite of all our efforts, it has been impossible for us to train them in imitation of the stiff automata of tragedy. Unity of place causes them to quiver with fear and scatter over the map of the world in a truly disheartening disorder. In the olden days, novelists and poets could be as contentedly ignorant of geography as a woman. Today, on every page, it is necessary for them to have their hand on a Balbi,[36] or at least a commercial traveler. And to add to those miseries, readers become impatient and yield their brows to furrows that might perhaps trouble us. After all, though, one is quite wrong to worry about the contractions of Monsieur's forehead and the narrowing of the gap between Madame's eyebrows. Literature is a little like love; to succeed in it, it's necessary to play the highwayman. So let us close the parentheses and resume the benign pace of the narrative.

One cold bright morning, Robert de Rolleboise was going along the main street of Ingouville and getting ready to climb the steep stairway of the coast. The air was keen, the sun was shining and alone in the sky. The superimposed stages of the coast, seen from the road to Montvilliers, offered a magnificent tableau, Oriental in appearance. The gardens, summer-houses and villas lost in tall trees gave the great hill the physiognomy of a mysterious dwelling haunted by perils.

When Robert had reached the middle of the rising road, he stopped. The Ocean had enlarged its circle beyond visual range, and the Seine, gaping like a gulf, was sparkling in the sunlight. The young man was slightly troubled by the scene and resumed walking. In fact, the locations in question were, for him, imprinted with poignant memories.

---

[36] Adriano Balbi's *Abrégé de Geographie* [Compact Geography] (1832), translated from the Italian, was a standard reference book in France, as it was throughout Europe.

It was in the face of this vast nature that a man had seized his destiny in a fatal hand. There were reflections in this light of love and hatred. One of those hours of life that render malevolence, plunging doubt into the soul, plastering a snigger over the mask, had extended its flow in this vicinity. With a bitter voluptuousness, he tasted the corrosive poison that a woman's mockery pours on a man's pride.

Noon had not yet sounded at Notre-Dame-du-Havre, so the great highway of the coast was solitary. One a few meager Englishwomen, attracted by the cheerful sunlight and the calmness of the air, were strolling with their elastic stride and little somersaults like trotting hacks. The shawls hanging down from their narrow shoulders formed frightfully regular diamond-shapes, for it is not an affair of trivial importance to drape oneself in cashmere. Few women succeed, especially outside Paris. Thus, the provincial puts on her shawl, the Parisienne throws it on, and the Englishwoman hangs it. Needless to say, only the Parisienne succeeds.

Now, those lines are merely a little digression from my subject, and Robert de Rolleboise is entirely innocent in their regard. Far from being occupied in criticizing the Britannic dress of those ladies, he immediately quit the coast by a road that crossed the plateau and led to the village of Sanvie, which one might imagine to have been modeled on a backdrop at the Opéra-Comique.

On the plain, in a clump of trees, the blue roofs of an elegant detached house appeared. As he approached that swelling, Robert hastened his pace. He was pale. The agitation of his heart was visible in his anxious eyes and quivering lips.

One of the apartments of the house had a seductive aspect. The sun was shining there; a woman was dreaming there. A ray of sunlight and a woman's dream are enough to make one of those sad poets with weak chests and cancerous souls lose his head.

A magnificent fire that substituted very well for the insufficient winter ration accorded by the day star was reverberating from the white marble plaques of the hearth. Among all the pictures on the wood paneling and the precious futilities of the mantelpiece, one remarked, next to the head of an old man drawn in pencil, a silver-framed miniature representing a woman: Monsieur de Rolleboise's mother.

Ophelia, whom we recognize immediately by her beauty, had disinterred from her face that complexion of sadness and pain in which she has previously appeared in the hateful room in the Rue des Quinze-Vingt. We left her in the latter misery, but we find her again, instead, in comfort if not in luxury. She even appears so pretty that we are tempted to give a sketch here of her costume and coiffure, but we will resist that temptation and the reader will get away with a momentary alarm.

Ophelia was magnificently beautiful.

When Robert came in she held out her hand to him with an indefinable smile.

"I was thinking about you, Monsieur de Rolleboise, for if I have a happy thought, it is you that has given birth to it. I don't know why, but today I'm pleased with myself; I woke up at the emergence of a dream that has lifted me up in the course of my poor existence, a dream that has illuminated me with a beneficent suspicion.

"Believe in dreams, Ophelia!"

"Yes, we believe in them out there, in our chilly Scotland. Alas, shall I see it again someday? Oh, you can't comprehend how much I love today's cold atmosphere. That sun devoid of heat reminds me of Caledonia, with its fogs floating over its dormant lochs. Oh, I beg you, Monsieur de Rolleboise, talk to me in our language—the one in which my father talked to me. I love illusions!"

The young man sat down next to her and took her hands in his. For a moment he contemplated her silently, utterly joyful in his meditation.

"Let's leave illusions for sad days and dark hours, Ophelia, and talk about reality. I too am emerging from a dream—I, alas, have one of those natures that dream without sleeping—in which you appeared to me as a blessed revelation, in which your image was more resplendent than a vision of ecstasy! I am gripped in the heart by an intoxication so dazzling, Ophelia, that I fear your voice. Oh, I you can't love me, don't tell me!"

The young woman uttered a faint exclamation of reproach. Immediately, however, confused by that impulse of her forgetful soul, she inclined her face into her two hands, opened like an arch. There was one of those intervals in which real life falls silent.

When Ophelia's hands descended once again into Robert's, her gaze, meeting the young man's was transfigured by an indescribable expression. All the ecstasy of her soul fell in magnificent radiance upon the heart of the man who loved her.

"Since the moment when I saw you, my entire life has changed; my sentiment has been illuminated by a new religion. I want to love you to my knees, for you are for me the earthly shadow of the Virgin Mary. A cloud on your face is an anguish for my soul; a smile renders me mad."

"Oh, don't love me like that, for exalted passions are deadly! Then, too, they're extinguished more rapidly. Alas, Robert, a woman is very feeble, and the thought of redescending one day into the inertia of the heart breaks her with anxiety. I owe you life; I'm afraid of owing you happiness."

"No, Ophelia, don't compress a rising sentiment in that fashion, and above all, don't present it as a consequence of gratitude. I demand more. Forget the past entirely. Look at me as a stranger passing by, arrested by your virginal beauty. Oh, you are beautiful, child, far more beautiful than you believe."

For a long time, our two young people said crazy things, trivial things, silly things; in brief, they exhausted all the old hyperboles of a love scene. As they are two serious individuals, we shall not take advantage of their distraction to follow them barbarically through the contorted meanders of their oaths and their ecstasies.

Robert, under the gaze of the beautiful young woman, savored his delights, delivered himself entirely to his happy aspirations: hygienic emotions that scrub the heart clean of all the lees of miserable sentiments. Certainly, far from mocking such things, they are enviable. Is not being in love what is desired in life—that frank amour which galvanizes a man, rendering him mad or magnificent? For every one of those grand and splendid passions, however, many counterfeits and exceedingly droll copies are drawn from the human heart.

Robert loved the young Scotswoman recklessly, but she, although she did not say a word or proffer any exclamation, adored him with a greater love. It is always thus. It is a law of nature. Nevertheless, in spite of that, once encounters a good number of young men who crush themselves with perplexities and doubts, who torment their poor mistresses to obtain a well-formulated confession: machines set in action, which believe that they are moving of their own accord!

But our young man forgot himself completely.

"Oh, if I were only permitted to suspend the course of my life and pause for longer in this moment! For I mourn the minute that passes, the joy that flows by! Are you not happy, Ophelia? Is there a shadow in your heart that I ought to brighten?"

"Alas! You can suffice for my love, perhaps, but my happiness...alas, that I doubt. Out of discretion, you never question me about my past. However, it is simultaneously horrible and beautiful—so horrible that I still shiver, so beautiful that it seems to me to be a lie!"

"No, Ophelia, I don't talk about it for fear of giving you pain. I remember that you wept the day before yesterday when I mentioned our strange conversation, a year ago, after supper."

"Yes, that evening I met the man who was to save me. A secret voice told me to go to him...to tell him everything, to cry for help. But I weakened...your indifference caused my resolution to fail. You asked me just now what my soul lacks. Robert, my father died doubting me. To destroy that doubt, yesterday, I would have given my life—and today, my love. Did you know my father?"

"Ophelia...that's the only name by which I know you."

"My name is Ophelia Firstland."

"Firstland!" exclaimed the young man. "Yes, that's true—that was the signature on the letter you left in my house in the Rue de Helder."

"A letter from my poor mother!"

"But don't you have a sister?"

"Olivia is my father's daughter, and now the wife of that man you saw at that supper."

Robert de Rolleboise, struck by amazement, stopped dead, his eyes staring at the floor and his face pale, making no movement. He was afraid of sensing that he was still caught in that same deadly circle.

"Oh, calamity!" he said, in a slow voice.

"Do you know Horatio Mackinguss, now?"

"Yes—yes, I know him. And he is my damnation, perhaps my doom!"

"The man is very wicked, then?"

"Wicked! Say terrible. Oh, if it's because of him that you've suffered, I tremble..."

"But I haven't done anything to him—I'm just a poor woman!"

"Woman...oh, child, that name alone condemns you in his eyes. Fatality! My God! And it's me who must defend her!

"But if you know Horatio, perhaps you've also seen my sister?"

"I've met her, yes."

"Was she alone?"

"With her father, the old Duke."

"It was a long time ago, then, since my father is dead."

"Dead! No, Miss, your father isn't dead!"

The young woman's physiognomy was radiant. She fell to her knees, her heart thanking God. Afterwards, standing up, she went to the mantelpiece, kissed a crucifix, then the portrait of the old man, and then the portrait of Robert's mother.

"Oh, you haven't deceived me? You assure me that I can see my father again, tell him everything, obtain his forgiveness? Oh no—don't speak, I'm afraid of what you're going to say. Perhaps it's a long me since you encountered him. Oh, my God, let it not be an illusion!"

"I saw the old Duke at his daughter's wedding."

"Oh, how that man deceived me! But God has saved me, my ordeals are over. I'll forget those five years of misfortune as one lets the memory of a feverish nightmare fall into the past, and calm will return to my soul. You'll take me to my father. Oh, how happy we shall be to see one another again!

" Happy...! Alas, my beautiful hopes are distracting my thoughts from the thought of a drama it will be necessary to relate to him. He will still love me, it's true...but he will shiver too..."

"Ophelia, I divine that there is an event in your life, the fatal influence of which has passed over your soul, and is troubling you."

"Yes, a great event."

"Which struck you, perhaps?"

"Of which I was the victim. Listen, Robert, you are my savior, the vanquishing angel who wrenched me from the bed of torture on which I was expiring. I therefore owe you the truth, for I can appear innocent before you. Oh, how my father will love you when I tell him what you have done for his child! We shall go to find him together."

"See your father, me! Oh no—never!"

"Why?" asked the young woman, astonished.

"Why? Oh, Ophelia, don't ask me that, and forgive me if I darken your joy, but I can't speak...and yet, I love you."

"But have you not saved me, then?"

"Saved! No, Ophelia, I haven't saved you! The evening when you went down into the street, there was only one hand that could be fatal to you, and it is mine! But I'm frightening you! Oh, don't listen to me—I'm mad. And you talk to me about your father! Oh, Ophelia, although I do not know your life and what you have done, he will forgive his daughter—but me, never!"

Before Robert's emotion, the young woman felt her heart fall back into doubt. She had quit one man who had deceived her frightfully by feigning affection. Was this one not another torturer, who, by means of love, was about to torture her heart? Was it in her destiny to exhaust all human dolor and anguish?

The young man perceived that vacillation, so he resumed in a calmer voice. "Yes, my beautiful friend, I'm cruel to sadden you like this. But I'm made thus; to begin with, I'm afraid. Certainly, I can see, by virtue of the past and the present, our meeting and your love, that is in our destiny to live or die together. An immense drama is enveloping us. For a long time, you have been condemned; as for me, the day when I saw you, my heart doomed me. To march surely in this trembling path, it's necessary for us to know one another."

"I'm ready to tell you everything."

"And I to tell you everything; for two people who love one another are but one, and to tell you a secret is not to divulge it."

"Alas! When you've heard me, you'll still love me and you'll commiserate with me, for I'm innocent.

"But if I tell you my life, will you still love me?"

"Yes."

"But I'm guilty!"

"Well, Robert, I shall forgive you."

Monsieur de Rolleboise kissed Miss Firstland's hand. The latter, after a moment's reflection, her head bowed over her rich bosom, began to speak.

"I was born in the highlands of Scotland, a few leagues from Fort Augustus in the Monaghlea Mountains, and brought up in Firstland Castle. The manor is built on the plateau of the highest peak of the mountain. From the battlements of the high tower, on summer days when the air is pure, one can see the two rivers that border the estate, the Findhorn and the Spey, like two silver ribbons.

"It is a very wild place; to find his flock, a highlander draped in his torn plaid, poorly shod in ragged brogues and wearing his cap with an eagle's weather, must go down a long way into the glens. No matter—I shall be happy to see our heather, our lochs and our mists again! France is very beautiful, Paris splendid, London insolent in its wealth, but the only abode that I desire is that of our poor fortress in Monaghlea!

"However, I suffered a great deal there; my eyes shed dolorous tears beneath that leaden sky! Yes, it's true; but it's there that my mother lies, my poor mother, who I can scarcely recall...she's a beloved shade who traverses my dreams, but reality never showed her to me. I was three years old when my father lost her. My early youth was sad: melancholy hours, the influence of which still lingers. As a child, I rarely laughed; as an adolescent, I became dreamy. I had scarcely reached my fourth year when my father remarried.

"He married Ophelia Cockburn. I was told that she would be my mother, but I didn't believe it, and from the very first day, I knew that I wasn't loved. Before my father, the Duchess did not caress me; in his absence, she treated me harshly; I was punished for the slightest negligence. I had no aversion for her, but I feared her. After a year of marriage, she gave my father a daughter. Olivia is six years younger than me. I don't know whether you know Lady Mackinguss intimately; at any rate, she's my sister, and I won't say anything about her.

"The more years went by, the more her mother hated me. Alas, she was a woman whose heart was hard—and I can say that because I often saw my father, when he and I were alone, talk about my mother and weep for the first Duchess. Oh, she hated me profoundly; pride and jealousy twisted her heart. She never forgot her hatred; her slightest actions were imprinted by it.

"As children, Olivia and I played in the courtyards. In summer, we often came in eating; then, I remember, my mother-in-law immediately offered me a drink; Olivia wept because her thirst was left unslaked. The water that was given to me was iced. I had a delicate chest. At meals, she spiced the food that was served to me excessively—but my body resisted the woman's malevolence.

"As she grew older Olivia recognized the advantages of my birth, and shared her mother's aversion to me. From the age of fifteen on, my life went by almost outside their intimacy. I saw my father; that was all. The long winter evenings went by sadly and slowly. Olivia stayed with the Duchess in their apartment. My father, sitting in his oak armchair by the fire, would read, look up at me with a smile, and then resume his reading. He didn't say much. He knew that I wasn't loved, but he dared not help me to understand, nor commiserate with me.

"I still recall that big, high-ceilinged room with its ancient arms suspended from the walls, its large fireplace surmounted by a stag's head, and the flagstones of the hearth carpeted with fox-furs. I sat on a low chair at the Duke's feet, and when the hours had chimed for a long time, becoming drowsy, I pulled the plaid that covered my shoulders over my head. Before we parted, my father made me say a prayer beside him, and then kissed me on the forehead. Then I left him, and the night brought me to another day, which went by in the same fashion.

"My stepmother's character was taciturn, false and wicked. Oh, don't be astonished by that word—I have the right to pronounce it. I was almost eighteen. For some months the Duchess had not spoken to me, but if we passed one another in a corridor I sensed that she turned to look at me with a gaze that frightened me.

"Our family life was solitary. Scarcely once a year did any guest enter our dwelling. So, knowing nothing about the world beyond the forests of our estates, I was content with my sad life and did not hope for any wider circle. I read. As a girl, I had recognized that fairy tales did not exist; as a young woman, I hoped one day to discover the falsehood of novels.

"In that epoch, Olivia's mother was about forty-five years old. Her beauty had fled. She was a Scotswoman ignorant of all worldly subtlety, who had only undertaken one journey in her life, from her father's house to her husband's. Our country is very backward in its civilization. Its customs are not obliterated overnight. It is a country that died young; its traditions are as sheer as its rocks.

"As she grew older, the Duchess of Firstland abandoned herself to a base passion: she drank.

"One winter evening, I had just left the Duke, occupied in reading the life of some saint in his large book with gilded binding. After having kissed me, he had retained me with him momentarily and, contrary to habit, after gazing at me with loving affection, his mouth murmured, as if yielding to a memory: 'You always remind me of your mother!' Then, when he had kissed me on the forehead again and wished me good night, I left him.

"It was a stormy night. Snow covered the countryside and the wind was chasing it all the way into the apartments. In a corridor, my lamp almost went out. Toward the middle of the corridor there was a wooden stairway that led to a part of the castle where no one lived. As a child, I had been afraid of that passage and went through it fearfully, hiding in the pleats of my maid's skirt. That evening, I saw a shadow on the steps, and I shivered involuntarily. It was the Duchess, my step-mother—my wicked stepmother, alas!

"As I went past her, her hand seized my arm and drew me along, I followed her. We climbed the wooden stairway, went along several corridors that I scarcely knew, and then stopped in front of a little door that was locked with a key. That door opened on to a stone stairway leading upwards in a spiral. I was afraid. My hand clung on to the door handle. But I was only a frail child, delicate and devoid of strength; the Duchess was robust and vigorous. I was effortlessly detached from the door and dragged up the steps. Not a word was uttered, nor a plaint.

"We reached the top. In front of us there was a door, broader than it was tall. Having opened it, the Duchess forced me across the threshold and closed it behind her. We then found ourselves in a large square room pieced by four openings devoid of casements. It was the inside of a tower directly opposite to the inhabited part of the castle. The tempestuous night frightened me, and any sound would have been drowned out by the voice of the squalls. The room had no furniture, except that, in the times of our distant forefathers, a massive and squat bed had been built there, which seemed to be part of the floor, and a low table had been transported there I know not how. The wood of those two forgotten items of furniture was blackened and hardened by antiquity. Overhead, thick beams supported the roof, which was creaking from time to time beneath the weight of the snow that covered it.

"The Duchess had undoubtedly been there already that evening, because there was a lamp burning, with difficulty, on the table. Next to the lamp I noticed a glass and several bottles. When I saw that I was alone, far from any help, with that woman who did not love me and whom I dreaded, I shivered and my teeth chattered. In a supplicant voice, my face pale, I asked her what she wanted with me at such an hour, in such a strange place. She did not reply. That mutism, suggestive of a reflected resolution, increased my fear.

"The Duchess took the lamp that I was still holding in my hand and put it on the table. Then seizing a rope, she tied my hands behind my back. I wept. She laughed. Her cheeks were covered with bright red blotches; her eyes were gleaming; she was almost drunk.

"When my hands were tied, she pushed me against one of the spiral columns of the bed and tied me to it with further cords that she put around my waist. Thus secured, I couldn't move; the bonds held me so tightly that I was bent forwards. When that was done, my father's wife went to the table, filled a glass with whisky, and drank it.

"'Ophelia,' she said to me, 'I don't like you. You're not my child; you're a stranger to me, and obstacle for my daughter. Your mother was a pauper who had nothing, with whom the Duke was stupidly smitten. I left my father's house rich, and it's only just that my daughter should do the same. Yes, I hate you, because you eat Olivia's bread here, because her father doesn't love her as he loves you, and because, after my husband's death, you will be mistress of the Firstland name and fortune. That's why I hate you.

"'You'll require, will you not, an English peer for a husband, while my daughter will have the right, at most, to some wretched rich merchant in Glasgow or Edinburgh. No, no— Olivia is my daughter; I shall give her your name, I shall give her your fortune; and for that, I'll take your life. Ha ha! My beautiful dreamer, who says that she has a weak chest but doesn't die...whom everyone prefers to her sister. Ha ha! How everything will change tonight!

"'Well, my dear friend, when one poses as you do as a melancholy chatelaine, one follows one's role to the denouement—one commits suicide! Ophelia, you're going to die tonight. You'll be found here tomorrow, and it will be believed to be a voluntary death. You'll be buried without priests and without prayers. But what does it matter to you, the angel of the castle, as your imbecile of a father calls you?—you have no need of them!

"'Look, read this! Wouldn't one think that it was your hand that traced these letters? And then, wouldn't that romantic phrase emerge naturally from your brain? *Reverie is a shade of sleep; sleep is a shadow of death; to dream forever, it is necessary to quit the Earth. Ophelia.* Well, tomorrow, they'll read that sentence, signed with your name and picked up close to your body. Ha ha! It's a long time that I've been formulating this plan! Come on, don't weep and don't pray to me—that's futile—but to God, which might serve you afterwards!'

"I burst into sobs and supplications—for, I confess, I was afraid to die thus by a horrible crime. I thought about my poor father, whom I'd just left and would never see again, my poor father who would blame, me, but who would be alone in praying for me. My imploring and desperate tears would have touched a torturer, but a hateful and malevolent woman is pitiless for a woman.

"During my cries and my pleas, the Duchess had picked up ropes and, climbing on to the table, had attached one to a stout beam. At the extremity, which hung at the height of her head, she formed a slip knot. 'I'm going to hang you,' she said, coldly.

"I was still moaning and begging. Oh, it must have been a frightful and heart-rending spectacle, for my executioner paused briefly in her preparations to dart a glance at me in which indecision was legible. I had a glimmer of hope; I asked for another death; I promised to withdraw from worldly life and go to France to die in a convent. The Duchess listened to me, but suddenly, she leaned over the table, filled a glass with liquor, drank it, and burst out laughing.

"My hope was extinguished; I was doomed.

"Before the pitilessness of that woman, my heart froze. My last thought of rescue fled, I bowed my head under the weight of my destiny and addressed myself to God. Alas, I still don't know whether I ought to say that, in snatching me from the death toward which my father's wife was dragging me, God saved me...

"During my interior prayer, I shall always remember, there was a sudden silence that impressed me. Outside, the storm died down; facing me, on the table, Ophelia Cockburn stopped laughing. In that silence, a secret voice emerging from my soul told me that Heaven was listening to me, and a gleam of hope, ignited by faith, was born within me."

At that point in her story the young woman paused. Her thoughts were content to follow the drift of a sweet memory rediscovered in the details of the terrible drama. After a silence that the listener respected, she placed her hand on Robert's arm with an entirely chaste confidence and said to him, with moist eyes. "You're religious, aren't you?"

"I respect all beliefs, for I hold that mine, which I love and defend, should be respected."

"Yes, Robert, believe. There are days when religion in the heart is necessary. I inherited from my mother a great faith in the protection of the Blessed Virgin. On the night of which I'm speaking, that faith was transformed into a fervent love and an ineffable gratitude—for the Mother of God saved me;

that's the conviction of my soul. She saved me, not to suffer, but for a better future.

"The woman had paused in her preparations. Holding the rope in her hands, her head pale and leadenly inclined on her breast, her gaze fixed on me, she reflected. Before dying, my mother had placed around my neck this locket, which I later attached to a cord woven from her hair, which my father gave me. It's not made of precious metal, but it's a doubly precious souvenir, for it has been blessed in Rome.

"Well, during that scene, turning my eyes dried by prayer away from the inert and cold gaze of my stepmother, I perceived my mother's locket shining on my breast. In my movements of despair and supplication, it had come out of my dress. I read this caption, fervently—the magnificent expression of veritable motherly love: *If you love my son Jesus during your life, in the hour of your death, I will save you.* I prayed, and I hoped.

"But what stopped that woman was not a thought of pity. She merely judged that, because I was taller than her, the slipknot might fall too far. The skeletal room in which that frightful drama was in preparation seemed bare to the gaze, entirely unfurnished. The Duchess looked for something. Her eyes, gleaming with intoxication, searched the darkness. Suddenly, behind the bed to which I was tied, she perceived an old wooden chair.

"She got down from the table, paying no heed to a few bottles that were knocked over by her dress, falling to the floor. She picked up the chair and climbed back on to her scaffold. Then, hoisting herself up on the old chair, she shortened the rope by means of a few knots.

"Forgive me if I go over these details slowly, for I share the horror that they inspire in you, but they're indispensable for the comprehension of the frightful scene. My stepmother was drunk, but with an intoxication whose almost-extinct excitement had left her dazed. Scarcely able to maintain herself on her scaffold, because vertigo was troubling her vision, she was holding on to the rope, the instrument of my execution. The noose was open.

"Mechanically, wanting to test it, she passed it over her head—but in the course of the movement that she had to make, she lost her balance, and her body leaned forward like a full sack tipping over. The rope retained her by the neck. In the movement that she made to bring herself upright again, the chair on which her feet were placed slipped off the table and fell, dragging the lamp with it.

"The darkness was complete. I screamed.

"The Duchess found herself hanging; her feet were not touching the table. I heard a kind of croak; then, my eyes adapting to the darkness, I perceived, in the faint moonlight, a body writhing.

"My situation was horrible. I writhed in my bonds. I shouted for help. It was futile.

"The movements ceased; my torturer was no more than a cadaver.

"I spent a horrible night in front of that dead woman, in that room where the snow, blowing in through the large windows, was freezing me. God had exacted justice and saved a victim, but I dared not thank him. I prayed for my father's wife.

"The hours went by. Alone, placed in front of that cadaver, whose face was peppered by the white gleam of snowflakes, I felt vertigo. Fear gave me new strength. By virtue of an extreme muscular contortion, I freed one of my arms from the ropes, and with that free hand, untied myself. Unable to see, stumbling at ever corner, shivering like a victim of hallucination pursued by a specter, I fled.

"I almost fell dead on the threshold of the room where my father was asleep. I was about to go in, to wake him, to tell him everything, but a sudden thought stopped me.

"Tell him everything! Present to his already uneasy mind the details of his wife's crime, the anguish that his daughter had just suffered! Oh, I don't know whether you understand, but I didn't have the courage. I spent the rest of the night praying.

"The next day, the whole castle was distressed by the Duchess' disappearance. I dared not talk to Olivia or return to that atrocious scene, for, and I thank Heaven for it, if I have had a suspicion since, it has never degenerated into a certainty. Olivia was doubtless unaware of the means of the crime premeditated against her sister, but, given the expression of her gaze weighing upon my face frozen with amazement and anguish, I've always suspected that she knew about the plan.

"Three days went by in fruitless searches. During those hours of tumult and anxiety, I had neither the strength nor the science to offer advice. That calm prostration, in the midst of the agitation that surrounded me went unnoticed, by the very reason of the universal preoccupation. But the denouement that I anticipated fearfully arrived. On the evening of the third day, my father, his face as white as his hair, came into the room where my sister and I were, and told us about the fatal discovery.

"The news of that death petrified all the castle's inhabitants. All thought of a crime was rejected, but the Duchess was not liked by those people, simple and superstitious minds, so many among them attributed the event to a supernatural power and considered it as a punishment. A suicide in our cold and austere Scotland is accepted as a divine malediction. So not long afterwards, it was repeated throughout the region, from the banks of the Findhorn to those of the Spey, that Firstland Castle was afflicted by misfortune, much as one says here that a house is on fire. Alas, misfortune devours more than fire!

"I mentioned the few lines, in imitation of my handwriting, that the Duchess had raced on a piece of paper, in order that my death should not be imputed to anyone else. Olivia's mother had the same name as me. It was therefore considered, rightly, that the words came from her hand—but my sister, who perhaps suspected what had really happened, kept the note.

"The imitation of the handwriting might give rise to a doubt. Olivia, who hated me as her mother did, attached herself to that insensate supposition. She placed the fatal note before my father's eyes with a letter I had written. My poor father, his head shaken by all the things that had been perpetrated around him, shivered at the similarity of the two handwritings. In the face of the doubt of the only heart on earth that loved me, I abandoned myself to my destiny and accepted the misfortune that had fallen upon me without a murmur.

"I could have taken my father by the hand and led him to the altar of the castle chapel and there, after having sworn on the holy Tabernacle that I would tell the truth, confessed everything to him. But, I repeat, I dared not. Never did I feel strong enough to say to that old man, whom I loved: 'Your wife, to whom you gave your name, the spouse hat you honored to the point of according her my mother's place, tried to murder me, your daughter!'

"The funeral of the Duchess of Firstland was held at night. Her body was laid with those of our ancestors in the family crypt.

"Since her mother's death, Olivia, although she had never given evidence of any hint of affection, appeared to have inherited my stepmother's sentiments toward me. Moreover, I confess, our characters are dissimilar. Although her elder, I always accepted as a natural law her predominance in the direction of the affairs of the household. Thus, she was never inactive. In many circumstances, and for causes that did not disquiet me to the extent of reflecting on the subject, she absented herself from Firstland Castle. The letters she wrote during these displacements sometimes came from Edinburgh, sometimes from Glasgow.

"You know my imaginative mind. I am one of those souls that solitude seduces, who live in an unknown world. It was the end of winter; sometimes the sun disappeared into our mists. The harsh nature about which I have spoken to you pleased me; the sad landscape harmonized with my sad thoughts. I had a habit, every day, of going down through a path in the grounds to the valley of the Findhorn. In the deserted places on the banks of the river I wandered pensively, suffering mentally but unoccupied, heartsick but without aspiration toward the sentiments that the restricted frame of our existence still left unknown.

"One day at dusk, two men took possession of me, and in spite of my unheard cries and my impotent efforts, put me in a carriage that departed immediately. I was alone but I couldn't escape because the doors were padlocked. The carriage traveled for three days. Toward the end of the third day, I saw the sea. I had traversed part of Scotland and all of England. When the post-chaise stopped, a man who almost never quit me thereafter took charge of me.

"That man told me that his name was Antares, and that he had been instructed to take me to Paris, but that I had nothing to fear from him. To all my solicitations and prayers he made no rely.

There was a small fishing-boat in the harbor, to which I was dragged. The next day, after a very bad crossing, we disembarked on the French coast. There, as I was completely ignorant of the language, Antares bought two places on a diligence, which brought us to Paris. I shall not pause here on the details of the mental sufferings that I experienced; you will divine them without difficulty. Pale and frightened, I wept incessantly. Then too, the harsh physiognomy of my companion frightened me and drove me to despair.

"'Is on my father's orders that you are acting?' I asked him, when we arrived in Paris.

"'No,' he said.

"'It's my sister Olivia, then, who wants me to disappear?'

"'Yes.'

"More skillful than her mother, my sister was completing her work, and taking possession of my fortune. Alas, it remains for me to tell you the most poignant part of the drama of my life, and it is with a blush on my face that I am going to reveal it to you. But the God who saved me from my stepmother, who attacked my body, did not abandon me in the face of the atrocious temptations invented by Olivia against me soul.

"We lived in a rather beautiful apartment in one of the better quarters of Paris. In the first days, I found at my disposal all the seductions of toilette of which a woman can dream. I pushed them aside. But one evening, a young woman dressed me strangely; my hair was powdered, my shoulders covered with necklaces, my arms with bracelets. I looked at myself in a mirror, and was frightened to see myself dressed in that fashion. Then a memory moistened my eyes with tears. That style of costume reminded me of the old portraits in the galleries of my father's castle.

"At supper, there were two women dressed like me. They were very jovial, and tried to bring a smile to my face. I perceived that the wine was intoxicating me and stopped drinking. Finally, midnight having chimed, I was put into a carriage with my two companions. After a quarter of an hour's journey, we got out in front of a large building, brightly illuminated. A crowd, composed of costumed and masked men and women, drew us inside. It was the Opéra ball. Can you understand my panic? Me, a poor girl abducted from the austere existence of Firstland Manor, suddenly pitched into the noise, the vertigo and the folly of the Opéra ball!

"I was stunned, and if I hadn't put my hands over my eyes, I would have lost my head. I wanted to run away. Having climbed a long, broad stairway I sought a refuge. I perceived an unoccupied box. I ran into it and there, alone, in the midst of the drunken cries and the coarse joy, in the din of the monstrous orchestra that was making the crowd bound, I wept. At the end of the night, Antares came into the box, in a bad temper, and took me away.

"Permit me not to go into all the details of the task that man sought to accomplish. There were infamies whose proximity could not tarnish me, the repulsion of which decided my death, and into which my memory does not have the courage to descend.

"Rather, let me tell you about a vision that illuminated my soul with hope and faith. It was about a year ago. One evening, Antares told me that we were leaving the next day. He did not speak to me on the way, and when I asked him where we were going, he did not reply. We crossed the sea in a matter of hours, and that circumstances, combined with the recognition among the people we encountered of the mother tongue, told me that we were in England. We stopped in London. I remained there for a week, hidden from all eyes. Then, one evening, I was put into a carriage on my own, which carried me away.

"It was dark. We went at top speed through the streets of London. Alone in the carriage, I leaned out of the window, looking at the houses, following with my gaze the rare pedestrians that we passed, and thinking about my father, who might perhaps be living in the city that I was traversing, while believing me to be dead. Then by the action of souls that live more in the unknown than reality. I started searching in the darkness, in the void, in the blackness of the houses. What I'm telling you now is a great strangeness of mind, is it not?

"Well, I don't know whether it was an imaginary creation, a product of the fixity of my brain, but all of a sudden, in the darkness, at a faintly lit window..."

"What?"

"Well, I saw my father! My father, who was reaching his hand out to me, as if to stop me...I uttered a cry...we turned a corner...everything had disappeared!"

"Ophelia, that might really have happened, for he has been in London for four years."

"Poor father! He too, then, thought it was a vision! You know the rest of my life of misfortune, the final atrocity of that monster who, having been unable to kill me by vice, was about to finish it by starvation. I have laid my destiny bare before you. Now, will you hide anything of our past from me?"

"I'll tell you everything."

"And when will you take me to my father?"

"Tomorrow."

As Rolleboise prepared to speak, however, a maid brought a letter. The letter was addressed to Robert and bore a Paris postmark. It contained these lines:

Monsieur de Rolleboise.

If, in two days after receipt, you will take the trouble to find yourself at the Castle of the Falls, I shall have the pleasure of introducing you to Madame de Lormont.

Horatio Mackinguss

"Tomorrow, we're going to see my father?" the young woman repeated, when Robert had folded up the letter.

"Tomorrow...I said tomorrow! Listen, Ophelia, in a week, when all this is finished, I will tell you everything. And then, if you forgive me, we will go to find your father, the Duke of Firstland."

"Oh! You said tomorrow!"

XXV. Nicotine

The British Isles, although governed by a monarchical apparatus, and although the aristocracy still enjoys its privileges, nevertheless constitute the country that accords most liberty to the individual. The common reserve that one encounters everywhere, and almost mistakes for insouciance, is in nature as well as in people. Thus, in regard to Scotland, there are a great many people in France who think that uncultivated and mountainous land is still the model of the landscapes that Walter Scott has depicted for us, while others see Caledonia furrowed with railways and canals and inhabited by honest manufacturers wearing garments like a stockbroker on the Bourse and paying more attention to "consolidateds" than to anything else. These two kinds of people are equally mistaken.

The English government has pierced roads, railways and canals, in order that progress can insinuate itself into those mountainous regions. Entirely commercial zones have resulted from that, but without impinging in any way upon the rude mores that rub shoulders with them. Glasgow is a city of four million souls, the railway goes though Perth and Dundee and steamers belch their smoke on Loch Leven, but a few miles from Glasgow, foxes and grouse are hunted and there is a celebrated falconry, Dundee shows you Macbeth's castle on Dunsinan Hill and Lock Leven is lost in the evenings in blue-tinted fogs, as in the days when Queen Mary was imprisoned there. The great lord lives on his lands, the industrialist in his factory. Those two individuals, the one leisured, the other active, met one another but never communicate.

In sum, the country has given birth almost simultaneously to Robert Burns, the man of dreams, and James Watt, the man of figures.

Scotland is, therefore, simultaneously a curious country and a country like any other. There are départements in France where the superstitious beliefs are more burlesque than those that the inhabitants of the Highlands recognize; there are cities in Scotland that offer more comfort than one would find in the middle of certain great cities in France. I am taking the trouble to establish this in order to demonstrate that a novel can unfurl some scenes in a Scottish castle without fearing the contumelious epithet of melodrama.

The Castle of the Falls, belonging to Horatio, as I said in one of the earlier chapters of this book, is built perpendicularly on the bank of the Clyde, a few miles north of Lanark.[37] In that locale, the landscape extends massive and rude. The horizon is limited by low mountains with shaggy pelts. Night and day, a continuous noise similar to the rumble of the Ocean makes itself heard. That is the Clyde Falls at Stonebyres, cataracts where the river falls vertically like an immense silvery curtain. Without being wild—for the land is cultivated—the vicinity of Horatio's dwelling is deserted.

Olivia had been constrained to follow her husband into the solitude of Lanarkshire. An obliging doctor had assured her that her native air would repair the fatigues of her childbirth—and Mackinguss loved the mother of his child too much to neglect such advice.

They day when we enter the Falls—as the estate was called—Horatio, Olivia, Antares and Lord Lodore were at the castle. Sir James Cawdor had announced his arrival for that evening. In order to give more clarity of the scenes that fol-

---

[37] "The Castle of the Falls" is not Stonebyres Castle, which had recently been remodeled as a Baronial mansion by its owners, the Weir (or de Vere) family, when the novel was written, and which the author might conceivably have visited. If he had, he would probably have been told that there had once been another castle nearby, located on the cliffs above the falls, known as Cairnie Castle, of which some vestiges still remained in the early 19th century, although none remain today. That seems to have been the inspiration for the Castle of the Falls.

low, it, is, I think, necessary to set in relief the dispositions of the heart of each of these individuals.

Horatio had not modified his plan, and was still proceeding calmly along the route he had mapped out. His child assured him of the Firstland fortune, but his wife prevented him from augmenting that fortune by a new alliance. That was, however, no more than a simple algebraic equation to solve.

Olivia's situation was quite different. That young woman, who had sacrificed all her sentiments to her pride, the inheritor of her mother's heart, had collided with the bronze character of her husband. For two years, beneath an apparent submission, she had been meditating a terrible revenge. Particularities very distant from her, by virtue of one of those bizarre laws of the workings of fate, were to provide the denouement of her drama. Those strange circumstances were about to link up with the designs hidden from Olivia by the hand of Antares.

That same evening, as I said, Sir James would arrive from London. That arrival worried Antares, for one of Antares' passions was named avarice, and avarice had counseled him not to pay Sir James the price of a certain secret—purchased, it will be recalled, in the Rue de Quinze-Vingts, in Paris. The man who was called the Jew thus had two reasons for fearing Horatio: first because of the Baronet, and secondly because of the disappearance of Ophelia, which he had refrained from confessing. There only remained one means of rescue: to appear to be serving Olivia, and by that means to serve himself.

Olivia lived somewhat apart from these men. Her Aunt Cockburn had not accompanied her. One of her maids, Suky, had died in childbirth in a seizure of terror caused by the apparition of her lover, the former horseguard, whom she knew to be buried in the cemetery at New Cross—this is a secondary episode, which I thought I could leave out of the story without impoverishment. Olivia, therefore, had no one with her but her faithful Hannah and her child's nurse. So she did not accept that state of isolation without a hidden agenda.

Antares resided in a rather remote room in the castle, but placed in the same diazome as Lady Mackinguss' apartment. He was rarely seen, especially by day. Enclosed in his laboratory, he was doing something.

One morning, Olivia went into the room where the Jew was working. He was the same old man that we have glimpsed in the hovel in Corbett's Lane in London. Enveloped in his quaintly-colored dressing-gown, his head covered by a heavy woolen bonnet, his eyes hidden behind spectacles and an eyeshade, his hands stiff and wrinkled, the individual offered an appearance of which it was difficult to take account. He had no age.

"I present all my respectful salutations to Milady."

"Good day, Antares. So you're working with your old books and alembics. You resemble an alchemist. Can you make gold?"

"No, Milady—but as I found these instruments, books, retorts and furnaces here, I'm doing chemistry to distract myself."

"You're lucky to be able to distract yourself. Personally, I'm reduced to coming to chat to you."

"I saw you out riding yesterday."

"Yes, with Hannah! My husband had promised to flush out a fox, but he was too busy."

"Ah! Milord was busy?"

"I say that because he sent me that excuse. After all, how do I know what is happening here?"

"But it's a Thebaid, Milady!"

"In appearance, perhaps. That's not what the peasants say, who only have the word *vampire* on their lips."

"Lanarkshire peasants! Men who believe in fairies!"

"Well, Antares, I, whom am not from Lanarkshire and don't believe in fairies, am nevertheless convinced that something is happening here. Last night I was at my window, and in the moonlight, I clearly distinguished two men carrying a body. They came into the castle by the door of the Falconry."

"A dead body?"

"I don't know. Unconscious, perhaps, but certainly a woman. I didn't recognize the men."

"What you say astonishes me, Milady—all the more so as I haven't heard anything."

"Or you haven't wanted to hear anything."

"Milady, I was awake in here all night."

"It smells very bad here."

"It's the odor of tobacco, Milady. I'm conducting experiments with that plant."

"What are you looking for?"

"What am I looking for? What I'm looking for, I found last night. Can you see, in this corner?"

So saying, Antares lifted a cover from a formless heap that as lying in the corner of the room.

"Oh my God! Where did those dogs come from?"

"The dogs are dead, Milady, as are the cats. I killed them with a drop of the liquid that you see in this phial."

"It's a very terrible poison, then?"[38]

"Lethal. Here, Milady, I'll procure you a means of distracting yourself. Take this phial and, with every precaution, try the effect of the toxin on the birds in your aviary. Only one drop, Milady."

"But I'd never dare touch it!"

"Oh, well-stoppered, it's inoffensive."

"And you say that a single drop would kill me?"

"Oh, I wasn't talking about a human being."

"But in order to be on one's guard against its effects?"

"Oh! I believe that for a human being…

"A spoonful would suffice?"

"Yes, yes, Milady…and might even be more than enough."

"It must decompose the flesh."

"It leaves no trace."

---

[38] The toxic effects of nicotine were immediately recognized by the chemists who first isolated it in 1828, Wilhelm Posselt and Karl Reimann.

"That's frightful! Good night, then, Antares."

"But you haven't taken it, Milady."

"What?"

"The phial…on a pullet, its effect is very curious."

"That's barbaric."

"On a rabbit, then."

"In fact, I might try it out on the fox that was caught in the shepherd's trap the other night."

"Two drops on the tongue, Milady."

"I thought you said a small spoonful."

"For a human, yes. But for a fox, that would be too much."

And the old chemist uttered an amiable snigger.

XXVI. Sir James' Amours

"So, Lodore, you'll be kind enough, as soon as Monsieur de Rolleboise arrives, "to take him to the apartment of which this is the key. You won't have any need to speak to me again this evening. I don't feel well—I'm going to sleep."

Lord Lodore went out. Sir James Cawdor remained.

"I'm going to sleep, Sir James."

Sir James established himself tranquilly in a profound armchair. Horatio looked at him in astonishment.

Without worrying overmuch about his host's surprised expression, the Baronet rang.

"Bring coffee for Milord, and a bottle of Xerès for me."

Then, as Horatio studied him intently in order to make sure of his sanity, he added, while casually adjusting his cravat: "You're drowsy—the coffee will wake you up."

"But I intend to rest. Are you insane, Sir James?"

"Not in the least. I have to talk to you about serious matters, that's all."

"Well, I'll see you tomorrow morning."

"The morning? I'm only serious in the evening, after my dinner."

A domestic placed a loaded tray within the Baronet's reach.

Horatio drank a mouthful of coffee. "What do you want with me, Sir James?"

"Money."

"But I don't owe you any."

"I know."

"Then permit me to remark, Sir James, that the manner I which you conduct your affairs astonishes me. You're always down to your last pound—and yet, I know you have no family."

The Baronet slowly filled a glass with Xerès wine, and drank it with the great seriousness that was characteristic of him.

"It's exactly that, Milord, that has ruined me. Independence is enormously expensive, especially for a humorist like me."

"Are you in love?"

"No, but I'm an Englishman to women; an Englishman who has cashmeres, an Englishman who is never amazed or suspicious of anything, an Englishman in Piccadilly's Royal Saloon in London and the Bal Mabille in Paris. Perhaps I'm the last Englishman."

"And you have mistresses who are ruining you."

"It's necessary to sustain one's reputation. Anyway, I prefer that to traveling. It costs less to lie down in the Breda quarter than on the slopes of Chimborazo. Between two follies, it's necessary to choose the less foolish. And then, I have traveled—because of a woman, it's true."

"Ah! You were pursuing her?"

"Not at all. I was running away from her."

"She was pursuing you, then?"

"Not in the least. It was fifteen years ago..."

"What—you're going to tell me stories?"

"Only in brief. I'm in a mood to talk. Then again, this Xerès is so seductive. Aren't you drinking, Milord?"

Horatio, who was beginning to find his friend's phlegmatic manner irritating, began striding back and forth, without appearing to pay any attention to Sir James' presence. The latter, after having emptied a third glass, started whistling a tune between his teeth. That little game necessarily attracted that attention of Lord Mackinguss, who stopped in front of the drinker and looked him full in the face.

"Yes, it was fifteen years ago."

"But in sum, Sir James, you have something else to say to me."

"In good time, Milord, in good time. Let my words flow at the caprice of my tongue, and you'll soon hear something that concerns you."

"Since that's the case, Sir James, at your ease!" So saying, he rolled an armchair up to the table, sat down, and set about sugaring his coffee with the resignation of someone heroically playing his part.

"Yes, yes, it was a good fifteen years ago. I still had illusions! I imagined that something else existed in life than Bordeaux wine and truffles; I almost doubted the stomach, that precious porcelain of human clay! Oh, I was very young. Be careful, Milord, you're putting too much sugar in; that's an error; personally, I take my coffee entirely bitter. One of my mistresses lived in Dover.

"You had several mistresses, then?"

"Three. A trinity necessary to my existence. So, I lead from the front, one candid amour for a young woman, one passion for a young woman, and one grotesque caprice for an ugly woman. That composes a whole whose regime suits my temperament very well. I'm like those people who breakfast on dairy products, dine on solid meat and amuse themselves at supper with odd delicacies. Men reputed to be eccentric are always very systematic. So, one of my mistresses was living in Dover."

"Was that one of your burlesque amours?"

"Perhaps. Anyway, she was an Englishwoman...a very droll Englishwoman. I loved her very much...after dinner. One evening, I had come from London to spend the evening with her. We were drinking tea, when we suddenly started arguing. I got carried away, to such a point that, without even finishing my tea, I grabbed my hat and left Miss Arabella's dwelling.

"I was furious, and I wanted to get away from Dover immediately, at any cost. I ran through the town like a madman. But it was late, there was no train, not a carriage on the road. I ran to the harbor with the intention of throwing myself in the sea and drowning myself, if I didn't have the strength to swim all the way to the shore of France. As I went along the jetty I heard the sound of a steam-engine warming up. I stopped. It was a boat about to depart. I leapt aboard. The next morning, I was in Ostend.

"While eating oysters for breakfast, an occupation interrupted from time to time by ill-tempered words—for my anger as following its course—I was accosted by a gentleman who knew me. He told me that he was going to Hamburg to eat scarlet beef. I went with him. From Hamburg we went to Rome, from Rome to Naples, from Naples to Constantinople. There we left Europe and went into Asia.

"Finally, one day, in Calcutta, three years after my abrupt departure from Dover, my ill-humor against Miss Arabella began to die down. I even thought about going back. In fact, two years after having left Calcutta, after having sojourned in Africa, Spin and France, I returned to Dover. Thanks to that five year absence, I expected to find Miss Arabella uglier, and that hope made me smile, for women are like Roquefort, the older they are, the more stimulating they are.

"It was evening. I came back utterly confused by my little escapade. 'Aha!' said the poor Miss, immediately. 'I knew you'd be back before long. Come on, sulky, come and finish you tea and thank me for having kept it warm.' And that was the only traveling I ever did in my life."

As the Baronet was no longer talking, Horatio said to him, with the greatest self-composure: "I'm still listening, Sir James."

Without paying the slightest heed to that strange complacency, the humorist returned to his bottle of Xerès, in which he was beginning to make a considerable void.

"Milord, I've come to ask you for money."

"I've already told you that I don't owe you any."

"And I've already replied that I know."

"They why come here to augment my fatigue?"

"Permit me, Milord—you don't owe me anything now, it's true, but it's probable that you're going to pay me three thousand pounds."

"Are you mad, Sir James?" exclaimed Horatio, getting up impatiently, in a bad temper.

"Calm down, Milord, or I won't answer for myself any more, I warn you."

"What do you mean by that, Sir James."

"I mean that if you don't start discussing business calmly with me, I'll send for a second bottle of Xerès and tell you another story. Milord, I want to talk to you about a person of whom you make use, but don't know."

"You mean Lodore. I know everything, and that's his business."

"No, it's not Lodore. Milord, six months ago I discovered a secret regarding Antares. That secret is of some importance, since the Jew consented to pay two thousand pounds sterling for my silence. But Jews don't much like paying. Antares thought he'd get out of it in time; he's mistaken. Now, that secret is of great concern to you, Milord."

"Really?"

"Really. I think that you won't haggle over paying three thousand pounds to know something that Antares consented to pay two thousand pounds to prevent you from knowing."

"But what guarantee do I have of that?"

"My God, the letter in which the man in question asks me for a little patience while imploring my discretion. You can read it, Milord. It won't tell you anything, but you'll understand the importance of the matter from the style."

Horatio took the letter from Sir James' hands and read it attentively.

"Then again," the Baronet continued, although his interlocutor was not listening, "I won't be sorry to do the nasty fellow a bad turn. He was the cause of my disappointment with regard to the young maiden of the Chariot of Fraternity."

"And what will the result of this revelation be?"

"Tee hee! Bad for Antares—and enlightening for you. One always likes to know the underside of the cards."

"Speak, then."

"Milord, one doesn't commit the same naivety twice. Before I speak, you're going to sign this order to the Harriss Bank in London to pay the agreed sum on presentation. Harriss is, I believe, your banker; it was the least you can do for the family."

"Don't permit yourself, Sir James, to make such reflections in my presence. Here's your mandate; now, I'm listening."

Horatio's physiognomy was presenting the contractions of an irritated impatience. The man, whose pride was an incessantly-seething ferment, suddenly learning that he had been the dupe of a man he thought dependent on him, felt his anger mounting. His eyes, like two burning coals, stared at the Baronet, who did not flinch.

"You've never been astonished by the scant communication that your brother, the Earl, maintained with society. Whenever you called in at his castle in Argyll, you never wondered where the good brother might be, who was never at home. It's necessary to be inquisitive about everything, Milord—permit me to offer you that advice. Now, this is where the Earl was: your brother, who, as you know, professes a perfect love for wealth, has become a Jew. Ah, you've guessed! My God, do you recall that letter your received from Argyll ten years ago, which indicated to you, in order to bring to conclusion certain delicate financial matters, a man named Antares, resident in Canongate in Edinburgh?"

"What, that Antares...?"

"Yes, that Antares, whose subsequently established himself in St. Giles in London, and then in Corbett's Lane, whom I also suspect of having trafficked in the Rue de Bièvre in Paris, that Antares is your brother. I know that you will allege, to attenuate your fault, the slight frequentation that existed between the Earl and yourself, but it's a fault nevertheless, Milord."

"But what you're telling me astounds me! That I've been tricked in that way! It's true that, except for my marriage, I've only encountered my brother twice in twenty years! Ah! The brother that I always despised is, then, as vile as I thought!"

But Mackinguss' irritation was contained with difficulty. He was marching precipitately, his teeth grinding and his fists clenched. The Baronet seemed calmer than ever; but then, it was not water that he was throwing on the fire.

"Oh, he's deceived you, it's true—but why get annoyed about it?"

"Why, the miserable hypocrite!"

"Yes, everybody is deceived to some extent. So it must be even more disagreeable to this that he has stolen from you."

"Stolen! Come on, let's have it—quickly!"

"Quickly…I'll get confused. Oh, I'm cleverer than I seem. So, would he be very astonished, that good Antares, if I assured him that your sister-in-law, Ophelia, is not dead, and that she escaped from him?"

"Ophelia is still alive!" cried the aristocrat, going pale.

"Yes, and perhaps she's now in the arms of her old father, as in the fifth act of a drama that finishes well, her old father preferring her to Milady. Oh, that would be disagreeable for both of you, but still…!"

"Sir James, are you certain of what you're saying?"

"I'm always certain of what I'm saying, Milord. Oh, why break that chair? Calm down. Yes, I'm sure of it. One doesn't die without being buried, and one isn't buried without a few petty scribbles at the Mairie. Oh, I've been to the Mairie—I'm a man of detail."

In Lord Mackinguss, however, a strange effect of anger was produced. He could no longer speak and his breath as hoarse. His terribly wide eyes had a coruscating fixity. Some kind of foam was whitening around his lips. He was panting, haggard and trembling, effortlessly breaking the objects placed within his reach.

Sir James emerged from his phlegm. He got up and slipped away without Horatio appearing to notice.

In the corridor, he met Lady Mackinguss.

"Milady, I don't know what's wrong with your husband, but he'll need a glass of water."

A thought crossed Olivia's mind. She went back into her apartment and poured water into a glass. From a little phial baring a close resemblance to the one that Antares had given her to carry out her experiments on foxes, she let a few drops fall into the water.

Perhaps it was a distraction perfectly natural at such a moment, and Milady doubtless thought that she was making use of a bottle of essence of orange-flowers.

At any rate, having done it, he headed for the room in which the Baronet had left her husband.

XXVII. Hydrophobia

I consider certain chapters of a novel as surgical operations recognized as inevitable. In those cases, the best thing is to have a sure hand and move quickly.

Horatio was in an armchair in the least well-lit corner of the room. Motionless, his head tense, his hands gripping the arms of the chair, he seemed to be listening, or waiting.

Olivia came in.

"What's the matter with you, Milord? Sir James has just told me that you're indisposed…here's a glass of fresh water."

At those last words, Horatio's eyes lit up, but he appeared to be containing an interior emotion. He stood up.

"Thank you, my beautiful Olivia," he said, drawing nearer to his wife.

Then, putting an arm around her neck, he inclined his head as if to give her a kiss on the shoulder.

The young woman uttered a piercing scream. Horatio had bitten her.

The memory of Mont-Dore's bite came to mind. Her husband was afflicted by rabies!

She tried to get away, but the madman closed the door. And there was a struggle, a pursuit, in which terror rendered the woman mad. Suddenly, at a moment when a table separated her from her husband, she opened a window and threw herself out.

Two people in the castle had heard Olivia's scream: the Baronet and Antares.

Sir James, who is decidedly one of the strong men in this drama, pulled the covers of his bed over his ears and went to sleep.

Antares, preoccupied with the slightest events that might erupt around him, ventured out of his laboratory and went as far as Horatio's room.

The latter, hearing the noise outside his door, and having no one on whom he could vent his rage, opened it and threw himself furiously upon his brother—who had not expected that turn of events.

There was a frightful struggle.

The window through which Olivia had thrown herself overlooked the Clyde.

XVIII. The Gold Coin

Robert had not forgotten that frightful night spent in Madame de Lormont's bedroom. He remembered it all the more clearly because, his passion being extinct, nothing remained to him in regard to that woman but an indefinable sensation hovering between aversion and scorn.

Rolleboise arrived at the Castle of the Falls in the morning. Lodore was awake. Without proffering a word, the Englishman beckoned to the traveler to follow him. After going through a few corridors, he opened a door.

"Please go in, Monsieur de Rolleboise; this is your apartment."

When Robert was inside, his guide closed the door and turned round. Although it was broad daylight, the room in which the young man found himself was dark because curtains were drawn over the windows. He made out a bed.

At the noise made by the door, the bed-curtains agitated, and a frightened voice cried: "Who's there? Don't come near me, or I'll kill myself!"

Gripped by astonishment, however, the voice fell silent. Then, after a moment's silence between the two individuals, one standing on the other lying down, one a young man and the other a young woman the latter exclaimed again: "What! You here, Monsieur de Rolleboise! But then, tell me where I am, why I've been abducted, what's going to happen to me. Oh, my God, perhaps it's you who have done all this! Speak to me then, Monsieur, for I'm going mad!"

Almost crazed by fear, Mathilde did not think about her position in front of the man who had loved her. Her upper torso and arms half-naked, she was leaning breathlessly over the edge of the bed.

That disorder, far from troubling Robert, merely made him smile. Very calmly, he came to sit on a chair placed beside the bed.

"You ask me, Madame, where you are. You're in my bedroom. Does that astonish you? Does the sight of me fill you with fear? Well, my God, I once found you, in almost identical circumstances, one night when a man came into your apartment, much more sober in your exclamations."

"What are you saying, Monsieur de Rolleboise?"

"Do you remember, Madame, the beautiful evening that I had the honor of spending in your company two years ago at Le Havre? Oh, I loved you dearly then! All night—a sleepless night—I dreamed about you. Because, seeing you beside that old man, your husband, I considered you almost as a child. I adored you like a virgin. Wasn't it the case that while I was dreaming thus, you, pale and calm, were resting tranquil, sleeping dreamlessly, and that a mere thought directed toward me would have tarnished the candor of your soul? Isn't that true, Mathilde?"

"Why are you speaking to me like this?"

"Why? Because the entire night to which I'm referring, I spent in your bedroom...because, that night, no one slept in the beds prepared for Monsieur de Bassens and me...because, that night, Monsieur de Bassens lay in yours...because, if I still wanted to, I could take my revenge!"

"Wretch, what are you saying. That Monsieur de Bassens, I can now admit..."

"Is your lover, I know."

"Monsieur de Bassens is not my lover, Monsieur, for I'm his wife!" said Mathilde, sitting up straight on the bed, proudly.

"Your husband...what, and Monsieur de Lormont...?"

"Monsieur de Lormont is my father-in-law. At the time when I encountered you, my husband, by virtue of events that are doubtless unknown to you, was obliged to leave France, incognito. He was traveling under a false name. That's the truth, Monsieur. Certainly, there are terrible correlations between certain individuals to whom, I can see, you have accorded every confidence, and me. Perhaps I could tell you about them in other circumstances, but today, Monsieur, I beg you, save me! Take me back to my husband!"

Robert remained pensive. Not that he was hesitating for an instant about taking the side of the young woman, but he was alarmed and bewildered by the new drama that he saw surging forth before him. The poor young man aspired to a calm life for everyone, and he had good reason. He rang.

"Someone will help you dress, Madam; I shall come to collect you in a quarter of an hour."

Hannah, the chambermaid, came in, in utter distress.

"Oh, my God!" she cried, in utter violation of English etiquette, "Oh, my God! I don't know what's happening here! Milady has disappeared, and I could hear noises all night in Milord's apartment."

Robert went out.

Ten minutes later, he came back, frightened.

"Madame, this house is accursed—let's go!"

"Robert, on your honor, I can follow you?"

"On my honor, you can trust me; as for yours, that's your concern."

They went out. The corridors and staircases were deserted. They did not encounter anyone in their passage. It might have been nine or ten o'clock in the morning.

Scarcely had they passed the last door in the courtyards than they saw someone on the road coming toward them. As Robert came closer, he thought he recognized the face. Suddenly, he exclaimed: "I'm not mistaken; it's the Vicomte de Saint-Loubès."

"In person, Monsieur de Rolleboise. Where are you going so early in the day? Ah, I recognize Madame! Accept my respectful salutations, Madame de Lormont."

"We're fleeing, my dear friend."

The Vicomte started. Indeed, I ought to remind my reader of the tendencies of that individual, of whom I had completely lost sight, and whose portrait can be found in the early pages of his book.

"Ah! Monsieur de Rolleboise, this is a practical joke! I'm traveling tranquilly in Scotland, like any bourgeois, and I encounter you in the heart of the countryside with Madame de Lormont. I ask you where you're going, and you tell me that you're fleeing! Oh, Monsieur, that's mischievous!"

"We'll explain later. Listen, Vicomte, how are you traveling in Scotland?"

"Why, in my carriage. It's waiting for me over there—for its necessary to confess to you that exceedingly unpleasant adventures have befallen me today."

"Well, you can tell us about those adventures later. Let's go to your carriage quickly and leave."

"Oh, you're making my head spin! I don't want, you hear, to throw myself into these old romantic ways. I don't want to! In fact, it would be too much! Scarcely will we be under way than you'll confess to me that we're being pursued, the horses will be forced, my post-chaise will break down...a complete chapter, in a word! No, no, Monsieur!

"Besides which, I have business at this house—a very stupid business! And truly, Monsieur de Rolleboise, I believe that your proximity has a terrible influence on me. In fact, for a month, I've been traveling without a hitch. I don't encounter any extraordinary landscape, no one tells me any legends, I dine in hotels as well as anywhere else, and not the slightest event happens to me, when, this morning, I don't know what evil spirit brought me toward the falls of the river that passes this way—the Clyde, I believe—to a place named Stonebyres...and while watching the foaming waters, have I not perceived, lying between two rocks, the cadaver of a woman?"

"Oh, my God! I know who it is!"

"Oh, now you're going to tell me that it's you who drowned her! In fact, I'd rather not know. So, I return to my carriage. Then I mention it to a peasant who was fishing in the vicinity. He's not at all surprised, and tells me that it's always the same when anyone comes to take up residence in the castle; it's vampires, he assures me. I don't understand it; I'm getting away!"

The poor Vicomte was expressing himself in a desolate tone that would certainly have amused his interlocutors if they had not found themselves differently disposed.

"And you're right, my dear friend, to want to turn back! Do you remember our last meeting?"

"Yes, at Bazas, where that accursed traveler started telling us stories!"

"Well, that traveler is in the castle."

"Good."

"You doubtless remember that his dog bit him."

"Yes—he called it Mont-Dore."

"Well, he's become rabid as a result of that bite. Don't go there—you'll be bitten."

"My dear Rolleboise, I don't understand any of what you're saying. Let me travel in peace. Adieu!"

"What! Adieu? But you're going to take us away…one doesn't leave friends in the middle of nowhere like that!"

Monsieur de Saint-Loubès was about to exclaim again, but his friend took him by the arm and dragged him to his carriage. The Vicomte resigned himself to it. In any case, he was in haste to get away from a place in which such extraordinary things were happening.

When all three of them were sitting down, and the coachman was waiting for his master to give the order to depart, the latter turned to Robert and his companion.

"Where do you desire to flee?"

"In fact," Rolleboise said, "I don't know. Where are we going, Madame?"

"To rejoin my husband."

"Where is he?"

"When I was abducted from my carriage we were on the road to Edinburgh. Perhaps he stopped before then, but he must be moving heaven and earth to get me back. Let's go to Edinburgh; we'll doubtless learn something there."

An hour later, the three travelers arrived at Lanark, where they breakfasted without any incident, which contributed somewhat to easing the Vicomte's mind. That evening, they reached the Scottish capital.

By virtue of the literary tendencies of its inhabitants, Edinburgh is an entirely French city. There is no slightly imaginative young woman in the city who does not eventually give birth to a pretty yellow volume ornamented with a nebulous title, nor a nubile man who does not write a book of legends, nor a serious intellectual who does not edit a magazine. The stupid, the bourgeois brains, those who cannot rhyme, are something else; they invent religions or raise falcons. One would never believe the number of religions that the British Isles produces.

The three travelers stopped at a sumptuous Hotel in Princes Street, almost opposite the monument raised to Walter Scott. After dinner, which consisted simply of at least four pounds of roast beef, which two waiters cleared away without difficulty, a York ham and a monstrous salmon, followed by an enormous beefsteak pâté, the Vicomte, almost suffering from indigestion, left the "parlor."

Left alone with Madame de Lormont, Robert walked back and forth for a while, and then placed himself at the window. Mechanically, he paraded his gaze over the tall houses ranked in twelve or fifteen stages, all brightly lit, up to the impregnable castle somberly outlined against the sky like a mountain.

Mathilde was sitting pensively by the fire, her eyes imprudently staring at the blazing logs. The inevitable kettle, with its swan's neck, was hissing continuously as its flanks were heated.

The young man and the young woman both felt a certain embarrassment. Robert closed the windows, because the cold air was becoming uncomfortable, and went to sit down next to the fire-basket.

"So, the proprietor of the hotel has given you precise information regarding Monsieur de Lormont? You're leaving for Glasgow tonight?"

"At midnight."

"We shan't see one another again?"

"Probably not."

"You've forgiven me, at least? And yet, Madame, I'm not entirely sure that I've forgiven you."

"What do you mean?"

"Listen, I'll talk to you with an open heart. I loved you with an insensate passion, the sight of you perhaps gave my destiny a bad direction, but frankly, I tell you today, that fever is extinct. However, there still remains something resembling a jealous sentiment. You know Horatio—it's him that had you come to Scotland, isn't it?"

"It's him."

"Madame, let's separate without any afterthought of doubt. Anyway, the man might well be dead by now."

"Monsieur Robert, there are two romances, two dramas in my life, one of which will never be divulged by my mouth, for it is terrible. The other only concerns me, and as, unfortunately, it responds to the suspicions that you have just voiced, I shall tell it to you. Your life is sufficiently experienced, I know, that that after you have heard me out you will not condemn me.

"I spent my entire youth—my girlhood, if you prefer—in Montpellier."

"Did Horatio Mackinguss not live in that town?"

"Alas!" she said, by way of reply, putting her head in her hand in order to collect what she wanted to say.

Robert remembered his first meeting with the man; so, in order to seek clarification regarding the atrocious story that opened this book, he added: "Did you not also know, in that same town, a Madame Noirtier whose son was killed in a duel some four years ago?"

"Noirtier…no…however, I believe there was some question, at the time of the waters, in Cauterets, of a duel that caused some noise in Montpellier. As it did not concern anyone I knew, though, I scarcely paid any attention to it. I'll return to that which regards me. Don't interrupt me again, I beg you; let me say this quickly, for it costs me more than you can believe.

"I was sixteen. I lived in my father's house, isolated, having no one but an aged relative for company, for I had lost my mother. I did not go out much, but we went to church regularly. When my aunt could not go with me, a maid accompanied me. Provincial towns, especially the smaller ones, as you know, have a population that changes so little that everyone knows everyone else by sight. For a few days, during the journey from our house to the church I had noticed a man—I don't say a young man, although his age was almost the same as yours is today; the expression on his face was not youthful. I'm not talking here about his physique, only his physiognomy.

"My aunt told me his name. He was a foreigner who often came to the locale, especially in winter; his name was Horatio Mackinguss. The man had noticed me. His gaze didn't trouble me, but weighed upon me. Encountering him made me anxious. I sensed that to in order to love a young woman, to express words of love, the man who was considering me thus would retrace his steps.

"I shall not waste time explaining to you how I received his letters, in what manner he forced me to take them; you know those means. For a long time, I did not respond. Finally, one morning, when my maid had gone back to fetch my missal, which I had left in my room, I slipped a letter furtively into the post-box.

"I did not love that man; I have never loved him. But I was very young; I only saw him; my existence was so unoccupied that it was impossible for me not to think about him sometimes. Finally, I repeat, I never loved him; I say this with all the more verity and frankness because I recognized that the man was handsome. In brief, he fascinated me: I was afraid of him.

"Well, Monsieur, that man took such possession of me, paralyzed my will to such an extent, that I was frightened. I deceived him; I told him on day that I loved him. Oh, he made use of an infernal means! Listen. I had replied to him, as I told you; I had asked him to leave me my youth, my soul's tranquility, to have pity on me. A letter, you see that was very imprudent on the part of a child. He demanded a rendezvous. When I encountered him, my gaze my gaze must have told him how wounded I had been by such a demand. Instead of offering me his apologies, he made demands. I tore up his letter angrily.

"That was in May. We were going every evening to the Mois de Marie. Horatio was there every evening. Once, I noticed an expression on his face that gave me a chill. An indefinable smile wandered over his lips, his eyes held me captive and prevented me from praying. When the blessing had been given, I got up immediately, for I dared not remain as one of the last people in the church.

"At the door, he approached me; I sensed that he wanted to give me a letter; I pushed his hand away, but he grabbed mine and would not let go until I had taken the piece of paper. It was heavy. Alone in my room, I unsealed it. It contained a hundred-franc gold coin.

"What the letter said approximately, was: 'Don't send this gold coin back to me via an intermediary; I shall not accept it; nor by post, because that is forbidden. You can easily go out one evening to pray alone. If you want to return this gold to me, I will be in the passages behind the church that night.'"

"That was an infamous means!"

"Wasn't it? What could I do? At any time, that man could say: *I gave her gold, and she has kept it!*"

"So you went to the passages at night?"

"Yes. There was a carriage; I was lost! Imprudently, after that, I wrote to him. He has my letters. It was by threatening to give them to my husband that he forced me to persuade the latter to come to Scotland. Then he had me abducted—why, for whom, I don't know. In sum, may God protect me! And you, since I owe it to you that I am rejoining my husband, safe and sound, I forgive you."

The next day, at ten o'clock, Monsieur de Saint-Loubès came down to the parlor. Robert was eating breakfast.

"Madame de Lormont?"

"Left last night by railway."

"Ah! Did she tell you her secrets?"

"No, I still don't know why her father-in-law was posing as her husband in France. Why did her husband flee?"

"He was condemned to death."

"Ah!"

"Yes, but the victim of a miscarriage of justice—or, rather, was sacrificing himself for the honor of the young woman he was about to marry. The true guilty party was Madame de Lormont's father. He rendered justice by enabling the young man to escape and committing a frightful suicide in the prison. It's a very long and complicated story. I'll tell it to you another day, if I have the courage. Will you have a cup of tea?"

"Gladly!"[39]

Horatio died of an attack of rabies. One day, his brother Edgard—Antares—one of the perhaps overly numerous evil figures in this books, sensed the first symptoms of that terrible disease, so he went into his laboratory, emptied a phial into a glass of water, drank it, and fell down dead.

The old Duke lived alone in his Highland castle, dressed in mourning, and asked God to reunite him soon with those he had loved in this world. He rarely emerged from his oratory, where a crucifix, an image of the Virgin and a portrait of his

---

[39] The author inserts a footnote: "A book is often a true Procrustean bed, so the demands of format have necessitated considerable suppressions here, and a simple summary."

daughter Ophelia rendered him strong by virtue of hope and memory.

It was a very moving scene—a commotion that might have killed him—when Ophelia, accompanied by Robert, came to throw herself into his arms, saying:

"I've come to console you for the death of my sister and weep with you."

The young woman introduced Rolleboise as her savior. The Duke embraced him, weeping—for he reminded him, he said, of poor Amadeus.

At those words, the young man shivered.

One morning in spring, four people were in the Duke of Firstland's drawing room. The old man, extended in large armchair, was warming his feet in the sunlight; Monsieur and Madame de Rolleboise—for there is no need to relate their marriage to the reader—were chatting at a table covered with albums and newspapers, and old Aunt Cockburn was reading the *Times* in front of the fire.

"Oh my God, that's strange!" she suddenly exclaimed.

"What is it, Aunt?"

"An extremely scandalous affair in the London court. Do you recall those frightful crimes committed in the cemetery at Kensal Green? Was it Kensal Green? No, New Cross… abominable…abominable! London is nowadays as depraved as Paris. In fact, this name is not unknown to me."

"What name do you mean, Sister?" asked the Duke, while Robert stood up to hide his disturbance from his young wife.

"Lord Lodore."

"Lodore…yes, I remember. Has he been convicted?"

"He's been hanged at Newgate."

"Was he a murderer?"

"Oh, much worse!"

"What, then?"

"A vampire!"

SF & FANTASY

Adolphe Alhaiza. *Cybele*
Alphonse Allais. *The Adventures of Captain Cap*
Henri Allorge. *The Great Cataclysm*
Guy d'Armen. *Doc Ardan: The City of Gold and Lepers*
G.-J. Arnaud. *The Ice Company*
Charles Asselineau. *The Double Life*
Cyprien Bérard. *The Vampire Lord Ruthwen*
S. Henry Berthoud. *Martyrs of Science*
Aloysius Bertrand. *Gaspard de la Nuit*
Richard Bessière. *The Gardens of the Apocalypse*
Albert Bleunard. *Ever Smaller*
Félix Bodin. *The Novel of the Future*
Louis Boussenard. *Monsieur Synthesis*
Alphonse Brown. *City of Glass; The Conquest of the Air*
Emile Calvet. *In a Thousand Years*
André Caroff. *The Terror of Madame Atomos; Miss Atomos; The Return of Madame Atomos; The Mistake of Madame Atomos; The Monsters of Madame Atomos; The Revenge of Madame Atomos; The Resurrection of Madame Atomos; The Mark of Madame Atomos; The Spheres of Madame Atomos*
Félicien Champsaur. *The Human Arrow; Ouha, King of the Apes; Pharaoh's Wife*
Didier de Chousy. *Ignis*
Jules Clarétie. *Obsession*
Michel Corday. *The Eternal Flame*
Captain Danrit. *Undersea Odyssey*
C. I. Defontenay. *Star (Psi Cassiopeia)*
Charles Derennes. *The People of the Pole*
Georges Dodds (anthologist). *The Missing Link*
Harry Dickson. *The Heir of Dracula*
Jules Dornay. *Lord Ruthven Begins*
Alfred Driou. *The Adventures of a Parisian Aeronaut*
Sâr Dubnotal *vs. Jack the Ripper*
Alexandre Dumas. *The Return of Lord Ruthven*
Renée Dunan. *Baal*
J.-C. Dunyach. *The Night Orchid; The Thieves of Silence*
Henri Duvernois. *The Man Who Found Himself*
Achille Eyraud. *Voyage to Venus*
Henri Falk. *The Age of Lead*

Paul Féval. *Anne of the Isles; Knightshade; Revenants; Vampire City; The Vampire Countess; The Wandering Jew's Daughter*
Paul Féval, *fils. Felifax, the Tiger-Man*
Charles de Fieux. *Lamékis*
Louis Forest. *Someone is Stealing Children in Paris*
Arnould Galopin. *Doctor Omega; Doctor Omega and the Shadowmen* (anthology)
Judith Gautier. *Isoline and the Serpent-Flower*
H. Gayar. *The Marvelous Adventures of Serge Myrandhal on Mars*
Léon Gozlan. *The Vampire of the Val-de-Grâce*
G.L. Gick. *Harry Dickson and the Werewolf of Rutherford Grange*
Edmond Haraucourt. *Illusions of Immortality*
Nathalie Henneberg. *The Green Gods*
V. Hugo, P. Foucher & P. Meurice. *The Hunchback of Notre-Dame*
Romain d'Huissier. *Hexagon: Dark Matter*
Jules Janin. *The Magnetized Corpse*
Michel Jeury. *Chronolysis*
Gustave Kahn. *The Tale of Gold and Silence*
Gérard Klein. *The Mote in Time's Eye*
Fernand Kolney. *Love in 5000 Years*
Paul Lacroix. *Danse Macabre*
Louis-Guillaume de La Follie. *The Unpretentious Philosopher*
Jean de La Hire. *Enter the Nyctalope; The Nyctalope on Mars; The Nyctalope vs. Lucifer; The Nyctalope Steps In; Night of the Nyctalope; Return of the Nyctalope; The Fiery Wheel*
Etienne-Léon de Lamothe-Langon. *The Virgin Vampire*
André Laurie. *Spiridon*
Gabriel de Lautrec. *The Vengeance of the Oval Portrait*
Alain le Drimeur. *The Future City*
Georges Le Faure & Henri de Graffigny. *The Extraordinary Adventures of a Russian Scientist Across the Solar System* (2 vols.)
Gustave Le Rouge. *The Mysterious Doctor Cornelius* (3 vols.); *The Vampires of Mars; The Dominion of the World* (w/Gustave Guitton) (4 vols.)
Jules Lermina. *Mysteryville; Panic in Paris; To-Ho and the Gold Destroyers; The Secret of Zippelius*
André Lichtenberger. *The Centaurs; The Children of the Crab*
Jean-Marc & Randy Lofficier. *Edgar Allan Poe on Mars; The Katrina Protocol; Pacifica; Robonocchio; Return of the Nyctalope;* (anthologists) *Tales of the Shadowmen 1-10*
Xavier Mauméjean. *The League of Heroes*

Joseph Méry. *The Tower of Destiny*
Hippolyte Mettais. *The Year 5865*
Louise Michel. *The Human Microbes; The New World*
Tony Moilin. *Paris in the Year 2000*
José Moselli. *Illa's End*
John-Antoine Nau. *Enemy Force*
Marie Nizet. *Captain Vampire*
C. Nodier, A. Beraud & Toussaint-Merle. *Frankenstein*
Henri de Parville. *An Inhabitant of the Planet Mars*
Gaston de Pawlowski. *Journey to the Land of the 4th Dimension*
Georges Pellerin. *The World in 2000 Years*
Ernest Pérochon. *The Frenetic People*
Pierre Pelot. *The Child Who Walked on the Sky*
J. Polidori, C. Nodier, E. Scribe. *Lord Ruthven the Vampire*
P.-A. Ponson du Terrail. *The Vampire and the Devil's Son; The Immortal Woman*
Edgar Quinet. *Ahasuerus*
Henri de Régnier. *A Surfeit of Mirrors*
Maurice Renard. *The Blue Peril; Doctor Lerne; The Doctored Man; A Man Among the Microbes; The Master of Light*
Jean Richepin. *The Wing; The Crazy Corner*
Albert Robida. *The Adventures of Saturnin Farandoul; The Clock of the Centuries; Chalet in the Sky; The Electric Life*
J.-H. Rosny Aîné. *Helgvor of the Blue River; The Givreuse Enigma; The Mysterious Force; The Navigators of Space; Vamireh; The World of the Variants; The Young Vampire*
Marcel Rouff. *Journey to the Inverted World*
Han Ryner. *The Superhumans*
Angelo de Sorr. *The Vampires of London*
Brian Stableford. *The New Faust at the Tragicomique;The Empire of the Necromancers (The Shadow of Frankenstein; Frankenstein and the Vampire Countess; Frankenstein in London); Sherlock Holmes & The Vampires of Eternity; The Stones of Camelot; The Wayward Muse.* (anthologist) *News from the Moon; The Germans on Venus; The Supreme Progress; The World Above the World; Nemoville; Investigations of the Future; The Conqueror of Death*
Jacques Spitz. *The Eye of Purgatory*
Kurt Steiner. *Ortog*
Eugène Thébault. *Radio-Terror*
C.-F. Tiphaigne de La Roche. *Amilec*
Louis Ulbach. *Prince Bonifacio*

Théo Varlet. *The Golden Rock. The Xenobiotic Invasion; The Castaways of Eros; Timeslip Troopers* (w/André Blandin); *The Martian Epic* (w/Octave Joncquel)
Paul Vibert. *The Mysterious Fluid*
Villiers de l'Isle-Adam. *The Scaffold; The Vampire Soul*
Philippe Ward. *Artahe*
Philippe Ward & Sylvie Miller. *The Song of Montségur*

MYSTERIES & THRILLERS

M. Allain & P. Souvestre. *The Daughter of Fantômas*
A. Anicet-Bourgeois, Lucien Dabril. *Rocambole*
A. Bernède. *Belphegor; Judex* (w/Louis Feuillade); *The Return of Judex* (w/Louis Feuillade); *The Shadow of Judex*
A. Bisson & G. Livet. *Nick Carter vs. Fantômas*
V. Darlay & H. de Gorsse. *Arsène Lupin vs. Sherlock Holmes: The Stage Play*
Séamas Duffy. *Sherlock Holmes in Paris*
Paul Féval. *Gentlemen of the Night; John Devil; The Black Coats ('Salem Street; The Invisible Weapon; The Parisian Jungle; The Companions of the Treasure; Heart of Steel; The Cadet Gang; The Sword-Swallower)*
Emile Gaboriau. *Monsieur Lecoq*
Goron & Emile Gautier. *Spawn of the Penitentiary*
Rick Lai. *Shadows of the Opera: Retribution in Blood; Sisters of the Shadows: The Curse of Cagliostro*
Steve Leadley. *Sherlock Holmes: The Circle of Blood*
Maurice Leblanc. *Arsène Lupin vs. Countess Cagliostro; Arsène Lupin vs. Sherlock Holmes (The Blonde Phantom; The Hollow Needle); The Many Faces of Arsène Lupin*
Gaston Leroux. *Chéri-Bibi; The Phantom of the Opera; Rouletabille & the Mystery of the Yellow Room; Rouletabille at Krupp's*
Richard Marsh. *The Complete Adventures of Judith Lee*
William Patrick Maynard. *The Terror of Fu Manchu; The Destiny of Fu Manchu*
Frank J. Morlock. *Sherlock Holmes: The Grand Horizontals; Sherlock Holmes vs Jack the Ripper*
Jean Petithuguenin. *The Adventures of Ethel King*
Antonin Reschal. *The Adventures of Miss Boston*
P. de Wattyne & Y. Walter. *Sherlock Holmes vs. Fantômas*
David White. *Fantômas in America*

Pierre Yrondy. *The Adventures of Thérèse Arnaud*

SCREENPLAYS

Mike Baron. *The Iron Triangle*
Emma Bull & Will Shetterly. *Nightspeeder; War for the Oaks*
Gerry Conway & Roy Thomas. *Doc Dynamo*
Steve Englehart. *Majorca*
James Hudnall. *The Devastator*
Jean-Marc & Randy Lofficier. *Royal Flush*
J.-M. & R. Lofficier & Marc Agapit. *Despair*
J.-M. & R. Lofficier & Joël Houssin. *City*
Andrew Paquette. *Peripheral Vision*
Robert L. Robinson, Jr. *Judex*
R. Thomas, J. Hendler & L. Sprague de Camp. *Rivers of Time*

NON-FICTION

Stephen R. Bissette. *Blur 1-5. Green Mountain Cinema 1; Teen Angels*
Win Scott Eckert. *Crossovers* (2 vols.)
Jean-Marc & Randy Lofficier. *Shadowmen* (2 vols.)
Randy Lofficier. *Over Here*

ART BOOKS

Jean-Pierre Normand. *Science Fiction Illustrations*
Raven Okeefe. *Raven's L'il Critters; Rave's Faves*
Randy Lofficier & Raven Okeefe. *If Your Possum Go Daylight...*
Daniele Serra. *Illusions*

HEXAGON COMICS

Franco Frescura & Luciano Bernasconi. *Wampus*
Franco Frescura & Giorgio Trevisan. *CLASH*
L. Bernasconi, J.-M. Lofficier & Juan Roncagliolo Berger. *Phenix*
Claude Legrand, J.-M. Lofficier & L. Bernasconi. *Kabur*
Franco Oneta. *Zembla*
L. Buffolente, Lofficier & J.-J. Dzialowski. *Strangers: Homicron*
Danilo Grossi. *Strangers: Jaydee*

Claude Legrand & Luciano Bernasconi. *Strangers: Starlock*